Carly Reagon completed a six-month course at Curtis Brown Creative and was shortlisted for the Lucy Cavendish College Fiction Prize in 2019. Her writing is inspired by her love of the Welsh countryside where she lives with her husband and three children. She works as a senior lecturer at Cardiff University, is a keen runner and singer, and has an interest in anything historic.

PRAISE FOR *THE TOLL HOUSE*

'If you like a good ghost story, put this chilling
thriller to the top of your list'
SARAH PEARSE, author of *The Sanatorium*

'Perfect for the spooky season. Be prepared
for some seriously good twists'
NATASHA PULLEY, author of
The Watchmaker of Filigree Street

'A satisfyingly good old-fashioned ghost story that
brilliantly echoes the likes of Susan Hill'
SUSAN STOKES-CHAPMAN, author of *Pandora*

'Tons of spooky fun'
OBSERVER

'Pacy and page turning ... will keep you up
long past the witching hour'
REBECCA NETLEY, author of *The Whistling*

'A beautifully written story tale of hauntings and grief.
Carly Reagon is one to watch'
C.J. COOKE, author of *The Lighthouse Witches*

'An unsettling and gripping ghost story that'll have
you looking over your shoulder until the end'
CARL THOMAS

THE
TOLL HOUSE

CARLY REAGON

SPHERE

SPHERE

First published in Great Britain in 2022 by Sphere
This paperback edition published in 2023 by Sphere

1 3 5 7 9 10 8 6 4 2

A CIP catalogue record for this book
is available from the British Library.

ISBN 978-1-4087-2645-7

Typeset in Garamond Three by M Rules
Printed and bound in Great Britain by
Clays Ltd, Elcograf S.p.A.

Papers used by Sphere are from well-managed forests
and other responsible sources.

Sphere
An imprint of
Little, Brown Book Group
Carmelite House
50 Victoria Embankment
London EC4Y 0DZ

An Hachette UK Company
www.hachette.co.uk

www.littlebrown.co.uk

For Steve

TWELVE MONTHS AGO

1

The house was further away from the town than Kelda had expected, a mile or so along the Old Turnpike Road. She'd spied it from a distance, a darker smudge against the dull green-brown of the autumn fields.

'It's over there!' Dylan pointed from the back seat of the car, telling her what she already knew.

Apart from the house and a wood behind, the landscape was featureless. A landscape she wanted to love but which left her feeling cold. All this space: the streams and little ditches, the flat fields used for growing cabbages and potatoes, the dead straight road. She fought the instinct to make a U-turn back into town, ring the estate agent and say she'd changed her mind. But after the effort of finding the place, she knew she couldn't do that. It was all she could afford, the leftovers from savings she'd put aside for university, five years living at home and working flat out in Tesco.

They parked beneath a shuttered bay window and got out, stretching their legs from the journey.

Dylan wrinkled his nose. 'The house doesn't look very happy.'

'What do you mean?' Although she knew *exactly* what Dylan meant. The photos on Rightmove had been deceptive, taken in a better light. The front of the house was dirty and there were weeds sprouting from the mortar. But it was more than that. There was something not quite right, something she couldn't pinpoint.

'It looks like it's crying.'

'Old houses often look like that,' she said, pushing the feeling aside. 'It just needs some TLC, that's all.'

The house sat squarely on the road, an old toll house from the time when the route had been busy. She could still read the tolls for various horse- or mule-drawn vehicles stamped in black metal above the bay window. Nowadays, the main road into Stonebridge – the town she couldn't quite see from here because of another larger wood – cut through the fields on the other side of the river, winding through an industrial estate. It was hard to imagine the Old Turnpike Road as it had been, busy with carts and carriages and horses spreading muck.

She glanced at the empty road, instinctively reaching for Dylan's hand.

Dylan pulled back. 'Mum!' he pouted. 'I'm not a baby anymore. I'm almost six.'

'Exactly,' she said. '*Only* six.'

'Can we go and get ice cream now?'

'Not until the estate agent arrives. Then I promise you, ice cream. Come on, let's explore the garden.'

They followed a path around the side of the house to the back. It was far from grand, smaller even than the house they'd shared with Mum, but perhaps that added to its charm, made it more homely? She peered through a narrow window into what seemed to be a kitchen: a sink with a dusty bottle of Fairy Liquid, a cupboard set in the wall, doorways leading off on either side. She tried to imagine living here, away from Mum and her childhood town, away from the job she hated. A new life with her own rules.

Behind her, Dylan was balancing on the pile of stones near the path.

'Look at me!' he shouted, wobbling. He spread his arms wide and sailed into the grass.

'Careful,' she said, smiling.

She crossed the path onto the lawn. Everything was unkempt: tangled bushes, shin-high grass, weeds instead of flowerbeds. But at least it was enclosed. She imagined Dylan playing here, splashing in a paddling pool or racing across the lawn with his Batman figures. She climbed onto the stones and looked over the garden wall. Apart from the small wood behind the field at the back, it was the same stark landscape as everywhere else.

When they'd finished exploring, they sat on the lawn, enjoying the early autumn sunshine and playing rock-paper-scissors until Dylan got bored. She plucked the long grass whilst Dylan hunted for sticks, thinking of the new job she'd found advertised on the internet, PA for a small market research company. She'd applied on a whim, not thinking she'd get it, but she'd been offered it there and then at the interview.

'Mum! Look over here!' Dylan was trying to prise something out of the wall, levering it with his stick. An earthenware pot, wedged in a crevice.

She pulled herself up, lethargic, like time had slowed down. Her limbs felt heavy. A feeling she could sleep right there if she allowed herself to. But Dylan was insistent. 'Come on, Mum.'

'Here, let me.' She walked towards him and wriggled the pot back and forth, getting dust on her hands, freeing it with a jolt.

'What is it?' he said.

The lid was crawling with spiders. Trying not to flinch, she lifted it off and laid the pot on the grass.

Blank eyes stared back at her. Perfect whites.

She gasped, drawing her hands away, almost toppling the pot.

'What is it?' Dylan tugged at her sleeve.

'Nothing.' She shook her head and looked again. 'It's just a pile of pebbles. For a moment, I thought . . . ' An odd feeling crept over her: there was someone there, someone watching them crouched on the grass. She drew an arm around Dylan and surveyed the empty garden.

'Thought what?' Dylan said. He dug his hands into the pot, the pebbles rippling through his fingers.

'Nothing. I'm just being silly.' The feeling deepened. A stirring in the pit of her stomach. Not some*one* but some*thing*. The house. It seemed to want her, need her, like it had claimed her already. Perhaps this is what it meant to call a place home? She looked across at the dull windows and crumbling brickwork. The house wasn't perfect, far from it in fact, but it could be hers. *Theirs.* And no one else's.

A creak as the garden gate swung open. She jumped up, stifling a cry. Behind them, on the path, was a man in a suit. 'Miss Johnson?'

She relaxed – it was just the estate agent, it *had* just been the estate agent – and dusted herself down. 'That's right. Call me Kelda. And this is Dylan.'

The estate agent beamed as he crossed the lawn.

'Pleased to meet you,' he said, ruffling Dylan's hair. 'Right young man, shall we take a look inside?'

1863

2

The silence is unnerving, a deadly hush, not even the hoot of owls in the wood. I climb the stairs, lantern raised high, watching my shadow as it dances along the banister. There's a stillness in the air, thick with the heat of late summer, only the flickering of moths in the shadowy light. I run up the last few steps and across the landing, throwing wide the bedroom door.

The midwife spins towards me. 'You should not be in here.'

I push past her to the bed, catching my feet on the clothes on the floor. My wife lies silently in a heap of twisted linen, her eyes shut tight as if she is praying.

Fear grips my chest. 'Why is she quiet?'

The midwife wipes her brow; the hours of attending to my wife have taken their toll.

'She needs cutting, that's why. The poor girl's exhausted. The shoulder's stuck. Look here.' She picks up a knife and points it at Bella's legs. There are marks on her thighs and darkness between them on the sheets. I had not realised the business of childbirth was quite so bloody.

I take hold of Bella's hand and squeeze it tight. No response. 'Hurry to the town,' I say, setting the lantern on the table. 'Fetch Dr Marsh.'

'Dr Marsh? That charlatan? I wouldn't trust him with my life, not with all his books and his grand ideas.'

'Good God, look at her! She needs a medical man. Someone with experience, with knowledge.'

'It's a mile and a half to the doctor's house. I've done the cutting before.'

A moan from the bed. Bella's eyes flick open, latching on to mine. A tremor of understanding. I reach over, snatch the knife from the midwife and hurl it at the wall.

'Now!' I scream. 'For God's sake, go now!'

'Sir, I must insist!'

'Damn you, woman. She's dying!'

The midwife crosses the room, drops her bloody apron in a heap, then gives me one last look before disappearing into the darkness.

'Bella!' I kneel beside the bed, brushing away the herbs laid on the pillows, sweeping a pile of white pebbles to the floor. A tinkle as they land. 'I am here. Do not be afraid.'

Bella moans almost imperceptibly, her cheeks the colour of milk. 'Please,' she whispers, little more than a breath. 'Please . . . I need . . .'

'Do not fret. She is gone and I am here. Your husband.' I reach for her hand.

'But the midwife . . . Where is the midwife?'

'Shush. Shush. Calm yourself. It is not such a bad thing, calling the doctor at a time like this.' My eyes stray to the herbs scattered on the floor; how much Bella trusts her own medicines. I squeeze her fingers. 'You cannot always rely on your herbs, my love.'

She sinks back into the pillow, her eyelids closing. I think of all the times I've watched her, running her hands over her swollen belly, wonder shining in her eyes at the life within. After all her losses, it's the one hope she clings to. She will do anything, *anything*, to protect this child.

The minutes slip by. Her hand grows clammy in mine. The silence deepens, only the occasional tremulous sigh. At last, I hear the clop of a horse outside.

I kiss Bella's damp forehead. 'He is here! Dr Marsh!'

The lantern light jumps ahead of me as I run down to greet him. 'Thank the Good Lord you are come.'

The doctor ties up his horse and follows me gravely into the house, swinging his bag. When he sees Bella, he frowns. 'You should have called me sooner.' He gets to work, lifting the hem of the shift that is hitched above her waist, grabbing hold of the baby's head. It's an unearthly thing, hairless and shiny with fluid.

'Go downstairs,' he says without taking his eyes away. 'Fetch me more water.'

I pick up an upturned basin from the floor and hurry down to the garden. It takes an age, lowering the bucket into the well, pulling it back up again. The sky is speckled with stars, but the house at my back is dark and brooding. Bella's blanched face swims in my mind as I slosh the water from the bucket into the basin, then stumble back inside, careless in my haste.

Water spills over the rim and splashes on the floorboards as I carry it through the house and up the stairs.

The bedroom has changed in the short time I've been gone. The stench is worse. The stillness near complete. Only the doctor's heavy breathing punctuates the quiet. I watch as he slides his fingers further beneath my wife's taut skin, expecting her to cry out, to protest. But she doesn't. She doesn't say anything. This time, she makes no sound at all.

Something snaps.

The baby slips from Bella's body like an eel, trailing its long silver cord and landing in the doctor's lap. He rubs it for signs of life, but there's no cry. No shuddering breath. Silently, he wipes his blood-bathed hands on a rag, then picks up the baby and carries it to Bella.

'I'm sorry,' he says, shaking his head as he feels for her pulse. 'It's as I feared. The strain was too much for both of them.'

I push the doctor aside, his words making no sense. 'Bella!' I shake her roughly, lifting her shoulders up off the sodden sheets.

Bella's mouth is open, but there is still no sound.

'My love.' The words choke in my throat as the truth jolts through me. My eyes flit to the baby at her side, laid in the crook of her elbow, its skin like curd. 'Please, don't leave me. Not like this. Not before our time is done.' I climb up next to her, not caring what the doctor thinks.

I close my eyes, shutting out the room, but it's still there in my mind. Not Bella but Ma, the night they laid her out; the same bed, the same dark covers, the same yellowed sheets. I remember Pa bending over me and lifting me away, his rough hands digging into my sides. But I wouldn't go, not that easily. I was only a child at the time, but I clung on to the body with all my might. They had to prise my fingers from her clothing, one by one.

I nuzzle into Bella, drinking her in, smelling the sweat on her skin and the grease in her hair, feeling the lingering warmth of her body through the thin weave of her shift.

Midnight slides towards morning.

Doors open and close. Words are spoken, soft as feathers. There is movement of pillows and linen and blankets. The lantern is long extinguished. A breeze from the window. The heady smell of late August.

Dr Marsh rouses me. Bella is tidied up and the baby is nowhere to be seen. The doctor looks tired. Red eyes, face as white as paper, his hands scrubbed clean of her blood.

'You need to let her go,' he says. He turns to the window, to the sound of coach wheels rattling towards the tollgate. 'There is work to do. It is time to start the day.'

NOW

3

'**M**ummy, I'm scared.'

Kelda forced herself awake, feeling a slither of cold on her bare arms as Dylan climbed in next to her. She drew an arm around him, knowing full well she shouldn't. Shouldn't set precedents. She should take him back to his own room, tuck him up in bed and tell him a story until he fell asleep again, but she couldn't let go of him, not yet. Too tired. Too comfortable. She nuzzled deeper, inhaling the smell of his Batman pyjamas and strawberry shampoo. It was the middle of the night, hours before dawn, before the rush of getting him dressed and breakfasted and strapped in the back of the car ready for school.

She consulted her alarm clock and groaned. 'Dylan, it's three in the morning.'

The thought occurred to her that Dylan never usually

did this, at least he hadn't for years. Not since he was a pre-schooler.

'I know, Mummy, but I'm scared.'

There it was again. The word that struck her more than anything: *Mummy*. Dylan hadn't called Kelda Mummy for months. She'd been Mum since they'd moved into the toll house. A growth spurt had sent her scouring second-hand shops for the next-size-up clothes and the name change had come with it. Mum not Mummy, which made her feel sad though she knew it was inevitable. The only time she was Mummy now was when there was something seriously wrong: the time he'd scratched his legs on brambles; the time he'd come down with chicken pox; the time Georgie had punctured his Batman football with his dad's screwdriver.

'It was only a bad dream,' she said. 'A nightmare. Come on, I'll take you back to bed.'

She peeled back the duvet and felt the floor with her feet. Dylan's hand seemed smaller in the dead of night, the moonlight shafting through the window on the north side of the house, enveloping them in stillness like they were doing something they shouldn't. Seven steps from her room to his, past the tiny bathroom. Now that it was just the two of them, she liked the fact the toll house was so small. Two bedrooms and a bathroom upstairs; a kitchen, lounge and hallway below. When Nick had stayed with them for a couple of months just after they'd moved in, they'd stumbled over each other, piling their things – her books, Nick's model kits, Dylan's artwork – in precarious mounds.

'Uncle Nick's coming for breakfast,' she remembered.

Dylan gripped her hand, not seeming to hear. 'I don't want to go back in there.' He froze by his bedroom door. She could see the window on the left, the one that looked over the garden and the wood and the miles of flat countryside.

'It's all right,' she said, going first, plumping his pillow, smoothing his duvet. Pat, pat, pat. 'In you get.'

He climbed in, still holding her hand. Reluctantly, she got in with him and shivered down beneath the duvet. She hadn't realised how cold Dylan's room was until now. It wasn't even proper autumn. She wondered whether it was too early to turn the central heating on. And there was something else. A smell above the muskiness. So faint she couldn't quite place it.

'What was the nightmare about anyway?' she said, stroking his hair.

'I wasn't asleep.' He turned away from her to face the wall.

'Of course you were asleep. Nightmares only happen when you're asleep.'

'I was awake. It was over there.'

He pointed over his shoulder, to where the lava lamp floated purple and silver against the wall beneath the window. The lava lamp she'd given him for Christmas last year, one of his stocking presents.

The smell was stronger now, unmistakable. Lavender.

'What was over there?'

'A woman. She was trying to get me. She had her arms stuck out like this.' He stretched his arms out into the darkness.

For a heartbeat, she faltered, but then she thought of the move, the new town, the change of school. All those fears that surfaced in the night-time. 'It's okay,' she said, folding his hands back beneath the duvet. 'Sometimes dreams feel real, that's all.'

She smoothed his hair again, the mop of brown curls that bounced across his forehead, over and over like she had when he was a baby, feeling him relax and eventually drop off to sleep. She knew she should get up and go back to her own room, double-check her alarm was set for the morning, but she felt herself drifting. Purple. Silver. The weird muddy Technicolor of sleep.

An hour later, she awoke with a start, wondering where she was and what had shocked her awake. She was in Dylan's bed, that was all. She'd woken herself. Just a dream that ran away from her before she could catch it, make sense of it; an impression, a feeling that she couldn't comprehend. The room was icy cold, and the lava lamp had somehow switched itself off. It was pitch black, like staring into a dark hole. Only the feel of Dylan next to her and the rhythm of his breathing told her where she was and that everything was all right.

She slipped out from beneath the covers, wrapped her arms around herself, and tiptoed back across the landing.

She spent the rest of the night tossing and turning, unable to sleep, wondering whether there was something wrong with Dylan. Earlier they'd had an argument and he'd got so mad, he'd thrown a saucepan at the wall. Maybe the nightmare and the bad mood were something to do with the school and the new teacher, Mr Yeo. Dylan hadn't taken to him like the teachers in his old school or Miss Reynolds in year one. She'd listen to his babble of criticism in the car on the way home, feeling guilty for making him change schools, change towns, make new friends: 'Mr Yeo made me eat all my lunch', 'Mr Yeo told me off for painting on my hands', 'Mr Yeo sucks'. Maybe Mr Yeo had transformed from villain to nightmare in the middle of the night? She'd always defended him in front of Dylan, but she suspected Mr Yeo was too harsh on the children. He seemed friendly enough when she met him at the school gates, but there was something old-fashioned about the way he called her

Mrs Johnson, though she'd made it clear she was Ms or Miss. Maybe she should talk to him. Or maybe the nightmare and the argument were one-offs, unconnected to school. After all, Dylan had said he'd seen a woman, probably a character from TV or one of his books.

She got up early and sat in the kitchen waiting for Nick. The kitchen was sandwiched between the hallway and the lounge, a tiny space with just enough room for a table and chairs.

'Hello?' Nick poked his head around the back door, making her jump. He was early.

'I made coffee,' she said, pleased to see him. He'd been away for a couple of weeks, a conference in Brighton, and then he'd been busy catching up on work. 'You sure you don't mind taking Dylan into school? Just I've got this meeting.'

'No really, it's a pleasure.' Nick smiled and sat down. 'I can pick him up, too, if you like?'

Nick looked at home in the kitchen, although it was too small for three people. They'd only lived there two months before he'd moved in for the summer after splitting with his wife. A late-night phone call in which she'd bailed him out before Rachel made him homeless. 'Of course you can stay,' she'd said, not really minding but worried all the same. They'd just been getting used to living on their own, their own routine, their own rules and no one else's. In the end, it had turned out fine. Nick had spent the whole time trying not to get in their way, and she'd spent the whole time trying to include him. She'd liked the chaos, the comfort of someone else in the house.

He picked up Dylan's football top which she'd been mending and smoothed the patch. 'I miss him,' he said.

She smiled. 'He misses you too.'

They took their coffees outside, a routine she followed

regardless of the weather, and sat at the picnic table. She was proud of what she'd done with the garden so far: growing apple trees along the fence, making flowerbeds, rehoming an old stone bench she'd found in a salvage yard.

'I'm worried about him,' she said to Nick. 'He had a nightmare last night. Said there was a woman in his room.'

'Not unusual for a six-year-old. The nightmare, I mean.'

'No. Except he hasn't had a nightmare for ages. It scared me, that's all. There was something about him that wasn't quite right.' She remembered the clammy feel of his skin against hers. 'He was terrified.'

Nick threw her a friendly frown. He thought she worried too much and was always telling her to chill, to let things happen. But it was easy for Nick. No commitments other than a job with a liberal interpretation of flexitime and a half-hearted girlfriend, a rebound from Rachel.

'Anything wrong at school?'

'He doesn't like his teacher.'

'Anything else?'

Kelda shook her head. 'Probably just me being silly. I'd better go and wake him.' She stood up and stretched, achy from the restless night. 'Pancakes for breakfast?'

'Let me do the honours. Pancakes are my speciality.'

Upstairs, Dylan was curled in a ball, hair springing across the pillow. She needed to take him to get it cut; yet another job, another expense. All the other boys wore it short, crew-cut short, but she didn't like the idea of Dylan all grown up like that.

'Dylan, wake up, time for school. Uncle Nick's making pancakes.'

He shifted in his sleep, refusing to wake. She glanced at the lava lamp, shifting purple to silver to purple again. It must have switched itself back on after she'd left.

'Wake up, Dylan.'

He opened one eye, then the other, testing them out, teasing her.

'Time for school. You slept late. Do you remember waking up in the night?'

Dylan sat upright, hair on end, pyjamas scrunched on his chest. He shook his head. 'I didn't wake up. I was asleep. It was night-time.'

Downstairs, Nick was wearing her 'Best Mum in the World' apron, tossing pancakes, at home with her lopsided cooker and plastic spatulas. She set out the plates whilst Dylan wrapped himself around Nick's legs.

'Hello, Uncle Nick!'

'Hello, cheeky monkey.'

Nick wasn't really an uncle, just an old friend from university. Kelda had met him in her first term, a drunken evening in the Students' Union. At twenty-three, she'd been considered a mature student, and as Nick was older too – he'd been starting the final year of his MA – they'd got talking. Everyone assumed they'd end up together, but Nick was too nice to be boyfriend material. They'd been friends for eight years now, losing touch only briefly when he was on a gap year in Germany.

Nick untangled himself from Dylan and hunted in the pantry for the golden syrup.

'You *are* coming on Saturday, aren't you, Uncle Nick?'

'Saturday?'

Birthday party, Kelda mouthed.

'Of course. Wouldn't miss it for the world. You're into *Frozen*, right?'

Dylan kicked him. A series of leg tussles which made her smile.

'I'm going to be seven.'

'Seven? Whoa!'

'And I like Batman.'

'Batman. Okay. Right. Will make a note.'

Kelda hurried them along, picking up the plates when they'd finished. 'Dylan. Teeth. Now.'

'Mum!'

'No arguments. Uncle Nick's taking you to school today and I can't trust either of you to be on time without me.'

After Dylan was gone upstairs, she washed the dishes, stacked them in the drying rack and sat down again. She was frayed from the night before and wished she didn't have to spend the day alternating between meetings and catching up on paperwork. It amazed her that the world ran on people like her, not actually making anything, just shuffling emails from folder to folder. But at least it was a job. Something that used her brain. Before, after she'd dropped out of university, she'd worked part time in a café for one of Mum's friends.

'Busy day ahead?'

'Just knackered.'

'What happened over there, by the way?' Nick pointed at the gash above the kitchen table, in the wall dividing the kitchen from the lounge.

'Dylan,' she said. 'Yesterday. We had an argument, he threw a saucepan. Honestly, he's different when you're here. Better. Sometimes I don't know if I'm doing the right thing.'

'That's quite a dent.' Nick stood up and ran his hands over the cracked plaster. 'More than a dent. You can almost see behind it.'

'I've been thinking of pulling the wall down anyway,' she said, pushing aside the thought that it *had* only been a dent, at least, at first. In the space of twelve hours, it seemed to have cracked open. 'Make it into one big room. Sort of open plan.'

'Wouldn't you need planning permission for something like that? How old is the cottage? 1700s?'

'Seventeen eighty-three. There's a plaque on the wall.' She ran herself a glass of water. 'Anyway, who would know? It's not like we're inundated with guests.'

Nick stretched and somersaulted his car keys. 'I'll give you a hand, if you like? After I've picked the monkey up from school.'

She came home early from the office. She was tired and Cassandra had said she could finish her work at home. She went upstairs, into the bathroom and ran the taps. Like everything else about the house, the bathroom was a work in progress. She had visions of pulling out the dated suite, ripping the tiles from the walls, putting in a proper walk-in shower. She'd go for a contemporary look rather than mock-Victorian, though she knew the latter was better suited to the house. White tiles with flecks of silver rather than the stark matt white that was currently here, which reminded her of tiles in public lavatories.

She poured in bubble bath and slipped her clothes to the floor. She was sticky. Still hot from the drive home. She got in, glancing at her watch through the bubbles. Dylan would be in after-school club right now. Dylan went to after-school club every weekday which made her feel guilty, but today at least, she needed the time to relax and officially she was still working. She'd do that later, sort invoices with a glass of wine when Dylan was asleep.

Lathering herself, she closed her eyes and ducked under.

It had been a hell of a day, sitting through meetings and taking notes, listening to Cassandra drone on, full of her own self-importance. Afterwards, Cassandra had pulled her aside. 'Everything all right? You seem to be a little – what's the word?' Cassandra had pretended to think, pretended to look concerned though Kelda knew it was just an act. 'Distracted.' In the background, Lucy had raised her eyebrows. 'I'm fine,' Kelda had replied. Even if she wasn't, she wouldn't tell Cassandra. Cassandra had laid a hand on her shoulder. 'Can't be easy being a single parent.'

She pulled herself up from the water, playing with the bubbles, moving them over her knees, making peaks. A feeling crept over her: of being watched, of someone else being in the room with her. She froze, the bubbles popping lightly on her knee. She was sure there was someone there. She could feel it. Someone behind her, staring at the back of her neck, her naked shoulders, the ripple of her spine. A feeling that she'd had before, the first time they'd seen the house. A feeling that she was *wanted*. She swivelled around, splashing water over the sides of the bath, onto the tiles. The bathroom was empty apart from herself. She was being stupid, of course there was no one there. She laughed nervously.

A sound cut her short.

She sat bolt upright, catching her breath in her throat, waiting, listening. It came again. The creak of the loose floorboard near the window in Dylan's room. She remembered Dylan's expression in the moonlight, the grip of his hand in hers. Her heart raced.

Mummy, I'm scared.

Silly. She was being silly. The house was old. Decrepit, Mum had called it. A million other things could have made a noise like that. It was probably just a pipe, something to do with running the bath. She closed her eyes and counted to ten before opening them again.

Everything was how it had been. Silent apart from the squeak of the bathtub against her back. Those awful white tiles. The smell of bubble bath. Lavender bubble bath. God, the smell was nauseating. She'd always liked it before or at least not noticed it; a gift from Mum along with a folding clothes rack when they'd moved in. She stood up and searched for her towel, ensuring everything was in place, that nothing had changed. But of course it hadn't, the bathroom cupboard was open just as she'd left it: Dylan's toothbrush was next to hers in a plastic cup, her make-up bag bulging with Superdrug bargains. She just needed to check the room next door, test the floorboard herself.

She pulled the towel from the rail and wrapped it around her. Another sound, this time from somewhere downstairs. This time it was real, not imagined, not just a creaky old pipe. She opened the bathroom door and stood dripping in the doorway, huddled in the towel, feeling the chill on her shoulder blades.

'Hello?'

Footsteps.

Silence.

Footsteps.

Someone was here. Someone was in the toll house. She felt light-headed. Sometimes the postman left parcels at the back door, the only door they used, but she'd already found a pile of bills on the mat when she'd come home, so the postman had been.

'Hello?'

She was out on the landing without remembering walking there, one hand on the banister looking down. For a split second, it was last night and she was crossing from her room to Dylan's. That smell again. Deep. Permeating.

Lavender.

A shadow fell across the stairs from the kitchen doorway. She suppressed the instinct to scream.

'Kelda, is that you?'

Immediately, she relaxed. Nick!

'I'm sorry,' he said, appearing in the hallway. She realised she was trembling. Just the temperature change from the bath. 'I called and called, but no one answered.'

4

————⚬⚬⚬————

'So, what do you want to do exactly?' Nick shone a torch at the hole in the kitchen, angling it one way then the other, peeling flakes of plaster away with his fingers. 'It's like there's a cavity. A wall hidden behind a wall.'

'It's because of the cupboard,' Kelda said, indicating the wall-length cupboard at right angles to the back door. 'I suppose whoever built the wall wanted to incorporate the cupboard.' She wasn't really in the mood for DIY. Except DIY was the reason Nick was here, bunking off work rather than pretending to read academic papers in his attic flat. She ought to play along with it. 'I suppose I could take the cupboard out and knock the whole wall through. Do you think it's safe? The last thing I want is to bring the whole house down on top of me.'

Nick went along the wall, tapping it with his knuckles. 'In my very unprofessional opinion, I don't think the wall has any bearing on the structure. This was obviously one big room at some point. Probably the toll keeper sat here all day watching traffic through the lounge window.'

She reached across to the top of the fridge and lifted down a bottle of wine. She didn't often think about the history of the house, although the estate agent had said it was 'interesting'. History was more Nick's thing than hers.

She opened the wine. 'Drink?'

'No thanks. I've an early start tomorrow, I'd better be off in a mo. Walter wants me in at nine.' Nick wrinkled his nose. Usually, he worked at home on his laptop rather than the university thirty miles away, the city where he'd lived with his wife. 'And Alexa's cooking tonight. She'd be furious if I missed it.'

She glugged wine into her glass. Alexa didn't often stay over at Nick's during the week so he was usually on hand to help after school. But Kelda hadn't seen Nick since Brighton. Perhaps things had moved on between him and Alexa.

'How's it going, the two of you? Do I hear the sound of wedding bells?'

'Hardly. I'm not divorced yet, remember?'

She screwed the top back on the bottle.

'You know her parents are traditional? I've only been introduced once and that was enough.'

'For you or for them?'

He grinned. 'For them, I think.'

She listened to his description of a wedding he'd attended in London, one of Alexa's cousins: the Greek Orthodox ceremony; the hotel they'd stayed in with the rest of the family; the pretence they'd booked two rooms not one.

'You should have seen the look on her mum's face when she caught us leaving the same room in the morning.'

She stifled a yawn; she'd heard the story before. She realised she wanted to talk about the house after all, she wanted his reassurance. She thought about the noise she'd heard from the bathroom, but she knew it had been nothing. Nothing at all. She'd feel stupid even mentioning it.

'Her mum went crazy.'

She swallowed a mouthful of wine. 'You're a grown man. You've been married. You *are* married.'

'Not according to Alexa's parents. I'm a fresh-faced college boy, apparently.'

She let him talk without really listening, wondering if this was cathartic for him, telling her about his love life and the difficulties of enmeshing himself with Alexa's family. She remembered when he'd told her he was marrying Rachel, giving her the details of the big church wedding. She wondered if he talked to Alexa about her in the same unconscious way.

As he talked, she watched Dylan through the window, dribbling a football around the picnic table, hair flopping over his forehead.

'What about you?'

'What do you mean?'

'Invited on any dates?' Nick nodded at her ancient laptop.

'Oh, you know.' She picked up her glass of wine, covering a smile. Someone *had* sent her a message on the dating app, but she wasn't going to tell anyone yet.

'Bet they're flooding in.'

'Actually, I can't keep up.'

'Anyone suitable? Do you need me to vet?'

She shook her head. 'I'm grown up, remember?'

He laid a hand on her shoulder. 'In my mind, you'll always be twenty-three.'

'And you'll always be—'

'A prat, I know.'

He gathered his keys and she wondered quite what she would have said if he hadn't stopped her. She thought again about the noise she'd heard in Dylan's room and wondered if she should say something after all. But there was nothing to say; it was just her mind playing tricks – she was stressed about her job, worried about Dylan – or, more likely, something to do with the house. Something structural.

'See you soon,' he said, pecking her on the cheek. 'And let me know what you decide about the wall.'

'Will do.' She glanced up at the gash. 'I'll have a think. But I probably ought to get a second opinion before we start knocking things down. Not that I don't trust you, of course.'

He grinned. 'Very wise. According to Alexa's parents, I can't be trusted at all.'

He was out of the door, running towards Dylan, tackling him for the ball, when she remembered: 'Saturday.'

'Saturday?'

'The birthday party.'

Dylan shot the ball into the imaginary goal between the apple trees and whooped. Nick turned to Kelda and smiled. 'Wouldn't miss it for the world.'

She got Dylan to bed early. He was tired though he'd never admit it, rubbing his eyes in front of the TV. She read him stories, perched on the side of his bed, then switched on his lava lamp, checking the lead trailing from the back to the wall. No loose wires. Since buying the toll house, she was proud of her achievements: wiring plugs, changing fuses, cleaning gutters, even getting rid of a family of mice. The memory of the mice still made her shudder. She'd caught them one by one using a humane trap, letting them free in the fields behind the wood, watching them dart from the trap. Flashes of brown. She had a phobia of mice, something to do with their tails, something to do with the way you only ever half saw them. The fields weren't far enough, Lucy from work had told her, but four months later, they hadn't returned.

'Goodnight, Batman,' she said, kissing him on the cheek.

Usually, Dylan made a show of wiping it off – *Aw Mum, yuk* – but tonight he closed his eyes and snuggled down into the duvet. A few minutes later, he was asleep. She sat for a while, watching the slow rise and fall of his chest beneath the covers, remembering the first time she'd held him, still wrinkled from birth, the skin of his fontanelle pulsing gently in and out. She'd realised at that point, she'd never been in love before, truly in love. Before Dylan, love had always been conditional, limited, a series of ifs and buts and maybes. But with Dylan it was different. Love was linked to his vulnerability, his need for her. She tiptoed out, wondering whether Dylan remembered the woman in his nightmare, but there'd been no sign he was scared. Just stress from the start of term, she thought.

Downstairs, she emptied his school bag. An uneaten apple rolled from the bottom of it onto the floor and wedged itself beneath the grate of the antique range. She fished it out and ran it under the tap. As far as she could tell, the range hadn't been used for years, probably not since Victorian times. There'd only been one other owner since, Mr Pritchard, the old man she'd bought the place from, who had moved to one of the retirement homes in town when his wife died. Before that, the toll house had been empty for decades. The estate agent had been quick to point out all the original features: the range, the fireplaces, the space in the kitchen wall for a safe, the toll board outside. No doubt he'd been trying to distract Kelda from the flaking paintwork and the peeling wallpaper and the general atmosphere of disuse. Kelda supposed she should make something of the range, make it into a real feature rather than a place to dump things on. One day, she'd sort the house out, transform it into the home she'd imagined when she'd first seen it on Rightmove, cosy but uncluttered, a place Dylan wouldn't be ashamed to bring his friends.

She bit into the apple, tangy, not quite ripe – one of the apples from the trees in the garden – and inspected the gash Dylan had made in the wall that seemed to have opened up. It was even bigger now that Nick had been playing with it and there was a smell. She leaned in. The smell of cold bricks. Something sweet floating on the edge.

She threw the barely eaten apple into the composting bag next to the sink. She couldn't clear the tang from her mouth. It was worse than unripe. There was something rotten about the taste. Something bad. She wondered whether she'd accidentally eaten something she shouldn't, a bug that had crawled into the middle of it. She rinsed her mouth with the wine she'd been lingering over since Nick left and retrieved the envelope still nestled at the bottom of the school bag. A note from Mr Yeo asking her to meet him tomorrow afternoon to discuss Dylan's behaviour. She downed the wine and poured herself another glass. Dylan hadn't said anything to her about his day, just the usual evasive comments about football and Georgie and Mr Yeo being a poo. She'd have to ask Cassandra if she could leave work early again tomorrow and she hadn't even done the work she'd promised to finish today. She pulled the other papers from his bag and opened them one by one. Paintings he'd created that afternoon. Paintings of her. She smiled at that, despite Mr Yeo's letter. She hardly ever wore dresses, but that's how he'd painted her: a long brown dress that reached to the floor, her hair sweeping over her shoulders.

She smoothed the paintings out onto the pile of artwork next to the box of Lego, her mind turning to yesterday's argument. It seemed stupid looking back. She'd asked Dylan to tidy his toys but he'd pretended not to hear.

'I wish you'd just listen for a change!' she'd snapped.

She'd watched as Dylan had deliberately spread Lego pieces further across the kitchen tiles.

'Georgie's got a playroom and a garden,' he'd said, running out of space.

A piece of Lego had jabbed her bare foot. 'We've got a garden.'

'Not a proper one.'

She'd winced as she'd stood on another piece of Lego. She was trying her best with the garden. She *liked* it. She liked the fact you couldn't see the road or the miles of empty countryside unless you stood right by the gate, just the back of the toll house and the wood behind. She liked the little stone bench she'd bought and the lip in the cottage wall where she could sit and watch Dylan play. She liked the idea she had for building a rockery from the pile of stones near the path. She had an idea for a bird bath too and a tree house for squirrels. The garden felt like hers. *Theirs.* Whereas the house still felt like it belonged to someone else.

'Come on, I'll help you,' she'd said, getting on the floor, putting the pieces into a plastic tub.

'Georgie's going to America at Christmas.'

'Lucky Georgie.'

'Can we go to America?'

'No.'

'Why not?'

She'd sat back on her heels and tried not to look frustrated. 'Because I thought we'd go camping next summer. Cornwall maybe. We could ask Uncle Nick?'

Dylan had pouted. 'Boring.'

'That's not very nice.'

'You never let me have any fun.'

'It's not about fun. We can't afford it. I'm not rich like Georgie's parents.'

'I wish you were. I wish we didn't have to live in this stupid house. At least at Grandma's there was a climbing frame.'

She'd gritted her teeth. Dylan hardly ever mentioned Mum. He never said he wanted to go back to their old house, their own way of life, living with Mum on the estate; he never talked about the rickety old climbing frame that Dad had erected years ago, a present for Emma. She'd thought he was happy here.

'You ought to be grateful,' she'd said. 'Some people have nothing. Some kids even have to live on the streets.'

'No, they don't.'

'Yes, they do.'

She'd snatched his Batmobile and thrown it into the plastic tub along with the rest. It was then that her phone had pinged with a message from the dating app. She'd picked it up and seen a photo of a man taken in the shadows. Even at a glance, he was obviously handsome. Dark hair, dark eyes. Next to the photo was a message, inviting her for a drink. She'd put the phone down – she'd read it properly when Dylan was in bed – at the same time as Dylan had jumped up and grabbed the saucepan.

'You don't care about me. All you care about is your stupid phone.' The shock of the saucepan smacking the wall had sobered them both. Dylan had started crying.

They'd hugged. Ragged sobs into her sweater.

'I'm sorry,' he'd said.

'It's okay. We're both tired. I shouldn't have shouted.'

She'd pulled his face back, wiped his tears with her sleeve.

'Shh, shh.' She'd pretended she couldn't see the dent he'd made, pretended it didn't matter about the wall.

But it did matter. She didn't like it. Didn't like the way it looked even wider now the night was setting in. She stood up and collected a torch from the pile of tools jumbled on top of the microwave, then peered in – that smell again – moving the torch up and down. There was something in there, catching the torchlight, reaching towards her through the gap. She grabbed a chair for a better view, climbed up and leaned over the table, bending down a little, peeling the plaster.

A face stared back at her, white as chalk.

She gasped, grabbing the back of the chair to steady herself, then looked again. Not a real face, just some weird sculpture on the inside wall.

She jumped down, thinking of the toolbox she kept in the garden shed. Perhaps she could find a chisel to chip away the edges of the plaster? She ran outside. Still just light enough to see, yet everything seemed murky. Corners she hadn't noticed before. Shadows. She took the toolbox from the shelf, startled by a spider that ran across her hand, found a chisel and went back inside.

The smell was pronounced.

Lavender and no, please God no, not mice. But of course there were bound to be mice somewhere in the house, you couldn't eliminate them entirely. And the smell was obviously coming from the hole.

She tapped the chisel gently around the edges, flecking the floor with plaster, coughing in the dust. She wiped her eyes, then shone the torch into the opening. The face stared back. A face with a long slender nose and narrow lips. Stared without seeing because the eyes were closed like the person was sleeping. But Kelda could feel it. Feel the face *looking*. Taking it all in, taking *her* in. Only this was a person's head made out of plaster, with dimples and smooth arches. Nothing else. No body, not even a neck.

She pushed the chair back under the table, wishing she hadn't looked, wishing she could erase the image from her mind. She found an old shopping list she'd written, left on the table, and pinned it over the hole with Blu Tack. Just some strange feature of the house, she told herself. But she didn't want to stay in the kitchen. She took her laptop to the other side of the wall, to the lounge, and sat in the bay window trying to work, but not managing more than a few columns on her spreadsheet.

At nine o'clock she went around the house, checking the windows, checking the front and back doors, bolting everything that was open. In the hallway she hesitated. A feeling she couldn't shrug off, the same feeling she'd had in the bath: that she was being watched, that someone or something was following her every move, that someone wanted her, though she wasn't sure why. The hallway reached right up to the ceiling on the first floor. Looking up, she could see the gallery landing, open on two sides apart from a wooden banister that ran along the width of the hallway, then turned right and followed the line of the kitchen wall below. If all the doors were open and she stood where she was now, at the foot of the stairs, she could more or less see the whole house. The landing allowed access first to Dylan's bedroom overlooking the garden, a tiny windowless bathroom, and her own slightly larger room at the front of the house with the toll board hanging on the outside wall. The effect should have been grand, but the space was small and narrow, and there was only one window on the landing, on the left at the top of the stairs. It was the part of the house she'd never liked. Probably just the wallpaper. Blue cornflowers on a white background reaching right up to the ceiling. She'd painted everywhere else, but it had seemed such a mission, painting the equivalent of two floors.

She tipped the remains of the second glass of wine back into the bottle and went to bed, exhausted from the night before. She tried to doze off, tried not to think how far away they were from the town, or about the wood behind or the endless fields. She turned on her side, pressing her face into the pillow. Go to sleep, she told herself, just go to sleep.

The white face in the wall swam in her mind. However much she tried, she couldn't get rid of it. It only made it worse trying to shut it out. She couldn't stop thinking about the narrow nose, those sleeping eyelids.

No, not sleeping, she decided, pressing her face deeper into the pillow. It was more final than that.

The person was dead.

5

~

1863

I'm halfway down the stairs, dazed from lack of sleep, dazed from the horrors of the night before, when an idea forces me back again.

Blocking the stairway, Dr Marsh stiffens. 'Bella is dead,' he says like he is talking to a child. 'Helen is with her now.'

I pretend not to hear, moving upwards, expecting him to step aside. But he remains steadfast, thinking, no doubt, of the job I have to do: the carriage waiting at the turnpike, the driver who's knocked three times on the front door, the horses snorting and shitting beside the porch.

'I want an image,' I say.

'A photographer? I can arrange—'

'No, not a photograph.' I think of the death images people keep on their mantelpieces and shudder with distaste. I want something more than that. Something to keep Bella here in the house. 'Come with me.'

I skirt around him, then climb back the way we've come, two steps at a time. The doctor hesitates, then follows me along the landing and into the darkened bedroom. We stand just beyond the threshold. In the far corner, by the soft flicker of a candle, Bella's sister, Helen, mumbles from a prayer book. She doesn't look up, though she knows we are there, stealing the light from the little window on the landing. Beside her is the bed: dark oak, green covers, fresh white pillows. Bella is laid out in her best dress, hair brushed and parted neatly in the middle, the dead infant wrapped by her side. Helen has been busy, not risking anything: the mirror is swathed in black crepe, the photograph of Bella and me on our wedding day face down on the chest of drawers, the clock on the mantelpiece stopped at just gone midnight.

Helen shifts at the sound of our footsteps, closing the prayer book and smoothing her skirt.

I walk to the bed and draw my fingers over Bella's skin, her forehead, her cheek, the little brown mole on her chin. Already she doesn't look like my wife. Too pale. Too stiff. Her skin more like wax than a real human being. It seems impossible that this time yesterday, Bella was pacing across the floorboards in the wake of her labour, her hair flowing long and free – so long she could sit on it – insisting it was too early to fetch the midwife, that she could manage the pain on her own.

Below us, the coachman shouts and raps the door knocker. I should do my duty and hurry down, take his coins and let him through the turnpike. Instead, I listen to his muffled curses with indifference, knowing he'll soon grow bored, turn his horses around and take the long way into town. I wonder how many others have knocked since Bella died, waiting to be let through.

Despite the doctor, despite Helen, a sob escapes my chest like a donkey's bray.

'Mr Walton,' the doctor says firmly. 'It is not unusual. A woman lost in childbirth. A baby born sleeping. You must have known the risk.'

I run my fingers over Bella's lips. So cold. So motionless.

'Bella was a good woman,' the doctor continues. 'She is with Sweet Jesus now. She is with the angels.'

I catch the scent of the herbs Bella laid out yesterday. The herbs she'd chosen for childbirth. Sage for her lady's place. Thyme for courage. Lavender for everything else. Always lavender. There is a half-drunk cup of tea, a herbal or plant concoction, on the table next to the bed and I catch a whiff, earthy and sweet. Helen hasn't been quite so fastidious in cleaning up as I'd thought.

'Her face,' I say. 'You can preserve it, can you not?'

Dr Marsh pretends not to hear.

'Her face,' I urge, indicating the line of her jaw, the round of her cheeks.

'What do you mean?'

'A mask. A death mask.'

The doctor clears his throat. The task is obviously not one he relishes, but I'm impatient. 'You've done it before?'

'Yes. But . . .'

'I will pay you well.' I draw a handful of coins from my pocket, yesterday's takings. The doctor suppresses a smile. For all his talk of angels, he is easily persuaded.

Across the room, Helen grips the chair arms in silent disapproval. She doesn't want anyone to touch Bella but herself. She wants things the way she has planned, no morbid mementoes, no meddling. Nothing that could accidentally trap a spirit. Just the lock of hair I saw her take earlier, cut with a pair of sewing scissors and secreted in her pocket. I glance at the covered mirror, the overturned photograph frame, the stopped clock. All the usual superstitions.

'I would have to act fast,' the doctor says. He points at the cheeks, the hollowed eyes, the lips settled into an almost-smile. 'The features change so rapidly, you see.'

I nod. Already Bella looks like another woman. 'Get what you need and come back as soon as you can.'

An hour later, Dr Marsh is back with a servant. Helen rises to her feet as he lays a bag at the foot of the bed and takes out a pot of grease and a wrap of bandages.

'You can find me downstairs,' Helen says, brushing the floor with her black skirts, leaving a tang in the air, bitter as vinegar.

The doctor gets to work, smoothing grease across Bella's skin, across her eyebrows and the hair above her forehead, an act so strangely intimate, I'm forced to pull my gaze away and watch the servant mixing the plaster of Paris instead. The doctor wipes his sleeve across his face, catching drops of sweat, then nods at his servant. The two men dip the bandages in the smooth white paste and lay them carefully over Bella's face. The doctor talks to me as they work, explaining the process. They will leave the bandages to set before creating a second layer. Too many layers now and the mask will sink and the impression made will be imperfect. When the second layer is set, the mould will be greased before filling with more plaster to create the mask. Then he tells me about the head shape, how the slight rise in the centre of Bella's skull indicates kindness, how the length of her forehead suggests an agreeable nature.

I turn aside, knowing I cannot watch any longer, cannot listen to the doctor's cold assessment of my wife. I leave him be and find Helen downstairs, wiping the furniture, boiling water on the range, gathering the sprigs of lavender Bella left on the windowsills. Everything is bathed in an unnatural half-light. The shutters are closed, and, befitting a death, candles rather than oil lamps burn on the kitchen table. The kettle hisses and spits into the dark as I fight the fury in my head. Helen has already made it clear she intends to stay here for the duration of the wake, sleeping in the chair beside the bed, muttering from her prayer book.

I walk to the bay window and throw wide the shutters.

'What are you doing?' Helen's voice is pinched.

'How am I to do my job if I cannot see the turnpike?'

She says nothing, just lifts the kettle from the range and fills Bella's best teapot, moving about the room like a shadow.

I walk out into the morning. Still only morning! The road is clear. The travellers – the wagons and coaches – have turned around and taken the longer route into town. Everything is bright. It hurts to look at the garden, the flowers, the apple trees, the neat rows of vegetables and herbs, the little rockery by the path. It hurts to see Bella's seat cut into the toll house wall where she would sit for hours, reading or sleeping or simply resting in the garden at the end of the day. It hurts to see life. To see trees and flowers and insects and birds, swaying and fluttering as if nothing has happened. *How dare they not know!*

I find the earthenware pot Bella kept on the window ledge and pull off the lid. Inside is a mound of white pebbles. Bella used to pick them from the stream, wading in, feet bare, until her skirts were wet. She liked the feel of them in her hand, so smooth and round. She liked to rub them over and over before tying them in a handkerchief and carrying them home. 'For good luck,' she'd say.

Now, I dig my hand into the pot, hoping to feel her presence, a whisper, a connection, but the stones are cold and hard against my fingertips. I replace the lid and leave the pot where it is, turning back to the toll house. The doctor is standing in the doorway with Helen, bidding her farewell with an ease that suggests they have been talking awhile. Watching me awhile.

'I will leave my servant with you, Mr Walton,' the doctor says, checking his watch, making no pretence he is not in a hurry. He looks drained, red-eyed, awake since the midwife roused him in the early hours. 'He knows what to do with the bandages.' He passes me a bottle. 'Laudanum. It will calm you, help you sleep. Just a few drops in a glass of wine.'

I wait until I hear the click of the garden gate before I turn back to the toll house. As soon as she sees me looking, Helen disappears into the kitchen. The limewashed walls are bright in the morning sunlight but the shutters are closed on this side of the house; it looks like a corpse with its eyelids shut.

'Bella!'

I drum my fists into the walls, breaking the skin, blood bubbling across my knuckles. Over and over, pummelling the cold brick, uncaring of the carriage clattering towards the turnpike and Helen hiding behind the stark white walls.

6

❀

NOW

On Tuesday morning, Kelda looked up from her desk to find her boss standing over her. She wondered how long she'd been there, watching her. Watching her doing absolutely nothing, just staring at her keyboard, trying desperately not to fall asleep. It had been another bad night, this time of her own doing. Something had woken her at three in the morning, the same time Dylan had woken her the night before, only this time it was something outside the house, not in. She'd listened hard, aware of the in-out of her breath, the rustle of her duvet, trying not to move, trying not to breathe more heavily than she had to. When it came again, she'd known what it was, just the wind lifting the iron knocker on the old front door. Rat-a-tat-tat, like someone wanting to get in.

After that, she'd lain awake, going over things in her mind.

Silly things. The presents she'd wrapped for Dylan's birthday. The party. The friends who'd said they'd come. She'd thought of Mr Yeo and the meeting but pushed it aside knowing that otherwise she'd never sleep at all.

'Ahem.' Cassandra drummed her nails into the top of Kelda's PC.

'Sorry,' Kelda said. 'I was miles away.' Silently, she challenged Cassandra to say something about single parenthood, but instead Cassandra handed her a file.

'A little project for you. I need all this typed up by tomorrow.'

Next to her, Lucy shifted in her seat.

'Do you think you could find the time?'

'Of course.' Kelda sat upright and opened the file. Pages and pages of handwritten notes. 'Wow, that's a lot.'

Cassandra smiled sweetly. 'If you don't think you'll manage . . . ?'

Lucy cleared her throat but Kelda willed her to be silent; they'd dissect it all next time they went out together for lunch. She thought of the afternoon visit to Mr Yeo which she hadn't mentioned, the invoices she hadn't finished from the day before. 'It's fine.' She stood up and collected her mug from the shelf. 'I just need coffee, that's all.'

Cassandra swivelled on her heels, back to her office. 'You're a star. I knew I was right to hire you.'

Mr Yeo was waiting for her in Dylan's classroom, stacking books on a trolley. Her spirits lifted at the sight of the artwork on the walls, the brightly coloured information sheets about this term's topic, the human body. For a moment, she saw another side to Dylan's teacher: a man who liked his job, who cared enough about his pupils to speak to their parents when he was concerned. She even felt sorry for him. All this care and attention only to be the butt of his pupils' jokes.

He shuffled the books until they were perfectly aligned. 'Can I help you?'

'Kelda Johnson. Dylan's mum.' She stepped forwards. The room smelled of industrial disinfectant and tangerines. 'I'm sorry I'm late. I had trouble leaving work.'

She'd finished the notes just in time, working through her lunch break, her fingers moving mechanically over the keyboard, not thinking what she was typing, the numbers, the lists, Cassandra's rambling comments. She'd even wondered if this was Cassandra's idea of a game, whether her boss had invented it just to see if she was capable. Ever since Dylan had come down with chicken pox a week into the new job and she'd taken time off to look after him, Cassandra had been watchful. At three fifteen, she'd slid the file into Cassandra's in-tray with a note to say she'd finished and needed to leave early for a doctor's appointment. She didn't want to have to explain to Cassandra about the meeting with Mr Yeo; she couldn't bear the fake sympathy, the loaded comments about parenthood. Cassandra had twins who were farmed out to nannies, two perfect three-year-olds who, according to Cassandra, were never any bother.

Mr Yeo glanced at the clock. Fifteen minutes late. She'd had trouble finding a parking place then got trapped by a group of mums gossiping at the school gate.

'Take a seat, Mrs Johnson,' he said, indicating one of the children's chairs.

She shifted uncomfortably in the tiny chair, attempting to regain a sense of control, a sense that she was a responsible adult.

'You asked to see me,' she said. 'And please, call me Kelda.'

She slid Mr Yeo's note from her pocket. 'You said you wanted to discuss Dylan's behaviour. Is there anything wrong?'

'No, not wrong exactly.' Mr Yeo fetched a sheet of paper from his desk and pulled up an adult chair opposite. 'It seems your son has a natural talent.'

'Talent?'

'As a poet.' He handed her the paper. She recognised Dylan's writing, large and not quite uniform. A poem entitled 'My teacher Mr Yeo'. She flushed with embarrassment.

'The rhyming's pretty good. Silly. Billy. Willy.'

She stared at the letters, willing them to rearrange themselves.

'Forgotten. Rotten. Bottom. But we still need to work on the limerick form. The anapestic meter. It falls apart round about here.'

He pointed at the word 'poo'.

Kelda shuffled uncomfortably. 'I see. Well, I think we can work on that.' What else was she expected to say?

'If you could, Mrs Johnson. You see, it all comes down to respect. If Dylan can't even show respect in year two, at the start of the academic year, he will be impossible to teach later on. These tender years are amongst the most important.'

'I understand.'

'It's just a small matter.'

'Yes. No problem. I'm sorry.' She was feeling like a child, taking the blame. 'I don't know what's wrong with him at the moment. He's unsettled. It's all very new still. The school. The town.'

'As I said, it's the start of the academic year. I'm sure it's just a matter of time. There's a group of them – Dylan, Georgie Watts, Ethan Jones – I'm keeping my eye on them all.

Please don't worry unnecessarily.' He scraped back his chair. 'Academically, Dylan is very bright. I'd hate for anything to get in his way.'

For some reason she thought of the toll house, the wind lifting the knocker in the dead of night, the plaster face. She reached for her bag on the floor. 'Well, thank you for your time. And sorry again. I'll have a word with him, ensure it doesn't happen again.'

Mr Yeo nodded. 'I'd appreciate that.'

She picked Dylan up early from after-school club. She'd intended to talk to him straight away, but he was happy, telling her about the game of tag he'd been playing and how he'd scraped his knee in the playground but not cried.

'Look,' he said, proudly showing her his plaster.

She decided to speak to him another time, after the birthday party, no point ruining things beforehand. Was it even that bad, a poem about his teacher, a few rude words, but nothing *too* rude? She reached for her phone, intending to text Nick. Instead, a message from Cassandra flashed on her screen:

Sorry I missed you earlier. Everything okay?

She lied and texted back that she'd not felt too well after the doctor's appointment and was on her way home. Will make up time tomorrow, she added.

'Can we have pizza for tea?' Dylan jumped the cracks in the pavement as they headed back to the car.

'Maybe.' She pushed aside the gnawing guilt about Cassandra and texted Nick as they walked.

'Oh, go on, Mum, special treat for my birthday.'

'It's only Tuesday.'

'But it *is* my birthday.'

'Not yet it isn't. Not until Saturday.'

He ran ahead, swerving lampposts, engrossed in a game about dragons.

Nick pinged a message back: he'd be over as soon as he finished work.

She put her phone away and ran after Dylan. 'Uncle Nick's coming round later,' she said, 'so you might be in luck.'

Dylan squealed. 'Pizza?'

'Only if you're very, very good.'

Back home, she logged in to her work account and tried to respond to her outstanding emails, but she couldn't concentrate. Dylan was in the next room, watching TV and playing with his Lego. She could see him through the doorway, lying on his front, legs at right angles in the air, feet swaying rhythmically to his favourite TV tune. To her left was the cavity wall. The shopping list she'd tacked over it had fallen off whilst she'd been at work and the gash seemed bigger. Big enough to put a fist through. She stood up, and did just that, meeting the cold edge of plaster on the other side. The plaster face. She hated the thought of it being there, watching her through the crack, surveying the comings and goings of the kitchen, but she supposed it was something she'd have to get used to, unless she ripped out the wall or filled in the hole.

She sat down again, trying to focus on the words on her screen, but it was no good. Instead, she called out to Dylan that she was going outside.

'Want to help me with a bit of gardening?' she said, poking her head into the lounge.

He shook his head and stared at the TV.

Outside, she gathered tools from the shed, then raked the leaves from the apple trees into a pile. She'd bought the trees from a local nursery at the beginning of the summer, having hacked back the brambles and weeds along the perimeter. It was one of the first things she'd done, more pressing than the house itself; stripped the garden bare, seen what she'd got for her money. It wasn't much. A straggly lawn, a couple of flower-beds that she would have to start again from scratch. She'd been in the nursery, trying to keep up with Dylan, when the idea of apple trees had occurred. She had to have apple trees. She'd grow them along the garden wall, she knew the exact place, she saw it in her mind like they were there already. Like they'd always been there. She'd splashed out and bought mature trees which, according to the nursery owner, would last her eighty years. Eighty years. She'd be dead by then but she'd decided it was worth it, spending money on something that would last. Maybe she'd been thinking about Emma. When they were little and still close, they'd pick apples from the tree next door and pretend to make cider, then drink the sweet-sharp juice, mimicking their father.

But now the trees annoyed her. The fruit was bad, even the ones which looked good from the outside. More than once, she'd put an apple in Dylan's lunchbox only to find he'd taken a couple of bites and discarded the rest. She'd tried making an apple pie, slicing through the bright white flesh, getting tangy juice on her fingers. But then she'd seen that the fruit was mushy and brown at the core. She couldn't understand it. Had she done something wrong when she'd planted the trees?

She picked one up from the lawn – green and shiny – and turned it over. Maggots wriggled through the decaying flesh on the underside. She dropped it with a gasp.

'Can I help you, Mum?'

She spun around. Dylan was behind her. 'Gosh, you made me jump.'

Dylan skipped to the shed and grabbed his little set of gardening tools. 'I'm going to do my archaeology.'

'Good plan, Batman.'

Twenty minutes later, she crossed to the compost heap, weeds and sticks bundled in her arms. Dylan wasn't where he had been, poking beneath the apple trees, his tools abandoned on the lawn.

'Dylan? *Dylan?*'

She dumped the weeds and walked into the house, into the lounge, but he wasn't there either. There was just the TV chattering on. She ran out again, feeling the chill of early evening against her face and hands.

Dylan was walking along the garden path, swinging his bucket.

'There you are! Where were you?'

'In the field.'

'What?'

'I went to see if I could climb over the wall. If the trees were low enough on the other side. But they weren't.'

'Dylan! I've told you before. You mustn't leave the garden! You mustn't wander onto the road. It's almost dusk!' Her eyes landed on the bucket. 'What have you got in there?'

'My archaeology,' he said, drawing it close.

They went back inside, Kelda pulling Dylan with her. Immediately, she knew there was something wrong. The kitchen was steaming up and there was a smell of burning. She sprinted from the doorway and yanked open the oven door. Wisps of hot smoke that made her eyes smart. She searched the room for the oven gloves but couldn't locate them, pulling a tea towel from the range instead.

'Shit.'

She threw the burned pizza from the oven onto the table, burning her fingers through the flimsy towel. She ran to the sink, turned the cold-water tap. Nothing. She twisted it harder. A sudden splutter, the old pipes cranking and gurgling.

'What's wrong, Mum?' Dylan peered beneath her arm.

'Nothing, I burned the pizza and then I burned myself, that's all.' Dylan turned to the mess on the table, his feast, his special treat. She thought he was going to cry. Instead, he ran towards her and wrapped his arms around her waist.

'It's okay, Mum. Maybe we can get a takeaway pizza instead?'

She looked at the crown of his head, his hair pressing against her blouse.

Suddenly, he released her and ran to the open door. 'There's someone here.'

The house had two outside doors though it was only really big enough for one: the one they used, leading from the kitchen into the garden, and the heavy one at the foot of the stairs that led into the outdoor porch, open on three sides apart from the two corner pillars. The porch sat too close to the road for Kelda's liking. When they'd first moved in, she'd taped a sign to the knocker, directing people round the back.

'Uncle Nick! Mum burned the pizza.'

Nick swung Dylan back into the kitchen.

'Just as well I brought crisps and popcorn then.' He dumped a plastic bag next to the blackened mess. 'I thought we could have a movie night? I've brought DVDs. *Scooby-Doo. Tom and Jerry. Toy Story.*'

Dylan squealed and attacked the plastic bag, pulling out the DVDs.

Is that okay? Nick mouthed above Dylan's head. *Sorry, should have asked you first.*

Perfect, she mouthed back.

'And I brought something for your mum too.' He leaned over Dylan's head and swung out a couple of bottles. 'From your text, you sounded like you needed a drink, and to be honest, after a day with Walter . . .'

'You read my mind,' she said. 'But tea first, okay? Pasta, then popcorn?'

Dylan wrinkled his nose at the pasta, then launched himself at Nick.

They waited until Dylan was in bed to drink the wine, then sat outside at the picnic table, watching the fading light and shrinking deeper into their coats. The days were still warm but the nights were getting colder, creeping in earlier and earlier. Kelda had lit a candle in a glass jar. A vanilla and coconut candle. Only it didn't smell of vanilla and coconut. It smelled of that other smell, the one that had been hanging around the house for days. Dust and dried herbs and mice and . . .

'I think it's quite good.' Nick handed her back Dylan's poem. She took it and folded it slowly, wishing she could meet his enthusiasm. 'Come on, Kelda, you've got to see the funny side. It's impressive for a six-year-old.'

She topped up their glasses, glad he couldn't see her properly, couldn't see how worried she was. 'I know, I know. I need to chill out.'

'I don't mean that.'

'You're right, though. I get so het up. I sound middle-aged. I *am* middle-aged.'

'You're thirty-one. Younger than me. You're practically a teenager.'

'Hardly!' She made a pretence of laughing though she knew he saw through it. 'It's just I feel this horrible pressure. Like everyone's watching me, waiting for me to fail, waiting for me to be the disaster parent they expect me to be.'

'Who thinks that?'

'Cassandra Parker.'

Nick groaned. 'God, not her.'

'And my mum.'

'Who you hardly ever see anymore.'

'And Emma,' she said, thinking about her sister, though she knew that wasn't true. Emma probably didn't think about her at all and, if she did, she probably wouldn't care what sort of parent she was. They'd been close once, when they were children, spending hours dressing up and playing dolls and disappearing into imaginary worlds. But something had changed between them when Dad left. Emma had been Dad's favourite, his for-ever-little girl. When he'd upped and left, Emma had been fourteen but she'd not understood it; in her mind, you didn't do that to the people you loved. She'd even packed a suitcase and followed him to the new address, only to be met with his new family, his soon-to-be new wife and soon-to-be stepdaughter. The last time she'd spoken to Emma, before they'd moved to Stonebridge, she'd sounded completely out of it, slurring down the phone, talking about Mum and Dad but not making any sense.

She drank the wine, feeling it warm her, numb her.

'You know it doesn't really matter what they think of you.' Nick put his hand on her arm. She saw his tanned skin, the wrinkles on his knuckles. 'And I promise you, this is just normal stuff, the normal sort of thing a kid Dylan's age would do. I'm sure I was far worse when I was six.'

'Really?'

'Really.'

She softened. 'Perhaps you're right.' She thought of telling him about the feeling she'd had the other night in the hallway and before that in the bathroom, the feeling of being watched. She'd already shown him the mask on the wall, hidden behind the plasterboard. He'd called it a death mask, which she hadn't liked; he'd seen something similar in a museum, the face of a criminal hanged for murder. The Victorians were like that, he'd said, handing her back the torch. Morbid as . . . well, morbid as death, he supposed. But the mask was tangible whereas the other was just a feeling, like someone walking on her grave.

She decided to try him anyway. 'There's something about this house . . . ' She broke off and shivered, feeling it watching them over their shoulders. 'It feels weird.'

'Weird?'

'I don't know. Since I found the face in the wall, the house sort of feels alive.'

'It's old, that's all. When I stayed here, I didn't feel anything odd.'

'Probably just me then.'

'Things always seem different when the seasons change.'

She tried to block her thoughts as she listened to Nick's stories of the places he'd lived in as a kid, his dad's failed attempts at DIY and damp proofing. But she struggled to follow him. The smell of the candle was nauseating. She saw the piled leaves on the compost heap, the apple trees shadowed against the garden wall.

She blew out the candle, realising how dark it had got, how she couldn't see Nick clearly.

He laughed. 'I can't see my drink.'

'Sorry, the smell. It was irritating me. I'll turn the kitchen light on instead.'

She stood up at the same time as he did. They bumped into each other, hands brushing. She took a half-step backwards. She ought to call it a day, make Dylan's lunchbox, tidy up the kitchen.

'I missed you when I was in Brighton,' he said.

She felt his breath in her hair; a subtle change in atmosphere. Without knowing what she was doing, she raised a hand and touched the side of his face, the stubble along his jaw line. She felt the dimple on his cheek that deepened when he smiled. She wondered if she'd dare . . .

He laughed as they bumped foreheads.

'Sorry,' he said. 'I can't see a thing.'

He was lying: it was dark but not *that* dark. She opened the door and switched on the kitchen light, casting a pale glow across the garden and the picnic table. The second bottle of wine stood half drunk between their glasses.

'I'd better be going,' he said. 'I've got loads on tomorrow. Walter is planning this conference . . .'

'And I'd better be getting an early night after the hash I made of today.'

'You're too hard on yourself. By the sound of things, you handled everything brilliantly.'

'Do you want to take the bottle back? Share it with Alexa?' The name jabbed against her tongue like a knife.

He shook his head. 'Save it for the weekend. You'll need it . . .'

She joined in, laughing nervously, ' . . . after the party.'

She heard him walk away down the path and only breathed steadily again when she heard the click of the garden gate.

7

The next day, Cassandra sent Kelda home as soon as she came in. It was a busy day in the office; Cassandra was expecting visitors and the last thing she needed, she said with a flourish of concern, was for Kelda to pass on her bug.

'I'll just have to welcome them myself,' Cassandra said. 'Or perhaps Lucy can be my PA for the day?'

Kelda drove home with a sense of guilt, hoping no one in the office would let slip about yesterday's meeting with Mr Yeo or the non-existent doctor's appointment. She even hoped she'd develop symptoms, but the only ailment was a throbbing head from last night's wine.

She unlocked the back door, wondering what to do with her unexpected free time. She thought about spending the day in the garden, planting the bulbs she'd bought for the spring, but instead, with a sigh of determination, she decided to attack

the kitchen. She'd been putting it off for weeks – there were
so many other things to do around the house – but it was the
place she spent the most time in apart from the lounge, as well
as the most chaotic.

She climbed onto the counter and started with the shelves.
Everything was mismatched, stuff forced on her by Mum. She
went through tins, throwing things out, kitchen gadgets she
knew she'd never use, Tupperware containers with missing
lids, old bags of pasta and out-of-date sauce. There was a model
aeroplane kit of Nick's that was still in its box and covered in
cobwebs. She dusted it off, thinking about last night, the feel
of Nick's skin beneath her fingertips, the wine on his breath.
'Men and women can't be friends without sex getting in the
way,' Emma had said years ago, when they were still teenagers,
like sex was something she did all the time. Maybe it was, but
for Kelda it had been an abstract concept back then, something
other teenagers did but not the ones like her, the ones concentrating on their grades.

She put the aeroplane kit on the table, imagining Nick when
he'd stayed with them, sitting in the chair near the cupboard,
coffee in one hand, superglue in the other. It was the only time
he used his reading glasses, when he was building models.
They made him look serious and academic. She pictured Dylan
sitting next to him, obediently handing him the pieces one by
one, trying not to fidget or get his fingers stuck with glue.

'Shall I take him out of your hair?'

'No. It's your kitchen. Anyway, he's being helpful, aren't
you, Dylan?'

Over the summer, Nick had talked a lot about Rachel, the
failed marriage, the wasted years. He'd talked like he was
someone much older. She'd felt jealous, not of Rachel but of

Nick. He'd had a proper grown-up relationship unlike the dates she sometimes went on, the occasional boyfriends she couldn't quite commit to.

Kelda pulled the last items from the shelves and laid them on the table, determined not to think about Nick and Rachel or what had happened last night. Right at the top was a heavy earthenware pot with a loose-fitting lid. She ran her fingers around its rimmed surface, wiping away dust and tracing the sand-brown clay, before removing the lid. Inside was a pile of white pebbles. She dug her hand into them, feeling how cold and smooth they were. She remembered Dylan finding the pot in a nook in the wall, the day they'd first seen the toll house. The stones were all the same, almost perfectly white. When they'd moved in, she'd put the pot on the top shelf in the kitchen and forgotten about it. Funny to think it had been there all these months, biding its time. She wiped it carefully and put it back on the shelf next to the cookbooks, then laughed at her own absurdity: biding its time for what?

The rest of the week, she went to work, batting away Cassandra's feigned concerns about her health, and counting down the days to Dylan's birthday. On Saturday, the big day, she spent the morning making sandwiches, slicing carrots into sticks and halving grapes, all the healthy stuff she knew the children would bypass in favour of crisps. Dylan's first birthday party in the new town and she wanted it to be perfect. The house was so small, she'd had to limit the guests to his six closest friends, but she hoped she'd made up for it with her preparations. She had a list of games to play including pass the parcel with a gift for every child, cake and party bags, speakers borrowed from Lucy to blast music into the garden.

'You've done a marvellous job,' Lucy said, giving her a squeeze as the guests started to arrive. 'They're all going to love it.'

Two hours later she was exhausted. Georgie and Ethan's mums had dropped off their kids without staying or offering to help. The rest of the parents had congregated at the far end of the garden, keeping away from the chaos. Only Lucy, who had come along for moral support, was at hand to help with the entertaining, handing out cake and twisting balloons into animal shapes.

Kelda took a breather in the kitchen, running herself a glass of water and glancing at her phone. Nick still hadn't arrived. Her mind wandered back to Tuesday night, the wine, the garden. She'd drunk too much, or rather she'd not eaten enough for dinner. The wine had gone to her head. She wondered whether she'd scared Nick off, whether he'd decided to play it cool for a while. Still, it wasn't like Nick not to turn up without letting her know. Even if he'd freaked out, he'd have made an excuse. Perhaps he was running late – very late – or perhaps he'd got the time wrong?

As the party wound to a close, she handed out the bags of sweets and toys and thanked the guests for coming. Dylan had disappeared upstairs with Georgie despite the fact she'd repeatedly called him down. She told herself not to be angry. He was over-excited, showing off, running everywhere in his new Batman trainers. He'd be a nightmare to get to bed later. Eventually, Georgie ran downstairs again at the sound of his mum's car.

'I hope he's behaved himself.' Mrs Watts leaned over the garden gate. 'Come on, Georgie, the car's still running. Say thank you to Dylan's mum.'

'Thank you,' Georgie's mouth bulged with sweets.

Kelda turned back inside. The house was a tip, bits of food crushed into the floor, apple juice from an upturned paper cup pooling on the table. 'Dylan?' Kelda called up the stairs. It had been a good twenty minutes since she'd seen him, since they'd sung him happy birthday and taken photos whilst he blew out the candles on his Batman cake.

'He's probably crashed out,' said Lucy. 'Too much sugar. You go and find him, I'll start clearing up down here.'

Kelda climbed the stairs and crossed the landing.

'Dylan, are you in there?' She opened his bedroom door and immediately stood on a pile of toys. The life-sized blow-up skeleton she'd given him as a present to go with the human body theme at school tilted towards her on the bed. But Dylan wasn't there. Her mind spun. Where the hell was he? It wasn't like Dylan to miss out on a party, even for a few minutes. She looked under the bed and in the wardrobe, calling his name.

A faint sound of sobbing came from next door. She ran to the bathroom, twisting the door handle. It was locked. 'Dylan! Is that you? Come out!'

She heard movement inside.

'Dylan! Please! I didn't know where you were. All the guests have left. Please open the door!'

The lock slid open on the other side. A crack of light. Dylan buried his face in her jeans.

'What on earth is wrong? I was worried for a moment. I thought you'd run off.'

He peeled back his face, red and puffy from crying.

'Someone broke my new glider.'

She looked behind him. His main present, a bright green glider, was snapped in two pieces on the floor. She bit her lip, swallowing her anger. She'd told him to leave his toys alone, to enjoy the party and stay downstairs. And now look what had happened! She wanted to say something, she wanted to show him she was cross, but she couldn't, not with tears running into his nose and snot smeared across his cheeks. Instead, she grabbed sheets of toilet paper and wiped his face.

'What happened?'

'Me and Georgie were fighting.'

'Fighting? What about?'

'My cake.'

'Your cake?'

She'd spent the evening making it. Chocolate cake which she'd covered in black icing with yellow bats. She'd been pleased with her efforts though it looked distinctly homemade.

'He said it was rubbish. Then he ran downstairs. So I looked for my glider. I wanted to show it to him. But I couldn't find it. I went in your bedroom and found my glider on your bed. Someone had snapped it in half.'

She picked up the two pieces and tried to fit them together, but she knew it wouldn't work, even with glue.

'You must have left it there earlier,' she said. 'And Georgie must have been in my room and broken it.'

'It wasn't Georgie.' He shook his head, convinced. 'He wouldn't do that.'

She sighed, knowing there was only so much she could say. Dylan had to learn who his real friends were. Still, it didn't stop the ache, the desire for everything to be perfect, for everyone to be kind and loving. 'I'll buy you another one. Come on. Let's go downstairs. Lucy's still here. She might have some more cake for you.'

By seven o'clock, Dylan was fast asleep on the sofa despite

her concerns he'd be difficult to get to bed. She switched off the TV and tried to feel happy, resisting the urge to pour herself a large glass of wine. She picked up her phone and stared at her messages. The last text from Nick was Tuesday afternoon, before they'd drunk the wine. It hurt that Nick had let Dylan down. Whatever Nick thought of her, this was Dylan's day. She texted, Missed you at the party, then flicked to the dating app without waiting for his response. She still hadn't replied to the guy who had invited her to the pub. She'd been meaning to do it, but something had stalled her. All the stuff with Dylan and the school, and then the party. She studied the guy's photo. He was standing under a tree, his features in shadow like he had something to hide. But what she could see of him was definitely good-looking. She typed a message, apologising for the delay and asking when he was free, then she threw the phone on the sofa. Exhausted, she bent over Dylan and lifted him gently into her arms. He murmured in his sleep and nestled into her chest.

'Come on, sleepy boy. Time for bed. You've had a busy day.'

Upstairs, she pulled the duvet over him and switched on the lava lamp, then watched the warm glow against the walls, the colours merging into one another, before tiptoeing out.

'No!'

She was halfway across the landing.

'Please, Mummy, I don't like it in here.'

She stepped back into Dylan's room and sat down on his bed. 'What's wrong, Batman? I thought you were asleep.' She smoothed the hair from his face. He stared eyes wide, forehead glistening with sweat. Stared like he wasn't seeing her, like he was looking through her and seeing something else. She wondered whether he was ill.

'I don't like my bedroom anymore.'

'Don't be silly. It's a lovely room.'

'Please, Mum, can I sleep with you tonight?'

She tucked the duvet around his shoulders and smoothed the pillow on either side of his head. 'I don't think—'

'Please!'

She sighed. She knew she shouldn't agree. She'd had such problems when he was a baby, getting him to sleep in his cot. He'd always preferred sleeping next to her, rolling towards her on the bed in Mum's house until he was as close as he could get. Mum had given her a book on the Gina Ford method, but she'd not had the heart to try it. For the first two years, she'd been permanently tired, permanently resisting Mum's efforts to instil a strict regime. It wasn't until he was three that he'd agreed to try a toddler bed.

He pushed the duvet away and grabbed on to her sleeves. 'Please!'

She sighed again. She really shouldn't but . . .

'Just because it's your birthday,' she said. 'As long as you promise me you won't ask me this every night?'

'I promise.'

She lifted him up again, carried him across the landing, and tucked him into her own bed.

'What's wrong with your room, anyway?' she said.

'I don't like that woman.'

She felt a chill down her spine, remembering his nightmare, remembering what he'd said about the woman standing in his room. 'It's just the light, the shadows. There is no woman. It's the lava lamp playing tricks. We could switch it off.'

He shook his head. 'The woman scares me. She's always trying to get me. I don't want to sleep there anymore.'

She leaned over him and kissed his forehead. 'It's your

dreams, that's all. When I was little, I got nightmares all the time, but you grow out of them, honestly you do. Shall I go and get Snuggy?'

He nodded and turned on his side.

She went back into his room, the room she'd painted magnolia, painting over the wallpaper, sticking it down where it had peeled away, though she knew she should have stripped it to the paint underneath. One day, she'd have to do it again, do the job properly. She rooted around the bed for the blue fluffy rabbit he'd had since he was a baby, that had been through the washing machine more times than she could remember. She found it rolled deep in the duvet, then straightened the bedclothes. It was then that she found them, her fingertips falling over their cold hard surface: three white pebbles tucked beneath the pillow. She picked them up one by one. Perfect ovals, worn smooth over the years, gleaming like they were still wet. Gleaming like tears. She thought of the earthenware pot in the kitchen. It was impossible Dylan could have climbed up there and lifted it down. Far too heavy and beyond his reach. He must have found them elsewhere, trophies from some game or other, something he'd played at school. She left them where they were, deciding she'd ask him about it another time, then closed his bedroom door.

Back in her own room, she tucked the rabbit beneath his arm.

'Goodnight, Batman,' she whispered. 'Sleep well.'

Dylan didn't stir, exhausted from the excitement of the day. But Kelda tossed and turned all night, images of pebbles and apples and Nick's face flitting at the edge of her consciousness.

8

❧

1863

I'm in the carriage behind the hearse, seated next to Helen, watching the horses with their black plumes making their way uphill towards the church. It is a cold drizzly day in early September, a turn in the seasons that I can feel in my bones. Helen sneezes and blows her nose. I look past her to the glass windows of the hearse, Bella's coffin jolting in time with the horses. Their tails sway, their heads toss, their breath clouds the air. The townsfolk have come out to watch, to pay their respects. No one has a bad word to say about Bella, but I feel the women's eyes on me as the carriage rattles up the street. They know what happened that night. I see the midwife amongst them, holding me with her eyes, just a moment, a flicker of breath, then she looks away and stares at the ground.

Helen sneezes again, drawing me away from the townsfolk,

back to the coffin. Before the funeral, before the procession to the graveyard, I found her asleep, exhausted from watching over her sister and cooking for the visitors who traipsed through the toll house to pay their respects: Bella's dour-faced mother and her uncles and aunts and cousins. I stepped around the sleeping Helen to the coffin on the bed. There were flowers everywhere and I thought how Bella would have liked that. She always seemed more at home in the garden than in the house, though it was I who spent my days outside, watching the road from the porch whilst Bella cooked and cleaned. In the days before we were married, when my father was still toll man, she would take me walking with her, miles and miles across the countryside. 'Look, Joe,' she would say, bending down at the side of a hedgerow, 'early violets, see how delicate they are?' Once, she brought a bird into the cottage with a broken wing, a starling with freckled feathers that made me jump every time it moved. A grown man by then, yet the starling made me jump! She nursed it back to health then watched with delight when it hopped on the garden wall and flew away into the fields. I remember her saddened by a mouse she'd caught, bloodied and lifeless, in a trap. After that, she'd put all the traps away and strewn herbs around the skirting boards instead. Torn sprigs of mint. 'The mice do not like it,' she'd said when I asked.

As I stood there, over her coffin, with the memories drifting around me like leaves, I realised Bella's body was beginning to smell. A whisper of decay above the flowers. I remembered when my stepmother died, how the smell would soon become unbearable, lingering long after the body had been removed, seeping into everything: the mattress, the sheets, the pillows. Now, I wanted to turn away but I could not let Bella go. I *would not* let her go. I grabbed Bella's hand, the fingers so cold, like sticks on a winter's day, and breathed on them hard, trying to re-kindle the life that had ebbed from her so quickly, so cruelly. But the skin was like leather, unyielding to my touch. I stared at the baby swaddled at her side, the baby she wanted more than life itself. How strange to think they would lie together for eternity.

Helen stirred in her sleep, reminding me I was not alone. That Bella and I would never be alone again. I walked to the chest of drawers, rattling the doors open one by one until I found what I was looking for: the small handbell my step-mother had used in her illness whenever she had wanted me to fetch her water or mop the beads of sweat from her brow. I wiped it clean with a handkerchief and placed it in Bella's hand in the coffin. If we were wrong, if she was sleeping deeply, so deeply her pulse was imperceptible, she would be able to ring for help. And someone would hear her, wouldn't they? The grave digger, the rector, the women laying flowers?

Now, the carriage halts behind the hearse and we dismount stiffly, following the pall bearers around the side of the church to the graveyard. The drizzle breaks into a proper downpour, rain darts off the graves. The mourners huddle beneath their black umbrellas, feet sliding in the mud as the rector begins his prayers.

'Earth to earth, ashes to ashes, dust to dust.'

I stare at the coffin, at the scattering of soil on the lid, listening for Bella, listening for the bell as they lower her into the ground. A sign. Something to tell me she has not left after all, that my prayers are not forsaken. A sparrow hops towards the grave, looking for worms, taking flight at the rector's stole flapping in the breeze. Is that you, Bella? Is that how you have chosen to come back to me? As a bird, as one of God's little creatures?

And then I hear it: the slight but unmistakable tinkle of a bell.

'Stop!' I stumble towards the grave, pushing the rector out of the way. 'She is alive. I heard it. She rang the little bell I placed in the coffin.'

The undertakers stop lowering the ropes. They look at each other, at me, at the rector. The coffin is suspended halfway down the hole. Helen releases her mother's grip and steps from beneath her umbrella. The rain catches her face.

'Joseph, no.'

'I heard it,' I say, and just like that, I hear it again. A faint but definite tinkle. I spin towards the mourners. 'You heard it too, did you not?'

The rector shakes his head, unsure. The mourners lean forward. One or two incline their heads as if to listen. The rest look horrified. Mutters of disbelief.

I wipe rain from my forehead. 'Pull the coffin back up.'

The undertakers hesitate, glancing at the rector who nods his assent, then heave the coffin back onto the ground. It lands with a thud, the ropes falling slack.

'Joseph, I said no.' Helen is between me and the coffin but I step around her easily, grabbing the grave digger's spade. I raise it high as Helen screams, then pitch it into the wood. There's a terrifying splinter. I raise the spade a second time. The rain bounces off my coat as the rector crosses his chest.

'I will get you out, Bella. I will set you free.'

I bring the spade down hard. The lid splinters in two. I grab the halves with my hands, the wood digging into my palms, and try wrenching them apart. But the wood is too thick; the finest coffin I could afford. I lift the spade a third time, plunging it deep. The wood cracks. Bella's mother sways and cascades to a heap on the ground. Swathes of black crepe on the sodden grass. The crowd gathers around her. Helen attempts to lift her to her feet. Someone else steps in to help.

'Where is the doctor?' I shout, ignoring the spectacle behind me.

Dr Marsh pushes his way through the crowd. Standing next to me, he stares at the bodies in the coffin, the wood broken around Bella's face, the wedding veil torn and gaping, the wrapped infant at her side. There is a deep gash on Bella's forehead where the spade must have cut in. She looks like wax, like an oversized doll, and the smell of death is worse. Putrid. Nauseating.

The doctor bends over, feeling for a pulse, and shakes his head, then he lifts the bell, fallen away from her hand.

'You heard it rolling, that's all,' he says. His voice is as wooden as the panels cut from the coffin. 'Come on, Mr Walton, I will take you home.'

'No!' I'm blinded by tears and rain. Scenes from the night of Bella's death spill like cards: holding the lantern, stepping into the bedroom, watching the doctor twist the baby from between her legs. I see the doctor's clothes splashed with Bella's blood, red marks on his forehead, his hands shaking. I remember how he'd sent me downstairs to fetch the water, how he'd wanted me out of the way. I swing towards him. 'I trusted you!'

The crowd shifts and mutters.

'You, a medical man! You were meant to save her. You were meant . . . ' My words dissolve in angry tears.

The doctor scowls. 'You do not know what you are saying!' His cheeks burn despite the weather. 'You have no comprehension of such matters. How could you? A mere toll keeper!'

My limbs stiffen. I remember the midwife's words: *I wouldn't trust him with my life.*

The rector steps between us and lays a hand on my shoulder. 'It is too late for blame,' he says. 'We need to bury her. We need to lay her to rest.'

I shrug him away, lifting my face to the black sky, imploring whatever God there is to help me.

The undertakers pick up the wooden panels and lay them gently over my wife's face. Rain stings my eyes and drenches my coat, but no one brings me an umbrella. The mourners turn away in drabs, scared and superstitious. Bella's mother is helped to the carriage in a half-faint. Only the rector remains, and Helen with her face like stone.

9

NOW

'You look nice, Mum.' Dylan peered around the bedroom door. Kelda was tying her top at the back. A black cropped halter-neck that sat just above her belly button. She wasn't sure if it was too much, whether she would be able to hold her stomach in for the whole evening, whether she would feel sexy or uncomfortable.

'Thanks, love,' she said. She pulled on a pair of jeans and felt better. Nice but not too dressy. She'd told Dylan she was meeting a friend in the pub and that Lucy was babysitting. Dylan had always got on well with Lucy. Lucy sometimes slipped him Haribos when Kelda was pretending not to look and let him play games on her phone. But it was the first time she'd babysat. One of the few times Kelda had gone out alone. The last time, Cassandra's birthday party in June, when she'd felt like a spare part and drunk too much to compensate, Nick had been on hand to help.

'Where are you going?'

'I told you, the pub.'

'With Uncle Nick?'

'No. Another friend.'

'What's her name?'

Kelda painted on lipstick then rubbed half of it off again with a tissue. 'It's not a her, it's a him. His name's Simon.'

'Can I come too?'

'No. It's a grown-up evening. You'd get bored.'

Dylan pulled a face and ran downstairs. She heard him below, chatting to Lucy in the kitchen. Kelda relaxed and selected a pair of plain stud earrings from her jewellery box. She'd been more nervous about leaving Dylan with someone she hadn't left him with before than the actual date, but she realised now, all that worry had been wasted energy. There wasn't anyone more solid, more easy-going than Lucy. They'd stay up past his bed-time, watching DVDs; Dylan would fall asleep on the sofa and Kelda would carry him up to bed when she came back home. She'd already decided to drive and not drink; it would be easier that way to get away quickly if she needed to.

In the kitchen, Lucy was ladling soup into bowls. 'Fab top, by the way.'

'Thank you. And thanks for doing the soup.' Kelda tugged the top lower at the front. 'Are you sure it's not too much?'

'It's perfect.'

She looked at her watch, too early to make a move, and grabbed Dylan's school bag from the floor for emptying. She tipped the remains of a sandwich into the bin and rinsed his lunchbox. Then she pulled out a fistful of notes from the bottom of his bag, the usual reminders about the correct uniform and the dates for half term. Folded with the rest was another handwritten note:

Dear Mrs Johnson, I would appreciate it if Dylan would refrain from bringing organic matter into the classroom in future. The school prides itself on a safe, hygienic environment for pupils, and we cannot risk undue contamination. Yours sincerely, D. Yeo.

She frowned, glancing over at Dylan, playing with his soup. Something else was at the bottom of his school bag, rattling about. She dug her hand in and pulled out a plastic container, the type they sometimes got with takeaway food. Inside were four small off-white bones.

'Dylan, what's this?'

Dylan dropped his spoon. 'Mum, I don't like this soup.'

'Never mind about the soup. What's in the container?'

Dylan grinned sheepishly. 'Just some bones.'

Lucy peered at the contents and pulled a face.

'I can see that,' said Kelda, 'but where on earth did you find them?'

'The other day, when I was doing archaeology. I found them in the field at the back of the garden. I took them into school for show and tell. Mr Yeo said he thought they were from a dog or a fox.'

'Well, I don't think he was very impressed,' she said, putting the container down and folding the note. 'You'd better ask me first before you take things in for show and tell. And finish your soup. It's your favourite. Lentil and tomato.'

'I told you, I don't like it.'

She sighed. 'Since when?'

'Since now.'

Lucy flashed her a sympathetic smile.

'Well, that's all there is. And Lucy's been very kind heating it up for you and buttering bread.' She smiled at the neat triangles on a plate. When he was a toddler, Dylan had only eaten bread in triangles. Triangles never squares. It had driven Mum mad.

Dylan pushed the bowl across the table, soup splashing over the side.

'Dylan!'

He picked up a triangle of bread.

'You can't just eat bread for tea,' she said, keeping the exasperation from her voice. She inched the bowl back towards him. 'Just try it.'

He pushed it away again. This time the bowl skidded to a halt as it reached the plate of bread, soup slopping on Lucy's perfect triangles.

'Dylan!'

'Leave this to me,' Lucy said, urging her towards the door. 'You go and have a lovely evening. Relax. Enjoy yourself.'

'I'm sorry. I don't know what's got into him recently.' Tears pricked the corners of her eyes. She should have known her going out would upset him. 'I can't leave you with him like this. It wouldn't be fair. I'll just let Simon know I can't make it after all.'

'Don't you dare! We'll be fine. Won't we, Dylan?'

Dylan said nothing, just made patterns in the spilled soup with his spoon.

Lucy turned to Kelda. 'Honestly, we'll be fine. I've brought up four children, remember?'

'I feel bad . . .'

'Just go.' Lucy opened the back door and handed Kelda her handbag.

'I've got my mobile on me if anything happens.'

'Nothing *will* happen.'

'I know, I know. But just in case.'

'Go!'

Kelda smiled, ran back to the table, ruffled Dylan's hair. 'Look after Lucy for me, won't you, Batman? I won't be long.'

She parked in the town centre, self-conscious in the cropped top, zipping her jacket up as she walked, slowing as she passed the turning to Nick's flat, wondering what he was up to. He'd texted her at midnight on the day of the party, apologising for not being there, saying he'd explain, that he'd call her as soon as he could. But since then, nothing. Not even a text. She glanced at her phone in case he'd texted whilst she'd been driving, or in case Lucy had tried to get in contact. Maybe Dylan had become really awkward and Lucy had changed her mind. But to her relief and, in the case of Nick, disappointment, there was nothing.

She reached the pub and scanned the tables, realising she was nervous. It would be so easy to walk straight out again and drive back home. It was Lucy who had set her up on the dating site, one slow afternoon in the office; she'd allowed Lucy to write her profile and upload a picture from her phone. It had been a laugh, that's all. She hadn't pictured this moment, how she'd actually feel when she got here, meeting a stranger for the sole purpose of falling in love.

Simon was sitting in one of the alcoves, tall and well dressed in a light chequered shirt, loose at the collar. He looked up from the book he was reading and waved her over.

'Hi,' he said, shaking hands. 'You must be Kelda. Can I get you a drink?' He felt for the wallet in his back pocket.

She wished she'd taken a taxi after all. She needed a drink, something to steady her nerves. Close up, he was distractingly handsome, the sort of chiselled good looks she only saw in movies.

'Sparkling water, please,' she said apologetically. 'I'm driving.'

'Coming right up.'

She sat at the table he'd chosen, under the low lighting, playing with a beer mat. She put her phone on the table and switched it onto vibrate, just in case Lucy phoned.

'So,' Simon said, when he returned with her drink. 'It's lovely to meet you at last.'

'You too.'

'You live in the town?'

'On the outskirts.'

'Hence the driving?'

'Hence the driving.'

They clinked glasses.

'So tell me about yourself,' he said, his voice low and silky. 'You're into sky diving, right?'

Kelda laughed. 'That was my friend Lucy. She wrote my profile.'

'I see.'

Her eyes rested on his book, *Wuthering Heights*. 'Actually, I'm more into reading than jumping out of planes.'

'I'm glad to hear it. I was worried you'd try to persuade me.'

She relaxed, letting him lead the conversation, telling her about his job as an orthopaedic consultant and living out in the sticks on the other side of Stonebridge. He was more interesting than she'd given him credit for when she'd viewed his profile, more intelligent, and she wondered if she sounded boring by comparison.

'What do you want to do, eventually?' he said, leaning closer.

She noticed how dark his eyes were, pools of deep brown. 'What do you mean?'

'Well, you're obviously clever. You must have a talent? A hobby? Something you want to pursue? You don't want to work as a PA for the rest of your life, do you?'

She thought of Dylan and the reason she'd left university early, never completing her degree, never pursuing the MA she'd dreamed of. She remembered the disappointment in Mum's eyes when she'd told her. The first person in the family to go to university and, according to Mum, she was throwing it away.

'I don't know,' she said. 'I haven't really thought about it before.'

'Well, you should.' Simon picked up his Coke and swirled it around his glass. 'You're still young. The world's your oyster, as my old man used to say. I can see you being a . . . ' He stroked his chin with his long fingers.

'Well, what?' She wasn't sure whether she was flattered or annoyed.

'Something mysterious. An oceanographer or an archaeologist.'

'Well, I like digging the garden.'

'You see! I was right. You'd be perfect, unearthing old bones.'

She thought about Dylan's tub of archaeological finds. 'I'm not sure . . . '

'I think you'd be amazing. Just look it up anyway. Far more fun than working in administration.'

'Maybe . . . '

She tried to suppress her irritation, remembering how Mum

had always tried to tell her what to do. But Simon wasn't anything like Mum. Apart from the bit about her non-existent career – and she supposed he had a point – he was charming. The conversation moved back to his work at the hospital and his medical training. He told her about his family and how proud they'd been when he'd announced, at the age of four, in the middle of Christmas dinner, that he was going to be a doctor.

At half past nine, she made her excuses. It was far later than she'd intended to stay out, and she still needed to take Dylan to bed – no doubt she'd find him curled on the sofa, already asleep – and Lucy would be wanting to get home. She'd resisted the urge to continuously check her phone, but she glanced at it now, just in case.

'I'll text you, okay?' Simon said, holding out her jacket.

'That would be lovely.'

'Perhaps we can go out again, sometime next week?'

'Sounds great.'

He leaned forwards and pecked her on the cheek.

Back in the car, her phone pinged with a text from Nick.

You okay?

She switched her phone to silent and threw it in the glove compartment. If Nick had something to say, he could phone her, not text. She moved her hand to the place where Simon's lips had touched her skin and felt a tingle deep down.

'How was it?' Lucy looked up from the sofa when she walked in and switched off the TV.

She shrugged off her jacket. 'Great. At least, I think. He was nice. Easy to talk to. Good-looking. *Really* good-looking. Where's Dylan?'

'Bed. Went up an hour ago. No problem.'

'No problem?' She'd had so much trouble getting him to bed recently. Ever since the birthday party, he'd refused to sleep in his room. A battle every night. She'd stand her ground at first, reminding him of his promise on the night of the party. But then she'd think of the toll house, the new school, Mr Yeo and his complaints, Cassandra and the new job; she'd think of Mum in the family home on her own and every night she'd caved, allowing him to snuggle in next to her like he was a toddler again. She'd wake early in the mornings to the feel of him at her side, his curls brushing her pillow.

'You're a star,' she said, flopping next to Lucy. 'How did you do it?'

Lucy grinned. 'Bribery.' She patted the cushions. 'Now sit down and tell me about the mysterious Simon.'

She stood at the edge of the garden, watching the taillights of Lucy's car disappear towards town. The Old Turnpike Road was silent. She listened hard. Not even the rustle of wind in the trees. She thought of the wood behind and the autumn-brown fields. The nearest farm was four miles away, the town over a mile, yet it seemed like more with the trees and the river. She ached for the High Street, for the sound of traffic and the glare of streetlamps, anything to remind her that other people existed, that it wasn't just her and Dylan and no one else for miles.

She went into the toll house and switched off the downstairs lights for the night. A sudden breath of lavender sent her coughing. She felt in her pocket for her mobile phone to use as a torch, then remembered she'd left it in the glove compartment. She didn't want to go out again, go rooting in the car, not in the pitch black. She fumbled for the light switch but couldn't find it. Couldn't find the bloody light switch, though she'd only turned the lights off moments ago. Instead, she found the hole in the wall with her fingers. The hole with the plaster face.

She jarred her thigh on the kitchen table as she stepped back a few paces, feeling along the wall until she found what she was looking for. She kept the light on behind her as she walked into the hallway and tiptoed up the stairs. She hated the stairs. Hated how narrow they were, how steep. It was the part of the house that had made her waver before signing the deeds. 'You could break your neck on those stairs,' Mum had said when she'd visited. She'd thought of putting a stairgate at the top, but Dylan had promised her it wasn't needed, that he was far too old for that sort of thing.

In her bedroom, she found her make-up bag on her bed, open though she was sure she'd zipped it, mascara and blusher cast on the duvet. She tidied it up then checked on Dylan, sound asleep next door, duvet thrown off as though he'd been fighting with it. She couldn't believe he'd gone to bed so easily. Lucy must have waved a magic wand. She pulled the duvet back on top of him.

'No!' he shouted, pulling himself upright.

'Shh, it's okay.'

'Get away from me!'

'It's okay, it's okay, it's only me. It's Mummy. You're dreaming.'

He softened and she brushed his fringe back from his damp

forehead, stroked his brow with her thumb until she felt his breathing grow slow and steady again. She sat there a while, watching the light from his lava lamp float against the wall. At one point, before the house had an indoor bathroom, the room had been slightly bigger, not quite as big as her room, but a room for a child. As she watched the light on the wall, she became aware of another colour spiralling across the paint. Thick streaks like a giant spider's web. At first, in the semi-darkness, she thought it was black, but the more she looked, the brighter it became. The redder it became.

How had she not noticed it before? She stared in disbelief, in horror, then stood up and ran her fingers along the nearest mark. It was smooth and she could smell it. Not a crayon or a felt tip, but the slight waxy fragrance of lipstick. Dylan must have taken the lipstick from her make-up bag and drawn across the walls! She froze, not knowing what to do, whether to wake him up, whether to shake him and ask him what the hell he'd been doing. But she couldn't, not when he was so settled. She thought about trying to wipe it away, but it would smear and look even worse in the morning.

The lava lamp faded to black then switched itself off.

She gasped, spinning back to the bed, unable to see a thing, her chest constricting. Short, shallow breaths, in and out. She had to get out of the room and she knew, instinctively, she had to take Dylan with her. She stumbled forwards, tripping over one of his toys, finding the bed with her hands. She wondered if the noise would wake Dylan, but he didn't stir. She cradled him in her arms and started to sing 'Twinkle twinkle little star'. A nursery rhyme she hadn't sung in years. 'How I wonder what you are.' She knew it was ridiculous, that Dylan couldn't hear her. But she had to do something to break the silence – the terrible deep silence of that room – as she wrestled her sleeping son from the bed.

He felt like a dead weight in her arms as she crossed the landing to the safety of her bedroom.

10

She dreamed that night though she wasn't usually a dreamer. She dreamed she was with Simon in a bar and he was buying her a drink.

'There you go,' he said, handing it over, 'a Bloody Mary.'

She looked at the garish liquid in her hand. She didn't drink Bloody Marys but it seemed rude to hand it back. She put the glass to her mouth, navigating the stick of celery, and it cracked, cutting her hand, slipping from her fingers. The drink spilled down her top, and pooled on the floor. Bright red liquid like blood.

'I'm going home,' she said, turning away from him. She picked up what she thought was a shawl and threw it on. Not a shawl but a baby carrier, the type with buckles you had to tighten. She put the baby carrier on and looked for Dylan. There he was, dangling over a bar stool, still a baby with wrinkly skin.

'Goodbye, Simon,' she said, fastening Dylan into the carrier, 'it was nice to meet you.'

She stepped into the street and pointed out the stars and the streetlights to Dylan. 'Look they're glimmering, see!'

She felt the carrier slipping, the buckles loosening, the clips on the front popping open one by one, but she didn't do anything about it, too busy looking at the streetlights, showing them to Dylan, thinking how they looked like flames, like oil lamps, rather than electric bulbs.

Smack.

When Dylan hit the pavement, she jolted awake, her pyjama top drenched in sweat. She threw back the duvet to cool herself, then turned on one side to check Dylan was okay. As usual, he'd worked his way towards her in the middle of the night and was still fast asleep. She thought about waking him, just to double-check that nothing had happened, but she knew she was being silly. Dylan was fine. She was fine. It had just been a dream, a nightmare, and it was too early to get him up for school, only just gone six. She remembered the lipstick she'd found scrawled across his bedroom wall and knew she wouldn't go back to sleep. And she couldn't lie there any longer with the memory of that dream going round her head.

She crept around Dylan in the dark, pulling on her jeans and a jumper, and went downstairs. The kitchen light was still on from the night before and the gash in the wall looked bigger. She could see the mask from the hallway door through the hole. She could see the lips, the closed eyelids. She was sure that hadn't been possible before. Before, she'd had to get up close and use a torch to peer inside. Maybe it was something to do with where she was standing or the angle of the kitchen light. She remembered how she'd lifted Dylan out of bed and carried him across the landing, how everything had been dark, impenetrable. How she hadn't been able to see the kitchen light, though the door was wide open into the hallway below.

But she was getting confused. She *must* be confused. There'd be a rational explanation, she just needed to be calm and think things through. She made herself coffee, then sat at her laptop, tapping her fingers on the side of the mug. She thought about the history of the house, the history she barely knew anything about, just that it had been a place for collecting tolls. She remembered what the estate agent had said, the history was 'interesting'. She'd not thought much about it at the time, just presumed he was talking about the tollgate, but what if it was more than that?

She typed 'Stonebridge Toll House' into the search engine and waited for the page to load. The first two results she'd seen before: the estate agent's website where the building was listed as 'sold' and an entry on Zoopla. There was only one other significant result: an article on the Stonebridge History Society website. She clicked to open it, waiting as the seconds dragged by for the information to load. The webpage was blank. She tried again, refreshing it over and over. Still nothing, just a heading THE OLD TOLL HOUSE followed by a blank space. She flicked through the rest of the site, scanning information about the medieval bridge, and the Tudor cloth trade, and a daughter of the local aristocracy who had mysteriously disappeared in the 1860s.

Frustrated, she took her coffee outside and sat at the picnic table. There was a bite to the air that made her think of winter, of dark mornings and early nights. She wondered what it would be like when the roads got icy, patches of black ice that you couldn't quite see. She imagined chipping at the windscreen first thing in the morning, fingers numb with cold, the toll house grey and watchful behind her; she imagined the car stalling, the tyres unable to get a grip; she imagined being stranded, having to walk to town along the perilous road.

She finished her coffee and grabbed her phone from the car where she'd left it. Her screen blinked with a message from Simon, thanking her for the evening and inviting her out to lunch at the weekend. On top of that, there was a missed call from Nick. She felt bad about the missed call and texted him back.

Everything okay?

He replied straight away, he'd always been an early riser, said it was the best part of the day.

Fine, just wanted to explain about Saturday. You free after work later?

She relented. She couldn't be angry for ever. Anyway, there was the small matter of Simon; if she did agree to meet him at the weekend, she'd need a babysitter. In which case, Nick could repay his debt.

Back inside, Dylan was in the kitchen, bed-hair flopped over his eyes, dragging his bare feet. She poured him a bowl of Coco Pops and sat next to him, watching him eat.

'Did you sleep okay?' she said whilst he finished his cereal and she made him toast. He nodded, still mute, still not quite woken up.

She took a deep breath. 'What happened last night?'

He grinned, dribbling chocolate milk down his chin. She resisted the urge to catch it with her finger.

'We watched *Batman*. Lucy gave me sweets, but she said not to tell you.' He giggled.

She spread peanut butter on his toast and cut it in half. She should eat something herself, though she didn't feel hungry.

'No, I don't mean that. I mean, what happened to your room?'

'What do you mean?'

'I mean the lipstick.' She told herself to be patient, not to jump to conclusions. 'The lipstick all over the walls.'

Something crossed his face, something she couldn't quite read. 'What lipstick?'

She rubbed her forehead. She hadn't had enough sleep and she couldn't deal with the lies on top of everything else.

'The lipstick on your bedroom walls,' she said as patiently as she could. 'I found my make-up bag open. You'd rooted through it.'

'I don't know what you mean.' He scrunched his nose up at the toast. 'I want peanut butter *and* jam.'

She flew at him, dragging him by his arm, pulling him up the narrow stairs and along the landing.

'Mum! You're hurting me!'

She loosened her grip. A moment of horrifying shame. What on earth was she doing? Then she saw his bedroom. The curtains were open – had they been open last night? – and the morning sunlight was streaming through, accentuating the red. It was worse than she'd thought. Lipstick everywhere, the incriminating tube abandoned on the carpet. She didn't know one tube of lipstick could go so far. Maybe it couldn't. Maybe he'd helped himself to more than one.

'You were angry that I went out,' she said, trying to see things from his point of view. 'You were angry that I got dressed up and went to the pub and had a nice time without you.'

'Mum, I didn't do it!'

'Well, who did then? The pixies?' She dragged her hands through her hair, trying to think. She wondered what Nick would say, whether he'd handle this differently. Of course he'd handle this differently, he'd know exactly what to say. 'I can't have you behaving like this. I really can't. I'm exhausted. I've got a long day at work. I haven't eaten breakfast . . .' She started crying, stupid thick tears rolling down her cheeks.

'Mum, I didn't do it.'

She stared through her tears at the blank expression on his face. For a moment, she believed him, really believed that he didn't have a clue about the marks on the wall. But then she realised that was worse. Far worse. Because if Dylan hadn't done it, and it couldn't have been Lucy, then that meant . . . No, she wouldn't think it. She wouldn't even entertain the thought there'd been someone else in the house.

She wiped her cheeks, bent down and hugged him, turning him around in her arms so they were facing each other. She felt him resist, leaning in the opposite direction. 'It would be easier, so much easier, if you just admitted it. If you said you were in the wrong. If you just told me you'd been into my room and taken the lipstick. If you said sorry.'

He pulled away from her, ran onto the landing and down the stairs.

She could hear him crying in the kitchen below. She went down after him, placed her hands on his shoulders. 'Please, Dylan. I'm worried about you. I just want us to talk about this.'

He pouted. 'I didn't do it. I didn't touch your stupid lipstick. I didn't draw on the stupid walls. I hate that room.'

'Dylan!'

He bent down to the pile of Lego under the table. She sighed;

she'd have to let it go for now. She still had to supervise him getting dressed and brush his hair. She couldn't send him off to school like this. Maybe she'd ask Nick to talk to him later. She'd leave the two of them together whilst she made dinner, sorted through the apples in the garden to see if there was enough good fruit to make a crumble. After missing the party, it was the least Nick could do.

11

1863

A week after the funeral, Dr Marsh appears at the tollgate. 'Good afternoon,' he says curtly, stepping from the road into the porch. His frockcoat is open, his cheeks flushed with the exercise of walking from the town. I'm sitting in front of the door on a spindle-backed chair, a good place for watching the road when the weather is fair.

'I have brought you something,' says the doctor. He passes me a package, his fingers ice-cold as they brush against mine.

'Is it her?' I stare at the brown paper, hardly daring to believe it, aching to pull the neatly tied ribbon and lay the wrapping aside. But I know I cannot with the doctor standing over me.

He coughs into his fist. Beneath his rosy cheeks, his skin is sallow, marked by middle-age. 'The mask. As you requested.'

He lingers, tapping his thumbs together, no doubt wanting his payment.

I stand up from the chair. 'Stay here. I will be back.'

I take the package inside and make space for it on the table in the kitchen, pushing aside the dirty plates and half-drunk tankards. My fingers quiver over the stiff cloth and the curling ribbon. I long to see it. To see her face. But not with Dr Marsh waiting outside.

Instead, I take a little key from the vase on the windowsill and open the safe in the wall beside the range. Then I count out the sum of money we agreed.

Outside, the doctor puts the money in his pocket.

'Good day,' I say, wanting rid of him. I step inside the door and make as if to close it.

'Mr Walton.' The doctor coughs again. 'There is something else.'

'Something else? Whatever can there be?'

I look past him at the empty road, willing a coach or a farmer's wagon to appear.

'You have been talking, saying things that would ruin my reputation if believed. You must stop this foolish gossip.' Dr Marsh talks with his hands. The same hands that pulled the dead child from my wife's body.

'No one could have saved Bella,' he continues. 'There was something wrong with her. I knew how she'd suffered before. The other children . . . ' The word dies on his lips.

'How do you know about the others?' I think of the babes who were lost before they even swelled her stomach, the ones she buried in the wood. *Poor little mites*, she'd say, the tears streaking down her cheeks, all the happiness draining away.

The doctor twists his lips. 'It is no matter. Only that there was something wrong with Bella. Wrong with her body. She was incapable of bearing a living child. There was nothing I could do. By the time I arrived, it was too late to save both the child and your wife.'

I stare at those hands, still talking on their own. 'I will not be silenced,' I say quietly.

The doctor steps forward, puts a hand to the door, stopping it from closing. 'Promise me you will desist from talking in this manner? I have worked as a doctor for many years, studied hard in my youth, trained first as a surgeon, then as a physician. You are grieving. Angry. It is understandable to a point, but my reputation—'

'Damn your reputation.' I slam the door closed, hard against his hand, then watch at the window, waiting for him to turn, to walk back towards the town. Eventually, his shadow crosses the pane, his frockcoat flapping in rhythm with his step.

I take the package from the table and carry it upstairs. Carefully, sitting on the bed, I pull the ribbon undone and lay the cloth aside. The mask is chalk-white, the resemblance to my wife uncanny. I run my fingers over her face like I did when she was alive, over the contours of her cheeks, the dimple on her chin, the crest of her sleeping eyes. So beautiful, she could have had anyone, but she'd chosen me, her poor simple Joe.

I lie down on the bed with the mask next to me on the covers, stroking the cool plaster, so smooth like marble, no memory of the doctor's bandages. I linger over the mole on her chin, the mole that quivered when she laughed. Not an ugly thing, but something that caught your eye, that broke the otherwise perfect symmetry. In the arch of her right eyebrow, there is a single hair. A tiny eyebrow hair pulled away in the plaster. My finger tingles as I touch it, so short, so fine, it is almost imperceptible. This tiny eyebrow hair, the colour of coal, is the closest thing I have to my wife. I touch my lips to hers – so cold, so unresponsive – wanting her in death as much as I did in life.

The afternoon darkens into evening. I fall asleep with my hand on the mask, my finger on the hair, the stale smell of bed sheets and waning memories drifting around me. Through my dreams, I hear the sound of coaches and wagons trundling past the turnpike, the drivers no doubt surprised to find it unattended. One or two coachmen call out, but most quicken their horses, and all I hear as I sink deeper into darkness, is the striking of hooves and the creak of carriages on the open road.

12

NOW

K elda couldn't concentrate at work, couldn't focus on what Cassandra was saying, what jobs she was being asked to do. She tried to make a to-do list but couldn't think straight and crossed it all out again. Lucy thought she was still buzzing from the night before, thinking about the date she'd had with Simon. Kelda didn't want to tell her the truth; she didn't want Lucy to think she didn't trust her, that Dylan's behaviour was somehow Lucy's fault when she knew it wasn't. When she accidentally deleted the files she'd saved yesterday, Lucy made her coffee and informed her it was a sure sign that Simon was the one.

'Do you really think so?' she said, remembering Simon's tanned skin, his dark eyes, so dark they'd appeared almost black in the pub. She thought of his collar bone, sharp beneath his shirt, the ridge of his shoulders.

'Definitely.' Lucy plonked a chocolate biscuit next to her coffee. 'You need the calories,' she said. 'You'll waste away. All skin and bones. Men like something to grab hold of.'

After work, she collected Dylan from after-school club and drove home. She asked him about his day, but he replied in grunts, mumbling something about Mr Yeo being a shithead.

'What did you say?' She thought she'd misheard him.

Louder, more confident: 'Mr Yeo was a shithead.'

She slammed the brakes at the traffic lights, almost missing the red light. Pedestrians wandered in front of her: kids sucking lollipops, parents lumbered with school bags and abandoned coats.

'That's a horrible thing to say. Where did you learn that word?'

'That's what Georgie's mum calls his dad.'

'Well, it's not very nice. It's horrible. Horrible. I don't want to hear you using that word again.'

She remembered the poem he'd written, the one she'd been keeping silent about. She wondered whether she should mention it now or whether he'd retreat entirely. They'd always been so close but recently things had changed; half the time she didn't know whether she was doing the right thing.

She watched him slip further into his seat in the rear-view mirror. 'It's Georgie's word, not mine.'

'You shouldn't listen to Georgie.'

'He's my best friend.'

'He's a bad influence.'

God, she sounded like Mum. How had that happened? How had it crept up on her without her realising? She remembered the words Mum had used, speaking to Emma: *Such and such is a bad influence, you ought to stay away from them. If you go behind my back again you're grounded for a month. If I catch you drinking in the park . . .* Emma and Mum had always argued, even when Dad was still around, but after he'd left it had got worse. Unbearable. Emma would call Mum a bitch to her face, sometimes worse, like she'd been blaming Mum for the fact Dad hadn't wanted to know her anymore. And Kelda would silently retreat to her room and shut the door and try to concentrate on her schoolwork.

'I just want the best for you,' she said, trying to soften things, trying to make him understand; the last thing she wanted was to sound like her mother. 'Sometimes our friends aren't who we think they are.'

She pulled up outside the toll house to find Nick's bike leaning against the garden gate. Dylan sprinted into the garden, 'Hi, Uncle Nick,' and clambered on his back. She watched as Nick piggybacked him around the flowerbeds, ducking beneath the trees, leaning over to allow Dylan to take one of the apples. She knew she should be angry with Nick but she couldn't stop grinning.

'Hello, stranger,' she said.

He gave her an apologetic smile. 'Good to see you. How you doing?'

'Come inside.'

He rolled up his sleeves and offered to help her make dinner whilst Dylan sat on the kitchen table, playing with the present he'd brought: a microphone that distorted your voice to a high squeak or a deep growl, to high-speed gibberish or a gaping drawl.

'Look, Mum, you can record yourself. Say something.'

She leaned over. 'Have you done your homework?'

He played it back, high, squeaky, like a mouse: *Have you done your homework?*

'No, not that. Say something fun.'

'Do you want chocolate ice cream or fruit crumble for pudding?'

Low, gravelly, a man's voice: *Do you want chocolate ice cream or fruit crumble for pudding?* The sound lingered in the room, making Dylan laugh. He jumped down from the table and went next door to watch TV.

'Thanks for the present,' she said. 'He loves it.'

'It was the least I could do, after missing the party.'

She chucked him a carrot. 'Chop that.'

'Look, I know it looks bad, it looks like I forgot, like I didn't care, but Saturday was awkward. Difficult. Alexa doesn't want me to tell anyone, but I feel I owe you an explanation.'

She chopped an onion and scattered the pieces into the frying pan. The oil hissed and caught at the back of her throat. She wiped her eyes. 'Go on.'

Nick looked serious. 'We were in hospital.'

'What?'

'Alexa had a pain in her stomach. It had been on and off for days. I'd told her to go to the doctors' but she wouldn't listen. She woke up on Saturday morning and it was really bad. She got up to use the loo and felt dizzy. Cut a long story short, we ended up in A&E. She'd had an ectopic pregnancy.'

'Oh gosh, I'm sorry.'

'Thank God I made her go in. It could have got really serious. Anyway, I meant to text you about the party, saying I wouldn't make it after all, but I couldn't get a signal in the hospital, and then things got sticky.'

'Sticky?'

'Well, you know what Alexa's like.'

She grabbed the carrots from the chopping board. She'd only met Alexa on a couple of occasions and wouldn't say she knew her exactly. Early twenties, dead straight hair, olive skin.

'She was arguing with the consultants, saying she wanted it out there and then, whereas they wanted to wait. She went crazy, threw the rule book at them. By the time I left, it was almost midnight.'

'Is she okay?'

'Alexa? As well as can be expected. A bit tearful. She didn't want a baby, not now anyway, and it was all a bit of a shock because we haven't been planning anything.' He blushed. 'In fact, we've been ultra-careful, because of her parents. But she also didn't want to lose it. If you can call it an "it". Apparently, at that stage, it isn't really a human being at all, just a bundle of cells. Anyway, it made us both think.'

'What do you mean?'

'Marriage.'

'You're not serious?'

'Yep.' He opened the fridge. 'What else for dinner? Mushrooms?'

'You're not seriously going to get married? You and Alexa?' She thought of the last wedding, Rachel's fairy-tale dress, the bridesmaids, the extravagant reception. She'd spent the whole day thinking it wasn't quite Nick.

'Why not?' He pulled out a block of tofu.

'Because . . .' She stared at the frying pan. The onions were catching at the bottom of it. 'Because you've only just met and you're still married to Rachel.'

'Minor detail. I'll get a divorce.'

'And Alexa's a kid!'

'A little harsh.' He took a knife and sliced open the packet of tofu. 'But I suppose that's the whole point. Her parents won't let her do anything. We thought if we got married then at least she'd have her freedom. At least we could sleep in the same room without her mother condemning us to hell.'

'But you're supposed to marry because you're in love.'

She stepped around him, pulling peas from the freezer, finding the soy sauce at the back of the cupboard. Maybe she'd got it wrong and Nick really was in love. She'd always assumed Alexa was just a bit of fun, a distraction from the tedium of life at the university. Alexa had been a research assistant on his last project and they'd got it together in the library. Apparently.

'You're burning that,' he said, nodding at the frying pan.

She moved it off the heat and picked out the blackened onion.

'I suppose, if you really mean it, then congratulations.'

'Thanks. And about last Saturday, I really am sorry. If there's anything I can do to make up for it?'

She attacked the block of tofu. 'Actually, I could do with some help at the weekend. I have a date.'

After tea, she showed him Dylan's room whilst Dylan sat at the kitchen table doing his maths homework. Nick let out a long slow whistle.

'Wow, he really went for it.' He ran his hands over the marks. 'You should be able to scrub this stuff off. Soap and water should do it.'

'I know, but why? And why won't he tell me?'

'I'll have a word with him, if you like?'

'Would you? It's just I can't seem to get through to him at the moment. I don't know if he was just jealous about me and Simon.' It seemed strange talking to Nick about Simon, but at the same time she was glad of it. Glad she had someone to talk about, just as he had Alexa. 'It's all my fault. I should have known it was too much too soon. The move. The new house. The new school. Now Simon.'

'It's not your fault. You deserve a life too.'

'But I should have known. I should have thought.'

He threw an arm around her and she felt the light scratch of his jumper against her neck. 'It's not your fault, okay?'

She nodded, though she didn't believe it.

'You stay here. I'll go and have a word.'

She heard him run down the stairs, calling for Dylan as she sat on his bed and put her face to the pillow. Lavender. She flipped it to the other side. A white pebble rolled onto the floor. She'd forgotten about the pebbles. She'd meant to ask him about those too. She picked it up, feeling how smooth it was. She supposed he'd found it in the garden. She looked up at the walls, at the mess, the pebble still in her hand. Something was written far up, further than she thought Dylan could reach – he must have pulled the chair from his desk or balanced on his beanbag – in long sloping letters. Joined-up letters. She smiled, despite the situation. At least Dylan was learning. The word said: *Bella.*

'I think someone wants to speak to you.'

She turned. Nick and Dylan were in the doorway. Dylan ran towards her and gave her a hug. 'I didn't do it, Mum. Honestly, I didn't. Someone else made the marks on the wall.'

She tried to read Nick over the top of Dylan's head. He shrugged.

Dylan wriggled from her grasp. 'Can I go and play Lego now?'

He ran away again without waiting for an answer, feet pattering across the landing.

Kelda sighed, feeling the exasperation creep inside her. 'You see? I don't know what to do. He won't listen. He doesn't understand how naughty this is.'

Nick sat next to her on the bed, picked up Snuggy, folded and unfolded the rabbit's ears. 'He's just a kid. Don't be too harsh on him. He was probably sleepwalking.'

'I guess. I never thought of that.'

'I used to sleepwalk all the time when I was a kid. Mum was always finding me in random places and taking me back to bed.'

She rubbed her forehead. She still wasn't convinced; she'd never known Dylan to sleepwalk, not even once. 'He even wrote a name. Is that possible? Can you do that when you're sleepwalking? He must have climbed on something to reach up there.'

She pointed at the word, except now she wasn't so certain, maybe it was just a scrawl, something that looked like a name but wasn't.

He stood up and traced the letters. 'Bella.' So, he saw it too. 'Is that someone in school?'

'I don't know.' She ran through a list of names in her head but she couldn't recall a Bella. 'It wouldn't be so bad – it wouldn't be *half* so bad – if he just admitted it.'

'He probably doesn't remember a thing. Remember the nightmares he's been having? You said it yourself, it's all linked. The new school, the new town, the nightmares, now this. It takes kids time to settle sometimes. That's all. Try not to worry. It probably looks a whole lot worse than it actually is.'

He stood up, walked to the window and rattled the latch,

ensuring it was firmly shut. He was right, she thought. He must be right. There was no other explanation.

That night, she double-checked everything: all the windows were locked, the back door was firmly shut, the front door which they didn't use was bolted at the top and bottom. She had to root around for the key for the front door, a heavy iron thing on a chain, shoved at the back of a drawer in the kitchen. She wondered whether this was the original key as she fitted it into the lock and turned it, hearing a deep clunk from within. She pulled the door open – a draught of midnight air – then closed it again, and turned the key the other way before sliding the bolts back into place. The front door was well and truly locked. It had always been locked.

She lay in bed staring into the dark, making out the shape of the wardrobe, the chest of drawers, the chair. Dylan had refused to sleep in his room again and her arm was around him though she knew it would ache in the morning.

She remembered the night they'd first moved in, how she'd lain awake then, too, trying to close her mind to the enormity of what she'd done: moving out here, to the middle of nowhere, to a leaky old house. It had been cold though it was March. A blanket heaped on her bed as well as the duvet. She'd listened to the wind batter the house from both sides, heard it whistle down the chimneys. She'd got out of bed and checked the old fireplace, checked it was properly boarded up, no hidden draughts whispering into the bedroom. She hadn't got round to hanging curtains, but everything was dark if not quite pitch black. They were too far away to see the lights from the town and where she'd expected a bay window to be, mimicking the one downstairs, there was a blank wall for the toll board outside. She'd got out of bed and crept across the landing into Dylan's room, feeling her way with her hands against the wall. In the glow of Dylan's lava lamp, she'd seen the peeling rose-patterned wallpaper that she hated, that she'd decided to paint magnolia along with the rest of the house. She'd lifted a flap near his bed, revealing the old paint behind, the colour indistinguishable in the almost-dark. She'd felt the cold even more, shuddering at the thought of him sleeping there alone, sleeping amongst other people's memories.

Wind forwards six months and she still wasn't sleeping.

The clock flashed to the hour. Three a.m. again! The time she always awoke. She was thirsty and knew she wouldn't get back to sleep without a drink. She rolled Dylan away and slipped out before he had a chance to roll back again. She felt for the door with her hands, turned the knob as silently as she could, then tiptoed along the gallery landing and down the stairs. In the kitchen she ran herself a glass of water, purposely not looking at the hole in the wall, keeping her back to that part of the room. She switched off the light and crept back again, across the hallway, feeling for the bottom of the banister.

A noise startled her. She paused halfway up the stairs and listened. A scratching sound followed by something scurrying across the floorboards. Mice. Cold air breathed against the nape of her neck. She thought of the old front door at the foot of the stairs and the tingly night air, but she knew it was locked, that there was no way through, that the ancient letterbox was jammed with old paint. She desperately wanted to return to bed, dig deep beneath the covers, warm herself up. But something held her in the dark, like someone was there, pinning her to the spot.

The feeling grew stronger. Not just a feeling, a *presence*. There was someone here, she thought, the same someone who'd watched her in the bath. Someone who wanted her, who wouldn't let her go. Inexplicably, she began to cry. She felt sorrow like she'd never felt before, like all the bad things that had ever happened to her rolled into one.

She jerked herself away, breaking the spell, then stumbled up the narrow stairs and ran across the two sides of the landing, not bothering to be quiet, throwing wide the bedroom door at the far end. She dived into bed, feeling the warm, reassuring shape of Dylan still fast asleep. She screwed her eyes shut, telling herself it was nothing. Nothing had happened. Nothing that she could put into words, that would make any sense if she tried to explain it. Nobody was here, they were quite alone, just the two of them. And yet she knew she would lie awake like this, her arms thrown around her son, for the rest of the night.

13

'Can I go to Georgie's on Saturday?'

Kelda was walking with Dylan into town after school. Dylan wanted a haircut, a grown-up haircut like the other boys in his class, and she'd relented though she knew she'd secretly mourn the loss of his curls.

'Georgie's?'

'For a sleepover. Georgie's invited me and Ethan. It's going to be so cool. We're going to have a midnight feast and play on the Xbox and swim in his indoor swimming pool.'

'Does Georgie's mum know about this?' Dylan and Georgie were always inventing elaborate plans without adult approval.

'She's going to call you.'

'I see.'

'Does that mean yes?'

'No. It means, we'll see. *If* she calls me.'

Dylan skipped ahead of her. He'd obviously forgotten that Georgie had broken his glider, and she was obviously meant to forget that Georgie's mum used words like shithead in front of children. She supposed she'd have to say yes if Georgie's mum rang; she just hoped Georgie would be nice and his mum would keep an eye on things.

Ten minutes later, she watched with dismay as the barber got out his scissors and lopped Dylan's curls off one by one.

'It tickles,' Dylan squealed as the barber brushed the fluff from his neck.

'Do you want gel?'

Dylan glanced at Kelda. 'Can I, Mum?'

She nodded and bit her lip.

'Yes please!' he beamed.

Kelda picked up a magazine and pretended to read, watching the barber over the top of the page, rubbing gel into Dylan's hair and spiking it up, making him laugh.

'Wow,' she said when he clambered down from the chair, sucking a lollipop. 'It looks great. Really smart.'

Dylan admired himself in the mirror as the barber swept up around his feet.

'I love it,' he said, giving her a squeeze. 'Thanks, Mum.'

The next day, Cassandra called her into the office. Kelda tried to think what she might have done wrong. They weren't often called into Cassandra's office; if Cassandra wanted something doing, she usually talked to them over the top of their PCs.

The office smelled of flowers and takeaway coffees. Cassandra's husband, who led the fieldwork side of the business, was always sending her flowers. Kelda wondered whether it was part of the show, whether the rest of them were meant to believe they were from grateful clients. This week's flowers were deep purple buddleia.

'Oh, hi, Kelda, take a seat. Just finishing this email.'

Kelda sat at the desk in the visitor's chair, reading Cassandra's Post-it notes upside down, the usual appointments and reminders.

Cassandra pressed the return button on her keyboard and leaned back, smiling. 'How's everything going?'

'Fine. Thanks.'

'Home life okay?'

'Great.'

'Your son enjoying school?'

'I think so.'

They sat in silence. Just get on with it, Kelda thought, drop the bombshell.

'October half term.' Cassandra clicked her nails together. Bright red nails like drops of blood. 'You've put in a request for annual leave.'

'Yes.' Kelda had already planned what they'd do: day trips to the city and the dinosaur park and the seaside; if the weather was good, they'd take picnics. She'd ask Nick, too, but he'd probably be working. Anyway, it would be nice, just the two of them, a chance to spend some quality time together.

'Lucy has requested that week off and so has Deb.'

'Right.' She could already see where this was heading.

'I need someone in the office to keep things ticking over, fielding emails, you know what I mean?' She played with the Post-it notes. 'Some of our new clients are very demanding. Unfortunately, I promised the twins I'd take them to Disneyland.'

'Disneyland?'

'I know. Not exactly glamorous. But they've got it into their heads. It's all they're talking about.'

'I see.'

'So, if you don't mind moving your annual leave to the week after?'

'The week *after*?'

'I couldn't ask Lucy because she wants to take her daughter away on holiday. You know her daughter's pregnant? A pre-baby break. And, of course, Deb has her boys.'

'But I've got Dylan.' She regretted it as soon as she said it. Already Cassandra didn't trust her. Besides, Lucy and Deb had worked for Cassandra for years; they'd earned their right to take annual leave when they wanted to.

'I know, it's unfortunate. But there are tonnes of clubs you could send him to. I wouldn't ask if I wasn't desperate. Maybe you could take a longer break at Christmas?'

'I suppose . . .'

'Think about it, at least. And there's the week after New Year. Maybe we could pencil that in too?'

Kelda said nothing, just stared at the Post-it notes.

Cassandra leaned over the desk and played with the flowers. 'I don't expect you to decide straight away. Have a think about it and come back to me.'

Kelda nodded and stood up. 'Anything else?'

Cassandra smiled. 'Only that you did a really good job with those last-minute notes I gave you the other day.'

When she returned from her lunch break, Kelda found a flyer on her desk: a half-term football camp for kids that cost a week's wages. She screwed it into the bin. She knew she'd have to say yes to Cassandra – it wasn't a request, it was a demand – but she was eking out the moment before she finally agreed. She'd bring Dylan into work with her and occupy him with magazines and colouring books and hope he wouldn't mind, she'd arrange a couple of playdates with Georgie and Ethan's mums, she'd plan nice things for the evenings. It would be Halloween and there was bound to be fun stuff they could do together. 'What did the witch want?' Lucy had asked earlier. Kelda had said something vague about booking annual leave, knowing that if she told Lucy the truth, she'd insist on cancelling her own break with her daughter.

Her phone rang as she was leaving the office. It was Mrs Watts inviting Dylan to the sleepover. Kelda replied that he'd love to, before dashing to the car, running late as usual. She worried that Georgie and Ethan would gang up on him. Worried, too, though she pushed it to the back of her mind, about staying in the house on her own. A week ago, she wouldn't have hesitated in inviting Nick over to stay, to sleep on the sofa in the lounge like in the summer. But it didn't feel right asking him when he had so much going on with Alexa. Besides, she'd arranged another date with Simon at the weekend. Perhaps, she thought sadly, she and Nick would eventually drift apart.

'Mum, did you say yes?' Dylan asked, as soon as he saw her, hopscotching his way across the playground. 'About the sleepover?'

She shouldered his school bag. 'As long as you promise to behave yourself?'

'I promise.' He ran around her in circles. 'Can you buy me new pyjamas? Georgie's got these ones which glow in the dark.'

She listened to his plans on the way home, feeling his

excitement, the thrill of being let loose in Georgie's big house with the American-style fridge-freezer and the pool-side bar with its never-ending supply of Coca-Cola and Sprite. When they got home, he ran into the garden and retrieved his football from beneath the apple trees, aiming it at the gate whilst she unlocked the back door.

A flash of movement in front of her, a mouse darting across the kitchen tiles. She screamed and jumped back.

Dylan abandoned his football. 'What is it, Mum?' He took her hand.

She held her breath and peered around the door, expecting the mouse to jump out at her.

'A mouse. I think.'

Already she was wondering if she'd imagined it. Dylan squeezed past her. 'Can't see anything.'

'You're right. My mistake. There's nothing there.'

How could a seven-year-old be braver than she was?

She settled him in the lounge with the TV and climbed over boxes into the pantry, an alcove at the back of the kitchen, lined with shelves. Yet another place that needed a good tidying up; things were still dumped from when they'd moved in, still waiting to be assigned their rightful place. She used a fold-up ladder to get to the top, then felt along the shelves until she found what she was looking for. Mousetraps. Even the sight of them made her shudder.

She took the traps down, wiped the cobwebs away with kitchen towel and baited them with bread and peanut butter. Then she folded away the ladder and took one last look at the shelves.

Next to the housekeeping jar where she kept her spare cash was a line of smooth white pebbles.

'Dylan,' she called, not daring to take her eyes away from them. She was inexplicably afraid they might vanish if she did. He poked his head around the lounge door. 'Do you know anything about these?'

She picked up one of the pebbles and held it to the light, glassy like the white of an eye, remembering the pebbles she'd found beneath his pillow.

'What's that?'

'I don't know. You tell me.'

He took it from her and rolled it in his palm. 'It's a stone.'

'I know that. Where did you get it from? And why have you left them all over the house?'

She read the blank expression on his face.

'Can I keep it?' he said. Before she could reply he was tucking it into his pocket and sprinting off.

She laid the traps on the floor, one beneath the sink, one beside the old range. She placed the trap on the floor beneath the oven door and stood up. A pebble rolled from beneath her feet, she must have accidentally carried it with her from the shelf. She turned to the wall opposite. There was one other thing she needed to do.

She rummaged through Dylan's artwork on the table. Felt-tip drawings of bats and magicians and creatures of Dylan's imagination. Paintings from school. The painting of her in the dress. There were several of those. She hadn't noticed them all before. Kelda in a long brown dress with a bunch of flowers fastened to her waist. She set them aside, and selected her favourite – not one of her, but a picture of bats flying over houses in a midnight sky. She placed the picture over the hole in the wall and stuck it in place with drawing pins this time rather than Blu Tack. Better, much better. Until she could afford a builder to pull down the wall, or until she somehow hacked the face off, this would have to do. She couldn't see the gap anymore, not even a shadow behind the picture. She couldn't see the face.

14

On Saturday, Kelda dropped Dylan off at Nick's just before lunchtime. She'd arranged to meet Simon in a café in the middle of town and, despite the fact it was a public space and she'd met him once already, she was nervous. Somehow meeting him for the second time was far more daunting. The first time, she could have run away if she'd wanted to, but now, Simon had her phone number and she'd told him where she lived. There was something unsettling about the whole situation, the unknown, the possibility of a future she couldn't quite see, only glimpses, suggestions. Could she really imagine waking up next to Simon in a year's time? In eighteen months? For the rest of her life?

She sat at a table near the window, watching the street, the Saturday shoppers, the joggers weaving between the pedestrians. Since Dylan had been born, she'd only been on a handful of dates, mostly set up by old school friends when she'd lived at Mum's. Nothing serious. Nothing that went beyond a few meetings. She'd felt afraid of getting too close, afraid of someone coming between her and Dylan though she'd known Mum disapproved of her solitary lifestyle. She wondered how she should greet Simon — a kiss, a handshake? — wondered if she should have been fashionably late rather than early, wondered if she should have waited for Simon to arrive before ordering coffee.

He turned up punctually at twelve o'clock. 'You're here already.' He looked surprised to see her, as though he hadn't expected her to turn up at all, and shook his coat off.

'You're privileged,' she said. 'I'm usually late for everything.'

He bent over and kissed her on the cheek. She felt herself blush as he handed her the lunch menu.

'So how's your week been?' she said, scouring the sandwich selection.

'Hectic, you know?'

She smiled though, really, she didn't know; she couldn't imagine what it was like working in a hospital, but she saw the dark patches beneath his eyes and a stain of what looked like wine on his sleeve. The first time, he'd been immaculate, magazine-perfect, but just for a moment, she saw something else, another side to the prestigious job and the frantic hours.

'Tell me,' she said, handing him the menu. 'What sort of things do you really get up to? Anything grisly?'

'Not really. The odd amputation.'

She grimaced.

'Mostly hip and knee replacements. I'm a dab hand at knees. It's my speciality. Brutal, mind you. Being a surgeon is a bit like being a butcher, only you fix people up after you've cut them open. And, usually, you don't eat them.'

She laughed. 'I'm glad you don't eat them.'

A waiter came over and took their orders, a stilton sandwich for Kelda, coffee for Simon.

'Don't you eat?' she said, mocking him.

He twisted his shirt sleeve so she couldn't see the stain. 'I'm not hungry. I was on a night shift. It messes with your metabolism. It takes me days to recover sometimes.'

'I'm sorry, I should have suggested another time.'

'It was me who suggested it.' He reached for her hand and lifted her fingers from the table one by one. 'Anyway, this is nice, isn't it? Being out, being together. Just talking.'

'It's lovely.' She threaded her fingers through his – long fingers, she thought, good for performing surgery – and felt her stomach flutter. 'I think I'll have wine,' she said, 'to go with the stilton.'

When the waiter came back, Simon ordered a bottle and two glasses.

'Did I see you with a little boy?' he said, pouring her a glass.

She stared in surprise. 'Dylan. He's my son.'

Simon smiled. 'I thought so. Only you didn't mention him last time.'

'No, well.' She picked at the salad garnish on her plate. 'You didn't ask.'

'I didn't know there was anything *to* ask. Not that it's a big deal.'

'He's a big deal to me.'

'Of course, he's your son.'

She took a gulp of wine, unsure where the conversation was going. She didn't like the thought of being watched, however innocently. 'Just, it didn't seem relevant to what we were saying. When did you see me? *Us?*'

'You were going into the barbers' on the High Street.'

'Aha.'

'I was on my way to work. I think I mentioned before, my village is five miles that way.' He pointed down the High Street towards the south end of town. 'This is the quickest route. A short cut.'

'I see,' she smiled. Of course it didn't matter he'd seen her with Dylan. She needed to relax.

'Tell me about him. What's he like? What's he into? I love kids. They're so much fun.'

'He's just a normal boy. Into football and Batman. Correction, he's *obsessed* with Batman.' Nick had taken Dylan to the cinema and she imagined the giant box of popcorn wedged between his thighs, the Slush Puppie balancing on the arm rest; she imagined him trying not to spill a drop on his favourite Batman T-shirt, the one he'd chosen for Georgie's sleepover. Simon smiled, seeming genuinely interested. 'He's doing well at school,' she said. 'He doesn't like his teacher, but apart from that . . . '

'He sounds great.'

'He is.'

'Maybe I'll meet him one day?' He reached for her hand again, his fingers locking playfully around hers. 'Maybe I could even take him out somewhere? Give you a break?'

She picked up her wine with her other hand. A rush of emotions she couldn't untangle; things were moving so fast. 'Maybe.'

The conversation wandered. They talked about Simon's childhood in the country, growing up on a farm with three brothers. She told him her own story, how she'd worked in the café and taken a computer course in the evenings; then before that, how she'd studied performing arts for a year at university.

'Then Dylan came into my life.'

'But you'll go back to university one day, won't you?'

She thought of Dylan in the cinema and smiled. Life had taken an unpredictable course. 'Perhaps.' She curled her fingers around his thumb and felt him lean in, wondering if he was going to kiss her properly this time. Instead, he moved a strand of hair from her eyes, making her giggle.

'Another glass?' he suggested.

'Better not. I'm driving later. And I've got to get back for Dylan. He's with a friend.'

'Well, how about we arrange something for the week after next? I promise I won't be so shattered, then. I'm on days next week. Time to reset my body clock.'

'All right. I'll call you.'

She collected her bag from the floor, insisting they split the bill between them, but he resisted. 'My shout. You can buy the next one.'

'So, how was the date?'

She was in Nick's attic studio, perched on his bed, watching Dylan messing about with a model Spitfire. To her right, on the bedside table, was a silver washbag and matching hair-brush. Everywhere she looked, there was evidence of Alexa: a vase of fake flowers on top of the TV; Nick's model village that he'd spent years perfecting, shoved beneath the bed; a jar of own-brand instant coffee on the window ledge. Nick was fastidious about coffee. *Life's too short to drink bad coffee*, was one of his sayings.

'Shh,' she said, indicating Dylan. 'He doesn't know it was a D. A. T. E.'

'I don't think he's listening,' said Nick. 'Too full of popcorn.' He grinned. 'And he can spell.'

Dylan turned around, smiled, then raced the Spitfire along an imaginary runway.

'I don't know,' she said, rubbing her forehead. She liked Simon, she really did, but it wasn't quite the fireworks she'd imagined. 'He's a bit old-fashioned. Wouldn't let me pay for my food.'

'Sounds dreamy. Will you see him again?'

She glanced at the washbag.

'Probably. I said I'd call him. Unless I get a better offer in the meantime.'

She meant it as a joke, but for a fraction of a second they locked eyes. She thought of the garden, the smell of candlewax and autumn air.

'Is it time to go to Georgie's now?' Dylan landed the Spitfire on her knee.

'Not quite. Thought we'd go for a walk in the park first.' She needed to clear her head. She didn't want to drive with the alcohol still in her system.

'Aw, Mum!'

'It's too early. It's only three o'clock. You're not expected there until six.'

'Can Uncle Nick come to the park too?'

'I don't think—'

Nick jumped up and grabbed his trainers. 'I'd love to. Beats reading journal articles.'

It felt good to be outside. It was another breathless day, hot for the time of year. Children rolled up their trousers and paddled in the lake. Only the leaves alongside the pathways reminded them it was autumn. Dylan ran ahead to the playground area and they watched from the railings as he monkeyed his way up the climbing frames, wrapped his arms and legs down the fireman's poles, swung on knotted ropes.

'He's growing up so fast,' said Kelda. 'One day he won't need me.'

'He'll always need you.'

'I'm not so sure . . .'

'And you're doing a brilliant job as a mum.'

'Thanks. It's just that . . .'

'What?'

'Something's changed recently. It's difficult to explain.' She thought of the pebbles she'd found that morning, in her side of the bed. She'd rolled onto them, felt them dig into her hip, waking her up. Dylan must have woken in the night and put them there. Except why hadn't she felt him move? And where was he getting them from in the first place? There was nothing in the garden apart from the rocks by the path, and it was impossible he'd found the pot on the top kitchen shelf unless he'd clambered on the work surface. Even then she doubted he'd reach.

'Try me.'

She sighed, glad of the children playing in front of them, the ice-cream van humming in the background, the groups of mums with their snacks and water bottles and packets of wet wipes. Out here, in the park, none of it seemed real.

'Things have been happening in the house,' she said. 'First Dylan had that nightmare. He thought he saw a woman in his room, not once but twice. Then I thought I heard someone else in the house when I was alone. The floorboard in Dylan's room.

It makes a funny squeak. And the electrics have been going haywire. Lights turning themselves on and off.'

She paused, waiting for his reaction, but he just looked blank.

'I got up in the middle of the night, and I swear I was being watched, though I didn't see anything. It was dark. I didn't hear anything either, apart from what I thought was mice. It was more a feeling. A knowledge. Like when you're walking down the street and you sense there's someone behind you.' She watched the two kids in front of them, just beyond the railing, on the seesaw going up and down. 'I know it sounds weird. Stupid. I can hear myself talking and I sound crazy even to myself. But for a moment, for a few seconds, it was real. There was someone else in the toll house, watching me in the dead of night. Wanting me. The same thing happened one day when I was in the bath. I felt even more naked than I was. I felt *violated*. Then, there are these pebbles.'

She had one in her pocket, one of the ones she'd found beneath the duvet. In the daylight it seemed dull. Nothing of any interest. Just an ordinary pebble that she could have picked up anywhere.

'I'm finding them all over the house, but Dylan says it's not him. He denies knowing anything about them.'

Again, she tried to read the expression on Nick's face but couldn't. At least he wasn't laughing. On the surface, he seemed to be taking her seriously.

'Something's changed in the house. Ever since Dylan threw the saucepan at the wall, ever since we found the . . .' She stumbled on the words, remembering what Nick had called it, a 'death mask'. 'Ever since we found that face.'

For the first time, he looked surprised. 'You think . . . ?'

'I don't know what to think! I'm not even sure I believe in stuff like that.'

'Stuff like what?'

The kids jumped off the seesaw, causing one end of it to squeal to the ground. 'I suppose, paranormal stuff. It feels as though whoever the mask belongs to, is still in there. That their spirit is somehow trapped in the toll house.' She stared into the playground, looking for Dylan, but couldn't see him, scanning the swings and the rock-face wall and the roundabout. She felt that familiar knot in her throat like she couldn't quite swallow, until she saw him on top of the pirate ship, waving. She waved back, softening her grip on the railing.

'If you don't mind me saying,' Nick said softly, 'you've not been happy recently, have you? What with your boss, and Dylan getting into trouble at school. Then there's the new house, the new town. All this, the feeling of being watched, is probably just stress. Maybe you should speak to your GP?'

'My GP?'

'Stress. It can do weird things. Completely mess with your body.'

'I suppose.' The idea sounded so strange compared to what was going on in her head. Could she be doing this to herself? Could she be making it up? She remembered how scared she'd felt in the dark on the stairs. Petrified. Nothing had caused it, nothing physical. Yet, she'd felt too scared to move. She'd had to tear herself away from ... well ... from nothing. What if this really was all in her mind? After all, she'd been so worried recently about Dylan, about his friendship with Georgie Watts, about the school. On top of that, she was stressed about her job, Cassandra's continuous demands and her suspicion that Kelda wasn't pulling her weight. No wonder she was out of sorts, maybe if she ate a bit healthier and got some exercise ...

'Or maybe there's a rational explanation,' Nick said. 'Maybe

Dylan's just playing a game with the pebbles. And maybe it wasn't the floorboard creaking. Maybe it was just an old pipe or the wind outside. And you probably need to get someone in, to check out your electrics. Sounds like there's a fault.'

'I guess.' She thought of the money it might cost. 'But what about the face? All this started when we found the face in the wall.'

'Just a weird feature of the house. It must have been there years, decades. No reason for it to start causing trouble now. Not that it *could* cause trouble. It's just plaster. I'll help you remove it, if you like? We could chip it off.'

She nodded, watching Dylan slide down the side of the pirate ship. 'Would you do me another favour?'

'What's that?'

'I've been doing some research on the internet, but I've not had much luck. Seems there's almost no information on the Stonebridge toll house. I thought you could see if there's anything in the university archives?'

He folded his arms. 'Won't that make things worse? Worrying about what I might find? Not that I *will* find anything.'

She shrugged. 'Sometimes it's worse, thinking there might be something out there, but not knowing what it is. Probably just me being silly. Or stressed. But it would make me feel better if you tried.'

'All right. If you're sure. But what about the guy who lived there before? Could you get in contact? Ask him too?'

She thought of the name on the paperwork: Mr Pritchard. From what she'd gathered from the estate agent, he'd moved into one of the retirement homes in town.

'Maybe,' she said. 'But he's elderly. I won't bother him unless I really have to. Unless I can't find out another way.'

She felt better now that the stuff in the toll house was out in the open. It had lost some of its power. She shielded her eyes from the bright sunshine and watched Dylan kick a pile of leaves beneath the tree, joining the other children searching for conkers. She knew she'd be all right, going home alone after she'd dropped Dylan off at Georgie's. She'd make herself something quick to eat, watch TV or read a book, go to bed with the lights on.

'Don't suppose you're free tonight?' she said, just in case.

He shook his head. 'Appointment with the future in-laws.'

She gulped. 'Have you told them?'

'Nope.' He rubbed his hands together. 'Tonight's the big night.'

She dropped Dylan at Georgie's house, a white-bricked mansion with an automatic gateway. Ethan was already there, spilling crisps over the cream shag-pile carpet, looking entirely at home.

'Come on,' he said to Dylan. 'Georgie's giving us turns on the Xbox.'

She bent down to kiss Dylan goodnight, but he turned away from her and ran after his friend. She handed his overnight bag to Mrs Watts, looking oddly glamorous in loungewear and fluffy white slippers.

'Don't worry about anything,' Mrs Watts said airily. Kelda had a feeling she was trying to get rid of her. She could hear Ethan's mum in the next room speaking to Mr Watts and she supposed they were going to make an evening of it whilst the children played, or rather got square-eyed looking at screens.

Mrs Watts moved to close the door. 'I'll phone if there's a problem.'

As soon as she got home, she checked the mousetraps. Both were empty, the peanut butter and bread untouched. She made herself toast and turned on the TV. *Enigma* was about to start, one of her favourite movies. She kicked off her trainers and put her feet up on the sofa. She'd watch the movie and not think about the house or the face in the wall; she'd not think about the fact she was alone, a good mile from the town with no one else around.

She texted Nick, Thanks for the chat earlier. Good luck tonight, then sat back and relaxed.

Her phone buzzed with a message:

Thnx, I need it. And don't worry about the other stuff

Other stuff.
She texted back a smiley face. She wouldn't think about the house tonight. After all, she'd done this plenty of times when Dylan was asleep, sat in front of the TV and watched a movie on her own. She'd be fine. Just fine.

She awoke to darkness. She didn't remember drifting off, but she knew where she was, in the lounge with her head on the cushions, the slight stickiness of the leather sofa beneath her jeans, the shutters barring the bay window behind her. The television had switched itself off – she must have leaned on the remote control – and she couldn't see a thing, not even the standby light at the bottom of the screen. She stared at where she thought the screen should be. Nothing but darkness. The lounge light and the one in the kitchen had switched them-selves off, too, though she knew she'd left them on. Purposely left them on. There'd been a power cut or she'd blown a fuse, maybe something to do with the toaster. She felt for her phone on the cushions. Battery dead, though she remembered charging it at Nick's. It had been a hundred per cent by the time they'd left for the park. What if Mrs Watts had tried to call her after the battery died? She put the phone in her pocket and stood up. The fuse box was in the kitchen and there were candles she kept in a box on the old range.

She crossed the room to the light switch, groping in the dark, and flicked it one way then the other. Dead. She listened carefully, not even a hum from the fridge-freezer, which meant it would be dripping by morning if the power wasn't restored. The thought of spending the entire night in the dark made her panic. She laid a hand against her chest and breathed deliberately through her mouth. In, out. In, out. She just needed to find the candles and the box of matches then make her way to the fuse box. She crossed to the range and felt the cold dusty metal with her fingers. The box was at the back, an old tin she'd found in the garden when they'd first moved in, which she'd supplied with candles and a box of matches for emergencies.

She prised open the lid, found the box of matches and struck one. The light glared in her hands, burning her thumb, causing her to drop the match. It went out. Darkness again. She lit another, hands trembling, reminding herself to breathe, then fumbled for one of the candles and coaxed the wick. She moved the candle around the kitchen, relieved when she saw things she recognised, the arc of the bread bin, the microwave, the metal tin with its assortment of knives and spatulas. Just the kitchen, she told herself, the kitchen you see every day, the kitchen where you make pancakes and school lunches, the kitchen where you sit and drink wine and read books. Nothing to be afraid of. You're just being stupid. Bloody, bloody stupid.

She hunted for the step-ladder, leaning against the pantry cupboards, and set it wide beneath the fuse box, starting at the sound of the metal legs scraping across the tiles and the candle swaying precariously in her hand, splashing wax on her fingers.

She stepped onto the first rung. A noise came from somewhere above. She halted, listening hard, conscious of the sound of her breath, her heart beating fast. It came again, a noise she recognised. The creak of the loose floorboard in Dylan's room followed by the slow tread of feet crossing towards the landing.

The candle dripped at an angle and hot wax seared through her jeans. She didn't dare move. Didn't dare scream. Her throat tightened. She couldn't get enough air. She thought she was going to pass out.

The footsteps sounded along the length of the kitchen ceiling then stopped. She waited. Waited to hear them cross the landing and descend the stairs, waited without moving, without breathing. There was nothing. No more footsteps, no more sagging floorboards, just the terrifying certainty someone else was in the house. Molten wax dripped on her foot, hardening on her sock. She stumbled backwards. She had to get out. She had to get to the car.

She made out the shape of the back door and ran towards it, catching her feet on one of Dylan's toys. She heard the splinter of breaking plastic. The candle went out as she dropped it, as her hands fell upon the latch. At the same time, the lights came on, the television in the next room blared into life. She blinked in the electric light. Normality. Except it wasn't normal at all. She stared at the kitchen tiles, at the empty mousetraps, at the broken toy, her gaze moving to the doorway that led to the hallway that led to the stairs, wide open, the way she always left it. She hesitated. She knew she should get out of the house, but at the same time, she had to check, she had to climb the stairs, cross the landing to Dylan's room, switch on the light. Even now she was doubting herself. What had Nick said? She was stressed, she should speak to her GP. It was all in her mind.

She looked for something to take with her and settled on the bread knife. She felt braver with the knife in her hand though she knew it would take all her courage to use it against an intruder and deep down she knew that there was no intruder, no one else at all; she was quite alone. She pushed the door into the hallway as far back as it would go and felt for the light switch on the other side.

The stairs were perfectly silent, perfectly still. At the bottom was the unused front door that led to the outdoor porch, bolted as always. She ran her eyes up and down the stairs and along the gallery landing. Nothing but the old brown carpet that had been there ever since she'd bought the place. She hated the carpet. She'd promised herself it was the first thing she'd get rid of when she could afford it. Nothing but those awful brown swirls covering the stairs and the shadowed bookshelf at the top on the landing piled high with junk and books she hadn't got round to reading.

She gripped the bread knife tighter, palms sweaty with fear. Just her imagination, wasn't it? After all, if she thought it was real, she'd have been out of the house minutes ago, she'd have telephoned the police, she'd have reported an intruder.

You've not been happy recently . . . Dylan getting into trouble at school . . . maybe you should speak to your GP?

She crept up the stairs, trying to make as little sound as possible. The house was silent. The night was silent. No wind. No owls. No rustling trees. She reached the landing and switched on the light, heart thudding in her chest. She walked the length of it, all the way to the far bedroom – her room – turning the light on, checking beneath the bed, inside the wardrobe, throwing her clothes off the chair. Then back again, into the bathroom, a few paces in and out to check behind the door. Lastly, into Dylan's room. She knew instinctively what she'd find. Or rather what she wouldn't find. There was no one there. No sign anyone had been there, just the walls, still scrawled with lipstick. She'd started to scrub it off, but not got far. It was harder than she'd thought. Stubborn, like it wanted to remain there. Her eyes rested on that name high up in joined-up letters: *Bella*.

She lowered the bread knife thinking how ridiculous she'd seem if anyone saw her now. Except, no one would see her because she was quite alone. She'd been alone all evening, hadn't she? She turned back towards the landing, catching the scent of lavender at the back of her throat.

'He's looking for you.'

The voice came from behind her. From Dylan's room. A woman's voice. Insistent.

Her mouth ran dry. She thought she might faint.

'He's looking for you.'

The lights flickered and went out. She stood completely still in the darkness, shivers of ice down her spine. That feeling again: sorrow and despair and escalating fear, wrapping itself around her, grabbing her throat.

'He's looking for you.'

She was drowning in sorrow, in the terror of what had happened here, of whatever was lurking within these four walls.

The lights blinked on again, flooding the toll house. There

was a noise behind her, something thumping. This time she cried out, clasping her hands to her mouth. She turned around slowly, terrified of what she'd find.

The microphone Nick had given Dylan for his birthday rolled across the floor as though it had been dropped, landing at the foot of the blow-up skeleton, red light flickering. It must have fallen from the shelf or the bed.

'He's looking for you.'

She grabbed it from the floor, fumbled for the switch, turned it off. Dylan must have been playing a game; he must have recorded the message and somehow it had switched itself on. That stupid microphone. She took out the batteries, fingers trembling, hurled it beneath the bed and ran down the stairs.

15

⌘

1864

One morning, when I'm upstairs combing my long hair, readying myself for the day ahead, I hear a knock on the door. It is early, not yet light. I curse. Not a carriage at this time, worse still the road surveyor or one of the turnpike trustees. But I know I must go down; it is my job to open the turnpike, to collect the tolls, whatever the hour.

'I am coming,' I shout. It's been months since the doctor's visit and no one's called since. Only the drovers and the coach drivers to be let through the gate, and the trustees to complain that standards have slipped, that the turnpike has been left open with no one to man it, that I have been found slumbering in the porch when I should have been working. *Mend your ways, or you will be out*, they say. There are plenty of folk who would be glad of the work. I throw on a shirt and fasten the buttons of my trousers. My feet are bare but they will have to do; whoever it is, is insistent.

I take the key from the hook beside the door and slide back the heavy bolts before opening the lock. Then, I inch it wide. A gasp of icy air brushes my skin and lifts my collar. Bella's sister is standing in the shallow light, basket over one arm. It has been so long, I don't recognise her at first, but then she tilts her head and I see the angle of her jaw, the narrow lips.

'Good day,' I say without inviting her in.

Helen takes one look at me and swings herself and the basket beneath my outstretched arm. In the kitchen, she tugs off her coat and gloves and sets the basket on the table, taking out a loaf of bread, some ham, some cheese.

'They say you are going mad,' she says, finding my jack knife and sawing a chunk of bread. 'They have been talking about you in the town, saying they will find someone else to keep the tollgate. You need to change your ways. At the very least, you should hire a woman to look after the cottage.'

I think of the mask lying on the bed upstairs. 'The last thing I want is a woman. I had the best woman!'

Helen ignores me, sniffing the air. The house smells. Reeks. No one to empty the piss pot. No one to clean the bedding or wash my shirts. No one to beat the rag mats in the garden. No one to pick herbs and dry them in the kitchen. The smell has become a part of me. A part of my sorrow. It inhabits the void in my heart, eating away at it, carving it deeper. Even the mice have returned, built their nests in the walls. Late at night, when the turnpike bars the road, I hear them scratching behind the skirting boards; I see them scurrying across the tiles in the kitchen.

'You need someone to do your washing,' Helen says, 'to

sweep the floors, to blacken the range.' She sets the bread on a plate and wipes the knife to carve the ham. 'You need to take better care of yourself. If you lost your job, you would have nowhere to go.'

Her skirts brush the floor, gathering dust. Just a movement. A whisper. But it takes me back to my childhood, to Ma treading softly across the tiles.

It's a warm summer's day, flies hovering in the heady air and buzzing at the window. Ma lifts the flap of my hiding place – a cloth thrown over the table – and coaxes me out like a shy animal.

'Joe, is that you?' A plate is nudged beneath the cloth. 'Here, I have fruit.' Slices of apple from the garden. Blackberries from the hedge.

'Has he gone?' I say.

She puts her head next to the plate and smiles. 'He is out front, at the gate. He will not be in again until luncheon, you have nothing to fear.'

I wriggle out on my knees and help myself to the apples. They're sweet and juicy, no sign of the bugs that will devour them later in the season. My father has taken his dark cloud away with him and the kitchen is warm and friendly again, my mother's domain. It spans the ground floor of the building, apart from the hall and the staircase and the entrance to the cellar, and is broken in two by a brick pillar. At one end is the range with its cooking pots and jars of dried herbs and bowl of eggs, at the other, a bay window with a ledge and various spindle-backed chairs, where Pa watches the road in the winter. Beside the range is a high-backed settle where I curl in the evenings with my head on Ma's lap, listening to her stories.

I'm halfway' through a slice of apple when the front door opens. Ma hurries me behind her, guarding me with her skirts. I bury my head in the thick warm cotton. There's a smell of wood smoke and hard work, soap and garlic. I cannot see Pa from where I am, but I hear him, sense him. Big boots. Large hands. A presence that fills the tiny space. Some days he is worse than others and today is a bad one.

'Where is he?'

I imagine Ma's face, pale but determined. 'What troubles you, Arthur?'

'The brat left the mail coach waiting.'

'Are you sure?'

I hear Pa unfasten his belt and wrap it around his knuckles. I imagine the colour creeping beneath his collar, blooming across his cheeks. 'Where is he? I asked.'

'I sent him into town.' Ma's voice is as steady as running water. 'He won't be back for hours.' She nudges me back beneath the table, but I'm slow to react, too clumsy, too noisy.

'Do not lie to me, woman.'

He shoves her out of the way.

'You!' he shouts, reaching beneath the tablecloth, dragging me upwards by my ear and twisting it.

'Arthur, be careful!'

'I trusted you,' he spits. 'I trusted you to open the turnpike.'

'I did,' I say, lying. I'd got waylaid. I'd been talking to the shepherd. I'd forgotten what I was supposed to be doing.

The belt comes down fast, lands with a thwack, missing me but catching the table. A mug rattles to the floor. The cat jumps from the chair to the window. Ma stares in horror. Pa flicks the belt again, anger sparking in his eyes. This time it lands on my shoulder, slashing my cheek as it falls. Red-hot pain flashes down my face, into my neck. Tears well in my eyes. I bend over in pain, in shock.

'No!' Ma shouts, placing herself between me and my father.

I hear her wrestling for the belt, but I cannot think clearly, the pain in my face is too sharp, too fierce. Everything feels far away, like I'm drifting. Spinning. I hear the belt swishing through the air again. I hear Ma scream. I hear Pa grunting. There's a horrible uncertain silence, then the sound of Pa's thick boots heading back the way they came.

'He is gone.' Ma lifts me from the floor and cradles me in her arms, her warm salty tears on my cheek, wetting the wound. 'Come sit on my lap. Let me see to that cut. Let me sing to you.'

'Joseph!' Helen's voice cuts through the years. 'You should eat something.'

'I am not hungry.'

'You are thin. Too thin. I will start believing the rumours.'

I humour her, taking a bite of the bread. It's good. The freshest food I have eaten in a long time.

'Why are you here?'

Helen spears a piece of cheese with the jack knife and drops it on my plate. Her manner is guarded, uncomfortable. Obviously, she'd rather not answer my question.

I take the cheese and sandwich it between the bread. 'Do not tell me this is charity?'

She shrugs as though it doesn't matter one way or the other what this is. 'Dr Marsh asked me to look in on you. He says he is concerned.'

'The doctor?' I spit out the words.

Helen puts down the knife. 'He is a good man. A Christian gentleman. You must not speak ill of him. You must not gossip with the drovers.'

She looks me up and down as if the wickedness inside me is visible, and for a moment, I see what she sees: my hair grown long, my beard untrimmed, my shirt stained, buttons missing from the cuffs. I have grown reedy, cannot be bothered with the business of cooking, eating whatever leftovers the farmer's boy brings. As long as I have beer to wet my throat . . .

'I am a grown man,' I say, pushing the sandwich aside. 'I have no need of charity.'

'But you need company,' she says. Her eyes roam my face, my shirt, the smudges on my collar. 'You are growing wild on your own. It is not a Christian way to live. You should take up another occupation to stop you from growing idle. You could repair shoes or stitch leather whilst you sit at the roadside.'

'Pah!' I strike the table with my hand, but she does not react. Instead, she picks up plates and piles them in a basin, then looks around for something to scrub with, her woman's eyes disapproving of everything she sees.

I throw myself in the chair beside the range and tug on my shoes. Daylight is breaking – the shutters at the bay window are never closed – and I see the long length of the turnpike road waiting for me. I want to tell Helen to leave. I want to tell her I am happy with my own company, that I do not need a woman to fuss over me and clean for me. Instead, I scowl and grunt and tie my laces. Then I open the front door and sit in the porch, waiting for the sound of hooves on the road. It's a quiet day and the road glistens with ice. I would rather be indoors, watching the road from the window, but not with Helen in the house.

An hour later, just when I'm pocketing pennies from a coach-man, she sweeps out with her basket.

'I will be back,' she says without meeting my eye. 'I will not forget my promise to the doctor.'

She walks away without bidding me goodbye. I watch her getting smaller and smaller as she nears the bridge to the town. Inside, she's left me the bread, the cheese, the ham. In some ways she is right, I think: I ought to take better care of myself.

I kneel beside the range and pile it with coal. Then, when the fire is blazing, I lay the kettle on the hob and wait for it to sing. My eyes stray from the red-hot coals to the Bible on the table next to the ham. The Bible I recognise as my stepmother's. I remember her sitting in the settle, the book at arm's length, squinting at the words, speaking aloud her favourite passages about judgement and eternal life, as if by doing so I might for-give her all the beatings and unkind words. I wonder if Helen has been leafing through it, trying to rid the house of whatever demons she believes I've conjured, or whether she has left it out for me to read. Whether this is another of Dr Marsh's requests.

I take the Bible in my hands and rip the pages out one by one, crushing them in my fingers and feeding them to the flames.

16

NOW

'I think I'm stressed,' Kelda said, crossing her knees. She was sitting in the doctors' surgery, looking beyond the GP to the car park outside. It seemed strange thinking about the house like it was a medical problem, an illness or a disease, something that could be cut out and discarded.

The GP looked at her kindly.

'I've got a lot on at work and there are some problems at home. Well, not problems exactly. My son, Dylan, he's just turned seven. He's going through a difficult phase. We've not long moved into the area and the transition has been, well ...' she stared at the car park, at the grey tarmac speckled with rain, '... difficult.'

'I see. I'm sorry to hear that. Is there anyone at home to support you? A partner?'

Kelda shook her head. 'It's just me. I've got a friend, Nick. He helps out sometimes but he doesn't live with us.'

She thought about the night of Georgie's sleepover, how she'd slept in the car. After what had happened in the house – the lights going out, the footsteps on the landing, the microphone playing that ... that message ... she'd driven into town, to Nick's street, and parked outside his block of flats. She'd waited for Nick to return from Alexa's parents', except when he did, he wasn't alone. Alexa, obviously drunk, was swaying on his arm. For some reason, Kelda hadn't considered that Alexa would come home with Nick. But of course she would. They were officially engaged. It was just a matter of time before they moved in together. She'd felt bad, intruding on their special night, and had driven to the park before they'd seen her. It had been dark, too dark. She'd found a secluded spot in the car park, reclined the driver's seat, pulled the blanket from the back seat and tried to sleep.

The GP glanced at Kelda's notes on the computer screen, her previous medical history, which, for the last five years, consisted of occasional prescriptions for the mini-pill. 'And how does the stress manifest itself?' she said. 'What I mean is, how do you feel?'

Kelda thought of the toll house, the way she'd felt in the dark when the lights had gone out. The next day, picking Dylan up from Georgie's mansion, bleary-eyed, freezing cold and wearing the same clothes as the day before, she'd promised herself she'd never sleep in the park again; she'd see her GP in the week as Nick had suggested. She'd thought about scrambling beneath Dylan's bed and checking the microphone, putting the batteries back in and playing the messages; at the same time, she couldn't bear to hear that voice again, even if it was just Dylan's voice distorted.

'It's hard to explain. It sounds stupid.'

'Try me. Believe me, I've heard all sorts between these four walls.'

Kelda took a deep breath. 'I've been hearing things. Things in the house. Footsteps. A creaking floorboard. I was in the kitchen and the lights went out and I swear someone else was in the house with me. Only, when I looked, there was no one there. The house is tiny. There's nowhere to hide. It was just me in the dark, but it felt like ...' Tears slid down her cheeks and she wiped them angrily with her sleeve. 'It felt like I wasn't alone.'

'Okay.' The GP smiled with the confidence of a professional. 'Anything else?'

Kelda shook her head. 'Just the feeling that someone's watching me, that there's someone else in the house besides me and Dylan, though I know there isn't. I just can't shake the feeling.'

'You feel anxious?'

'Sometimes.'

'What about sad? I mean, really sad?'

She thought of the feeling she'd had, standing on the landing with the bread knife in her hand. Like the whole world was against her, like nothing would ever be right again.

'Sometimes.'

'Let's take your blood pressure.'

Kelda rolled up her sleeve and stared at the white walls, the medical textbooks on the shelf above the doctor's head, whilst the fabric tightened around her arm.

The doctor ripped off the blood-pressure cuff and put it back on its stand. 'A little high, but not dangerously high, just something to keep an eye on.' She typed a few notes on her screen then leaned back in her seat. 'I don't think we need to worry too much at the moment.'

Kelda felt the relief drop from her shoulders. After Saturday night, she'd worried there was something seriously wrong with her.

'When we feel anxious, our bodies go into fight or flight mode. We experience things like dry mouth, racing heartbeat, rapid breathing. Sometimes we experience more unusual symptoms, too, such as hallucinations and paranoia. Of course, these can also be symptoms of more serious problems, so we need to be vigilant.'

'You don't think I'm going mad?'

'I think you're stressed, like you said. You need to relax.'

'Okay . . .'

The GP smiled. 'Most people come into my surgery expecting me to hand out pills. But some of those pills can be highly addictive and they're not always the most appropriate solution. I don't want to head down that path yet. Instead, I'm going to suggest you try a relaxation course.'

'A relaxation course?' She realised she'd wanted the pills after all, the quick fix, something that would make her feel like she was getting on top of the situation.

The GP rifled through the papers on her desk and handed her a flyer. 'Here. Have a read. There's a number on the front you can ring to book yourself in. It's a self-referral system.'

Kelda nodded and folded the flyer in half. 'Thanks.'

'Anything else?'

She shook her head.

The GP tapped more words into her computer. 'Come back straight away if things get worse. It's important you look after yourself. Eat well and exercise.'

*

She drove home via the fruit and veg shop, stocking up on bananas and oranges and a large bag of spinach. The doctor was right, she needed to look after herself. Recently, she'd had too many late nights. Too many hours staring into the dark, watching the alarm clock flash from three to four to five o'clock in the morning. In her bag was a mountain of work from Cassandra which needed completing before she picked Dylan up from after-school club. She'd sit in the kitchen, eating oranges, not thinking about the house or the fact she was alone. Since Georgie's sleepover, there'd been nothing untoward. She'd been grateful for Dylan running around the place, still on a high, talking non-stop about Georgie's house and Georgie's swimming pool and the midnight feast they'd eaten in Georgie's bedroom.

She pulled up outside the toll house, beneath the bay window. It dominated the front of the house. Above it was a rusty metal sign, set in a slight alcove, detailing the tolls to be paid, BY ORDER OF THE TRUSTEES OF STONEBRIDGE TURNPIKE TRUST.

She'd got so used to looking at it over the months, she'd almost forgotten what a unique piece of history she'd bought. The sign, if it was original, probably belonged in a museum.

She went inside, keeping the door open just in case, pulled the file of work from her bag and took her laptop to the kitchen table. She cut an orange into quarters and tried not to drip juice on the file.

Two hours later she was bored. She put the file down and studied the doctor's flyer. The relaxation course didn't sound like her type of thing – deep breathing and meditation – but maybe that was the point: trying something new, shaking her-self up in a good way. She dialled the number on the front of it and spoke to an Irish woman who invited her to the group on Thursday.

She put the phone down, feeling better for taking control, doing something rather than just mulling over her problems. Still bored, she cut open another orange. The knife caught her finger, a short sharp jab. Blood rushed to the surface. She sucked it, wincing at the pain, eyes wandering to the open door.

She jumped.

A woman was sitting on the picnic table in the garden, knees bunched in her chest, arms wrapped around each other, eyes focused on the house. Watching her.

She flew to the garden. 'Emma! You gave me the shock of my life. I thought you were a . . .' She couldn't find the word, couldn't grasp the fact her little sister was here at the toll house. 'I thought you were a . . .'

'What?' Emma grinned. She looked older, thinner. Lank hair and dirty jeans. There was a large holdall dumped on the grass beneath her feet. She jumped down from the table.

'Emma, what the hell are you doing here? Why didn't you ring? Why didn't you tell me you were coming? How did you get here? Don't tell me you drove?'

'I took the train and then I walked.'

Kelda wondered how long it had been, how many years. They didn't even exchange birthday or Christmas cards anymore. They'd more or less lost contact, even Mum had stopped trying to keep track of Emma. Kelda had assumed Emma's life was too busy, too chaotic, for family.

'But what are you doing here?'

She knew she should invite her in. She should be nice, make a cup of tea, make a pretence of being pleased. She *was* pleased, just it had been so long, and the few times she'd heard from

Emma over the years, Emma had been drunk, ringing in the middle of the night and slurring down the phone.

'I got chucked out of my place. I had nowhere to go. I rang Mum and asked her for your address. Can I come in?'

Kelda hesitated, knowing she had no option.

'Yes, of course. Though I've got to leave in half an hour. The school run. I have to pick up Dylan . . . ' She watched as Emma looped the strap of the holdall over her shoulder, staggering under the weight.

In the kitchen, Kelda closed her laptop and pulled out a chair. 'Tea? Coffee?'

'Water for me, thanks.'

'Okay.'

She boiled the kettle anyway and made herself a cup of tea. She wondered whether she should open a packet of biscuits.

'I'm starving. Is there toast or something?'

'Toast? Of course.' Kelda put two slices in the toaster. 'So, how are things? Apart from losing your flat, I mean?'

'Oh, you know.'

Kelda hovered by the toaster, remembering how, as children, they'd played together for hours, how easy it had been between them. Or had it? Maybe she wasn't remembering right. Maybe over the years she'd forgotten about the bickering, the squabbling over toys.

'So what happened?' Kelda said, planting the toast on the table.

Emma took a bite. 'Mmm, Marmite. You remembered.'

Kelda sat down opposite her and cradled her tea.

'If you must know, Luke threw me out.'

'Luke?'

'My boyfriend. My *ex*-boyfriend.'

'I see.'

'I slept on the landing for a bit, but then the landlord found out and went crazy about health and safety.'

'Right.'

'I lost my job a few months ago, so I was relying on Luke.'

'Why didn't you get another job? Another place to stay?'

Emma looked solemnly at the toast, then pulled off a long tail of crust. 'Not easy when you don't have any qualifications. When your last boss refuses to give you a reference and spreads rumours about you that aren't true.'

Kelda sucked her finger again. She'd been good at school, conscientious, straight As for GCSE, four As at A-level. Emma had been set to follow, but then, after Dad left, she'd got in with the wrong crowd, started staying out late. Sometimes she didn't come home until the next morning and there'd be a row over breakfast. Even then, Kelda had stuck up for Emma, tried to mediate between her and Mum, tried to make Mum realise it was just a phase, Emma was just upset about Dad and being a normal teenager. Except it wasn't just a phase with Emma.

'So, what are you going to do?' she said.

Emma glanced at the holdall and Kelda realised she knew the answer already.

'I don't suppose I could stay here for a while?' She pulled at her necklace, a white stone dangling from a leather cord. 'Just until I sort myself out, get a job in the town, find a cheap flat.'

'I'm not sure . . .'

'Please, I wouldn't ask if I wasn't desperate.'

'But Dylan . . .'

'He won't mind. He must be five by now. We can get to know each other.'

'He's seven.'

'Seven. Yes. Of course. I was forgetting.' She put the crust in her mouth.

'Talking of which, I'd better go and get him.' Kelda hesitated, wondering what to do, whether to take Emma with her. But she needed the drive there on her own to sort her head out. She'd have to leave Emma here. She'd have to trust her. She stood up and looked for her car keys. 'I won't be long. We'll talk about that other issue – the issue of you staying here – later.'

She was glad to be out of the house, glad to be with the other mums waiting outside the school gate for the crocodile of after-school-club children, swapping notes about half term and Halloween. On the way home, she told Dylan they had a visitor.

'She's my sister.'

'Your sister? I didn't know you had a sister. I thought there was just one of you. Like there's just one of me.'

'Well, we're not very close. Not anymore.'

'A big sister or a little sister?'

'A little sister. She's called Emma. You can call her Emma too.'

'*Emma.*' He tried out the name like it was something exciting, a new toy, an interesting sweet. 'Is she staying for tea?'

'Yes, I think so.'

'Is she nice?'

'Of course she's nice. She's my sister.' She watched him in the rear-view mirror, drawing a letter E on the window pane, and frowning.

'Does she look like you?'

'I don't know. I don't think so. You'll find out for yourself soon enough.'

'Why haven't I met her before?'

'You have. Only you were a baby at the time. And then Emma moved away.'

Back home, she found Emma on the sofa, watching TV. She jumped up when she saw them and ruffled Dylan's hair. 'Hi, Dylan. I'm your Auntie Em.'

'Hi.' He collected a heap of Lego from the kitchen table, suddenly shy. 'Mum, can I go upstairs now?'

'Yes, of course.' Normally, she'd admonish him for being rude, but today, she was relieved. It was the first time in ages he'd volunteered to go to his room. She'd spent Sunday afternoon with a bucket of soapy water, going over and over the wall, washing the lipstick off inch by inch, revealing the magnolia beneath, scrubbing at the name last of all. Close up, it was just a scrawl. Random lines that looked like 'Bella' but weren't really. She realised how mistaken she'd been. Mistaken about the whole thing. Suddenly, none of it had seemed real: the footsteps across the landing, the certainty there was someone else in the house, the overwhelming terror. All in her mind. A horrible daydream.

'Cute kid,' said Emma.

'Yes. He can be a bit shy at times.' She put plates on the table for dinner. Three plates. No point asking Emma if she was staying. She reached for the wine bottles on the top of the fridge, then hesitated, knowing she shouldn't.

'It's okay,' Emma was by her side. 'I'm dry.'

'Really?'

'Really.' Emma sighed. 'I know what you're thinking. You think I'm going to cause trouble, I'm going to be drunk all the time. But actually, I haven't touched a drop for months. I've even had counselling.'

'And the other stuff?'

'Drugs?' Emma shook her head. 'Not for years.'

Kelda relaxed, opened the fridge and pulled out a carton of apple juice. Perhaps it wouldn't be so bad having Emma around for a few days, having another adult in the house. Perhaps it would even stop the weird stuff from happening. Her eyes fell upon a pile of pebbles Dylan had been playing with over breakfast that morning, heaping them into mounds.

'How about you stay until the end of the week?' she offered.

Emma beamed. 'Really? Oh, Kelda, I knew I could count on you. Are you sure?'

She nodded, embarrassed. 'You'll have to sleep on the sofa. There are only two bedrooms. Mine and Dylan's.' Dylan hadn't slept in his room for days, but it was his private space and she wanted him at least to have the option of sleeping there. 'And there are rules. No swearing. No smoking in the house. And you'll have to help with the washing-up.'

'You sound like Mum.'

'No, I don't.'

'Yes, you do.' Emma giggled. 'All right, I'll help with the washing-up, if you insist.' She bent down and unzipped the holdall, bringing out a handful of clothes.

Kelda turned back to the fridge and tried to think what to cook with the bag of spinach. Her phone vibrated in her pocket: a message from Nick, wanting her opinion on something he couldn't explain by text.

Can I come over Thursday evening?

She remembered about the relaxation course and realised she'd be in town; she could meet Nick afterwards for a drink.

She'd been planning to ask Lucy to babysit again, but now that Emma was here . . .

She watched her sister sort through her washing, doing the sniff test, sorting the really dirty clothes from the less dirty ones. She remembered Dylan as a baby in Emma's arms, screaming until Kelda came to the rescue, wriggling from her grasp like his life depended on it. But things had changed. Emma had changed. She closed the fridge door, wondering whether Dylan would take to her, wondering how much she could really trust her sister.

17

---ᘓᘓᘓᘓ---

On Thursday evening, Kelda drove to the church hall in the centre of town. She was early for the relaxation course and unsure what to expect. She sat in the car park, fingering the flyer, watching the clock on the dashboard. Part of her wanted to reverse the car and head straight back the way she'd come. She'd felt good since Emma's arrival; having another adult around made her feel safer. There'd been no weird feelings in the house, no sounds that weren't really there. Or rather, anything she had felt or heard, she'd been able to push to the back of her mind. Just the usual creaks and moans of an old house, she'd tell herself, nothing more. She'd even coped with the mess, Emma sprawling her stuff everywhere, surprising given she didn't have much to sprawl, leaving cigarette packets on the table, though Kelda had specifically asked her not to smoke in the house. Despite all that, Emma had helped with the chores, cleaning the bathroom and making lasagne one night after school. She'd watched Emma and Dylan together with interest. Dylan didn't seem to mind Emma being there, though he hadn't particularly taken to her either. He kept to his room though he still refused to sleep there, playing with his Lego, emerging now and again to show them his creations.

She checked the time again – three minutes to – and wondered what was happening at home right now. She'd left Emma with instructions: Dylan could stay up until she came home as long as he changed into pyjamas. There was homework that needed completing and, after that, there were DVDs and popcorn and crisps. Anything to make the evening run smoothly. But now she was panicking. What had she been thinking, leaving Dylan with her sister? Emma had volunteered before she'd even asked her. 'It would be a chance to get to know him,' she'd said, when Kelda mentioned going out. She didn't tell Emma about the relaxation course, only that she was meeting a friend for a drink in town, which was partly true. She'd agreed to Emma babysitting because it had seemed rude not to, and Emma had promised she'd be on her best behaviour. But now that she was away from Dylan, she wondered what on earth she'd done. The Emma she knew didn't look after children, had no interest in them.

She dialled Emma's mobile. 'Emma?'

'Hi.'

'It's Kelda.'

'I know that.'

'Is Dylan all right?'

'He's fine. He's right next to me. We're making popcorn in the microwave.'

'Has he done his maths homework?'

Emma groaned. 'Give us a chance. You've only just left.'

'Okay, okay.' She watched the dashboard clock hand flick to the hour. She had to go. 'Homework first, then popcorn, all right?'

'Chillax. He's fine. We're both fine. And yes, I'll make sure he does his homework.'

She took the keys out of the ignition and locked the car.

The relaxation course was being held in a room at the back of the church hall, beneath glaring strip lights.

'Hi, you must be Kelda?'

She recognised the Irish accent, the same lady she'd spoken to on the phone.

'That's right.'

'Grab one of the mats. We'll be starting shortly.'

She sat on a yoga mat in a circle with eight other people, mostly middle-aged women, a couple of men. The walls were plastered with notices about the local toddler group and there was a smell of gym kits and playdough. The man next to her leaned over from his mat and tried to make conversation, telling her about the day he'd had and how he really needed a drink. She smiled in sympathy; she'd sink a glass of wine right now.

'Right, everybody.' The Irish woman sat on a cushion in the centre of the circle. 'We've a newcomer today, so I'm going to go through the basics, the breathing techniques.' She switched on a CD player.

Wind chimes. The sound of waves.

'Everybody, lie down and close your eyes.'

Kelda tried to concentrate, tried to listen to what the Irish woman was saying. She hadn't realised how tired she was. All those sleepless nights. She felt the yoga mat beneath her sink into her back, seeming to become part of her.

'I'm going to count down from ten to one and by the time I get to one, you're going to be totally relaxed. Ten, nine, eight . . . '

She was drifting. A different time. A different space. She felt so heavy; such an effort to move. She smoothed her hands down her dress, a long blue dress she didn't remember owning, soft as silk. Her hands fell upon the curve of her belly. So big, so firm. She realised she was heavily pregnant. The baby must be due soon with all that weight. It was a struggle to walk, her bones seemed to click inside her, rubbing together. Everything ached as she heaved herself up the narrow stairs, one foot slowly after the other, stopping midway to catch her breath.

She felt someone beside her. Not the man lying next to her on the yoga mat, but someone much taller with black hair and almost black eyes, hand beneath her left elbow, helping her up as she grabbed the banister on the other side.

'Thank you for your kindness.'

The voice she heard wasn't hers, though she spoke it, though she felt the words in her mouth, felt her tongue against her teeth.

She was drifting again, away from the voice, away from the woman climbing the stairs. She was looking down, as if suspended from the ceiling, being shown something else. She was looking down at Dylan's room. She could see his bed, not the white Ikea bed he'd had since he'd been a toddler, but a heavy iron bedstead with a stained mattress and no sheets. No Batman duvet cover either. Where was Dylan? She searched the room from her position on the ceiling, feeling the panic slide around her chest. She couldn't see him anywhere. Shouldn't he be in bed? It was dark. She could hear an owl in the wood through the window. Dylan should be in bed, yet he wasn't there, and she had a horrible sickening sense that something was wrong. She wished she could dive down into the room and look for him properly, but she was trapped. Immobile. Frozen to that spot on the ceiling, where someone was holding her, showing her what had happened there. She saw something else. Something stealing across the walls, across the dirty mustard-coloured paint, subtly at first, then in bright red splashes.

Blood.

She could smell it. That sour tang. And something on the edge of it. The smell she'd recently detected in the house – that seemed to have permeated everything . . .

She screamed and opened her eyes. Not Dylan's room but the room in the back of the church hall. Everyone was looking at her, pushing themselves upright. Someone laid a hand on her arm, making her flinch.

'You okay?' It was the man who needed a drink.

She pulled her arm away. She couldn't bear anyone holding on to her like that.

'I'm sorry.' She scrambled upright and grabbed her bag, aware of everyone staring at her, open-mouthed. The Irish woman stepped towards her, but she didn't want her, she didn't want anyone. She pushed open the swing doors and ran down the corridor, into the car park, drinking in the cool night air. She fumbled for her car keys. What the hell had happened to her there in the hall? She remembered hearing the Irish woman's voice, she remembered following the instructions, thinking she may as well try to relax, to make the most of the session. *Square breathing*, the woman had called it in her soft lyrical accent. Breathe in for four. Hold for four. Breathe out for four. Hold for four. Repeat. She remembered her body sinking into itself. She remembered the woman saying something about tensing her muscles, then letting go, one by one. She remembered the woman counting backwards from ten. After that, it was a blur. A dream. Had she fallen asleep? She had a memory of blue silk, of a man with dark eyes, of a terrible feeling she'd lost Dylan. A memory of being pinned to the ceiling in his room.

'Are you all right?'

She spun around. The Irish woman was behind her, ghost-like in the dark. 'Yes. No. I don't know.' Kelda dropped the car keys and picked them up again, shaking. 'I just needed some fresh air.'

'You screamed.'

'Did I?'

'Yes.'

Kelda shook her head. 'I'm so sorry. I smelled something, something weird. And I think I fell asleep.'

The lady laid a hand on her shoulder. 'It's me who should apologise. I should have mentioned, I use essential oils in my sessions. Bergamot. Geranium. Lavender. They're meant to be relaxing.'

'It brought up a memory,' she said, though she wasn't sure whose memory it was, hers or the lady in the blue dress's or someone else's altogether. 'A bad memory.'

'A bad memory?'

'Yes. At least, I think. Maybe, it was just a dream. I don't know.' She rubbed her face. She wasn't making any sense.

'Do you want to come back in? I can explain to the others. We don't have to use the oils?'

'No, no. I don't think I could. I'm meeting a friend . . . '

The woman glanced behind her at the hall. 'I have to get back to my class, I'm afraid. Will you be okay? Can I call your friend, ask them to meet you here?'

'I'll be fine, honestly. It was just a shock. A panic attack or something.'

'Okay, if you're sure?' The woman hesitated. 'About the memory. Maybe you should tell someone about it? Sometimes just telling the story helps.'

'I will. And sorry again.'

The woman smiled. 'No need to apologise. This has been . . . well, let's just say, nothing like this has ever happened in one of my sessions before.'

She was early to meet Nick, a good half-hour early. She sat in the pub, drinking Diet Coke, trying not to replay what had just happened in her mind, trying to think of something else completely. She phoned Emma again, to check Dylan was all right. 'Fine,' she said. '*Still* fine. We're snuggled up on the sofa watching *The Lego Movie*.' She found it hard to believe: Dylan and her wayward sister on the sofa together, watching a movie. She said she wouldn't be long, reminding Emma to phone if Dylan became upset or if anything happened. Anything at all. 'Okay,' Emma said. 'If a spaceship lands in the garden and aliens try to abduct him, I'll let you know.'

By the time Nick walked in it was already quarter to eight. 'You're late.'

He held up his hands and she realised how accusatory she sounded.

'Sorry,' she said. 'Bad day. I've left Dylan with my sister.'

'Your *sister*?'

She filled him in on what had happened, how she'd found Emma outside, sitting on the picnic table, how Emma had nowhere to go, how she'd promised Emma she could stay until the end of the week.

'And what about you?' she asked. 'How are things with you?'

'Oh, you know.' He looked tired. Probably Walter working him too hard at the university.

'Let me get you a drink. What do you want? Lager?'

She went to the bar. It was a quiet pub on Nick's side of town, decorated with upside-down musical instruments and furniture suspended from the ceiling. She ordered Nick a drink and a bag of crisps to share.

'Hello.'

She turned. Simon was behind her. Simon with a book in one hand and a glass of wine in the other. She felt her cheeks flush.

'I thought it was you,' he said, 'but I didn't want to disturb you with your friend.' He looked pointedly in Nick's direction. Kelda swallowed hard; she couldn't quite believe Simon was here, in the same pub as Nick and her, on a Thursday night.

'Nick's an old friend from university,' she said, rushing her words, feeling she needed to explain. 'Come and join us. I'll introduce you.'

'No, really. I wouldn't want to intrude. I was just here reading my book, relaxing after work. It's been a bit of a day. I was in theatre all afternoon.' He cleared his throat. 'Unfortunately, we lost the patient.'

'Lost?'

He stared into his drink like he wanted it to swallow him. 'It happens sometimes. We deal with a lot of complex cases. Elderly, mainly. Sometimes they don't pull through because there's other stuff going on, not just the thing you're dealing with. One minute you're fixing someone's hip, the next you're dealing with a cardiac arrest.'

'I'm sorry.'

'As I said, it happens. You get used to it. Only this one was slightly different. This one was a child.' He drank deeply from his glass. 'Anyway, don't let me keep you from your friend.'

She hesitated. She wanted to ask him more, she wanted to give him the chance to talk, but she sensed he just needed to be alone. *A child.* She thought of Dylan and shuddered inwardly. 'Are you sure you won't join us?'

He shook his head and she saw his hand tremble lightly on the stem of his wine glass. 'Not tonight. I wouldn't be good company. I'll phone you over the weekend, okay?'

She took the drink back to the table and opened the packet of crisps to share.

'Don't tell me that's him?' said Nick.

She glanced over her shoulder. Simon was frowning at his book. 'Why? What's wrong with him?'

'It *is* him.' He grinned.

'You mean Simon? Yes. I didn't realise he'd be here. I invited him to join us but he said he's reading his book. Bad day at work by the sound of things.'

'He's *tall.*'

'I suppose so.'

'And good-looking, if you're into that sort of thing.'

'What sort of thing?'

Nick slurped the top of his pint. She imagined Simon lifting his head from the book and watching them from his table near the door. She wished he'd leave, though it had been nice to see him. Nice but weird. She wondered how long he'd been here, whether she'd missed him when she first walked in, whether he'd been watching her all this time.

'I bet he's really serious,' said Nick.

'He's a surgeon. He's meant to be serious. Imagine someone cutting you open for a laugh. Anyway, let's talk about something else. Let's talk about the reason you dragged me out here tonight.'

'I didn't drag you out. It was your suggestion.'

'You said you wanted my opinion on something.'

'Oh, that.' Nick waved a hand. 'It was nothing. I was having a mad moment, that's all. Forget it.'

'Okay ...' She didn't quite believe him. There were bags beneath his eyes and the buttons on his shirt were done up wrong. But she wasn't sure how to ask, or rather, this all felt too strange, being in a bar with Nick. Usually he came to hers, or she went to his, and usually there was the business of making dinner and supervising homework and getting Dylan ready for bed.

'I know where I've seen him before,' Nick said suddenly.

'Who?'

'Simon. He was in here the other day. Tuesday lunchtime to be precise, when I was grabbing a sandwich. I bumped into him at the bar. Literally bumped into him. Or rather, he bumped into me. He was drunk.'

'Don't be stupid, it couldn't have been him. He was working on Tuesday.' She remembered the text she'd received on her lunch break: Simon asking how she was as he dashed between theatre sessions. 'Maybe it was you who was drunk?'

Nick grinned. 'Probably.'

'Anyway, I thought we weren't going to talk about Simon? Tell me about work. Tell me about anything. I could do with the distraction.' She felt a breath on her back, but it was just the door opening and closing onto the street. When she looked behind her, Simon had gone. She relaxed.

Nick smiled. 'All right . . . '

He told her the story of his week so far, his research with Walter, an article he was writing. She tried to concentrate, but she couldn't stop her mind from wandering back to the church hall, to the lady in the blue dress climbing the stairs, to the blood splattered all over the walls in Dylan's room.

'I don't suppose you managed to find out anything about the toll house?' she said, interrupting.

He frowned and shook his head. 'Sorry. Work's been crazy-busy. It's at the top of my to-do list for next week, I promise.' He sipped his pint and put it down again, leaving a line of foam on his upper lip. 'Why, has something happened?'

She took a deep breath. 'The other night, when I was alone in the house, I thought I heard footsteps walking across the landing.' She realised she could smell it again, here in the pub, beneath the tang of beer and furniture polish, though she knew it was impossible that the smell could have followed her.

'Footsteps?'

The smell was stronger. Pervasive. She shot up. 'Can't you smell it?'

'What?'

'Lavender.'

He shook his head.

'You must be able to smell it.' She looked beneath the table, behind the chairs; she scanned the walls for a plug-in air freshener. But there was no explanation. 'Look,' she gathered her car keys, 'I'm sorry, I've got to go. I've got to get back to Dylan.'

'Kelda, are you okay?'

'Yes. No. I don't know. It's just I don't like the thought of him alone there with Emma. Let's have a drink another night instead?'

He stood up, looking worried. 'You'll be all right on your own?'

'I'll text you as soon as I get in.'

She grabbed her bag, her mind racing. Still that smell, stronger now. She had to get away, back to the toll house. She shouldn't have gone out without Dylan in the first place. She thought of the dream, his bedroom covered in blood, that rickety old bedframe, the mustard-coloured walls. Mustard-coloured yet she'd painted them magnolia. He hadn't slept all night in his own room since before the party, but what if Emma had somehow persuaded him there, put him to bed and turned off the light? She thought of Dylan alone in the dark. Alone in *that* room.

She ran out of the pub, into the street – it was still light though she'd expected everything to be dark like the darkness crowding her mind – then drove home as fast as she could, accidentally driving through a red light, slamming on the brakes at a crossing. Calm down, she told herself. Nothing has happened. Nothing is going to happen.

She parked beneath the bay window as she always did, then raced into the garden and through the back door.

Dylan and Emma were sitting at the kitchen table, building a Lego aeroplane.

'Hi, Mum. Look at this,' Dylan said, pointing to the cockpit. 'It's so cool. Auntie Em's so good at Lego.'

Emma beamed. 'Nice drink?'

She wasn't listening. She could smell it again. She could smell lavender. She went around the windows, sliding them open, allowing the fresh air to rush in. She brushed her hand against a pile of white pebbles sitting on the window ledge above the sink. A patter like hail as they fell against the ceramic.

'Mum! It's cold!'

'That's better.' She stared at the pebbles.

Emma shivered. 'You all right?'

'Fine, fine.' She composed herself. 'Looks like you two have had a nice time.'

'We have.' Emma looked at her strangely, seeing through her, knowing there was something more than she was letting on. It hadn't been quite so long after all. 'How's Nick?'

'Nick?'

'Didn't you say you were meeting Nick at the pub?'

'Yes. Sorry. Nick's fine.' She reached in her pocket and sent him a quick text, then glanced back at the sink, at those tiny white pebbles, like tiny white teeth. Human teeth. She picked them up one by one, hating the feel of them, wet from the sink, and threw them out of the open window.

'Mum, can I go to bed now? I'm tired.' Dylan stretched his arms. He rarely asked to be taken to bed, usually she had to cajole him, but it was late. A good half-hour past his bedtime.

'Yes, sure. Say goodnight to Emma.'

'Goodnight, Auntie Em.'

'Goodnight. Can I have a hug before you go?'

Dylan pulled a face as Emma wrapped her arms around him.

'Come on, Mum,' he said, pulling himself away and heading for the door. 'I'm going to be a big boy tonight. I'm going to sleep in my own room.'

She heard his feet on the stairs as he ran up to the landing.

18

❧

1864

I dream I'm standing beside the turnpike, waiting for Bella with her basket of goods. I'm eleven years old, too young to have romantic interests according to my stepmother, and Bella is only fourteen, but I have waited for this moment all week, waited to linger over Bella's basket and take my pick of her fruit.

'Poor Joe,' she says when I help myself to an apple.

I take a bite. It is bright and crisp, but not as sweet as the apples my mother used to grow on the trees in the garden. My stepmother has let the trees go to ruin and, more often than not, the fruit is left to rot where it falls.

'I am not poor,' I say, indignant, wiping the apple juice from my chin.

Bella reaches out and touches my cheek, making me blush.

'Poor Joe,' she says again. No one calls me Joe, not anymore, not since Ma died. But I find I do not mind it at all when Bella calls me that name. I wonder what she means, whether she feels sorry for me when she says I am poor, whether I should be flattered or ashamed. I want to ask her, I try to think of the right words, but I am only eleven, not used to such talk. By the time I've plucked up the courage, she's turned her attention to my stepmother who's appeared over my shoulder, quibbling over the price of a pound of cheese.

The dream spirals into darkness. I try to find Bella, try to return to the turnpike on that midsummer's day, but the harder I search, the deeper she hides. It's like she is afraid of something. Like she is trying to slip away. Water running through my fingers.

I jerk wide awake. The curtains have been closed since the day Bella died, but the sun steals through a crack in the middle. I sit upright. The mask is where I left it on the bedside table, on one of Bella's lace squares, but there is something else, something that wasn't there before. Three white pebbles circling the plaster head. I hold them in my hand, like I am holding silk. I'm almost not surprised, though I should be. I should be petrified.

'Why do you collect the pebbles?' I asked one day when Bella emptied yet another handkerchief of shiny white stones onto the kitchen table.

'Why not?'

She sorted through them, a pile of white ones, a larger pile of grey ones and cream ones.

'People collect feathers or shells. Not stones,' I said. 'Not all the same stones anyway.'

'I like them. They are perfect. It's taken millions of years to make them this way. This small, this round, rolled over and over on the riverbed. Someone told me that these tiny pebbles were once great rocks, smashed together to create smaller ones. What we are left with is the pearl.'

'Yes, but why keep them?'

'For strength,' she said lightly, 'and protection. They are my lucky charms.'

I watched her more closely after that, wondering what she meant. I'd see her rolling the pebbles in her palm when she thought I wasn't looking, and whenever the pains came and another child was lost. I noticed she kept only the smoothest, the most perfect pebbles, stowing them in an earthenware pot in the garden. The others she tossed into the wood or the fields to be churned by the plough.

And now I find them, three perfect pebbles on the pillow. I turn them in my hands, wondering what this means. Has Bella come back to me?

I'm gripped by the idea. She is here! She has come back! I throw off the covers, tear my nightshirt from my head, pull on yesterday's clothes and run downstairs. I dart into the kitchen.

'Bella, where are you?' My voice rattles around the empty shelves, across the unswept floor.

I throw wide the shutters, peer beneath the table, behind the settle. I look in the cupboard and the pantry, then unbolt the back door. A sparrow hops from one of the apple trees, but I cannot believe it is Bella, not this time. This time, she has come back to me in the flesh. I know it. I feel it. I spin back to the toll house. The door is wide open, and the moment I step inside, I know something has changed.

There's a smell, something floral. It drifts on the breeze from the little patch in the garden, into the kitchen. The spicy-sweet smell of witch hazel. I think how Bella used to tie flowers to her waist with a ribbon. Not witch hazel but lavender. Fresh in the summertime, dried in the winter, to aid digestion and to promote good sleep. She wasn't one for paying the doctor or the apothecary, preferring her own cures, her own herbs. *More powerful than the doctor's knife*, she would say, showing me the sweet berries of nightshade or the dainty daisy-heads of camomile.

The witch hazel is a sign – I'm sure of it! – it flowers bright as stars next to the patch of winter grey lavender. She is so near now, I can almost feel her; her hand in mine, the soft creases of her palm, drawing me closer, leading me to wherever she is hiding.

But where?

Through the house again, checking beneath the bed, inside the wardrobe, checking in the little room that was mine as a child's, that still contains the rickety bedstead and the bowed mattress, yellowed with age, and the mustard-coloured walls. Checking the porch. Walking the perimeter. Walking into the wood behind. Surveying the fields.

Not here! Not here!

Bella, how can you tease me like this?

I feel the madness rising as I go once more around the house and the wood. The hour is late and I should be watching the road but I have no care for horses and donkeys and coachmen. My belly groans. My heart aches. I feel the three white pebbles in my pocket and wonder what else it can mean, whether I've got it all wrong, whether this is just a game. I think of the coffin splintering under the weight of the grave diggers' spade, the gash on Bella's forehead, the veil torn in half, the same veil as in the photograph. I think of the bell fallen from her hand.

She tried to ring for me. Ring from the dead. I haven't got it wrong at all! Her poor wandering soul has found its way home, all the way from the graveyard.

'I will find you,' I say to Bella. 'I will find you wherever you are. And then we can be together again. Safe, like your pebbles!'

There's the sound of carriage wheels on the road outside.

I run to the front door and fling it wide. My hair is uncombed, my shirt tails hanging loose. Quickly, I muster some sort of order as the coachman reins his horses.

'Is this the Stonebridge Road?'

I do not answer at first. I *cannot* answer. So strange this everyday question, compared to the tumult in my head. I nod in the direction of the town.

'Stonebridge is a mile from here,' I say woodenly, before doing a quick count of his wheels and offering him my price.

The coachman hands me his coins.

'Good day to you,' I say.

I watch the carriage trundle past the turnpike. The day is fair now, set to be bright, though there are still ice patches on the road. By luncheon, it will be busy with the usual wagons and carriages. There's no more time to look for Bella, I must sit here and wait and watch the road.

19

NOW

'I'm so bored.' Emma was sitting at the kitchen table, flicking through the job pages of the local newspaper. 'How about we go out? Do something?'

Kelda looked up from packing Dylan's lunchbox. She'd asked Emma about her plans the night before, but she'd been evasive. She liked Stonebridge but it was too small; she was sorry to put Kelda to all this trouble, but she had nowhere else to go. She'd let slip about Luke, too, saying he'd shattered her confidence, that he'd been mean from day one. Kelda had been sympathetic though she'd failed to grasp the whole picture. Emma seemed confused at times, changing the story, sometimes Luke had a temper, other times he just seemed dull; how much was true and how much was Emma's imagination, she couldn't work out. At some point, she knew she'd have to be firm. This wasn't a long-term solution. Emma had been here a whole week; she hadn't misbehaved as far as Kelda was aware, but the toll house was too small for three people. It had been different when Nick had stayed. Nick had fitted in easily, seeming more a part of the family than her sister. But with Emma, the place seemed to burst.

'What sort of something?' she said.

Emma shrugged. 'I dunno. Anything. You must do fun stuff sometimes.'

Kelda put a tangerine next to the sandwiches. The school had a healthy eating rule. No crisps. No chocolate bars. No sweets. So many rules and things to remember. 'Yes, of course we do fun things, only . . . '

'A trip to the beach or a night out? You could invite your boyfriend.'

'My boyfriend?'

'Nick.'

'I told you, Nick's an old friend from university. Not a boyfriend. He stayed here when he split with his wife. He works at the university in Lincoln, and after the summer, he just sort of stuck around.'

'Sounds like he stuck around for more than just a job.'

'I don't think so . . . '

'Only retired people move to Stonebridge, unless they've an ulterior motive.'

'*I* moved to Stonebridge.'

'Exactly.' Emma turned the page and ran her finger down the columns. 'Of all the places you could have moved to, you chose to come here. Near Nick. You like him too. I can tell by the way you talk about him.'

'I don't talk about him. And of course I like him, just not like that. Anyway, he's engaged again.'

Emma flicked her eyes up from the newspaper, as if to say, yeah whatever. 'Well, invite Nick and his fiancée then. You must have other friends too?'

'One or two.' She thought about Simon in the pub, how he'd resisted joining her and Nick at the table. She imagined introducing him to Emma, how handsome he'd look standing next to her. They'd had another date at the weekend, when Dylan had been at football practice. When they'd said goodbye, he'd leaned over and kissed her, kissed her properly this time on the lips, lingering for a second or two, moving his tongue against hers. It felt like he was flicking a switch.

'One or two is fine,' said Emma. 'We could make an evening of it. A pub crawl. It's about time you let your hair down.' She glanced at the lunchbox.

'I'm not sure. What about Dylan?'

Emma sighed. 'Okay, the beach then?'

'What about the recreation ground? You could come with me on Saturday, watch him play football?'

'S'pose.'

She closed the lunchbox. It might be good for Emma to meet the other mums. It might be good for her, too, force her to be sociable. She thought of the house, the voice that still played over in her mind, the voice from Dylan's microphone: *he's looking for you*. Her rational brain told her it was just Dylan's toy, but still the memory of that evening unnerved her. Although the house had felt more settled recently, she'd still wake up every night and stare at the shapes in her room. Just a wardrobe, she'd tell herself. Just a chair. Just the mirror against the wall. Nothing else. Nothing untoward.

'How's the job hunting going?' she said, taking her mind off it.

Emma put the newspaper down. 'Seems I'm not qualified enough for anything.'

'Maybe you need to do some training – a computer course or something, like I did?'

Emma twisted her lips. 'I've seen this course. A catering course. It's the only thing I'm really good at. But it costs an arm and a leg.'

Kelda put Dylan's lunchbox in the fridge. 'You know I'd help if I could? I've still got a few savings, but there's the mortgage and Dylan . . . '

Emma folded the newspaper. 'Of course. I'd never dream of asking you for money.' Her phone buzzed on the table and she picked it up, smiling, before tapping in a message.

The rest of the week, Kelda was occupied with work, too busy with Cassandra's new clients to think much about the toll house. In the evenings, when she did have space to think, she set about cleaning the place with vigour, hoovering and dusting and bringing down the cobwebs. In her mind, it was a way of making a claim on the house. This was her home now, hers and Dylan's. When they'd first moved in, she'd cleaned everything meticulously, going around the whole house, into corners, into cracks with the nozzle of the vacuum cleaner, but when she'd finished, the results had been disappointing. Still that air of dilapidation, of a place unloved. She supposed it was the damp; there was only so much she could do internally when the outside was cracking.

On Thursday evening, she came home to find Emma in Marigold gloves, scrubbing the skirting boards.

She grinned at Kelda. 'Spick and span, as Mum used to say.'

Kelda smiled at the memory. Every Saturday morning, they'd hear Mum downstairs wielding the hoover, a warning for Kelda and Emma to keep out of her way. Mum believed in traditional family values, or rather, as she'd let slip one year after too many Christmas sherries, she believed Dad would keep loving her and stop straying if she looked after them all.

Kelda shrugged off her jacket. 'Here, give me a cloth.' She started from the other end, working towards Emma, still thinking about Mum. 'It was weird when Dad left, wasn't it? I mean, it was weird for me, but it must have been even stranger for you. I was so focused on my A-levels, but you were younger and Dad's favourite. I should have looked after you more.'

Emma played with her necklace, fingering the little white stone with her Marigold glove. 'It doesn't matter. All that was years ago. We were kids.'

'It does matter.' Kelda scrubbed harder, wondering how the house had got so dirty in the space of seven months. 'Looking back, I was selfish. I couldn't stop thinking about my exams, how annoyed I was that Dad had chosen that particular moment to leave. I remember feeling really angry that Mum's crying was keeping me awake at night, stopping me from getting a good night's sleep when I had my exams the next day. I was just thinking about myself. I never stopped to think about you or Mum.'

Emma dipped her cloth in the bucket of soapy water. 'I was okay. I coped in my own way.'

Her own way. Off the rails, that's what Mum had called it.

Emma shook the hair from her eyes. 'Anyway, Dad made it quite clear he didn't want me when I showed up at his new house. When he introduced me to his new daughter.'

'I'm sorry.'

'Not your fault. Just one of those things.'

'But it must have hurt.' She remembered the note Emma had left on the table, *Gone to find Dad. Don't worry about me*; how Mum had fussed about the fact it was a school day when she'd found it, covering up how scared she was; how sorry and embarrassed Emma had looked when she'd returned that night with her bag still packed. 'I was meant to be the responsible one,' Kelda said, wondering if things would have turned out differently if she'd taken care of Emma, if she'd sacrificed her grades for her family. 'The one everyone expected to do well, but I didn't think you might be suffering too. At least, I didn't think how painful it must have been finding Dad like that.'

Emma wrung out her cloth. 'As I said, it doesn't matter. Anyway, you're looking after me now, aren't you?'

On Friday, Kelda came home to find Emma and Dylan outside in the garden. Emma had picked Dylan up early from school and together they were stringing up fairy lights and bunting.

'What's going on? Why's Dylan home already?'

Emma jumped down from the picnic bench. 'Surprise!'

'I don't understand . . .' Kelda put her bag down on the path. 'Looks like you two are having a party or something.'

Emma grinned. 'We are. Tonight. A house-warming party just for you.'

Kelda shook her head, confused. She turned to Dylan.

He blushed. 'Auntie Em said not to tell you.'

'We went through your address book,' Emma said, standing back to admire her handiwork. 'We've been scheming all week, haven't we, Dylan? We invited a few friends.'

'Friends?'

'Just one or two, like you said. Remember? You agreed, we'd have some fun.'

'Wow.' She didn't know what to say, what to think. She put her arm around Dylan, pulling him close, certain it hadn't been his idea. She was tired from work, tired from the strain of the last few weeks. She wanted to settle down with a book and a glass of wine, not this.

Emma rattled off on her fingers. 'Nick and his fiancée, Georgie and Ethan and their mums. Lucy from your work.'

Kelda tried not to look horrified. Lucy hadn't breathed a word about it in the office. She imagined Mrs Watts all glammed up, passing judgement on their junk-shop furniture and tiny rooms.

'Oh,' Emma beamed. 'And Simon.'

'Simon?'

'You left his number on a scrap of paper in the kitchen. He seemed important because you drew a little heart.'

She felt the colour rise to her cheeks. 'But I hardly know him!'

'Well, here's your chance.'

'But . . . I . . . ' Kelda glanced at Dylan. 'Didn't Mr Yeo mind?'

'Who?'

'Dylan's teacher. Whisking him out of school like that?'

'That old fogey? I turned on my charm, said Dylan had the dentist.'

'You didn't?' Kelda cringed at the thought of Emma in the school, in her low-cut top and skinny jeans, chatting up Mr Yeo.

Dylan tugged at her arm. 'Mum, don't you like it?'

She smiled down at him, trying not to look cross. 'It's beautiful. Stunning. It's just that . . . ' She shook her head. It really was beautiful. Fairy lights had been strung from the kitchen window across to the apple trees. Leaves had been raked into a pile. Candles had been placed in jars on the picnic table and the wall ledge, and Emma had dragged out the old garden burner and cleaned it up, setting it on the indent in the grass. She hadn't noticed the indent before, a lip in the lawn, sloping down towards the wall beneath the apple trees, almost as if the lawn was sinking. She wondered whether the lawn really was sinking, whether there was something underneath it, pulling it down. An old well, perhaps? Strange she hadn't noticed it before.

'You do like it, don't you?' Emma said, running her hand over the burner. 'I knew you'd like it. And no one's going to get cold either when we light this old thing.'

Kelda picked up one of the jars, recognising it as one of the old jam jars from the larder, a remnant from Mr Pritchard, scrubbed clean and fitted with a tealight. Emma had worked hard. Despite the unexpectedness of the situation, the toll house, or at least the garden, felt friendly again. Friendlier than it had done for weeks.

'I've got pizza dough resting in the kitchen and wine chilling in the fridge and orange juice for the non-drinkers,' Emma said.

'Homemade pizza. Wow.'

Emma smiled sheepishly. 'As I said before, it's the only thing I'm good at. And after putting up with me for the last two weeks, it's the least I could do.'

Dylan released himself from her arm and raced his Batmobile over the lawn. 'Mum, it's going to be amazing. Auntie Em's even bought lemonade.'

'Lemonade, lucky you.'

Emma blushed. 'I'm afraid I raided your housekeeping jar. Come on, let's show you.'

Inside, there were packets of crisps and pretzels ready to be emptied into bowls, wine glasses lined up on the table, bottles of beer and wine in the fridge. Resisting the urge to pour herself a large glass, Kelda went upstairs and ran herself a bath.

'What are you going to wear?' Emma poked her head around the bedroom door.

Kelda was still in her towel, standing in front of the wardrobe. She wanted to tell Emma to leave, that she needed five more minutes to herself, to process the idea of the party and the imminent guests. To tell herself Emma was doing her a favour rather than interfering. But Emma had already sat down on the bed, legs crossed like the teenager she remembered.

'I don't know. Jeans. A black top.' She pulled out the cropped top from her wardrobe, the one she'd worn when she'd first met Simon.

Emma screwed up her nose. 'Boring. Let me have a look.' She jumped off the bed and rifled through her wardrobe, pulling out various work tops and jumpers she wore for slobbing around the house. 'You really don't go out much, do you?' said Emma. 'Hold on. I might have just the thing.' She ran to the landing where she'd stowed her holdall and returned a few seconds later with a strappy blue vest.

'It will suit you perfectly,' Emma said.

'It will be freezing!'

'No, it won't. We're going to light the burner, remember, and you can always wear a jacket on top. You'll look perfect. You always were the prettier one.'

Kelda pulled it over her head, thinking about Mrs Watts and her designer loungewear, thinking about Simon in his expensive shirts.

'See,' said Emma, straightening the straps. 'It picks out the colour of your eyes.'

Kelda smoothed the silk against her waist, unsure.

'You could dress it up with a necklace.' She opened Kelda's jewellery box on the dresser and rooted through it.

'This.' Emma held up a string of aqua blue glass beads.

'I don't know . . .'

'It will make you look really sophisticated.'

'Too over the top. What about the silver cross?'

Emma frowned, then unclipped her own necklace, the one she'd worn since she'd arrived, the little white stone on the leather cord. 'Okay then, have this. It's an opal, my lucky charm. It will look perfect. It will give you good luck for the party.'

'You sure?' At least it was less showy than the beads.

'Positive. And we could pin your hair up. Like this.' Emma twirled it in her hands and piled it on top of Kelda's head. 'You'll look gorgeous.'

'I still don't know . . .'

'Wow, Mum. You look different,' Dylan said, poking his head around the door when Emma had finished. He ran out again, racing his Batmobile along the banister.

'Ready?' Emma asked, beaming.

Kelda took a deep breath, hoping her hair would stay up with all the pins. 'Ready.'

She followed Emma down the stairs. Emma ran ahead, her tiny slip of a body disappearing into the kitchen. Kelda slowed, taking her time, still not keen on the idea of a party. In the hallway, she pushed wide the kitchen door, expecting to find Emma inside, busy with last-minute preparations.

Instead, the back door was wide open and in front of it, blocking the light, was Simon.

20

❧

1864

Every day, she leaves me the pebbles, a perfect circle laid around the mask. I feel her getting stronger, bolder. I look for her in the faces of those who pass the turnpike, the old lady nodding in the back of a cart, the fresh-faced drover, the farmer's boy selling me eggs. Sometimes I fancy I catch sight of her in the arch of a nose or the swell of a breast or the curve of a cheek. But never fully. She likes to tease me, to play games. Suggestions. Hints. Nothing more. When they say the dead are shy, they are right.

I take to wandering the fields as Bella used to do, breaking the ice with my boots, walking until my head hurts with the cold. I'm in attendance at the turnpike less and less. Carriages and carts idle through the open gate without paying. Sometimes, I spend all day walking, nothing in my belly but the determination to find her, to seek her in the places she used to love. At other times, I sleep in the porch, head nodding over my shoulder, exhausted from yet another wakeful night listening out for her in the dark. Cartwheels clatter through my dreams. Horses neigh. I dream of her; I dream that I am touching her, clinging to her as though my soul depends upon it, digging into her soft flesh. Then, I am awakened by the wind or the sharp clop of hooves or, as today, Helen come to see how far I have fallen.

'Joseph, you are worse! What ails you so?'

I watch Helen from the settle as she sets the kitchen right. I see the way she looks at me, the way she casts her eyes over my dishevelled appearance, the pale haunted look of a man who barely sleeps.

'Mr Turnbill has been speaking of you in the town,' she says. 'He has been airing his disapproval. He wants you out of here. There are others who feel the same way.'

I pretend not to listen. Mr Turnbill is one of the trustees, a man of wealth and influence. A pink-faced man with a pot belly.

'Dr Marsh continues to express his concerns.' She puts her hands on her hips. 'Does it not worry you, Joseph? Does it not rally you to action? The doctor is a good man, but the others. The others. They would gladly see you cast from this house!'

Her words are like the rain, running off my shoulders. What matter if they drive me from the toll house? I am still a young man but I am not long for this world. I know it. I feel it. Soon Bella will call me to follow her. Why else the pebbles? Are they not a sign of the life beyond? The perfection and steadfastness of what awaits?

'I will be back next week,' Helen says, sighing, her forehead furrowed. So serious, so joyless. So unlike her sister.

'Do not trouble yourself.'

'It is not my trouble. It is my duty.'

'To whom?'

'To the doctor.'

I jump up, slamming the settle with my palm. 'It was at the doctor's hands that your sister died. And yet you persist in defending him.'

She stares at me, her eyes like daggers. 'Bella was not a well woman. You know that. She could not safely carry a child.'

I pace across the tiles. 'What else has the doctor been saying? What other deeds has he bid you do?'

'Nothing. None.' The colour rises at her throat. 'You speak without knowing what you say.'

'And you speak like a fool!' I sink back into the settle, thinking of the mask upstairs. 'He has deceived you with his fine words, that much is clear.'

She sweeps up her basket without a further word and marches to the door, her lips pinched tight.

I breathe more easily when she is gone. I sit at the turnpike, too exhausted to wander the fields, listening instead for the traffic. As if to punish me for my slovenliness, the day is busy. I have no time to dwell on the pebbles I found this morning: a line along the window ledge and another smaller line around the brimming earthenware pot in the garden. I eat little, make little conversation with those who pass, with those who try to cajole me into a lower price. Be gone with you all, I mutter in my head.

By nightfall, my pockets are heavy with coins. I shrug off my jacket and count the day's takings. I'm sleepy, head bent over the table, the lantern burning low. A mouse scurries along the table but I don't even flinch. Everything is fuzzy, the light from the lantern blurring in my eyes.

I awake to the dead certainty Bella is in the house. Nothing I can put into words, just a sense. A knowledge. I fumble to relight the lantern, dripping oil on my hands, scorching my fingers with a match. At the same time, I hear the swish of a skirt. I jump up, startled, and raise the lantern to the doorway leading into the hall. She is there, I am sure of it. I run across the tiles and wrench open the door.

Nothing to see.

I raise the lantern higher, inspecting the steep narrow staircase leading to the upstairs rooms. A shadow skims against the landing wall then disappears. There's a renewed sense of stillness. I run up the stairs, two at a time, snatching my breath at the top. I trace the wall with my hands, along the peeling paintwork, trying to find a sign of her. I lean against the wall, feeling the cold against my cheek, before stumbling from one room to the other: the room that was mine as a child, full of memories both bitter and sweet; the larger room where she died, and my father before her.

The rooms are silent apart from the wind cursing the walls and howling down the chimneys. I remember when my father died, watching the coffin leave the house feet first so as not to call me with him. If only Bella had called me with her! Willingly would I have gone! I make my way back to the landing, to the banister, crashing to my knees at the top of the stairs.

I bow my head, overcome with exhaustion. Oh Bella, why do you punish me so? Why do you tease me?

I sink my hands into the rag-rug on the landing, clawing my nails into the old cloth. Then I pull at my hair, tugging out fistfuls, sending the thin strands dancing down the stairs in the lantern light.

I lay my face on the rug and close my eyes, willing sleep to come to me, for Bella to awaken me in my dreams. But my mind is cloaked in darkness, not light.

I'm jolted awake. There is a noise I cannot quite catch. My heart thuds, my throat runs dry. I pull myself to my knees, listening to the sounds of the house, the mice scratching in the hallway, the wind curling its way through the letterbox.

Then I hear it again and I know it is not a dream, not Bella either.

Someone is at the front door, rapping the knocker.

21

NOW

‘God, you gave me a shock.’

Simon stood in the frame of the back door, in black jeans and jumper.

‘I'm sorry,’ he said, taking a step forward. He seemed too tall for the toll house, seeming to dominate the room, making her feel squeezed as he handed her a bunch of flowers, orange and yellow carnations. ‘You look amazing.’

‘Thanks.’ She took the flowers and planted them in the sink, then hunted in the pantry for a vase. She felt nervous, self-conscious in the blue top and necklace.

‘What a great place,’ he said. ‘An old toll house, is that right?’

‘Yes. There's a sign outside, above the bay window, listing the tolls.’

Emma appeared from the lounge. ‘Hi, I'm Emma, Kelda's

sister, the one who phoned you. I can show you around, if you like? Give you the guided tour?'

'That sounds great.'

Kelda grimaced. 'It's very small and not very exciting. A drink instead?'

Simon turned back to Emma. 'A guided tour, then a drink. If that's okay with you?'

'Cool. We'll start upstairs.' Emma headed towards the hallway. 'This way.'

Kelda heard their feet on the staircase and across the landing, the loose floorboard in Dylan's room, the sigh of her own bedroom door which she'd closed on purpose. She tried to relax and not mind about the party, tried not to mind the thought of someone she barely knew glancing over her things. If anyone was to show Simon her bedroom, it should have been Kelda. But she supposed it was bound to happen sometime in the evening. There was only one bathroom. Guests would be coming and going, up and down the stairs; someone was bound to be nosy and look in. Emma hadn't thought about that, or presumed Kelda wouldn't mind.

A few minutes later Emma and Simon were back in the kitchen.

'It's fascinating,' Simon said, running a hand over the old range, then tugging open the oven door, fingering the cool iron. 'It must be like living in a museum. A tiny museum.'

'I suppose.'

He put an arm around her waist. 'You've got something really special here.'

'Thanks.'

Her phone vibrated from the work surface. She released herself from Simon and swiped to unlock it. A moment to realise her mistake: not her phone but Emma's, the same make but scruffier, dirtier. She saw a message from Luke, Emma's ex-boyfriend.

Miss u, babe. When r u coming home?

She scrolled to the message before, knowing she shouldn't, but still angry about Emma and Simon in her room.

Can't stop thinking about u, Emma had replied to an earlier message, It's so boring here. I've sorted K. Believes every word I tell her.

She bit her lip, watching Emma and Simon out of the corner of her eye, joking about something to do with the kitchen. What did Emma mean, *I've sorted K*? She scrolled further: more messages from Luke. Emma had replied to every single one of them, jokily, chattily, despite all the time she'd spent moaning about him, saying she never wanted to see him again, telling Kelda how he'd called her a bitch and taken her money.

She put the phone on the work surface, silently seething. Had it all been lies? The sob story about Luke? The landlord throwing her out? The lost job? She glanced at Emma, opening a bottle of wine from the fridge, pouring a glass for Simon who looked charmed by her attention. What did Emma really want from her? She remembered the conversation they'd had about the catering course, how insistent Emma had been that she wouldn't take Kelda's money. *Too* insistent.

'I don't drink,' she was saying, pouring herself an orange juice. 'At least, not often, only on special occasions.' She pulled a packet of cigarettes from her pocket. 'Want one?'

Simon shook his head.

'Suit yourself. I'd better go into the garden.' She looked over at Kelda. 'My sister doesn't approve.'

Kelda watched Emma through the back door, sitting on the picnic bench, smoking. Unlike Kelda, she hadn't changed for the occasion: the same skinny jeans, the same tight-fitting top, hair wound loosely into a bun like she didn't really care.

'I'd never have put the two of you together as sisters,' said Simon, following her gaze. 'Though I suppose there's a family resemblance. The same shape of head. The same bone structure.'

'We're very different, that's why.' She had an image of skulls. Of dead bodies. But she supposed it was just Simon's way of talking. She poured herself a large glass of wine. 'To be honest, we haven't seen each other in years. It was a bit of a shock, her turning up.'

'She didn't tell you she was coming?'

'Nope.' She played with the straps of the blue top, wishing she'd opted for something more casual, something more *her*.

'By the way,' he dug in his pocket and pulled out a plastic Spiderman figure, 'I bought this for Dylan. I thought we could get to know each other. As I said before, I love kids. I just don't have much experience.'

Dylan ran out between them from the lounge, pushing past Simon, squealing about Georgie's mum's car. Kelda laughed, attempting to sound light, attempting to push the thought of Emma and Luke from her mind. 'Well, now's your chance, if you're lucky enough to catch him.'

She drank wine, relaxed, got used to Simon's arm around her shoulder. Emma was in the kitchen, making pizzas, shooing her away whenever she tried to help. Nick turned up with Alexa and the two of them squeezed onto the wall ledge, Alexa in leather trousers and heels talking with Ethan's mum. Kelda tried to avoid Nick's eye. Not long ago, they'd sat here at the picnic table, drinking wine. Something had happened that night. Happened and not happened. She remembered brushing against him in the dark, touching his face with her fingers; she remembered how he'd not moved away. A moment of madness, yet she couldn't shake the feeling it had changed things between them.

Emma brought out plates of homemade pizza and set them on the picnic table. She grinned at Kelda, wiping her hands down Kelda's 'Best Mum in the World' apron. 'I hope you like it.'

Kelda looked at the neat triangles dripping with cheese and wondered if the party was Emma's idea of a joke, a secret challenge, seeing if Kelda would rise to the occasion. She wondered whether Emma would text Luke later, laughing about her behind her back, telling him how she'd got Kelda all dressed up. She heard the tinkle of the garden gate and turned with relief to find Lucy battling with the hook.

'Sorry I'm late.' Lucy handed over a bottle of prosecco.

'I'm so glad you're here.' Kelda drew her into a hug. 'I was beginning to feel like a stranger in my own home.' She looked over at Alexa and Nick sitting by the burner, Nick balancing pizza on his lap, Alexa beautiful and exotic in the fairy lights, the lace of a pink bra just showing beneath her top. Over by the apple trees, Simon was talking to Mrs Watts, explaining something with his hands, looking at once awkward and engaged. A shadow crossed his face, like a side of him she didn't know, but it was just the leaves overhead, shuddering in the breeze.

'I was sworn to secrecy,' Lucy said, looking up at the bunting. 'It looks beautiful. And so do you.'

Kelda squeezed her arm. 'Emma and Dylan have been working hard. Come on, I'll introduce you to my sister. And there's pizza. Loads of pizza.'

She made introductions then went inside to get Lucy a glass.

'Everything all right?' Nick appeared in the doorway, swinging an empty bottle of beer.

'Yes, fine.'

He helped himself to another beer from the fridge. 'Actually, I've got something for you.' He pulled a sheet of folded paper from his back pocket. 'It's the research I've been doing on the house.'

'You've found something out?'

'Yes.' He looked up at Dylan's painting on the wall, covering the gash, then put the paper back in his pocket. 'Only this isn't the right time. I don't want to spoil the party. Not that it's anything to worry about. I just don't want to distract you. Maybe sometime next week? We could meet in town for coffee?'

'Okay.' She wanted to ask more, but Nick was right; this wasn't the right time.

The door swung open behind him. Emma burst in, giggling, holding an empty plate. 'The guests are ravenous. Time for more pizza.'

By midnight, there were five of them left. Georgie's mum had been the first to leave, remarking on Kelda's pretty little hobbit house before packing Georgie into her four-by-four. Lucy had made her excuses next, followed by Ethan and his mum. Then Dylan had gone to bed, her room this time, 'just in case'. He'd told her about Georgie and Ethan and the games they'd been playing as she'd carried him upstairs. She'd kissed him on the forehead and switched on her bedside light. 'I'll be up soon,' she'd said.

They huddled around the picnic table, burning more candles, drinking more wine. The burner was almost out and in the diminished light, the evening seemed to fragment like in a dream. Emma was telling a story, something that had happened years ago, an incident when they were children: Kelda had fallen off a fairground ride, a kid-sized rollercoaster, and broken her arm. The way she told it, it sounded funny. Everyone was laughing. Kelda saw the delight in Emma's eyes. The acceptance. In front of Emma was a half-drunk glass of wine. She wondered when that had happened, at what point in the evening Emma had switched from orange juice to alcohol.

'Kelda was always so clumsy,' Emma said, lighting another cigarette. 'Do you remember, Kelda? One day you tripped over and knocked out a tooth.'

'I remember.'

'And another time, you got your leg trapped in the back of a chair. You were playing horses and Dad literally had to saw you out.'

'Yeah.'

Nick topped up their glasses. 'I haven't heard any of these stories before.'

Emma raised her eyebrows. 'Really? I thought you two were close?'

'We've known each other a long time, that's all,' Kelda said. She felt Simon beside her, shuffling in.

'The way Kelda talks about you, it's like you're practically married to each other.'

Kelda glared at Emma, mentally kicking her in the shins. Alexa leaned against Nick, who reached over and attacked the last slice of pizza, unfazed.

'What if we had a partner swap?' Emma said brightly. 'Kelda and Nick. Simon and Alexa and me,' she giggled. 'A three-some.' She turned to Simon. 'Bet you've never had a threesome, have you?'

'Emma!' Kelda glared at her sister. Why wouldn't she shut up?

'What?'

'You're talking rubbish.'

'No, I'm not. I'm making complete sense. It would be fun, liven things up a bit. I'm only saying what everyone else is thinking.'

'No one's thinking that.'

'Aren't they?' Emma turned to Nick. She was drunk, Kelda thought, far drunker than the rest of them. She must have been drinking whilst she made the pizzas. Stupid of her, to have left all that wine at Emma's disposal.

'I'm not thinking anything,' said Nick.

Emma laughed. 'Oh, come on. Don't pretend you haven't dreamed of shagging my sister.' She ground the cigarette out onto the table. 'It's obvious. The way you look at her. The way she looks at you.'

'Emma!'

'What's wrong, Kelda? Are you afraid of the truth?'

Alexa stood up. 'I think it's time we made a move.' Nick stood next to her, wobbling as he searched for Alexa's handbag.

'He's a good kisser,' Emma giggled into her wine.

Kelda flared. 'What?'

'Nick. He's a good kisser, at least he was the last time we met in your halls of residence. You'd passed out. Too much vodka, if I remember correctly.'

Nick closed his arms around Alexa. 'That was years ago.'

Kelda shook her head, trying to clear the fog of alcohol. Her one year at university had been a blur, too much drinking, not enough sleep. She remembered the time Emma had come to stay; she remembered introducing her to Nick, but that was about all. She fumbled beneath the table until she found Alexa's handbag and passed it over. 'Can I get you anything else? A glass of water?'

Alexa smiled, tight-mouthed. 'No, thanks.'

'I think we're all a little worse for wear.' Simon pulled on his jacket. 'I'll ring for a taxi. Perhaps we could all share?'

'I'm sorry,' Kelda said.

Simon smiled. 'Please don't apologise.'

'What's fucking wrong with you all?' Emma fished for her fag packet. 'The evening's only just started.'

Kelda swung. 'Isn't it time you went to bed?'

'Went to bed. What? Are you my mum or something? Why don't you just relax?'

Kelda snatched up a couple of empty wine glasses, her mind ticking over Emma's words. Emma and Nick. Her halls of residence, the autumn term not long after she'd met him. It was all coming back to her. She'd been ill, really ill, too much vodka and Coke. 'Some of us have jobs to go to,' she said, trying to regain a sense of the person she was now. 'Some of us are responsible adults. Some of us are parents.'

Emma shrieked and cupped a hand over her mouth, giggling. Everyone stopped what they were doing, stopped battling with their coats, and stared at her.

'There's only one parent here that I know of,' she said.

'Emma, please.'

'You mean you haven't told them? You haven't even told the perfect Nick?'

Kelda looked at Nick, at Simon, at Alexa, saw their blank expressions.

Emma drew on her cigarette, then blew out a long tail of smoke. 'Dylan's not Kelda's son. He's mine.'

Nick stepped forward. Hesitated. Stepped back again.

Emma waved the cigarette. 'Oh, I know what you're all thinking. Kelda's the one who drives him to school, who packs his lunchbox, who tucks him into bed at night. But I was the one who pushed him out. And let me tell you, it hurt. It bloody hurt.' She sat upright, seeming to collect herself. Suddenly, tears were streaming down her face, crystals in the candlelight. 'And now you can think what you like. You can think I'm a terrible mother. But it was the hardest thing I've ever done in my life, giving my baby away to my sister.' She reached for her glass and drained it in one gulp before pouring herself another.

'Kelda.'

Kelda turned to find Nick at her side, wishing he could make her disappear, wishing it was just the two of them, that she could explain everything to him properly.

'Are you going to be okay with ... ?' He nodded at Emma. 'I can stay longer if you like?'

She shook her head. 'Take Alexa home. I'm so sorry.'

'It's okay, I know she's lying.'

'She's not lying. She's telling the truth. You were in Germany and it was just easier to pretend Dylan was mine when you came back.' She remembered how Mum had hated the idea of a scandal, people knowing Kelda wasn't really Dylan's mum. But more than that, Kelda had wanted to protect Dylan; no one had the right to know the truth before he did. As for the father, no one knew that, not even Emma. It could have been one of several. For a panicked moment, she wondered whether it could even have been Nick, but that was impossible; the time they'd met in her halls of residence had been months before Emma fell pregnant.

'I'm sorry I never told you,' she said. 'Mum wanted me to

give him up altogether. But I couldn't. I just couldn't. There's no way I would have let Emma hand him over to a stranger.'

'It's none of my business. I—'

'But I should have told you. You're my best friend.'

He laid a hand on her shoulder. 'I'm sorry. I have to take Alexa home.'

She waited until she heard the click of the garden gate. Simon and Nick and Alexa, subdued and bewildered, piling into a taxi. Simon had been all politeness, saying he'd call her, but she'd had the sense he couldn't wait to get away. Nick had just been embarrassed and shocked. And Alexa. Poor Alexa, after everything she'd been through. She wished she had a clear head as she entered the toll house, stepping around the debris from the party. Emma had passed out on the sofa in the lounge, breathing heavily, smelling of cigarettes.

'Mum.'

She turned to the staircase. Dylan was still in his clothes, the way she'd tucked him into her bed; she'd been too drunk, too full of the party to bother with his pyjamas and teeth brushing.

She came forwards and ruffled his hair. 'What are you doing up at this time, Batman?'

'That lady,' he said.

Suddenly, she felt perfectly sober. 'What do you mean?'

'Upstairs. That lady I saw before. She's in your bedroom.'

22

∽

1864

I pull myself upright and listen, wondering whether I dreamed it after all, whether this is another of Bella's games. But then, the sound comes again. A sharp rapping at the front door. I stagger to my feet, pain jabbing my head where I pulled out the hair, and pick up the lantern where I left it burning on the rag-rug. I need a drink of water but whoever it is, they're insistent. I lean on the banister as I stumble down the stairs.

Someone shouts.

I reach for the jack knife in my pocket. At this time of night, there is no telling who may be calling. A thief. A murderer.

The shout comes again, 'Sir! Are you in there?'

I slide back the bolts and turn the key, then edge open the door. A young man stands within the porch.

'Thank the Good Lord,' he says when I hold up the lantern. His face is red-raw from the cold and a drip has formed on the end of his nose. 'We have walked a long way and my wife has taken ill.'

Behind him, in the shadows, I make out a woman. She steps forward beneath the shelter of the porch and lifts the hood from her head. I can barely speak. The same height, the same build. As she nears the door, I see the tight bulge of her stomach. She sees me looking and immediately folds her arms across her cape. I lean against the door frame, dizzy with shock. It is her, I am sure of it, come back to me in the guise of another woman.

Words swim around my mind but I am unable to catch them, unable to form a sentence, to ask the young man what he wants. I stow the knife in my pocket, knowing I have no need of it after all.

'Sir, my wife here is unwell.' The young man takes hold of the woman's gloved hand. His own hands look frozen to the bone. 'Is there any chance we can rest here a while? Fetch a doctor? I can pay. I have money. We were making for the town, but I do not think my wife can make it. We only have the moonlight as our guide and my wife says she cannot take another step.'

My wife. I almost laugh, the way he makes claims on her, as though she is rightfully his. But I know I must be patient, play his game until I think of a way to be rid of him.

'Of course,' I say, standing aside and letting them in. The man is rough and has the look of a commoner. In the dim lantern light I see the distant marks of a childhood pox. The woman, on the other hand, is dark-haired and good-looking. Her cape is well fashioned, and beneath it, I see the blue silk of a fine dress. Bella, I think, you have chosen well, though this man, this ruffian, is a poor interloper.

'Come and sit in the kitchen,' I say. 'I will light a fire and bring you something to drink.'

'Thank you, sir, my wife will be grateful.'

I lead them through. The woman takes the largest chair, sliding off her cape, cradling her bulbous stomach. There's a thin line of sweat on her brow and she looks exhausted. The man, on the other hand, perches on the settle, anxiously playing his fingers on his knee.

'Thank you,' the woman says. Her voice is so distant I wonder if I imagined it, the same warm notes, the same kindness. She speaks again, mustering a weak smile. 'You are very kind. You are a true Christian gentleman.'

I am filled with wonder, with sweet desire.

It is Bella's voice.

23

NOW

'What do you mean, there's a lady in my bedroom?'

Kelda wished to God she wasn't drunk; wished she could replay the whole evening from the beginning; wished she'd never agreed to the party in the first place.

She stroked Dylan's cheek. 'It was one of the guests,' she said. 'Probably looking for the bathroom, or just being plain nosy. Maybe it was Emma, checking you were okay?'

'It wasn't Auntie Em or any of the others.' He turned away from her, refusing to meet her eye. 'It was that other lady.'

'Come here,' she said, sitting at the table, drawing him onto her knee. But he resisted, kicking away from her. 'It's okay. I believe you. You're safe. What did the woman look like?'

'Dark,' he said. 'Dark clothes. And she had a spot on her chin.'

'A spot?'

'Like the one you've got on your back.'

'You mean a mole?'

She thought of the guests. No one had a mole as far as she could remember, at least nothing visible. Dylan must have been dreaming again. Or maybe he was mistaken. He said she'd been wearing dark clothes; Alexa had been wearing black trousers, it could have been her.

'Come on,' she said. 'Let's go upstairs together.'

She caught hold of his hand and led him out of the kitchen.

'I don't want to go up there.'

'It's okay. All the guests have left now. It's just us and Emma.' She looked up the staircase to the landing, more nervous than she sounded. There was no other option. She had to take Dylan to bed, they could hardly spend the night in the lounge with Emma or curled up with blankets in the car. A guest had been in her bedroom, that was all – probably Alexa – and Dylan had woken up and got confused.

'Was there anything else?' she said. 'Anything else you noticed about the woman? The guest?'

'She was wearing a dress.'

'Okay.' She tried to think rationally. The only guest wearing a dress had been Georgie's mum but she'd left hours ago.

'It had flowers hanging from it,' he said, pointing to his waist. 'Just here. And she smelled of yucky perfume. She told me to get out.'

'What do you mean? Out of bed?'

'No. Out of the house.'

She faltered, her eyes travelling to the bookcase against the wall at the top of the stairs, the bathroom door wide open, Dylan's room on the left, her bedroom on the right. She remembered the message that had played through the microphone, the woman's voice, warning her away. Panic spiralled through her mind, but whatever she did, she couldn't show Dylan she was afraid. She'd pretend everything was okay; she'd look after him as she always had, ever since she'd seen him as a tiny baby on the hospital ward, in the white cot with the green blanket, crying for milk, crying for his mother. His mother who didn't want to know, who was curled up in a bed sheet, saying she couldn't cope, that she couldn't take him home, that she was a mess, that he was better off without her in his life. Emma hadn't even known she was pregnant until she was five months gone. Five months! And then, when she'd found out, she'd telephoned Kelda, the big sister she hadn't spoken to in months and bawled her eyes out.

She squeezed Dylan's hand. 'It's all right. Hold my hand tight and I'll show you there's no one there.'

She took him into the bedroom, switched on the main light, helped him out of his day clothes and into his pyjamas. Then she made a show of looking in the wardrobe and under the bed. 'See, there's nothing. Just our reflections in the mirror. No woman. No monsters. Only Snuggy.'

She picked up the fluffy blue rabbit from the floor, dusted him down and handed him over.

'In you two hop. I'll be there in a minute, just need to brush my teeth.'

She tucked the duvet around him before checking the rest of the house – the bathroom, Dylan's room, the lounge, the kitchen, beneath the stairs – checking all the doors and windows were locked and bolted. Then she ran herself a large glass of water. God, what had happened tonight? They'd all got so drunk and Emma, Emma ... She tried to remember the look on Nick's face when Emma had accused him of wanting to sleep with Kelda; tried to remember exactly what she'd said about being Dylan's mum. She wished she could remember everything clearly, picture things as they'd appeared in the candlelight beneath the sway of the apple trees. All those candles, burning deeply in their glass jars like they belonged to another time.

She put the glass down on the worktop. Something was lying beside the old range: a folded piece of paper, weighted to the floor by a pile of white pebbles. She tipped the pebbles onto the tiles and opened the page, recognising Nick's university letterhead: the information Nick had wanted to give her, but then changed his mind. It must have dropped from his pocket, and somehow, incredibly, the pebbles had fallen on top of it. Beneath the letterhead, he'd written, '*Stonebridge Herald* 1864'. The rest of the page was a photocopy, a newspaper clipping in old-fashioned font. She sat down and read the headline:

HORRIFYING MURDER: THE TRIAL AND SENTENCE OF JOSEPH WALTON, TOLL HOUSE KEEPER OF STONEBRIDGE

Her heart pumped fast as she screwed the paper in her fist and dropped it on the table. She wouldn't look. She wouldn't read any more, not tonight. She staggered to her feet, her mind flashing to the stairs, the bookcase, the shadows on the landing. Oh God. Dylan! He was alone.

Clumsy with drink, she stumbled into the hallway, up the stairs and across the landing, finding her way in the darkness. She crawled into bed next to Dylan, still in the blue silk top, her jeans kicked off on the floor. Her head spun, the words she'd read orbiting round and round. *Horrifying Murder. Joseph Walton. Toll House Keeper.* A memory of Dylan's voice cut through the madness. *She told me to get out. Get out. Get out.* She felt something beneath her, pressing into her thigh. Digging deep beneath the duvet, she pulled out a fistful of pebbles.

24

1864

'Sir . . .' The man stands up from the settle. He looks at his wife who, already, is closing her eyes. He steps towards me and lowers his voice. 'May I speak to you alone?'

I nod. 'Indeed. Whatever I can do to help you.'

The woman seems barely conscious of our movements as I lead the man through the back door and into the garden. The night air prickles. Through the window, I see the woman reclining her head against the back of the chair, tilting it at an angle, wetting her dry lips with the tip of her tongue, just as Bella used to do. I ache to go back to her, to boil her some broth, to find a blanket for her knees. Not to stand out here, talking.

The man looks at me squarely. A servant, I think, seeing him for what he is. Not a husband. This man has taken advantage of his position; he has seduced this poor lady and forced her to come away with him. Anger flares in my belly. I am not so readily fooled!

'Sir, I am very worried about my wife. Do you know of a good physician? She has been complaining of pains, but it is still too early, far too early for the baby.'

I think of Bella, how she wanted a child more than life itself. Even more than she wanted her husband.

The man walks down the path and looks around the side of the house, as though a doctor might, perchance, be walking this way in the moonlight. But there is no one about at this late hour. Not a soul in sight this far from town. Only me and the woman and the midnight dark.

I pick up a stone, not one of Bella's pebbles, but a jagged rock from the rockery. The man is still talking about his wife and her need for a doctor. My eyes flash to the window, to the warmth within, the woman resting her sweet head against the back of the chair.

'Is the town far?' the man says, still turned away from me, looking at the road.

'Not far,' I reply.

I weigh the rock in my hand, one palm and then the other. Then, I take a step forward and drive the rock hard into the back of the man's skull.

25

NOW

Kelda awoke with a start, realising she'd slept through her alarm. It was broad daylight and her head hurt. She'd been too drunk to close the curtains, too drunk to find her pyjamas. She wrapped a hand around her stomach, feeling it churn, feeling the smoothness of cheap silk against her waist, her bra jabbing painfully into her ribs. She still had the sound of her dream in her head: someone knocking on the front door, footsteps on the path in the garden, someone screaming.

She sat upright and reached for her glass of water, draining it in one. Dylan turned over in his sleep and grabbed hold of her arm, pinning her beneath the duvet.

'It's okay,' she said when he wouldn't let go. 'Go back to sleep.'

Last night came back to her in nauseating waves. The drinks on the picnic table. Emma's revelation. Simon and Nick and

Alexa piling into a taxi. She looked at Dylan wriggling in his sleep, oblivious to everything that had happened outside. She'd not planned to tell him he was adopted, not planned to tell anyone, until he was eighteen. She still wouldn't tell him now. He was too young to understand. It wouldn't be fair.

She remembered when she'd first taken him back to Emma's – a tiny bedsit in an unfamiliar city – when they were still pretending things would be all right, that Emma would somehow find it within herself to be the mother he needed, before the social workers got involved, how she'd sing to him at night, rocking him in her arms or pacing the tiny flat, trying to get him to sleep. 'You're too young,' Mum had said to her when she'd told her about the adoption plan. Mum had been angry at both of them: Emma for getting pregnant and embarrassing the family, forgetting that Dad had already done that years ago; Kelda for shouldering herself with the child. 'You haven't even finished university. You wouldn't know what to do. How could you know? You've never been a mother before.'

Too young but not as young as Emma. She'd let Emma go back to her life in the city. As far as people knew, Kelda was Dylan's mum and always had been, and no one would ever know otherwise unless she chose to reveal it. Emma had seemed relieved, grabbing at the chance to walk out of Dylan's life. 'Not for ever, Little Man,' she'd said, blowing him a kiss goodbye as he'd gurgled in his cot back at Mum's. But as the years went by, it had seemed that way. Kelda couldn't remember the last time Emma had sent Dylan a birthday card.

She bent down and kissed his head, peaceful now beneath the duvet. He shifted slightly. She felt the warmth of his breath and smelled the soapiness of his hair and skin, promising herself she'd never get so drunk again.

She crept downstairs, not wanting to wake Emma, not sure what she would say or how she'd act towards her. The photocopy Nick had dropped was waiting for her on the table, screwed in a ball the way she'd left it last night. She hesitated before picking it up and smoothing it out. Beneath it, inexplicably, was a circle of white pebbles. She sank into one of the kitchen chairs, weighed down by a sense of inevitability. This time she read the article in full.

HORRIFYING MURDER:
THE TRIAL AND SENTENCE OF
JOSEPH WALTON, TOLL HOUSE
KEEPER OF STONEBRIDGE

On Tuesday 12TH April, Joseph Walton, toll house keeper, was brought before the Assizes court in Stonebridge to stand trial for the murder of Miss Helen Drake. The deceased was a spinster, thirty-five years of age and daughter of a Stonebridge grocer. She is thought to have visited the toll house on the morning of 24TH February as was her custom following the death of her sister, Isabella Walton. A coroner's enquiry found that Miss Drake had been stabbed repeatedly in the back with a jack knife on the landing and subsequently toppled to her death down the stairs.

The first witness was a maid by the name of Minnie Selbridge who chanced to see Miss

Drake depart her residence above the grocer's shop at eight o'clock on Wednesday morning. A short exchange followed whereupon Miss Selbridge assisted Miss Drake in retrieving items fallen from her basket. This was reported to be food for the prisoner who had lived alone in the toll house since the death of his wife, Isabella, last year. Miss Selbridge reported that Miss Drake was cheerfully disposed, unaware of the grave danger to which she was heading.

The second witness was Mr Henry Turnbill, trustee of Stonebridge Turnpike Trust, who arrived at the toll house just after ten o'clock in the morning. Mr Turnbill had called to speak with the prisoner, whose slackness and general wretchedness had been observed by passers-by since his wife's death. Finding the turnpike unattended, Mr Turnbill knocked on the front door to no avail. The door was ajar, and Mr Turnbill could see the landing and the staircase. On opening the door, he saw what at first appeared to be a sack of coal at the bottom of the stairs, but on second inspection, was found to be the dead body of Miss Drake. Mr Turnbill at once restrained the prisoner and made haste to the police station.

The third witness was the police constable who attended the scene with a brother officer and Mr Turnbill. The prisoner was found locked in the cellar where Mr Turnbill had

restrained him earlier following a short struggle. On questioning, the prisoner muttered
over and over that he did not know what had
happened and could not remember what the
deceased had been doing there.

The prisoner, on cross-examination, was
incoherent and unable to provide a motive
for his crime nor a defence. Several character
witnesses spoke generously of the prisoner
who, they said, was harmless but eccentric.

The jury retired for thirty minutes before
returning to announce the verdict of guilty.
The sentence was delivered by the judge who
addressed the prisoner, declaring that he
was utterly convinced of his dreadful crime
and that it was with great pain that he pro-
nounce the awful sentence of hanging from
the neck . . .

Kelda put the photocopy down on the table. She should
have known. She should have known something bad had
happened in the house. She should have researched the place
properly before she'd bought it, only she'd been so desperate to
leave Mum's, she'd not given the history of the place a second
thought. She looked up and saw Dylan's picture, covering the
hole in the wall. Was the mask behind it an image of Helen
Drake? Except that didn't make sense. Why hang her death
mask in the house where she was murdered? Thank God she'd
put something over it. It was like the mask had been trying
to get out, the wall breaking open, inch by inch. Impossible,

incredible, yet that's how it seemed. She re-read the words on the photocopy. *Miss Drake had been stabbed repeatedly in the back with a jack knife on the landing.* She thought of the stairs, the awful brown swirling carpet. Suddenly, she couldn't stand it. She couldn't stand any of it.

She stood up and threw the photocopy in the bin, then picked up the pebbles that had lain beneath it. She opened the back door and threw them in the garden. Whatever the hell they meant, whatever power they possessed, she wouldn't let them mess with her and Dylan anymore. She went around the house, as silently as she could, tiptoeing around Emma and Dylan, looking in boxes and along the edge of shelves, sweeping whatever pebbles she found into her hands. Then she went outside and threw fistfuls of the gleaming white stones over the garden wall.

Back inside, she heard Emma stirring and went into the lounge. Emma was lying on the sofa, head in one hand, flicking through her text messages with the other. She smiled at Kelda.

'Hi.'

'Hi.'

Kelda pulled back the shutters and opened one of the panels on the bay window.

Emma shot upright and rubbed her arms. 'What did you do that for?'

'It's morning.' There was a line of pebbles on the sill that she'd missed. She hurled them out of the window.

'I know it's morning.'

'And it's Saturday. I have to get Dylan up in a minute, get him ready for football.' She stared at the clothes on the floor, the cigarettes scattered where Emma must have dropped them last night, one half smoked and ground into the coffee table. She went into the kitchen and boiled water for coffee. Emma followed, still clutching her phone.

'Anything wrong?'

'Wrong?' Kelda spun towards her. How could Emma not know? How could she not see what she'd done? She grabbed a packet of coffee and slit it open with a knife. 'You throw a party at my house without asking me first. You spend all my housekeeping money. Then you insult my guests and tell everyone about Dylan, that he's not really my son, that he's adopted, when he doesn't even know it himself, and you ask me what's wrong?'

'Jesus, Kelda, I thought you liked the party. Calm down.'

'Calm down?' She piled coffee into the cafetière.

'It was just a bit of fun. The bit about swapping partners. Everyone was being so dull. And I'm sorry about the other bit. About Dylan. I shouldn't have said anything. But it doesn't really matter, does it?'

The kettle screeched to a boil. 'Of course it matters.'

'Why?'

'Because no one knew. And it wasn't for you to tell them. We agreed, didn't we? We agreed Dylan wouldn't know until he was eighteen. We agreed, for Dylan's sake, to say he was mine. We agreed that I'd be his mum and you'd be his auntie.'

'I know all that. Of course I know all that. I'm not stupid.' Emma tapped away at her phone then put it in her pocket. 'But what I said last night doesn't actually change anything, does it? It was just words.' She opened the back door and lit a cigarette. 'Honestly, Kelda, you can be so stuck-up sometimes. I should have known this was a mistake.'

'A mistake?'

'Coming here, playing happy families.'

Kelda plunged the top of the cafetière, splashing boiling water and coffee granules over her hands. She winced.

'You don't *do* anything,' Emma said, waving the cigarette. 'You just go to work and come back again and watch telly and then have a go at me for trying to liven things up.'

'Leave then, if it's so boring. Go back to Luke.'

'Luke?' Emma pulled a face. 'He hates me. I hate him.'

'Not according to your texts. Apparently, you two can't wait to be together again.'

'What?' Emma's hand sprung to her back pocket. 'Have you been snooping through my phone?'

'It was on the work surface. I thought it was mine.'

'You bitch!'

Kelda slopped coffee into her mug. 'It was an accident.'

'You're just like Mum. Worse than Mum. Even Mum wouldn't stoop that low.'

'As I said, it was an accident.'

Emma blew smoke into the garden. Beyond it, Kelda could smell the autumn, the unmistakable stench of dead leaves and rotting apples.

'Why did you come here in the first place?' she said.

'I told you. I had nowhere else to go.'

'Was it about the money? The money for the catering course? Were you hoping I'd eventually cave, give you the money anyway? Was there even a course in the first place or were you lying about that too? Is this what you and Luke do? Feed people a pack of lies, hoping they'll feel sorry for you and open their wallets?'

Emma leaned against the door frame, lifting the cigarette to her mouth, taking her time. 'This isn't about me, is it? This is about Nick. You're jealous about me and Nick?'

'What?'

'That time in your halls of residence, when you'd passed out on the sofa. You had no idea, did you? Well, for your information, it was just a kiss. Nothing more. Just a stupid drunken kiss.'

'I don't care what happened between you and Nick.' Her head hurt even more. She pulled Dylan's football kit from the pile of washing beneath the table. 'I think you'd better leave,' she said, shaking her head, trying to clear the fog. 'I'm sorry, I just can't see this working out. I'm taking Dylan to football in a couple of hours, you can pack your things and leave then. If you need any money for the train . . . ' She unclipped Emma's necklace, the one with the little white stone, and handed it back.

Emma stared silently at the apple trees, playing with the opal.

Kelda inspected the patch she'd sewn on the sleeve of Dylan's football top. 'And since you asked, this isn't about Nick. It's about me and Dylan. We need our own space. The house just isn't big enough for three of us.'

Emma shrugged. 'Suit yourself. It's not like I expect much from this family anyway. First Dad. Then Mum. Now you. I thought you were different, but you're exactly the same. Here,' she tossed the necklace back at Kelda. It missed and slid beneath the kitchen table. 'You can keep the necklace. You need it more than I do.'

'What do you mean?'

'This house. This fucking weird house. I'll be glad to see the back of it.' Emma stepped into the garden and disappeared.

Kelda followed, shading her eyes from the sun. The picnic table was still lined with glasses from the night before and an empty wine bottle glinted in the wet grass. She followed the path to the gate. Emma was already on the other side.

'Stop!' she said, reaching for the latch. 'What do you mean about the house being weird?' She felt light-headed, in need of water and something to eat. Her fingers stumbled, catching on the latch, making her wince.

By the time she reached the road, Emma was jogging towards town.

'Please!' Kelda shouted after her. She glanced at the car, knowing she couldn't drive yet, couldn't leave Dylan on his own. She needed coffee and breakfast. Besides, Emma would be back, if not now then later, to collect her things. She'd talk to her then.

She turned back to the toll house, silent and watchful in the early morning.

Just her and Dylan alone.

26

⌒

1864

The man drops to the floor like a sack of flour. I throw the stone at the wall beneath the apple trees – I'll think what to do about it later – then pick up my lantern where I left it on the path. Lifting the latch of the back door, I hear the man behind me, moaning softly, bubbling spit and blood.

I leave him where he is and walk inside. The dark-haired woman turns her head towards the door but doesn't open her eyes. The likeness is striking. The same wave of hair, the same milky skin, the same round cheeks. I search for the mole on her chin but it's not there. Of course, Bella wouldn't come back to me just as she was. That would be too easy.

The woman's eyes are closed but she is not asleep. Her fingers roam across her belly, across the fine blue silk, just as Bella's used to do, remarking on the kick of a foot or the punch of a hand. But this woman – this version of my wife – is silent.

I tiptoe around her, as noiselessly as I can, setting the kettle on the range to make tea. Her eyes flick open when the kettle accidentally knocks against a pan and I see the gleam of fever within, her eyes glazed and unfocused.

'My husband . . . ' she begins.

I silence her with my finger against her lips. Dry, thirsty lips on my skin. She pulls her head backwards, startled by my boldness.

'Shush, you must conserve your strength,' I say, thinking of the body outside, the pock-marked man face down on the path. I decide to play her game. 'Your husband has taken my lantern and gone to fetch a doctor.'

'A doctor?'

'He is very concerned. He said you are to rest here until he returns. You are not to exert yourself. You are not to attempt to walk to the town.'

'Sir, I cannot presume on your kindness like this.' She pushes herself up from the chair and I see the effort it takes, the sweat beading on her forehead. A moment to catch her breath, then she takes one faltering step towards the outside door. 'I . . . I . . . ' She falls heavily against my arm.

'Upstairs,' I say. 'You need to rest. Your husband will not be long.'

'I do not want to trouble you.'

'It is no trouble at all.'

I lead her to the other doorway – towards the stairs – as she mumbles about the journey and how far they've walked and how her husband is a good man and they have friends in the town yonder and they will pay me for my kindness. Her vowels are clipped, betraying her good breeding; the voice Bella would have had had she been born in more fortunate circumstances.

'Do not talk, so,' I say. 'You will tire yourself out. As for money, there is no need.'

We reach the foot of the stairs and she hesitates, pulling back.

'Your husband insists that you rest,' I say, seeing the panic in her eyes.

She nods as if resigned to her fate, as if she has no choice, then grips the banister and pulls herself up onto the first step. I walk behind her, steadying her with my hand, my arm below her left elbow. Halfway up she halts, clutching her stomach.

'I cannot go further.'

'It is not far, just a few more steps.'

'I do not have the strength. There is a pain.'

I urge her upwards. 'It is not far at all.'

She leans more heavily. 'Sir, you are very kind. You are indeed a true Christian gentleman.'

Upwards we go, the woman leaning on me the whole way. I feel the weight of her, the weight of the child. I see her shadow against the wall, cast by my lantern. The details may be different, but the shadow is the same. The shadow is Bella. My heart thumps as we near the landing then cross the rag-rug. The woman looks at the open doorway on the far right – the doorway to the bedroom – and tightens her grip on the banister, her face as pale as moonlight.

'Not there.' The woman stares in horror at the bedroom door. 'I have a feeling. I cannot explain . . . ' She trails off. It's as if she has a vision of what happened the night Bella died. She cannot repeat it. She cannot let her baby go the same way. She cannot return to the place she was lost. I look for some sign to guide me, tracing the floorboards for pebbles, feeling for them in my pocket, but to no avail.

'Is there some other room?' she asks, eyes focused on the door ahead, the child's room, the one that was mine. Her voice is small and quivering.

'Indeed,' I say, guiding her along the landing. 'But it is a poor room. A servant's room. I would rather you rest in the other.'

'No. No!'

She stumbles to the room ahead, dripping with fever and the effort of climbing, grabbing my hand. I push wide the door with the other. The room is unkempt. A single bed with a sagging mattress, stained with years of bed-wetting and childhood illnesses. Dust on the floor. Peeling mustard-yellow paint. She stops and glances over my shoulder, at the door closing behind us. I feel her hesitancy, her doubt, though she doesn't have the strength to resist. She sighs and lowers herself onto the bed, half falling. The bed groans like the wind around the house.

'I will get you water,' I say, playing her game. 'And pillows. You must rest before the doctor arrives. He is an excellent doctor. You have nothing to fear. Then, when you are feeling better, you must come downstairs and have something to eat. To fortify you for the rest of your journey.'

I leave her, head laid on the mattress, legs tucked beneath her dress.

Downstairs, I clear crumbs from the table and set out clean plates and a pitcher of wine. I take a cloth and shine the cutlery. I place walnuts in a bowl and lay out the ham my sister-in-law left this morning. Everything must be pristine. Perfect. I will let the woman rest awhile, then lead her downstairs and we will feast. A celebration for her homecoming! And then, then ...

After an hour, I am impatient. I go upstairs, cross the

landing, push wide the door of the little bedroom. The woman is fast asleep on the bed. I try to rouse her, shaking her by her shoulders, calling her by her real name – Bella – but all she does is groan. I leave her be and go downstairs again, watching the clock above the mantelpiece turn to midnight.

One o'clock.

Two o'clock.

Just before three, I go upstairs, unable to hold out any longer. I place the lantern on the floorboards. She is still asleep where I left her, breathing deeply, the colour in her cheeks returned a little.

I sink down on the bed and stroke the hair from her fore-head. Her skin is soft, softer than I remember and smells of rose water. Her hair has the scent of geraniums. She shifts beneath my hand. I lie next to her, running my fingers down the length of her body, caressing her arms through the thick fabric of her cape, touching her stomach, marvelling at its roundness, feeling the full curve of her breasts. 'Bella, Bella,' I moan over and over. My lips find the soft lobe of her ear, teasing it between my teeth, then biting down, overcome with longing, with desire.

She yelps. Jerks upwards.

I stretch out a hand. 'I'm sorry, I didn't mean to hurt you. Lie down again. Please.'

She pushes herself up from the bed and stumbles towards the door. The fever has lifted and she looks more human, more like the hesitant woman who hid behind her husband in the porch.

'It is only me,' I say, patting the mattress. 'Your true hus-band. You have nothing to fear.'

Her face twists in confusion and becomes something else. Some*one* else. 'You are not my husband.'

She fumbles for the door handle but I am faster than she is, blocking her escape.

'Bella! My love! Do you not recognise me? Do you not see who I am?'

She edges towards the wall, feeling for it with her hands. 'I am not who you think I am. Please, let me go.' Fear contorts her face, her eyes widen, her mouth parts as if to scream.

I lunge towards her, grabbing her arm, but she twists away with surprising force and slaps me hard.

'You witch!' I cry, hand to my cheek.

'Please.' She is humble again, a pawn in my hands. 'I need to find my husband.'

Something snaps inside me. The burn of my cheek and the tears in my eyes have made me see clearly. The way she speaks of her husband. The terror in her eyes. Not Bella at all! This woman has deceived me! She is but a poor impression of my wife. I feel for the jack knife in my pocket and spring it loose.

'You tricked me!' I snarl, feeling the coldness creep inside my bones. 'You made me believe you were Bella!'

'Please, sir. Don't hurt me.'

She cries out, stumbling sideways until she is trapped in the corner of the room beneath the window. A floorboard creaks beneath her feet, a horrible wrenching sound like someone screaming in pain. She stretches out her hands as if in invitation, as if accepting her fate, then, at the last minute, wraps them around the child in her belly.

She screams and the blade flashes.

27

NOW

The recreation ground was on the opposite side of town. On the pitch, the boys were playing five-a-side. Kelda stood next to Ethan's mum near the stands, holding a lukewarm cup of coffee she kept forgetting to drink. Ethan's mum was gossiping with the other school mums about Mr Yeo: he'd been spotted in town with a blonde half his age.

'Maybe she's an ex-pupil of his?' Ethan's mum spouted, setting the school mums gossiping again. 'Apparently, he spent the whole time talking to her boobs. She can't have been much older than eighteen.'

'Maybe it's his daughter?' Kelda offered.

Ethan's mum ignored her and continued her theory about Mr Yeo being a pervert.

Kelda stared at Dylan kicking the turf on the side of the

pitch. She was hungover but trying not to show it, glad that Ethan's mum had left the party when she did, before Emma had launched into her accusations and the party had fallen apart. She couldn't think straight, couldn't concentrate on the game of football, the mums gossiping, the dads cheering over each other, the coaches shouting instructions.

She pulled her phone from her pocket, scared of what text messages or missed calls might be waiting for her, but there was only one text, a message from Lucy saying she'd had a great evening.

She hovered over the keypad, composing a text to Nick then deleted it, unsure what to say. She wanted to talk to him about the old newspaper article, but it didn't seem right even to text him after what Emma had said. She thought of Simon which was somehow easier; what had happened last night was embarrassing but not the end of the world. She tapped a quick message into her phone, thanking him for coming and hoping he'd had a good night. She thought of apologising for what Emma had said, but wasn't sure whether it mattered, whether he'd even remember. He'd been quite drunk himself, knocking back the wine, though she was sure he'd said he was working today, or at least on call.

She put her phone in her pocket and scanned the pitch for Dylan. He wasn't in the place she'd last seen him. She looked again, searching more closely amongst the groups of boys, the coaches running back and forth between the games. When she still couldn't see him, she ran over to Georgie who pointed in the direction of the kiosk. Dylan was buying a bottle of cola with the money she'd given him earlier.

'Hey, Batman. You okay?'

He handed his pound over to the kiosk lady then unscrewed

the bottle top, spraying fizzy drink all over his hands. She pulled a tissue from her pocket and mopped it up.

'Stop it, Mum,' he said, pulling away from her. 'I'm fine.'

'You sure?'

He wiped his eyes with the back of his hand.

'You don't look all right to me,' she said gently. 'Is it Georgie?'

Dylan stared at the ground, kicking the grass again.

'Georgie says we live in a pigsty.'

Kelda sighed, picturing Mrs Watts in her fluffy white slippers, gossiping with her husband over breakfast. 'Georgie doesn't know what he's talking about. He's probably never seen a real pigsty. Anyway, who cares what Georgie thinks?' She swivelled him back towards the pitch. 'I can't wait to see you play. You must be on next. You don't want to miss it.'

'I don't want to play today.' He wiped his eyes again.

'Is this about Georgie?'

'No. I just don't want to play.'

'You'll feel better once you get out there. You'll enjoy yourself. I promise you.'

'But I don't want to go back on the pitch.'

She poured the dregs of her coffee onto the ground. 'Let's go home then, no point staying here if you're not going to play. I'd better tell your coach.'

'No.' He grabbed her arm, spilling the fizzy drink on her jeans. 'Not home. I don't want to go back there. Can we go to Uncle Nick's flat?'

'Not today, I'm afraid.' She thought of Alexa, of Nick just waking up, making Alexa coffee, laughing off what Emma had said about him and Kelda and his drunken night with Emma years ago.

'What about the dinosaur park?' she said. She desperately

didn't want to go back to the toll house either. 'We could take a picnic, spend the day there?'

Dylan's face lit up. 'Really?'

'Really.' She blanked out the thought of how much it would cost. It would do her good, clear her mind of the night before, stop her thinking about Emma and Nick, stop her thinking about the murder. She could switch her phone onto silent and chase after Dylan in the park. 'But we'll have to go home first. Collect a few things. Thick coats for a start. It's freezing.'

Back home, she found the door wide open, Emma's holdall on the kitchen table, bulging with clothes and charging leads and make-up. Just as she knew she would, Emma had come back.

'Is Auntie Em going away?'

Kelda hung up her jacket. 'She has to go home.'

'I thought she was staying here for ever?'

'No, not for ever. She just came to visit us.' She put an arm around his shoulder, not realising until now how much he'd taken to Emma.

'Was that the reason you were shouting?'

'What?'

'This morning, before I came down for breakfast. Before Auntie Em went out for her walk.'

'No, love. That was just Mummy and Emma being silly.'

'Is Simon your boyfriend?'

She rubbed her face, unable to keep up with the conversation. 'I don't know. Maybe. Do you like him?'

He stuffed his hands in his pockets. 'He's okay. He tried to play with me and Georgie, but he wasn't very good. He didn't know how to play kids' games. Can we go to the dinosaur park now?'

She laughed. 'Yes, we can. But not until I've made the sandwiches. Egg mayonnaise or cheese and ketchup?'

'Both.'

Dylan pulled off his football boots, scattering grass and mud
on the kitchen tiles, then he skipped to the hallway, yanking
his football hoodie over his head. She opened the fridge and
pulled out a block of cheese, then hunted for the mayonnaise.

Dylan screamed.

She dropped the cheese, slamming the fridge door shut.
'What on earth . . . ?'

She ran to the hallway and gasped. Emma was lying at the
bottom of the staircase, hair over her face, legs curled beneath
her on the floorboards.

'Oh my God.' Kelda knelt down and moved Emma's hair out
of the way. Emma moaned and opened her eyes.

'Emma, can you hear me? What happened? Say something. Please.'

'Kelda . . . '

'Are you hurt? What happened?'

'It hurts. It really hurts. I think I've broken something.'

'Where? What?'

Emma closed her eyes again. Kelda felt for her phone, aware
of Dylan over her shoulder, eyes wide with shock.

'It's okay. I think Auntie Em fell down the stairs. She must
have tripped.' Her eyes flitted to the landing, to the curl of the
banister, to the shadow skimming the bookcase, disappearing
beneath Dylan's bedroom door. She swallowed hard. 'I need to
call an ambulance, just to check she's okay.'

She tapped 999 into her keypad.

'Emergency, which service?'

She glanced back at the landing. Still again. Just the light from her bedroom window and the tiny one at the top of the stairs. On the right, Dylan's bedroom door was firmly closed. Had she left it open or closed this morning? She couldn't remember.

'Hello? Is there anyone there?'

She became aware of the woman speaking to her on the other end.

'An ambulance,' she blurted out, looking at Emma, seeing the way her right arm twisted away from her at the wrong angle. 'I need an ambulance. There's been a horrible accident. My sister . . .'

Tears coursed down her cheeks, into her mouth, blurring her vision.

'Mum,' Dylan was saying. 'Mum, are you all right? Will Auntie Em be all right?' At the same time, the woman on the phone was trying to speak to her, trying to find out where she was and what had happened. She squeezed Dylan's hand.

'The toll house on the Old Turnpike Road. My sister's had a fall. I think she fell down the stairs.'

She spoke to someone else, someone on the medical team, answering his questions as best she could, trying to prise the information from Emma. Yes, Emma was conscious. Yes, she was talking. She was in pain and she couldn't move her right arm but she was lifting her head. When she put the phone down, she smiled at Dylan. 'They're coming. They're on their way. The ambulance will be here any moment.'

Emma lifted her head again, wincing with the effort. 'Thanks.'

'Shh, don't talk. Save your energy.'

'It really hurts.'

'I know. Don't talk.'

They waited, the three of them at the bottom of the

stairs, Kelda staring at the minute hand on her watch, Dylan squashed into her.

Emma breathed through her teeth. 'I'm sorry, Kelda. I'm really sorry.'

'It doesn't matter.'

'I had a drink. I was angry with you. I was in your bedroom getting some things, some beads from your jewellery box. I was going to take them with me.'

'Shh. It's okay.'

Emma turned her head on the carpet, eyes flitting to the top of the stairs. 'Something happened. I was drunk. I had a coffee in town, then I came back here and found a bottle of wine in the fridge from last night.'

'Shh.' She felt Dylan next to her and wished Emma would stop talking.

'I was in your bedroom, looking at the beads, deciding which ones I liked best, which ones you wouldn't notice were missing, when I felt something.'

Kelda turned to Dylan. 'Can you go to the lounge and fetch me a blanket from the sofa? We need to warm Emma up.' Dylan nodded and disappeared.

Emma opened her lips, dry and cracked at the corners. Kelda could smell the wine and cigarettes on her breath and wondered whether she'd stopped at the one bottle or found something else.

'There was someone in your room,' she said.

'What do you mean?' A whisper. She didn't want to know. She couldn't bear to hear what Emma had to say and she didn't want Dylan to hear either. But still she had to ask.

'A woman. Standing in front of the wardrobe, watching me playing with the beads. A woman in a long dress, with flowers tied to her waist, staring at me like she saw through me, like she knew exactly what I was doing.'

'You'd been drinking. You were seeing things. Probably your own reflection in the wardrobe mirror.' She didn't dare look up at the landing now, but she felt it, that thing that was here in the house, that wouldn't leave her. She heard the names in her head again, from the old newspaper clipping: Helen, Henry, Minnie, Joseph, Isabella. Isabella Walton, the toll keeper's wife. She'd thought she'd not known those names before, but she realised she'd been mistaken: Isabella. *Bella*: the name written in lipstick on Dylan's wall. The name that no amount of scrubbing could obliterate.

'No.' Emma shook her head, wincing in pain. 'It was real. Not my imagination. Not the drink. I swear it. The woman was standing there, looking at me.'

'But how did you fall?'

'I had to get out. I couldn't stand it. The way she was judging me for taking your things. She shouted at me. She told me to leave. I'm sorry . . . ' Tears spilled down her cheeks. 'I'm so sorry. I was mad at you, that's all. I wanted to teach you a lesson.'

'Shh, shh.' She laid a hand against Emma's face. So cold. So horribly cold. She looked behind her for Dylan, past the kitchen and into the lounge; he was battling with the blanket on the sofa. She willed the ambulance to hurry. She didn't know how much longer she could stand it, crouched there at the bottom of the stairs, listening to Emma ramble on about things she couldn't allow herself to believe.

'Here you go,' she said, when Dylan came back with the blanket. She tucked it around Emma, careful not to make things worse. 'It won't be long now.'

'I'm freezing.'

'You'll soon warm up. Listen, I think I can hear the ambulance.'

Dylan ran to the bay window. She heard him clamber onto the back of the sofa, looking out, then racing across the kitchen tiles. He darted past the table, past the cavity wall where she'd pinned his picture above the gash, the felt-tip drawing of the bats and the midnight sky. As he opened the back door, the wind caught a corner of the picture and lifted it down, pulling the drawing pins with it. From the hallway, she watched it land on Emma's holdall on the kitchen table. The gash was bigger than ever. Gaping. She could see the plaster face behind it, staring at her. Staring at the two of them at the bottom of the stairs.

Outside, she could hear Dylan gabbling to the ambulance crew, calling them round the back, telling them proudly how he'd been the one to find her.

She looked down at Emma, and gently squeezed her good arm. 'They're here,' she said. 'The ambulance is here. Everything's going to be all right now.'

28

✷

1864

I'm out of the house, not bothering to pull on my coat, my shirt loose and spattered with blood. The man is where I left him on the garden path, no longer moaning or bubbling spit. Dead as the night. I run to the shed and search amongst Bella's pots until my hands fall upon the handle of a spade. At the same time, the lantern burns low where I left it on the path and eventually dies altogether. I fumble in the dark, feeling cobwebs against my palms, yanking the handle from amongst the other tools until it's free. Then I run back inside the house and light another lantern. Even with that small effort, I'm breathless. My head throbs. My veins feel like they are on fire. I tug my shirt over my head and bundle the blood-soaked cotton into the oven. I will make a blaze later in the grate, tear the shirt to shreds and burn it.

Outside, I heave the man into my arms, then drag him onto the frost-covered grass. The man is thin, a wasted thing, but he is heavier than he looks. I study the lawn, the gentle slope towards the wall, the flowerbeds untended since Bella died, the well with its coil of slack rope. But what am I thinking? I cannot bury the bodies in the garden, the earth would soon give me away. It is far too dangerous.

I jam the jagged stone I used earlier into the rockery, then wait for Bella to give me a sign, to tell me what to do. I wait and wait, every nerve in my body singing, knowing she will come. I listen hard, hearing the gentle whisper of the wind in the wood and the hoot of an owl. Beyond that, there is nothing. The night is silent. Unfriendly. But maybe that's the point. Maybe that's what she is trying to tell me: bury the bodies not here but in the wood.

I drag the man back to the path, then run into the house and up the stairs. The stench is worse than ever. A rotten, devilish smell. The house feels cold and hostile. A mouse skitters in front of me, across the landing, disappearing into the room on the left. The child's bedroom.

The woman is slumped in the far corner, still cradling her belly, her chest and throat slashed bright red. Bright red on the walls too. How can there be so much blood? I move the lantern up and down the mustard-yellow paint. Flecks everywhere as though the woman's soul has poured itself out and gushed all over the bedroom. A bloody mess, but somehow fitting, here in the room where I wept when Ma died, when Pa beat me, when my stepmother sent me to my room to repent. All that pain, all that anger, turned to blood. I reach out and touch it with my fingers, tracing the blood splatters across the paint, feeling the pain of all those years wrap around my heart, squeezing it like a rope.

I lift the woman by the arms, humping her onto my shoulder, the child within weighing her down in protest. Her stomach thumps my chest as I stagger across the landing, her arms swinging at my back, her heels click-click-clicking together. By the time I reach the head of the stairs, I'm exhausted. My body screams at me to give up, to go to bed, but I know I cannot. I cannot risk my sister-in-law calling at the house, or a passer-by nosing his way into the garden at first light. I tell myself to be strong, that I *am* strong, just as Ma used to tell me. *You are stronger than him*, she used to whisper, nodding at Pa.

I take a deep breath and begin the slow descent down the stairs, through the kitchen and into the garden. There's not a soul to be seen, no lights save for my lantern hooked to my waist, but I keep my head low anyway. I will have to pass the front of the house and around the left side to reach the wood, then go back again for the man and a spade to bury them.

The woman slips from my grasp and lands with a thud. I'm in the field that lies between the house and the wood, a small area of wasteland. I heave the woman back over my shoulder, my hands slippery with sweat, her stomach banging awkwardly against my chest. Behind me, the toll house is a shadow in the moonlight, and I can just about make out the line of the garden wall. There is a small patch of land just beneath it, on the woodland-side which is neither field, nor garden. A place shaded by the apple trees on the other side.

Why not there? I think. Why carry the bodies all the way to the wood?

I allow the woman to slide back onto the ground, then grab her by the ankles, the leather of her boots yielding beneath my fingers, soft as cloth. I can smell the tang of boot polish and that other scent, stronger now, heightened in the dark: the geranium oil in her hair. Everything about her is at odds with the fate that has befallen her. She wasn't intended for this, for the long walk in the night-time and the violent end. She was intended for ballrooms and dancing, fine food and good wine, a long and happy life, eventually a grave in a family vault. So much for that, I think, dragging her slowly to the spot beside the wall, knowing the farmhands never plough this close to the toll house. The ground is rough and uneven. Last summer, the field was thick with wheat, but the harvest is long over, and the field will be left fallow this year.

I leave the woman where she is and go back for the man, a heavier but less awkward load. Then, I find a blanket from the bottom of the wardrobe, thick with cobwebs and smelling of long-gone winters. Bella used to press herbs into the wool – lavender and rosemary – but the herbs have disintegrated and when I press the blanket to my face, it is cold as the frost.

I set the lantern down against the back of the garden wall and get to work. No easy work either with the ground so hard. My chest is shiny with sweat, still bare against the freezing night air. The work fires my muscles but the sweat chills me, running in rivulets down my skin. By the time the sun rises, I'm shaking. I think of the grave diggers at Bella's funeral, the hole far deeper than this, but I can go no further, no lower. I have used every ounce of my strength and I'm running out of time.

I heave the bodies into their shallow grave, the woman first, the man cradling her on top, then toss the blanket in after them, not quite covering their heads but too tired to care. The excitement of earlier has gone and all I am left with is numbness and exhaustion. The woman stares up at me, above the head of the man, above his smashed-in skull, her eyes still open, one hand stretching forwards as if trying to escape. For a heart-stopping moment, I think she is still alive, that I didn't do the job properly. But then I see that her eyes are completely lifeless. Just vacant holes.

I fill the earth back in as fast as I can, then, just as I'm levelling the ground, the rain starts to fall, thawing the frost, lightly at first like thousands of tiny kisses, then harder, faster. I throw the spade on the grass and allow it to soak me. Beautiful, merciful rain! Above me, above the graves, beside the garden wall, the apple trees shake the water from their leaves. I shoulder the spade and pick up the lantern, then walk the short distance to the toll house, just as the first coach rattles its way along the Turnpike Road.

29

NOW

'How are you feeling?' Kelda looked down at Emma in the hospital bed, arm supported in a sling, wincing every time she moved.

Emma groaned. 'Bloody awful.'

They were on the orthopaedic ward of the general hospital, a white room with curtained-off compartments adjacent to a nurses' station. Kelda played with the bed sheet. 'I called Mum,' she said quietly.

Emma shot up, despite the pain. 'Jesus, Kelda, you don't lose any time.' She hooked her good arm around the sling and breathed deeply. 'It even hurts to breathe. It's like there's a knife stabbing me in the arm.'

'I'm sorry.'

'Are you?'

Kelda sat down on the bed and sighed. 'I really am sorry – about calling Mum, I mean. I knew you wouldn't want me to do it. But you need someone to look after you. And I can't. I just can't. Not with Dylan. It's just not practical. The house isn't big enough at the best of times and you can hardly sleep on the sofa now.'

Emma lay down again and turned her head towards the window. 'If it wasn't for the consultant, I'd be out of here like a shot.' The consultant wanted to see her before she left, then X-ray again in a couple of days. It was an awkward fracture that might require surgery. Emma must have trapped it on the banister as she fell, or else fallen on top of it. Beside all that, she was still feeling dizzy, which was why they'd wheeled her up to the ward; she'd blacked out when she'd landed at the bottom of the stairs, for how long, no one knew.

'I hate this place.' Emma looked out of the window. 'The nurse is a complete cow. When I asked if I could go outside for a smoke, you'd have thought I was asking for the moon.'

'She's only trying to help you,' Kelda said. She wished she wasn't here. Emma obviously didn't want her around, but she couldn't leave until Mum arrived. Mum who was hurtling down the motorway, rallying to the cause, pretending the years of Emma's absence from their lives hadn't happened.

'Where's Dylan?' Emma said.

'With a friend.'

'Nick?'

'No. Lucy.'

'Look, Kelda.' Emma anchored her good arm onto Kelda's. 'I know I've been a bit of a shit. I know I shouldn't have said what I did about you and Nick. But I think I'm right. I think you *do* like him, and he likes you. That's why I said it. That's why I didn't tell you that I'd kissed him when I came to your university. I didn't want you to be jealous. I was trying to make things happen for you. Despite everything, I care about you. You're the only sister I've got.'

'It's all right.' She followed Emma's gaze: the multi-storey car park, the towers of various hospital buildings, the colourless sky. She thought about Dad and Emma and how close they'd been; how betrayed she must have felt when he left and took up with a new family.

'Simon's nice on the surface, but he's not the right one for you. I don't trust him.'

'What do you mean?'

'I was watching him at the party. There was something about his eyes. He creeped me right out.'

'You can't judge someone by their eyes.' But inwardly she faltered. She remembered the dream she'd had, the night they'd first met. There was something about Simon she couldn't put her finger on. Despite all the time they'd spent together, she still wasn't sure she could trust him. Had she been stupid? Reckless? She looked down at Emma, clutching her arm. No, she thought firmly. Simon was a doctor, an upstanding member of the community, and Emma was just jealous.

'Just be careful, that's all. I've made a mess of my life, but I don't want you to do the same with yours. Think about it, won't you? Think about Nick. Even if you reckon I'm just talking nonsense. Promise me, you'll think about him?'

She released herself from Emma's grasp. 'I need a coffee. Want one?'

'Latte, if you're buying.'

Kelda bent down to retrieve her bag. 'And yes, I'll think about Nick.'

She met Mum in the corridor, looking old and worried, wearing a dress Kelda remembered from their childhood, one of the ones she used to drag out for church.

'Kelda, you look tired. Where's Dylan?'

'With a friend.'

Mum threaded her arm through Kelda's. 'What on earth's happened?'

Kelda filled her in as best she could – the sanitised version, not mentioning the drinking or the text messages to Luke or the fact she'd had to ask Emma to leave, only that she'd turned up one day out of the blue, tripped and fallen down the stairs. Mum tutted. 'And I thought she wanted your address to send Dylan a birthday card.' She went on ahead, guessing, no doubt, there was more to the story than Kelda was letting on.

Kelda followed signs to the coffee shop, through a warren of similar-looking corridors. The last time she'd been in a hospital, Dylan had been a few hours old, named after the anaesthetist who'd given the epidural. She'd leaned over the plastic cot and lifted him out, still fast asleep, fists clenched above his head, scared she'd trip over something or he'd lurch from her arms. Instead, he'd blinked awake and she'd stared down at him in wonder, feeling his little legs twist beneath the green blanket, his hands opening and closing, perfectly safe and content. Such a long time ago now, so much had happened. Now, it was hard to think of a time before Dylan.

She bought coffees for the three of them and took them back to the ward. Mum was already there, sitting on the bedside chair, trying to make sense of Emma's medical notes.

'All jargon to me,' she said, closing the file.

Emma was propped upright on the bed, still looking out of the window as Kelda handed round the coffees.

'You'll come home with me,' Mum said. 'I know we haven't always seen eye to eye, but it will be different this time, we're both adults for a start. You can have your old room. I'll get the bed ready. You'll have your own space.'

Emma stared silently at the multi-storey car park, the queue of cars shuffling in and out.

'I'm sure we'll find our way,' Mum continued. 'It won't be for ever, just until you're better, until you've recovered from surgery. And then we can make plans.' She played with her hair as if suddenly conscious of how she looked; how she might appear to the daughter she rarely saw. 'It will be lovely having you back again.'

For a moment, Kelda felt sorry for Mum. All alone in the family home with no one to care for, to clean for.

A nurse pushed through the curtains wheeling a blood-pressure monitor. 'All good,' she said a few minutes later. 'The consultant will want to see you again, but then you can probably go home. You'll be staying with your sister?'

The nurse looked at Kelda who hesitated, unsure what to say. Unsure whether she was expected to rescue Emma again. She remembered when Dylan was born, how Mum had taken it upon herself to organise everything, even from a distance.

Emma pulled her gaze from the window. 'No. I'm staying with Mum.'

Mum beamed. 'She's having her old bedroom. We're going to have a great time, get to know each other again, aren't we?'

The nurse smiled and wheeled the obs machine back through the curtains. 'Great. A bit of TLC and you'll be right as rain.'

Mum stood up. 'Well, I'll leave you girls to chat whilst I use the ladies'.' She said it like they were still teenagers, like they still had their secrets about friends and parties and which boys they liked.

Kelda smiled at Emma when Mum had gone. 'Thanks,' she said. 'It means a lot to Mum, and it won't be for ever.'

Emma grimaced. 'It'll be torture.'

They laughed. For a moment, they really did seem like teenagers again.

'Can you get me some more water?' Emma said, wiping her eyes. 'The coffee's disgusting and all this laughing's making me feel sick.'

'All right. But don't try escaping whilst I'm gone.'

Kelda took the plastic jug from the bedside table and went to the nurses' station. She thought about Simon, how orthopaedics was his specialty, how this must be his ward. Perhaps the nurse would know if he was here?

'Excuse me,' she said, not quite sure whether this was permitted, whether she was overstepping the line. 'I have a friend who works here. Simon Morris. I don't suppose he's on the ward?'

She remembered Simon talking to Emma in the kitchen about his job, explaining all the gory bits. And after what Emma had said about him creeping her out, she needed to see him; she needed to know that Emma was wrong.

The nurse, the same one who had been in to see Emma, shook her head. 'Simon Morris. Don't think I know him.'

'He's a consultant. Orthopaedics.'

The nurse sucked the end of her pen. 'Nope. Can't place the name and I've worked here twenty years. I know the team inside out. You sure you've got the right department?'

'Definitely. Orthopaedics. Apparently, he does all the knees.'

'That'll be Mr Parsons, not Mr Morris. Does Parsons ring a bell?'

Kelda shook her head. She was sure she had the right hospital, the right department, definitely the right name. The nurse must be mistaken. She thanked her anyway and asked for water.

'She'd been drinking, hadn't she?' the nurse said, handing back the refilled jug.

'Yes. It wasn't normal. Not at that time of day, anyway. At least, I don't think so.'

'She was lucky. Really lucky. It could have been far worse, a fall like that. She could have broken her neck.'

Back on the ward, Kelda poured Emma a glass of water. 'Here you go.'

'I've been thinking,' Emma said, cradling the glass in one hand. 'I've been trying to remember what happened before I blacked out, before I fell down the stairs. Everyone thinks I was drunk, that that's how I tripped, but it didn't happen like that.'

Kelda retook her seat on the bed.

'Someone was on the landing,' Emma said. 'Not the woman I'd seen in the long dress. The woman in your bedroom. Someone else.'

'But the house was empty.' Kelda remembered the shadow disappearing beneath Dylan's bedroom door.

'There was a man. I didn't see him. I *felt* him. He was there, at the top of the stairs, on the landing. It felt like he'd been waiting for me all this time, waiting for the right moment when no one else was around. He wanted me out of the way. As if me just leaving wasn't enough. He wanted rid of me, completely. I felt him, not physically, I felt . . . ' Emma pulled a tissue from her jeans and blew her nose, blinking back tears. 'Shit, I don't know what's wrong with me.'

'You felt what?' Kelda pressed.

'I felt the man's sadness. Like all the bad things that had ever happened to him. All the unhappiness he'd ever felt.'

Kelda shuddered, thinking about the night she'd got up to get herself a glass of water, how terrified she'd felt, standing in the middle of the stairs.

'How did you know it was a man if you didn't see him?'

'I don't know.' Emma pushed the tissue back in her pocket. It was only now that Kelda realised Emma was wearing the blue silk top, the one she'd left crumpled on the bedroom floor, beneath a baggy T-shirt. For a split second she saw the lady in blue again from her dream. 'Only I felt it, I felt a male presence. And believe me, I've had enough experience of that in my life.' Emma laughed weakly. 'But this man, this thing. He wasn't . . . ' She fished for the words. 'He wasn't *real*, if that makes any sense?'

Kelda nodded, feeling light-headed. 'What happened after that?'

'I don't know. I was on the edge of the stairs and I knew I had to get away from the man but at the same time, I was held. Like he'd got me trapped. Like I couldn't move my feet. And then suddenly I was falling.'

'You tripped over something?'

'No.' Emma looked at her steadily, soberly. She put the glass down on the table. 'No. I didn't trip. I was pushed. The man pushed me.'

Kelda telephoned Lucy on the way back to the car.

'Everything all right?' Lucy asked, sounding concerned.

'Fine. Emma's going to stay with Mum for a few weeks. She's broken her arm, rather badly.'

They talked about the hospital and Dylan and what he was up to, reading comics and helping Lucy make a chocolate cake.

'Look, I hope you don't mind me saying,' Lucy said as she was about to hang up, 'but you seem a bit stressed. Last night at the party, I was worried about you, you looked exhausted. Lovely with your hair done up and that nice blue top, but exhausted. Of course, it's not my business to say anything and tell me where to go if you like, but I think you need a break.'

'I'm a bit tired, that's all.' Kelda pulled her car keys from her bag. She was in the hospital multi-storey, a spiral of concrete and metal signs.

'It's more than tired, though, isn't it?'

'What do you mean?' She unlocked the car door.

'As I said, it's none of my business, but how about you and Dylan stay with me for the week?'

'Oh, Lucy. That's so kind of you, but really we couldn't.'

'Why not? Mike's away on business and the house is too large for me on my own now the kids have flown the nest. It might not be much of a holiday, but it would be a change of scene, and I promise you, I wouldn't get in your way.'

'But it wouldn't be fair on you. We're not exactly tidy.'

'It would be lovely for me, honestly, and I don't care about the mess. I hate it when Mike goes away, I fall to pieces.' She laughed but Kelda detected an edge of nervousness. Funny, she'd always thought Lucy was so sorted.

'Think about it,' Lucy said. 'I'd love to have Dylan around the place too. He's great fun. Even with cocoa and flour in his hair.'

Kelda promised she'd think about it, just as she'd promised Emma she'd think about Nick, though Nick still hadn't texted her and she couldn't bring herself to text him instead. She put the phone down and drove out of the multi-storey onto the street. *I didn't trip. I was pushed. The man pushed me.*

She couldn't get Emma's voice from her mind, the sincerity behind it. Pushed, it was impossible. Yet was it? She thought of everything that had happened in the toll house over the past few weeks, beginning with the face she'd found in the wall. Things hadn't felt right since. Like someone was watching her, waiting for the right moment, just as Emma had said. But the right moment for what? She wondered if she'd ever felt settled in the house. Hadn't there always been an underlying unease? Wasn't that the reason she hadn't made it their home; hadn't bothered sorting through the junk or unpacking all the stuff pressed on her by Mum; hadn't bothered buying nice things for it? She'd had the sense that it wasn't really hers, though her name was on the deeds, though she'd presumed, until recently, they'd stay there until Dylan was at least in high school. Only the garden had felt like home, the picnic table, the flowerbeds, the apple trees she'd planted.

The apple trees. She pictured them as they'd seemed to her last night, a fan of dark leaves against the old stone wall. Most of the fruit had fallen now and lay rotting on the lawn. However thorough she was, raking the leaves, tossing the apples onto the compost heap, she'd always find more, shiny on the upper side, maggot-ridden underneath. It was like the ground was bad, like the ground was seeping into them.

She was cold. Leaves drifted across the road as she drove. Pedestrians were out in their thick coats and hats. She turned the heating up to maximum, feeling the hot air circulate around the car, fiddling with the vents, angling them down towards her feet. She flicked one the wrong way and blasted hot air in her face. A second later, it was freezing. She fumbled with the vents again, tilting them away from her. Too late.

Freezing cold air in her eyes. And a smell, unmistakable. A smell of lavender.

She felt as if she was suffocating, drowning in the scent.

She slammed on her brakes and sat in the middle of the road, winding down the windows, breathing deeply. Behind her, someone blasted their horn.

She turned off the heating and concentrated. The engine had stalled. She turned the ignition on again and put the car into first gear. The smell had dissipated, just the usual faint smell of strawberry air freshener and dashboard polish.

By the time she reached Stonebridge, she was desperate to get out, to stretch her legs, to stop concentrating on the traffic. She didn't want to go back to the toll house, not yet, and she wanted to mull over Lucy's offer before she went round to fetch Dylan. For a crazy moment, she thought about phoning Simon, seeing if he was free for a coffee. But then she remembered what the nurse had said. Simon Morris didn't work in the hospital, she'd never even heard of him, and she'd worked there twenty years. It was almost as if Kelda had made Simon up, this perfect person with his perfect job and flawless good looks. But of course she hadn't. She'd got the wrong hospital or the wrong department, that was all. Maybe he'd changed his surname on the dating site, didn't want to confuse his professional life with his personal one. There'd be a rational explanation; she'd phone him later, but not now, not until she'd sorted her head.

She parked the car outside the parish church, nothing in mind, just the need to be somewhere, if not quite familiar, then comforting. She didn't attend church regularly anymore, she'd grown out of the habit when she went to university. But there was still something reassuring about the dull grey stone, the weathercock on top of the spire, the angled gravestones. She could still remember the smell of hymn books on Sunday morning, Mum and Dad getting on for a change, parading their daughters in their matching dresses. She walked through the lychgate and tried the door. Locked. A notice pinned above the knocker reported a number of thefts in the area; if she wanted the key, she'd need to call at the vicarage. Instead, she wandered into the graveyard.

The graves were old – there was a cemetery on the outskirts of town for all the new burials – mostly nineteenth century, a few older ones with letters that were impossible to read. She wondered what she was doing here. It wasn't comforting at all, just morbid. After everything that had happened, a graveyard was the last place she needed to be. But she was drawn. There was something here she *had* to see, though she didn't know what or why. Something to do with the smell of lavender in the car.

She closed her eyes, took a deep breath and let it out slowly, letting out everything that had happened. The same dull grey day. The same hum of traffic. She saw an indistinct grave on the north side and knew that's what had drawn her here, a feeling so strong of being pulled, she knew she had no option other than to walk over and read the inscription.

IN LOVING MEMORY OF
ISABELLA WALTON
DIED 28TH AUGUST 1863
AGED THIRTY-FOUR

The grave was the same as all the others, but she knew the name instantly, knew why she'd been called here. The name of the toll keeper's wife. In a pot, in front of the grave, was a glass jar with a handful of lavender sprigs, and around it a perfect circle of white pebbles. She bent down and picked one up and held it in the palm of her hand.

'What do you want? What the hell do you want from me?'

No answer. The graveyard was silent. Only the traffic on the High Street and a plane flying low overhead. Yet, everything suddenly seemed terrifyingly real. Not just her imagination. Not just stress from her job. Of all the graves she could have walked to, she'd chosen this one. Or rather, the grave had chosen her. Isabella Walton had chosen her. And the lavender and the pebbles were to do with Isabella. Not Helen Drake. Not Joseph the toll house keeper. Not Dylan playing a silly game.

Isabella. *Bella*, the name in red on the wall.

Her fingers trembled as they closed around the pebble. She wished she'd never come, wished she'd never got out of the car, wished she'd driven straight to Lucy's and told her she was coming over and that she and Dylan would stay the week after all.

She pulled her phone from her pocket and dialled Lucy's number, trying to ignore the smell, the smell that was now more pronounced than ever, here in the graveyard.

'Lucy, is that you? It's Kelda.'

'Kelda. Everything all right?'

'Fine.' Kelda hurried back to the car. 'Just ringing to say thank you for the offer and, yes, we'll stay for the week if that's still okay with you?'

'Of course. It will be lovely.'

'I need to go home first to get our things.'

'Okay, take your time. We're fine here, aren't we, Dylan? We're doing some painting.'

She heard Dylan in the background, shouting some message she couldn't quite hear.

'Tell him I love him,' said Kelda. 'I'll be over as soon as I can. As soon as I've been back to the toll house.'

30

⤫

1864

As soon as I'm able, I leave the turnpike and walk to the back of the toll house. It's a grey soulless day, cold even for the time of year. I hug myself in my jacket and breathe warmth into my hands. I'm exhausted – I haven't slept since the night before last and I feel ill with a fever – but I know I should be alert, that the danger may be yet to come.

As soon as I see the ground behind the wall, I realise my mistake. The ground dips around the lip of the grave. I observe it from different angles, walking this way and that, hoping I am wrong – that it is just the sleepiness in my eyes – but the more I look at it, the more I realise it is true. I stamp the ground with my boots, trying to smooth it out, to make the lip less pronounced. At least the grave lies in the shadow of the apple trees. I can see no reason for anyone to come this way, save to pilfer apples later in the year. Even then, there are better pickings in town.

I look down at my footprints and curse my stupidity. I shouldn't be out here. I should leave things be. Why draw attention to the very thing I am trying to hide?

Back at the turnpike, I find a cart driver nodding over his mule. He's drunk though it is not even midday, his cheeks flushed with wine. The same cart driver who passed this way at first light. He tells me in muffled tones that he has been to the market; his cart is loaded with empty baskets and it is evident from the drink in his belly that his morning's been profitable. He lingers by the turnpike, his mule impatient, snorting and tossing its head. I humour him awhile, pretending to listen to his tales, his breath foul and thick with drink. Obviously, he is in no hurry. He lifts a flagon from beneath his seat, pulls out the stopper and gulps loudly, before swinging it in my direction.

'No, thank you,' I say curtly. 'You'd best be on your way. They say the weather is taking a turn for the worse.'

He snorts into his sleeve as though he doesn't quite believe me. As though he knows something else is afoot. Panic wraps around me and I force it away, force myself to breathe more evenly. My secret is safe. It's just the lack of sleep making me imagine things.

'Good day to you,' I say, turning back to the porch, wondering how many others I will need to please before the day is out.

I watch him go, nodding in rhythm with his mule. When the road is completely quiet, I set about the task that's been plaguing me all day. I take a rag and a bowl of water to the upstairs room. The blood has dried to a reddish brown over the floorboards and walls. I dip the rag in the water and get to work, scrubbing hard, over and over, removing a layer of paint as I go. I take the bowl to the kitchen and pour the sordid liquid out of the window, before refilling it from the jug and taking a block of soap from the pantry. I remember Bella scrubbing the kitchen, humming to herself as she worked. I remember the smell, sharp as lemons; Bella used to soak her cloths in vinegar. I hunt amongst the shelves until I find a dusty bottle and lift it down. The smell, when I open it, reminds me of the spring, of insects humming above the flowerbeds and fresh linen flapping on the line.

I've a sudden image of Bella in the garden, hanging out the laundry. Hanging out her monthly rags, pegging them discreetly beneath the bed sheets. I see her opening the earthenware jar where she keeps the pebbles, taking one in her hand and passing it over her empty womb.

The memory dazzles me. I stagger from the pantry. Everything seems brighter, almost blinding: the red of the kitchen tiles, the white of the basin, the silver of the sky outside. I look for any sign of her, any pebbles, but there is nothing. No pebbles either beside the mask upstairs. There's a stillness in the house that I've only just realised. Pain claws my stomach, my bones feel like chunks of ice. I feel alone, truly alone, for the first time since she died.

Oh, Bella, do not desert me now!

As if in answer, a single white pebble rolls from beneath the mask, across the bedside table and onto the floor, stopping at my feet. I pick it up, shaking, and press it to my lips, but it is hard and unfriendly. A remonstration rather than a comfort. I put it in my mouth, willing it to soften, to crumble into chalk, but it is as cold and unyielding as marble.

I resume my gruesome work, scrubbing with the soap and

vinegar until my hands are raw. I stand back. My head throbs with lack of sleep and makes me giddy but there is no longer any sign of what occurred here last night. I pour the last of the bloodied water out of the kitchen window, then push the sordid cloths into the oven with the blood-stained shirt.

That night, I doze upright in the settle. A fitful, feverish sleep full of dreams: the woman in the blue dress; the man with his smashed-in skull, lying out in the rain, blood running from the hole in his head like a river; the cart driver nodding over his flagon of wine.

A noise rouses me from my slumber. I blink into daylight and stand, stretching, aching from my restless night. At the same time, there is knocking at the front door. Immediately, I am on my guard. Has someone found me out?

I tell myself not to panic; it is just someone come to pay their toll, to request that I open the gate. But as I turn the key in the front door, hearing it clunk in the lock, I am breathing hard.

'Who is it?' I say.

Outside, peering up at me from beneath a huge black umbrella, is Helen. She sweeps around me without a word, into the house, her eyes as bright, as watchful as lanterns.

31

⎯⎯∞⎯⎯

NOW

K elda didn't want to go back now that she'd made the decision to leave. The toll house looked grey and ominous from the road. She parked where she always did, outside the bay window, beneath the sign that notified travellers of the toll, and sat in the car, making a list of stuff she needed in her head; she'd go in, grab a few things, get out as fast as she could. You can do this, she told herself sternly. It's no big deal. It's only been a few hours.

She left the gate open, walked quickly through the garden and unlocked the back door. The house smelled unloved, though she'd spent the last week cleaning it. A smell of damp and dust and washing that had sat too long in the machine. And mice. She glanced at the traps. Still empty, just a couple of droppings near the range, as though the mice were playing games with her. The work surface was still cluttered with glasses and plates from the night before, and Emma's holdall was still on the kitchen table, beneath the gash in the wall. Beside it was Dylan's mound of artwork. She halted at the sight of his latest drawing, the one she'd only glanced at yesterday, pulling it from his school bag: Kelda in a long dress, with flowers tied to her waist. Except it wasn't Kelda at all. A round face, with large round eyes, and long black hair down to her knees. It could have been anyone, except she knew it wasn't.

She was wearing a dress ... it had flowers hanging from it ...

She looked at the drawing beneath it, something else he'd done at school. The same woman, the same big eyes, the same purple flowers. Only this time, there was someone else next to her. A man, much taller than the woman, in a long dark jacket. A blank face apart from two black eyes staring out of the paper. Sweat pricked her forehead. Something about the man wasn't right, the way Dylan had drawn the eyes. The woman had pupils set within the whites of her eyes, whereas the man had two black holes.

She put the painting down and hurried to the stairs, pausing in the place she'd found Emma. No sign of the accident, just the brown carpet with its hideous swirls and the empty staircase and the wallpaper with the little blue cornflowers.

I didn't trip. I was pushed. The man pushed me.

She took a deep breath. She had to go up the stairs. She had to walk across the gallery landing. She needed to get clothes from her wardrobe and school clothes for Dylan. She had to go into the bathroom and get their toothbrushes and toothpaste and her make-up bag.

She ran, conscious of the sound of her feet on the stairs, every creak and sigh, then along the length of the landing and into her bedroom. Her jewellery box lay open on the bed where Emma had left it, beads strewn across the duvet. She bent beneath the bed and pulled out a suitcase, throwing it on top of the beads. Then she yanked open the wardrobe door and bundled a few work tops and trousers into the suitcase along with a fistful of underwear. She hurried along the landing to the bathroom next door, dragging the suitcase behind her, hearing the rattle of wheels on the carpet, then back in the direction of Dylan's bedroom. The door was still closed, just as she'd seen it earlier when she'd been waiting for the ambulance. She remembered the shadow across the bookcase, the way it had disappeared beneath the door. She wished she had something to hold on to other than the suitcase, some weapon to protect herself; at the same time, the threat didn't feel earthly. It was just as Emma had said: *He wasn't* real, *if that makes any sense?*

She grabbed the door handle and threw it open. The light settled on the remains of a game Dylan and Georgie and Ethan had been playing during the party, a tower of Lego, toy cars piled one on top of the other. The lava lamp had been left on, but apart from that, the room was still. Eerily still. Dust motes hovered in the air and the curtains hung unmoving in the semi-opened window. It was like a room that hadn't been lived in for a very long time.

She moved slowly, as though she feared disturbing something, as she gathered Dylan's school uniform and clothes from the wardrobe. She reached under his bed and pulled out his Batman trainers, catching sight of the microphone but leaving it there. Then she turned to the bookcase and selected a few books for his bedtime story. Something caught her attention on the shelf below: a collection of small white bones, the ones she'd seen before in the plastic container, that Dylan had taken into school for show and tell. Only this time, he'd lined them up: four small bones that fitted neatly together, one on top of the other, gradually getting thinner. She felt her mouth running dry as she glanced across at his blow-up skeleton. Not a fox or a dog as Mr Yeo had suggested. The bones looked just like a human finger. Quickly, she took a photo with her phone, then pulled the suitcase back along the landing and towards the stairs. Despite the impulse to get away, she felt exhausted, barely able to move; that unnerving sadness that didn't belong to her, that belonged to someone else, some other time. She felt like she was sleepwalking, like she couldn't wake up properly, like it was happening to someone else.

I felt the man's sadness. Like all the bad things that had ever happened to him. All the unhappiness he'd ever felt.

She stood still in the middle of the landing. A feeling like she was being held by invisible hands, like someone didn't want her to leave. Then, she jerked herself into action. She had to get out of here, away from those bones and whatever else was in the house. She had to get back to Dylan. She wouldn't be the next victim. Not like Emma. Not like Helen Drake. She ran down the stairs, the suitcase bumping the steps behind her, awkwardly, dangerously, then yanked it through the kitchen to the back door, catching the wheels on the table legs, wrenching off one of the little rubber rings.

Outside, she drank in the chill autumn air. The garden was still set up for the party, the bunting and fairy lights sagging between the trees, wine bottles huddled on the table. She thought of last night, Mrs Watts talking to Simon beside the apple trees, clutching her wine glass as her heels sank into the lawn. She remembered the look on her face, the look on *his* face. She'd not understood it at the time, it had just seemed so strange, the two of them together, the two most dissimilar people in the world deep in conversation. She tried to shrug it from her mind, but it held her like a vice: Simon had looked like a guilty man. She stared at the dip in the lawn where they'd stood, sloping towards the wall, going beneath it, like something was pulling the grass down on the other side. The dip was worse today, unmistakable, like the ground was trying to tell her something.

She shoved the suitcase in the boot of the car, then walked around the back of the toll house, along the outside perimeter. Behind the garden was the field and a little footpath leading to the wood. The field had recently been harvested and, with the recent rain, the ground was a mud bath. She followed the garden wall, careful not to slip, until she came to the apple trees just showing above the other side.

The ground was sunken. No mud, just a bare patch of grass. She must have explored here before but not noticed it or not remembered. She walked over the uneven ground, unsure what she was doing, thinking about Dylan and the bones on his bedroom shelf. Wasn't this where he'd found them, that day she'd been gardening and he'd gone around the back to investigate the wall? Something caught her eye. She toyed with it with her foot, turning it over and over. A single dirt-encrusted bone just like the others. She fished for her phone, thinking she could ask Simon. Whatever her doubts about him, he'd know, wouldn't he? An orthopaedic surgeon would know immediately what they were.

She checked her text messages – no response from the one she'd sent him earlier – and dialled his number. Immediately, it diverted to a pre-recorded message:

'This number is no longer is use.'

She tried again, thinking there must be a mistake or she'd pressed the wrong button, but again the same message, the same generic woman's voice informing her the phone number didn't exist. She thought of Simon the night she'd found him in the pub with his book, telling her about the day he'd had, the patient he'd lost, the child. *It happens sometimes*, he'd said; *we deal with a lot of complex cases.* She thought of the nurse sucking the end of her pen, insisting there was no Simon Morris at the hospital. She thought of Emma and the way Simon freaked her out, something about his eyes.

She left the bone where it was and ran to the car, driving as fast as she could back into town. It was late afternoon, getting dark already, the sky clouding over. The traffic was heavy, people finishing their shopping or picking their kids up from sports clubs. She sat at the traffic lights, inching forwards, impatient. On the opposite side of the road was a stretch of alms houses converted into retirement homes, the place where the old owner had moved when his wife died.

When the traffic lights changed to green, she turned right rather than straight on to Lucy's and parked round the back. There were nine alms houses altogether and another modern bungalow connected by glass walls and labelled WARDEN'S HOUSE. Before she could question herself, she rang the doorbell.

'Hello.' A smartly dressed woman opened the door and smiled. 'How can I help you?'

Kelda glanced at the alms houses. 'Sorry to bother you, but I'm looking for the person who used to live in the toll house.'

'The toll house?'

'On the Old Turnpike Road.'

The woman smiled kindly. 'Do you have a name?'

Her mind went blank as she tried to picture the paperwork.

'I'm afraid not, only that he moved to one of the retirement homes when his wife died. I'm the new owner and I was looking into the history of the place and thought he might be able to help me.'

The woman drew a scrap of paper and a pen from her pocket. 'I'm the warden. I can ask around if you like?'

'Thanks. That would be really helpful.' And then she remembered. 'Pritchard. Mr Pritchard, that's the name.'

The woman smiled. 'I think I can help you out on that one. Let me take your phone number.'

She let herself unwind, huddled in a blanket in Lucy's conservatory, thinking she should say no to the wine Lucy was uncorking but knowing she wouldn't. Dylan was already asleep, excited about his new room, content to sleep on his own for the first time in days. She knew Lucy was happy for her to sit, to drift with her own thoughts, without the obligation of talking, but she remembered what the lady had said at the relaxation class. Sometimes it helps to tell the story. And so she began, telling Lucy how she'd found the mask hidden in the walls, then everything that had happened since. Lucy sat patiently, handing her a glass of wine, not interrupting.

'You must think I'm mad,' she said when she'd finished.

Lucy shook her head. 'Despite what people think, I'm not a complete sceptic. It's all an act, anyway.'

'What is?'

'My happy-go-lucky attitude. Before I met Mike I was a complete mess. It's only Mike holding me together.'

'You're not a mess. You're one of the most sane people I know. You've brought up four successful children. You're—'

Lucy held out a hand, stopping her. 'Something happened to me, a long time ago.' She poured herself a large glass of wine and settled back in the sofa. 'Before I met Mike I was living in student digs. Turns out it was the site of an old children's home. There'd been a terrible fire there in the 1950s and, one night, I dreamed it.'

'What do you mean?'

'I dreamed of the fire. I dreamed of the children screaming and burning to death.'

'Oh God, that's horrible.'

'It got worse. Every night, I'd dream exactly the same dream except in more and more detail. I'd see the faces of those poor children. I'd see—' She broke off and wiped the corners of her eyes. 'Anyway, you don't want to hear all that. The point is, I couldn't find a way out. I couldn't get my money back from the landlord and my parents didn't believe me, they thought I must have read about the fire before dreaming it, though I swear I hadn't. I didn't even know it had been a children's home until afterwards. My parents said it was my overactive imagination.' She played with the tassels on her throw. 'I should have known there was something wrong with the place when I first moved in.'

'Why?'

'Because of the lights. They'd switch themselves on and off, sometimes flickering for hours. Sometimes the TV and cooker refused to work. I got the landlord to get an electrician in to check it all out, but he couldn't find anything wrong.'

Kelda thought of Dylan's lava lamp and the television and the way her phone had drained of battery in the dark.

'Some people believe that ghosts mess with electromagnetic fields, taking energy from things like TVs to . . .' Lucy laughed, though she sounded deadly serious, 'to power themselves up. Of course, a lot of other people, like my parents, think that's complete rubbish. But Mike believed me. Mike was just a friend back then and he let me stay at his, in a sleeping bag on the floor. He looked after me. I used to wake up every night, screaming, for months.'

'I'm so sorry. I had no idea.'

'Why would you? It was years ago. I hardly think about it anymore. I'm only telling you because I'm scared for you, scared of you going back to the toll house. I don't believe things just stop because time's moved on. Some things remain. Sometimes terrible things happen and they stay there. You said there'd been a murder. Well, what if the murderer's still there?'

'You mean . . . ?'

'Joseph Walton. The man they hanged in 1864. I don't believe people just disappear because they're dead. Energy has to go somewhere.'

Kelda pulled the blanket around her shoulders, thinking of Dylan's painting: the man with black eyes. It made sense what Lucy was saying, but at the same time, it was impossible. 'What about the woman? The woman who told Dylan to get out of the house?'

Lucy sipped her wine. 'I'm no expert, but it sounds to me as though she's a different case altogether. She's warning you away. She's trying to tell you to get away from the toll house. She knows what the man is capable of.'

That night, she lay awake in one of Lucy's spare bedrooms with the wine humming through her veins, surrounded by the smell of clean sheets. Whatever doubts she'd had about the toll house,

Lucy had sealed them. She'd only go back to get their things and tidy the place up, then she'd put the house on the market and rent somewhere else. Financially it would be a struggle, but somehow she'd make it work, she'd take on a Saturday job whilst Dylan went to football and out with friends, and, as a last resort, she'd ask Mum for help. It wouldn't be for ever, just until she sold the place. And then she'd be free of it.

She closed her eyes and huddled down in the duvet, her heartbeat slowing. It was going to be all right. She wasn't going back. She'd put the whole episode behind her just as Lucy had done with the children's home. Somehow they'd come out of this stronger.

She turned on her side and tried to believe it as the rain pattered lightly on the skylight.

32

✧

1864

Helen sweeps around me without a word, out of the rain and into the toll house. I follow, watching as she unpacks her basket on the kitchen table, the usual offerings of meat and bread. Then she sets to work, tying an apron around her waist and pouring water from a jug into a basin.

'Really, there is no need,' I protest, knowing she is intent on her industry whatever I say.

She takes no heed and surveys the dirty dishes, the knives and forks abandoned on the table, the half-drunk mugs of beer. Her disgust is palpable. She sweeps a hand across the window ledge and tuts. 'Have you no traps?'

'Traps?'

'For the mice?'

I walk away from her in the direction of the porch. The mice are my sole companions. They alone know my secret. If they are to die, they will do so at my hands, not Helen's.

'What use have I of traps?' I say.

I leave Helen searching the pantry shelves and stand outside, watching the road. Silent today. No carriages. No carts. Just the gentle drum of rain on dirt. The cold wraps around me like a second skin. I am numb, only half conscious, uncaring of Helen in the house or the wind in the trees or the rain dripping over the roof of the porch.

Eventually, I turn inside to fetch my jacket. Helen hums to herself in the kitchen and clatters about with pans and brushes. I cannot bear her devotion, her happiness. I cannot stand to listen to it. I catch one of the traps she's laid by the range with my boot, sending it skittering across the tiles, but she pretends not to notice.

Upstairs, I pull on an old jacket belonging to my father and a pair of fingerless gloves unravelling at the cuffs. I stare at the mirror above the dresser, barely recognising myself. My hair is long and thin, my beard straggly, my eyes sunk like two hollows. I look far older than my thirty-one years. I run my hands over my head, pulling out strands of hair, weaving them between the tips of my fingers. There's comfort in the feel of it tightening against my scalp, the tingle of pain as it yields. Over and over, until there is a neat ball of hair in my glove.

I become aware of something behind me in the mirror. Helen in the doorway as rigid as stone. I turn, about to remonstrate, to demand that she leaves me be, when something catches my eye. Something Helen is holding.

She says nothing, just lifts it up for me to see. Soiled rags. A blood-stained shirt.

'I found these in the oven,' she says, her voice quivering, the lightness from earlier gone. 'I wasn't sure what to do. I didn't know whether to . . . ' Her voice fades to nothing. She stares at me, right in my eyes, as if she knows everything. As if she can see what happened that night.

'Joseph?' she asks, begging me to tell her otherwise, to contradict her.

I stride across the floorboards and lift the soiled rags from her hands, bundling them beneath my arm, inwardly cursing my stupidity – I'd meant to burn them, but I'd been so weary, I'd forgotten – then crossing the landing to the stairs.

'What have you done?' she whispers, following. 'Joseph, what have you done?'

'It is nothing,' I say, knowing how unconvincing I sound. Knowing that she sees through me. I halt, hand on the banister. 'I hurt myself, that is all.'

'But so much blood.'

'I said, it is nothing.'

'How . . . how did it happen? You must have hurt yourself badly.'

I spin around to face her, feeling for the jack knife in my pocket.

'Are you still hurt? Do you need to see a doctor? I will fetch Dr Marsh.'

'No. Not the doctor.'

'Joseph. He is a good man. We have an understanding. He will not charge you a penny if I speak to him.'

'An understanding?'

There's a tell-tale rose in her cheeks. 'I wanted to tell you before.' She blushes fiercely. 'But he insisted we keep it quiet. We are soon to be married.'

She bends to pick up one of the cloths that has fallen from

my arm. One of the cloths I used to scrub the walls. Her words sting in my head. Married. To that man! I think of all the times she's been here, her meddling, her judgement, carrying out the doctor's bidding.

'We must bathe the wound ...' she says, examining the cloth. 'The doctor has instructed me in the basics of medicine.'

She traces the stains with her fingers, realisation darkening her features.

'Joseph?' She looks up at me, pleading for whatever horrors she imagines not to be true. I flick the knife from its handle.

Then she turns away, as if she cannot bear the sight of me.

Everything swims. I step forwards, my heart thudding wildly, and plunge the knife deep between her shoulder blades.

She staggers to the wall, then back towards me, stumbling on the rag-rug, unable to control her feet. There's a strange rattling sound from her throat. I pull the knife from her back, then stab again. Her knees buckle, then miraculously right themselves. I grab the knife where it's fallen on the rug and jab it through her dress, again and again. She lurches forwards, reaching the top of the stairs, gripping the banister where I've stepped aside, her knuckles white. With one final effort, she pulls herself up to face me, the knife still sticking out of her back. Pale eyes like a maimed animal, clouding over. But there is something else. Something beyond the pain: a look of determination. She will not let this happen, not to her.

She opens her mouth to speak, but blood bubbles out. It's so easy. *Too* easy. All I need is to give her a gentle nudge. She topples sideways, knocking against the banister as she falls.

I stare at the body at the foot of the stairs, the knife crushed between her shoulder blades, her legs stuck out like pins beneath her skirt. It's completely quiet. No moaning, no death throes. I get to work, grabbing the cloths and the shirt dropped on the landing, running down the stairs, over Helen, uncaring if she is dead or alive, through the kitchen and into the garden.

The rain has stopped. Milky sunlight slopes over the wall. A pale rainbow hovers distantly beyond the fields. I walk to the apple trees and bundle the stained rags into a nook in the wall. Then I wipe my gloved hands down my trousers and turn back to the toll house.

Inside, a breeze slices through the kitchen and I realise the front door is open as well as the back. I hurry to close it, thinking how I must have left it that way when I came in for the jacket. But then I see something else in the hallway. *Someone* else. Mr Turnbill, one of the turnpike trustees, is standing just inside the doorway, leaning over Helen, his face contorted with understanding. I turn and stagger back the way I've come. I need to get out. I need to get to the fields. I need to run. But he is quicker than me, nimble despite his portly frame, and I've grown weak of late, much weaker than I'd realised. He grabs me by the throat and thrusts me face down over the kitchen table, sending the food Helen left out for me flying to the floor, grappling with my arms, twisting them together. I cry out in pain.

'You brute,' he snarls, flecking spittle on my neck. 'What has happened here? What has happened?'

'I . . .'

He bashes my head hard against the table, then fumbles with something behind my back.

'They said you were gone to the devil,' he says, binding my arms with his belt. 'And they were right.'

He forces me upwards then pushes me back through the kitchen, past the body at the bottom of the stairs, to the cellar doorway at the far end. I kick out as the leather of his belt cuts into my wrists.

'You brute,' he hisses again, when I catch him. He forces my head beneath the doorway and shoves me inside. I fall to my knees, feeling the ridge of the topmost stair, knowing there is no way out other than the door by which I entered.

'I'll be back,' Mr Turnbill growls, 'with the constable.' He closes the door and turns the key in the lock.

It's dark. Midnight dark. I hear Mr Turnbill's footsteps along the corridor followed by the closing of the front door. It won't be long before they come for me. I twist my wrists one way then the other, rubbing them raw in my attempt to free myself. The belt digs harder. Firmer. The pain becomes unbearable. I lie on one side, with my face to the step, breathing in the dust and cobwebs and hearing the scrabble of mice, waiting for a sign, waiting for the feel of a white pebble in my hands, waiting for the comforting smell of lavender. But there is nothing. Nothing.

33

NOW

'Thank you so much for agreeing to meet me.'

Kelda stood in the foyer, a square of glass and concrete connecting the warden's bungalow to the alms houses. Heat was pumping from the radiators and she felt hot and uncomfortable. She took off her coat and looped it over her arm, looking for somewhere to place it.

Behind her, the warden busied herself with a bundle of keys on the desk. 'Shall I leave you to it?' she said. 'You can either sit here, or, if Mr Pritchard prefers, you can use his living room.'

Mr Pritchard planted himself in one of the armchairs. 'Here will do just fine.'

'Great.' The warden gathered her keys. 'If you need anything,' she looked at Kelda, 'I'll be in the warden's bungalow.'

'Thank you.'

Kelda took a seat opposite Mr Pritchard, resting her coat over her knees. She'd had a phone call that morning. Mr Pritchard, who had lived in the toll house between 1952 and 2014, was willing to meet her, briefly, at lunchtime.

'Thank you,' she said again. 'I really appreciate your time.'

Mr Pritchard stared at his tea-stained slippers. 'What's this about then? Something wrong with the house?'

'Something wrong? No, not exactly.'

'Sold as seen.'

'Of course.' She cleared her throat. 'This isn't about the state of the property.'

'Oh. What then?'

She wished she'd started somewhere else, made some comment about the weather or asked him about the alms houses or whether he'd always lived in Stonebridge, but it was too late now. She had half an hour before she was expected back at the office. Cassandra was already in a foul mood; next week it was half term, which meant a rush of last-minute jobs before she took the twins to Disneyland.

'I was researching the history of the toll house,' she said. 'I wondered whether you knew anything about it, about the people who lived there in the old days?'

'Oh, you're on to that.' Mr Pritchard flicked crumbs from his sweater onto the floor.

'If you can tell me anything, I'd be grateful.'

He folded his arms across his chest. 'Well, I suppose you've bought the place now, so there's no point in hiding it. Had a hell of a job, I did, trying to sell.'

'I'm sorry, I don't understand.'

'The murder in the Victorian times. Expect that's why you're here? Turns out people are superstitious. Don't want to buy a place that's had any sort of trouble. In the end I had to ask the local history society to take the information down.'

She thought of the blank page she'd found on the website and forced herself to smile. 'I guess, I was just after anything that might explain . . . ' she took a deep breath, she may as well say it, 'anything that might explain the sense there's someone else there. Someone watching me. A presence on the landing and in the little bedroom.'

Mr Pritchard dug his chin into his sweater. She wondered if he'd even heard her. In the background she heard the blare of someone's TV, the opening and closing of a door. She glanced at her watch. She ought to hurry, grab some lunch to eat at her desk.

'That was Glenys's room,' he said.

'Glenys?'

'Our daughter. She died.' He coughed into his fist and she saw his wedding ring, cutting into his finger.

'I'm sorry,' she said, wondering if she should carry on.

He shook his head. 'It was a long time ago. Time doesn't change what happened, but it dulls the pain. Go on, ask me whatever you like.'

She took a deep breath. 'Did Glenys ever talk to you about the room? Did she ever feel anything in there? Anything odd?'

Mr Pritchard lifted his head and looked her in the eye. 'She wouldn't sleep there when she was little. Always crawling into our bed in the middle of the night. My wife, Ellen, was too soft. We didn't have central heating back then, not like nowadays. I suppose Glennie was cold.'

'Cold?'

'Of course, it all changed when she was a teenager. Teenage girls want their own space. They don't think they need their parents anymore.'

She thought of Dylan asleep in her bed, curled like a cat beneath the covers.

'She died when she was sixteen. Fell down the stairs. We were out in the garden and she must have tripped. Ellen found her when she went back in. She died in hospital.'

A finger of cold snaked its way down Kelda's back.

'It was hard after that. I was working long hours at the quarry and Ellen was scared staying in the house on her own. There was a face on the wall. A plaster face.'

'The death mask?'

'That's right, or something like that.' He coughed again, banging his chest with his fist. 'She became convinced the mask was watching her. So I boarded it up.'

'It was you who made the cavity wall?'

He nodded. 'Ellen wanted me to hack the face off completely, but it didn't seem right. It was part of the building's history. I suppose it was something to do with the murder.'

'Did you ever find out whose face it was?'

Mr Pritchard shook his head. 'Ellen felt better after I made the new wall. I wanted to move from the toll house altogether seeing she wasn't happy there, but she insisted we stay, said it was Glennie's home. I don't think she ever got over Glenys's death. But when Ellen died, there didn't seem much point staying in the toll house. I was finding it hard climbing the stairs, my lungs aren't as young as they were, and I needed company. I didn't want to grow old there by myself.'

'So, you moved here?'

'That's right. Got my own bungalow and a warden if I need anything. People to talk to if I want.'

Kelda looked out of the window. A couple of pensioners were

sitting on garden chairs, blankets over their knees, reading the newspapers.

'Do you know about the grave in the churchyard? The toll keeper's wife, Isabella Walton?'

Mr Pritchard played with his wedding ring. 'So, you're on to that as well?'

'I found myself there one day.' She hesitated, wondering whether to go on or not. But the clock was ticking, her lunchtime was almost up; she might only get this one chance. 'It felt like I was being called.'

Mr Pritchard folded his arms. 'Ellen used to leave flowers at the grave. She said she could smell them in the cottage. She thought Isabella was trying to communicate with her.' He laughed like the whole thing was ludicrous. 'Poor Ellen. Lost her mind in the end. She became absolutely convinced about Bella. When she got too poorly to walk, she made me visit the graveyard myself.'

'It's you who leaves the lavender in the glass jar?'

Mr Pritchard smiled and she wondered what he really thought, whether he really thought Ellen had lost her mind.

'It's my way of keeping Ellen alive. Seems strange, doesn't it? Placing flowers on another woman's grave? But it's what Ellen would have wanted.'

'And the pebbles? The white pebbles?'

'That's what Ellen used to say. Always going on about the pebbles. She said they were for protection, like a charm or a symbol. They made her feel safe. Before she got ill, she did some research in the library, read up about the Victorians. They were obsessed with stuff like that, magic and charms and whatnot. White meant purity. Stone meant strength. Then there was the lavender. The Victorians thought flowers had a language of their own. According to Ellen's books, lavender was a sign of distrust. She became convinced Bella was using it as a warning, telling her not to trust the house, to stay on her guard.' Mr Pritchard shook his head. 'Sounded like a lot of hocus pocus to me. But you women are different, aren't you? You believe things.'

She sat at the traffic lights, willing them to change, foot hovering above the accelerator. Cassandra would be watching the office clock, expecting Kelda to return any minute. She'd have to skip lunch, eat biscuits at her desk. In the end, she'd spent far too long talking to Mr Pritchard. He'd not wanted her to leave, telling her about his life before he came to Stonebridge, his childhood before the war. She supposed he was lonely, even in the centre of town, even living in the alms houses; still missing his wife.

The lights turned to amber. She glanced at the line of shops on her right, tapping her thumbs on the steering wheel.

Simon was coming out of the bookshop. Simon with a bag tucked under his arm, striding in the direction of the river.

The car behind her beeped, forcing her to move. She jumped through the lights, swerving right into a side street, and parked on double yellow lines. She locked the car, tugging her coat on as she ran. The High Street was bursting with people, blocking her view. She weaved between the office workers sipping coffee from plastic cups, eating sandwiches, talking, laughing, passing the time of day. She realised she'd lost him. Or maybe she'd been mistaken and it had been someone else. Someone who looked like Simon from a distance but wasn't. She slowed her walk. Now that she was here, she may as well buy lunch.

She opened the door to the sandwich shop.

Simon was in the queue. She saw his duffle coat buttoned to the neck, a pair of well-cut jeans. Definitely Simon. He turned as if he sensed her. A moment later, he was pushing past her, through the door, mumbling his apology to the other customers.

She ran back onto the street, shouting at him to stop.

'Simon, it's me!'

He increased his step, disappearing amongst the shoppers. She knocked into someone and apologised, helping them pick up a bag from the pavement. When she looked up again, Simon had vanished.

She consulted her watch. She should be at her desk by now, she should be ploughing through Cassandra's diary and making phone calls. But to hell with Cassandra.

She ran along the edge of the road, skirting the pedestrians on the pavement. A car sounded its horn as the traffic swerved around her, but she didn't care. She wouldn't let him get away, not this time. She stopped for a moment to catch her breath, scanning the road. Simon was striding ahead, the blue haze of his duffle coat disappearing down a side street.

She ran to catch him. The side street was empty apart from Simon, a single narrow road near the river, with tall, red-bricked residential buildings. The expensive area of town. Most people would be out at work, she thought, seeing the empty driveways and parking spaces. Simon looked over his shoulder and broke into a run. He was so tall, such long legs, there was no way she could catch him. She felt a stitch jabbing her side, forcing her to slow. At the same time, the bag he was carrying broke. Books slipped through the plastic and cascaded onto the pavement, one or two splashing into a puddle. He hesitated, before turning around.

'Simon!'

She knew she should let him go, but she couldn't. She had to know why he was trying to get away from her, why the nurse had known nothing about him, why his phone number was no longer in use. It was like he didn't exist, like she'd dreamed him up, like he was a shadow rather than a real person, and yet here he was in front of her, grappling for the books on the pavement.

She ran the last few metres. 'Simon!'

He froze like a hunted animal, a couple of books in his arms. 'You can't just run away from me.'

He left the rest of the books where they were and stood up. His hair was a mess, all over his face, not the immaculate Simon she was used to seeing, who'd stood beside her at the party, arm curled around her waist. It occurred to her she hardly knew him. She regretted being here, regretted being alone in this deserted street with the vacant driveways. She clasped her car keys in her pocket.

'I tried to phone you,' she said, her voice shaking. 'But your number wasn't recognised. And then I asked about you in the hospital.'

'In the hospital?' His face drained of colour.

'Emma broke her arm. I asked the nurse. She said she didn't know who you were.'

A book slid from his arms and joined the others in the puddle. 'Oh God.' He leaned against the garden wall behind him.

'I don't know what to think,' she said. 'It's like I made you up, a figment of my imagination. Except you're standing here in front of me.' She thought of the toll house, the feeling of some-one else there, the person Emma had felt on the stairs. The man.

Tears crowded her eyes. 'Who are you? Who the hell are you?'

He stepped towards her.

'Keep away from me.' She was trembling; she hadn't realised she was so afraid. She remembered Emma's words: *he creeped me right out.* 'I don't know who you are. I don't understand . . .'

He put the books down on the wall and fumbled for something in his pocket. For a horrible moment, she expected him to reveal a weapon, a knife or something worse. She felt waves of dizzying panic. But instead, he pulled out an identity card. An NHS staff card with his photograph and name: Mr Simon Morris, orthopaedic consultant.

'I am who I say I am,' he said, still holding out the card. 'It's just I haven't been exactly truthful about everything else.' He put the card away and sat down on the wall, staring at his ruined books.

'What do you mean?'

He took a deep breath. 'I really do work in a hospital. Or, at least, I did. I worked at a hospital south of London for ten years. I was good at my job, well respected. But then,' he swallowed hard, 'then, I lost a patient.' He hung his head, his dark hair flopping forwards, obscuring his eyes.

'I'm sorry,' she said, unsure what else to say.

He waved away her sympathy. 'There was a series of issues – hospital politics and stuff like that, a colleague seemed to have it in for me, making trouble for no reason. And then I made a fatal error. It was six o'clock in the morning, emergency surgery. A road traffic accident. The patient, a little boy, died. I was tired, over-worked. It was the end of a very long night shift, I shouldn't even have been there but I was stepping in for a colleague. There were complications.' He rubbed his temples like the pain was still there. 'But still, it shouldn't have happened. Or rather, it could have been avoided. Basically, I messed up.'

'I see.' A breeze rippled across the puddles, lifting the pages of the books. 'What happened after that?' She looked at the manicured garden behind the wall, the pebbled driveway, the trees and well-tended bushes reflecting the sort of life Simon should have been leading.

'I was suspended whilst they investigated the case. The colleague who'd been making trouble, who should have stuck up for me, did everything he could to get rid of me, almost got me struck off the medical register. In the end, a junior colleague came to my defence, but it was too late by then. I resigned before they fired me. My career was over in the space of one exhausting night. I haven't worked since. I moved out here, to a part of the country where I wasn't known, hoping to find work. Any kind of work. I would have been happy working behind a bar or in a café, but of course I don't have any experience of anything like that.'

'Can't you get a job in a different hospital?'

Simon shook his head, staring at his ruined books. 'When you kill someone – even by accident – it stays with you. It drives you mad. You wonder if you might do it again, whether the pattern will repeat itself without you meaning it to. I can't let that happen. I can't work as a doctor ever again.'

She sat down next to him, feeling the cold brick through her skirt, trying to untangle her thoughts. She wasn't sure if she was angry with him for lying or sorry for him for what he'd been through. 'Why run away from me?'

'At the party someone recognised me.'

Immediately, she thought of Mrs Watts, the shadow on Simon's face beneath the apple trees. She knew what that had been now: a guilty conscience.

'It was just bad luck. A coincidence. Her husband is business partners with one of the patient's relatives. Turns out I should have changed my name after all. I was sure she'd tell you and I didn't think you'd want to know me after that. I couldn't bear for you to know the truth about me, so I decided to disappear.'

She shook her head. 'She didn't say anything to me. She didn't breathe a word.'

He buried his neck in the duffle coat. 'It was only a matter of time. It would have come out in the end. I'm sorry. Really sorry.'

Her phone vibrated in her pocket but she ignored it. Probably Cassandra demanding to know what she was up to.

'I was scared of you,' she said, wondering whether she was frightened even now. 'I thought you were crazy. Worse than that, I thought you might not exist at all. I thought you were a ghost.'

He laughed sadly. 'No. Not a ghost. Just a very stupid man.'

She jumped off the wall and picked up his books. 'I'd better get back to work,' she said, handing them over. 'It's freezing out here, for a start.'

'Of course. And thanks for these.' He piled the books in his arms. 'I think I'll take a walk to the river, clear my head.'

She held out her hand, knowing there was no going back. 'Goodbye,' she said.

'Goodbye – and thank you. Thank you for listening.'

She walked away, head buzzing. All the things he'd told her, bragging about his work, how busy he was, how he was on nights and couldn't focus, how he could only meet her at such-and-such a time because he was on call. She remembered the night when she'd bumped into him in the pub, the night she'd had that vision in the church hall, how sad he'd seemed about losing his patient, how convincing. A lie or part-lie. She felt alone. Truly alone in this quiet corner of town. No Nick. No Emma. No one to talk to except Lucy back in the office.

Lucy who had been kind enough already, letting them stay for the week, offering them the house for the week after as well, over half term whilst she was away with her daughter, whilst Kelda sorted out what to do with the toll house.

She walked back to the car, breaking into a run. Twenty minutes late already. She played her answerphone message as she lifted the parking notice from her windscreen, cursing her bad luck, expecting it to be Cassandra ranting on the other end. But it wasn't. It was Mr Yeo.

There'd been an incident with Dylan.

34

❧

1864

The cell is a tiny room near the governor's office. There is a shelf and a hammock and a rough woollen blanket. Four paces to the window, four paces back to the door, two paces across. The window is thick glass divided by a wrought-iron bar, distorting the world outside, but if I press my face close, misting the pane, I can see the square in front of the gaol and the road leading to the larger market square on the left.

I've been standing there for hours, with my nose pressed against the pane, when the gaoler shuffles in with his band of keys.

He bends down and picks up the piss pot, screwing his face up at the contents. He takes it out and returns a few minutes later with water at the bottom of it.

'Cleanliness is next to godliness,' he grunts, reciting one of the governor's mottos. He hands me a bar of soap and watches as I scoop the water from the piss pot and splash it over my face.

When he's gone, I crouch on the floor, wrapped in my blanket. There's nowhere to sit and it is freezing cold. No fireplace. No lantern by which to warm my fingers. I sit with my head on my knees, thinking about the trial in two weeks' time. Will the judge be lenient? Will the jury believe my story there was an intruder in the house? I think of Helen, that look in her eye, that cold determination, as I pull the blanket tighter around my shoulders, finding no warmth even now.

Despite the cold, I slip into sleep. A wretched dream-filled sleep. I'm almost glad when I'm jerked awake by a cramp in my leg. I stretch and relieve myself in the soapy water, then crouch down again, trying to get comfortable. My limbs are stiff as boards, my head aches with the cold. Eventually, I hear the gaoler's key in the lock. This time, he walks in with a tray of food. A slab of coarse bread and a bowl of soup.

'Cold today,' he informs me as though it might have escaped my attention. He blows on his hands after setting down the tray, then hesitates, frowning like he's battling some inner demon. 'I will see if I can find you an extra blanket.'

He returns a few minutes later with a blanket rolled beneath his arm and places it on the floor. He glances at the untouched soup.

'It will warm you,' he says, tapping the tin bowl with his foot, slopping soup over the sides and onto the tray. I pick up the spoon and force the thin grey liquid between my teeth. The gaoler watches me, talking all the while, telling me about his wife and his two strapping boys and the babe that is due any minute.

'Large as a house,' he says of his wife, patting his stomach.

I stare at the spoon, no longer listening to his words. I'm back in the field behind the toll house, standing over the grave. There is rain in my hair and sweat on my chest. I look down at the woman, her hands flopped over her belly where I let them fall, protecting her unborn child even in death. I feel the spade in my hand. I see the lantern casting ghostly shadows. Beneath her, in the dirt, is the pock-marked man . . .

'That's better,' says the gaoler as I take another mouthful of soup. He is in a good mood today, intent on keeping me company.

The soup tastes even fouler than it looks. I spill some on the blanket and watch as it seeps into the wool. I think of the stains on the rag-rug, the fingerless gloves soaked with blood, Helen lying in the hallway. I think of the look on her face before she fell down the stairs. Stubborn. Horrified.

I take another mouthful.

The gaoler leaves me alone again, disappointed no doubt by my lack of conversation. I've no appetite despite a growling stomach, so I take the blankets to the far side of the room and huddle beneath the window. I drift again, unsure whether I am awake or asleep. I see a room that smells of warm milk; a wooden horse on a chair beside the bed; a book of fairy tales. Ma bends over me and lifts me into bed, smoothing the blankets.

You are ill, Joseph, she says. *You haven't been well for a long time. You haven't been well since your wife died.*

I see a mole on her chin that wasn't there before. A mole that gets larger and larger as I stare. That quivers when she laughs. I reach out to touch it, but it jerks away from me. Not Ma, I think, but *her.*

'Joe!' she says, running away from me and laughing. It's the days before we were married. The days we would find ways to slip away from Bella's parents and walk in the fields; the days before my temper got the better of me. 'Come and catch me, Joe!' Not just my mother in her looks, but in her kindness and gentle ways. I run after her, grabbing hold of her warm skin, holding her tight.

She laughs again. 'Not so rough, Joe. You are hurting me.'

And there it is, when I release my grip, my handprint etched upon her arm.

I force myself awake, blinking into the gloom and scrambling to my feet.

'Bella?' I call. 'Where are you? Why have you left me? Will you not come back to me?'

My eyes dart around the room, looking for something, anything to show me that Bella has not abandoned me completely, that I wasn't just dreaming. I tip the tray over with my foot, sending the soup spilling across the floorboards. The piss pot goes the same way. I watch it roll, emptying its contents before clattering to a standstill.

'Bella?'

The door springs open. The gaoler glares at me, at the mess I've made. Outside, the clock in the marketplace strikes the hour. Not the square outside the gaol, but the place where they carry out the public executions.

'We'll be having none of that,' he says, like he is talking to a wayward child. 'If the governor finds out you are causing trouble, there is no telling what he might do.' He reaches for the piss pot and knocks it against my head, causing me to stagger backwards. I press my hands over my ears, my head spinning, as the darkness seeps deeper.

35

NOW

'I'm sorry to call you in like this, Mrs Johnson.'

Kelda sat in the children's chair in Dylan's classroom, trying to ignore the vibrating phone messages from Cassandra in her pocket. She should have texted her, explained she was running late back from lunch, but she'd been preoccupied, first with Mr Pritchard, then with Simon.

'I came as soon as I could,' she said. 'I was worried when I got your message.'

The classroom clock said two fifteen; her forty-five-minute lunch break was steadily creeping towards an hour and a half. She'd already seen Dylan outside, in his PE class, doing star jumps and jogging on the spot. She'd been relieved he was all right – she'd presumed he was sick – then annoyed Mr Yeo had called her out for seemingly no reason.

'I should be in work . . . ' she continued.

'Yes. I do understand parents have other commitments.'

She wished he'd sit down rather than pace around the room.

'Dylan disappeared this afternoon.'

'What do you mean, disappeared?' She'd only just seen him, waved at him on the sports field after she'd parked the car badly on the pavement. 'I saw him outside. It doesn't seem like he's disappeared to me.' She couldn't help thinking of Simon, how he really had disappeared and then reappeared as someone else, someone she didn't know at all.

'Just after lunch.' Mr Yeo picked up a ruler and tapped it in his hands. 'We had half the school looking for him, that's when we telephoned. Obviously, there are procedures in place for this sort of incident. Not that such incidents occur regularly.'

'I'm sure . . . '

'Miss Reynolds, the year one teacher, found him.'

'Where?'

'In the games cupboard.'

'In the games cupboard? Why?'

'He was hiding.'

'From whom?'

'I took him aside. Naturally, as his class teacher, it was my role to intervene. I tried to make him understand the serious-ness of the matter.'

'And?'

'He called me a rather nasty word.' Mr Yeo pinched his lips together and stabbed the ruler into his palm. 'He called me a . . . ' he swallowed, 'a shithead.'

She felt herself blushing. 'I'm sorry. I don't know where he would have picked up something like that.'

'Obviously, whatever goes on at home is none of my business ...'

'I can assure you, we don't speak like that at home.'

'... but I can't have that sort of language in the classroom.'

'No. Of course. I'll speak to him straight away.'

'I'm not naive.' Mr Yeo put the ruler down on the desk. 'I worked in an inner-city school before this. Believe me, I've heard it all. I just don't expect it from *this* school. Dylan hasn't made a very good start this term. He's disruptive. He doesn't listen to anything I say. He seems to be a law unto himself.'

'It's been a difficult few months for him.'

'I'm sure you appreciate the gravity of what occurred. It's not just the bad language. We can't have children disappearing like that. We were minutes away from calling the police. We had to lock the school gates, alert security. Some of the children were crying. They thought something really bad had happened.'

'I'll talk to him tonight.'

'The last thing anyone wants is to have him excluded.'

'I'm so sorry, once again.'

She stood up to leave. Cassandra would be going spare, probably writing out Kelda's dismissal notice and bitching about her to anyone who would listen. And right now, more than ever, she needed her job. She was halfway out the door, about to run to the car, when something occurred to her. She turned back to Mr Yeo.

'Did anyone ask him?'

He looked up from the jigsaw of a human skeleton he was tidying into a box. 'Sorry?'

'Did anyone ask Dylan why he was hiding in the cupboard?'

'Well, naturally ...' Mr Yeo picked up part of a cardboard skull.

She felt the blood rise to her cheeks. 'Did you bother to ask what he was afraid of? Why he was so frightened that he ran away and hid where no one could find him?'

Mr Yeo looked at her blankly.

She stood a little taller. 'If this happens again, perhaps that's the first thing you should do?'

She didn't mean for the door to slam, but it echoed down the corridor as she ran. Ran to the car, passing Dylan on the sports field. She wished she could run to him, take him back to Lucy's, ask him what the hell was going on, but she knew she had to get back to work, invent some sob story. She needed the money; without the money there was no escaping the toll house and she couldn't bear the thought of ever going back.

'How kind of you to join us this afternoon.' Cassandra flew out of her office as soon as she walked in.

'I'm sorry. The school phoned. Dylan wasn't feeling well. I've just dropped him off with a friend.'

Lucy flashed her a look of concern as Cassandra drilled her nails on Kelda's monitor.

'And didn't you think to phone? To let someone know where you were? I've left about three messages.'

'It all happened really quickly when I was out grabbing lunch. I panicked.'

'I almost cancelled my trip,' Cassandra said. 'I thought I was going to have to cancel the flights and let the twins down. They're so looking forward to Disneyland. I was just about to cancel when you walked in. You see, I didn't think I could trust you.'

'It was a one-off. It won't happen again. I promise you.'

'But I *can* trust you, can't I?' Cassandra stopped her drilling. 'Next week, when I'm away, I can trust you to be here? To run the show for me? Because otherwise . . . '

'Of course.' Kelda fired up her PC, determined to look busy however late in the day, however much her head was buzzing with what had happened at the school and before that with Simon and Mr Pritchard. 'I promise you, next week, everything will be perfect. And I'll make up the lost time from today. You'll have nothing to worry about.'

'Good.' Cassandra swivelled on her heels. 'Because I'd hate for you to be wrong.'

'What happened at school, today?' she asked Dylan later that evening. Lucy was out, purposely leaving them alone on the pretence of needing some essentials from the supermarket. She switched off the TV with the remote control, making him listen. Dylan stuck out his bottom lip and fiddled with the Lego on his lap.

'I had a phone call from Mr Yeo. He was really worried about you. He said you'd disappeared and then, when he found you, you said something rather rude.'

Dylan shrugged like she was making a fuss about nothing. She felt like shaking him. Screaming. Why couldn't he see this was important?

'Listen, Dylan. You've got to start behaving. You've got to start listening to Mr Yeo. I know you don't like him, but he's your teacher and you need to show him respect. I can't have you speaking to him the way you did and I don't want you picking up any more bad words from Georgie. I've a mind to speak to his mum.'

'No!' He kicked out at her, catching her chin. She drew back in horror.

'Dylan!'

He threw the pile of Lego from his lap onto the floor and ran out of the room. She hesitated, telling herself to stay calm, act rationally. No point making things worse than they already were.

She went after him, hearing his room door slam. 'Dylan, let me in.' She tried the handle, but already he'd drawn the lock. All Lucy's bedrooms were fitted with locks, from when the kids had grown up and wanted their privacy. She felt the fear again, the horrible creeping fear that never quite left; the fear of losing him; the fear of something terrible happening that was out of her control. The same fear that had accompanied her the first time he'd crossed the road without holding her hand, the first time she'd handed him over to a babysitter, the first day of primary school.

'Dylan, I need you to come out from there straight away.'

She heard sobbing from the other side. 'If you don't come out, I'm going to confiscate your Batman Lego.' She tried to think what was on the other side that could possibly hurt him. Just pillows and duvets and a wardrobe stuffed with Lucy and Mike's winter clothes. Oh God, the wardrobe. What if he crawled in there and closed the door and couldn't get out? 'Dylan!'

The door flew open under her weight.

Dylan jumped back, startled. She drew her arms around him, burying his wet cheeks in her jumper.

'Don't ever do that again,' she said. 'Locking yourself in like that, it could have been dangerous. Something could have gone wrong and I wouldn't have been able to help you.'

He was crying so hard he was shaking. 'Don't take my Lego.'

'No, I won't take your Lego, but you need to listen to me. What happened this afternoon? Why were you hiding?'

'I was playing a game.'

'A game?'

'Hide and seek.'

'Ah, I see.' So that's all it was. Just a game that had gone wrong. Why the hell hadn't Mr Yeo managed to glean this essential piece of information? 'The whole school was looking for you,' she said, trying to ignore the fact it had almost cost her her job. 'Didn't you hear them calling?'

'Yes.'

'Then why didn't you come out?'

'I didn't want to be found.'

'Why?' She held him gently by his shoulders. 'Why, Dylan, why? Mr Yeo was worried. Miss Reynolds was worried. I was worried. Who were you playing with? Georgie?'

He shook his head. 'I was playing hide and seek with the man. He told me to hide first. He was going to count to a hundred then come looking for me.'

'What do you mean, the man? One of the teachers?'

'No.' He looked straight at her. 'The other man.'

She felt sick. There'd been an intruder in the school. She'd have to go back, speak to Mr Yeo, speak to the headmaster. She breathed hard, thinking of a stranger amongst the children, pretending to be friends.

'Look, Dylan. This is important. Really important. What did he look like?'

'Big eyes. The same man I saw before. The man I've been drawing. I was playing tag with Georgie but then Georgie went off with some of the other children and I was left on my own. Until the man found me.'

She remembered the drawing she'd found, the one with the man with big black eyes. But it was just his imagination. An imaginary friend. She ought to be relieved but instead she felt worse. Far worse. 'But why did you hide in the games cupboard?'

'I felt safe in there.'

'Safe?'

'I didn't have to think of anything. I liked the smell of the footballs. I knew the man wouldn't find me with the footballs. I was scared of him. He said he was cross with me. He said he didn't want me around anymore. He told me to hide well or he'd break my neck like he broke my glider.'

'Broke your glider? Oh, Dylan.' She blinked back tears, imagining him curled up amongst the sports stuff, playing on his own, playing with some imaginary monster. 'It sounds like a horrible game. A horrible place to hide.' She held him tight, wishing she could make everything better. 'We'll get through this. Whatever's going on, we'll sort it out. We'll find a way through together, okay?' She felt him nod against her shoulder. 'This man you said you saw who was playing hide and seek, was he pretend? Like a made-up friend? Or a made-up monster?

Dylan drew his face back, pink and tear-stained. 'He was just like you, Mum. I told you already. The man I saw before. The man from the toll house. He said he'd been looking for me. He said he'd followed me all the way to school.'

36

❦

1864

The cell for condemned prisoners is even worse than the one near the governor's office. There is a narrow platform for a bed and a tiny slit of a window high up, too high up to look out of. I spend my days lying on the bed, unable to get comfortable, twisting my body this way and that, feeling my bones dig into the hard wood. The nights are the same, only worse. No sleep. No dreams save the ones that haunt me in the daytime. Sometimes, I press my hands around my neck, wondering what the hangman's noose will feel like, whether death will be fast or mercilessly slow. Harder, harder, pressing on my Adam's apple, feeling my pulse fight against my fingers until I'm forced to stop, spluttering into the dark cell.

When I close my eyes, I see the courtroom again: men and women craning over one another in the public gallery, trying to get the best view, their mouths twisted in a mixture of excitement and disgust; the prosecutor in his robes, beads of sweat running along his forehead; the maid swaying behind the witness stand, head bent low, hands trembling.

'And how did Miss Drake appear to you when you saw her on her way to see her brother-in-law?' The prosecutor taps his thumbs together impatiently.

'She appeared happy, sir.'

'Did she say why she was happy?'

The maid consults her shoes. 'She said, she thought spring was on the way. That's before it rained.'

The maid blushes fiercely as a titter ripples through the public gallery, silenced in a moment by the judge's frown. Then she disappears. A puff of smoke. A conjuror's trick. In her place is a man, chest held high, ruddy cheeks. Mr Turnbill is redder and puffier than I remember. He swims before me in my dreams, looking me straight in the eye like he's inspecting a dead rat before tossing it in the gutter.

'Can you describe where you found the prisoner?'

'He was in the kitchen, walking towards the hallway.'

'In the kitchen? So, he would have heard everything that was going on in the house?'

'Yes.'

'He would have heard, for example, Miss Drake crying out at the presence of an intruder?'

'Yes.'

'He would have heard her cry out as she was stabbed?'

'Yes.'

'He would have heard – heard with ease – in fact, he may even have *seen*, her body tumbling down the stairs after the awful attack?'

'That's right. The kitchen is adjacent to the hallway and the door between the two was open. He was perhaps six paces away when he first appeared. The toll house is very small.'

'Can you describe what the prisoner was doing when you saw him?'

'As I said, he was walking.'

'The prisoner was walking? Not attending to the deceased? Or at least *hurrying* to investigate the clearly audible occurrences in his house?'

A moment's hesitation. I see the disgust in his eyes as they flash towards mine. He means to see me damned. 'That is so. He was walking calmly.'

I scramble through the other images in my mind, the images of *that* day. Standing on the landing, the blood stains on my gloves. Straddling the stairs two at a time, leaping over the body. Bundling the stained cloths into the garden wall. The sense of exhilaration. Of power.

The cold wraps itself around me as I blink into the dank cell and shiver in my blanket. I pull at my hair, sending a scattering of strands onto the floor. A brief moment of comfort, of reprieve, as my scalp tingles, then I close my eyes again, pressing my fingers hard against my lids. The courtroom is gone. The darkness threatens to consume me.

I stand, swaying and dazed by lack of sleep, feeling along the walls of the cell, searching for a sign from Bella, anything to tell me she hasn't deserted me completely. That this darkness is not all I have left. But there's nothing, just the cold brick and the seeping damp. I fall to my knees, groping along the floor, feeling the corners of the bed, hands falling on nothing but dust and grit. 'Where are you?' I cry. A flicker of light. A moment's breath. I see someone else, hovering above me: the judge with his red robes and white wig. I reach out to grab him, to bring him down, to crush him with my palms, but my hand falls into thin air. He laughs at me and steps aside, lifting a square of black cloth to his head.

'*How many times do I have to tell you, Joseph?*' he says like he is scolding a puppy. '*How many times?*'

I must be ill, feverish. The cold binds itself to my muscles, eats into my bones. There is no one here. No judge. No Mr Turnbill. No maid. The room spins. I hold on to the bed, then – with what seems like a colossal effort – empty the contents of my stomach onto the cell floor.

There's vomit all over my hands as I scream, thrashing my body against the bed, pulling at my hair, calling for the one person who eludes me, who refuses even to meet me in my dreams. 'Bella!'

The gaoler bangs on the door. 'Shut up, ratbag,' he shouts through the grate.

I curl into a ball on the floor, closing my eyes again, seeking her in my dreams, trying to picture her as she was. Not a plaster mask, but a real person with soft skin and warm lips. The girl who would bring me fruit, the young bride who shared my bed, the dutiful wife.

She's not here, Joseph, says the cold dark voice in my mind. *She's left you to rot.*

37

NOW

On Monday of half term, Kelda sat in the office alone, addressing Cassandra's forwarded emails as best she could. Even from Gatwick, Cassandra was checking up on her. Kelda was exhausted. Another weekend when Dylan hadn't wanted to play football. Another weekend when she'd failed to tease out of him exactly what was wrong. He didn't want to talk about school anymore or the game of hide and seek or the man he'd said he'd seen, and she'd been so worried, she'd hardly slept. Should she speak to Mr Yeo again? Should she take Dylan to see the GP? Should she call the police? He'd gone round to Georgie's house to play on Sunday afternoon which at least had been normal, and she'd sat with Mrs Watts in the Wattses' designer summer house whilst Georgie and Dylan shot at each other on the lawn with Nerf guns.

'So, you're thinking of selling up?' Mrs Watts had said. 'You know we've got a couple of properties up for rent, if you're interested?'

Kelda had listened politely to Mrs Watts's description of a three-bedroomed house in the centre of town and another four-bedroomed mansion, or so it sounded, in the countryside.

'Give me a bell if you're interested,' Mrs Watts had said, attacking a packet of Viennese whirls.

Kelda had wanted to scream: *Isn't it obvious I can't afford much more than a shoebox?* Instead, she'd said she'd give it some thought. Realistically, until she managed to sell the toll house, she didn't have the money to rent somewhere else. At the same time, she couldn't bear the thought of ever going back, especially considering Dylan's state of mind. But she also knew she couldn't stay at Lucy's for ever, however much Lucy insisted she didn't mind.

She sat at her desk, trying to work through the problem, figuring out how far her money would stretch. Now that she'd replied to most of the emails, there wasn't much to do; no meetings, no visitors, no diary to manage.

An email pinged into her inbox: one of Cassandra's high-profile clients asking for her help. The data Cassandra had promised hadn't materialised and he needed it for a board meeting that afternoon. She was glad to have something to focus on, to take her mind off the house. She hunted through Cassandra's files, extracting the correct data and transforming it into an accessible format. She thought about Dylan as she worked. He was with Lucy and Mike, helping them to pack for their holiday, a pre-baby break with their daughter, but she had most of the day before Lucy dropped him off at the office.

'Are you sure you don't mind me staying another week?' Kelda had asked when Lucy handed over a set of keys.

'Not at all. You'll be doing us a favour. You can stay as long as you like, you know that, don't you?' They hadn't mentioned the house again, or what had happened to Lucy years ago, but she knew the real reason Lucy didn't want her to go back to the toll house.

It was half past ten, plenty of time to sort out Cassandra's client before Lucy dropped Dylan off. She spent the rest of the morning sending emails and making phone calls.

'You're good at this,' Cassandra's client said when she'd resolved the issue. 'Have you ever thought about setting up on your own?'

'On my own?'

'Your own business?'

'Not really.'

'I can put you in touch with a few contacts, if you like? Surely you don't want to be working for the likes of Cassandra Parker all your life?'

The thought buzzed around her head as she ate her lunch, picking her way through a salad from the deli next door. Could she really leave Cassandra and set up her own business? Not market research, but something that really interested her? She scribbled down the number of Cassandra's client and folded it into her wallet, just in case. Maybe one day when Dylan was older . . .

In the early afternoon, Lucy telephoned the office. 'Kelda, I'm so glad I caught you.'

'Are you all right? Is Dylan okay?'

'He's fine. Absolutely fine. Nothing to worry about. It's just my daughter called. She was having on-and-off pains all week-end. Then, this morning, her waters broke.'

'Oh God . . .'

'I know. She's only seven and a half months pregnant.'

'Can't they do something? Can't the hospital stop it?'

'We're on our way there now. Seems we'll have to cancel the holiday.' She heard the worry in Lucy's voice. 'I'm just ringing about Dylan. We were on our way to the office when we saw your friend Nick.'

'Nick?' She hadn't spoken to Nick or texted him since the party. She'd been too embarrassed to get in touch after what Emma had said, and she supposed he felt the same way, or he was ignoring her out of loyalty to Alexa.

'Yes, I hope you don't mind. He was out in town, so we stopped the car and asked if he could help. He said it wasn't a problem and he took Dylan home with him. I hope we did the right thing?'

'Yes, fine.' She hadn't told Lucy about what had happened at the party; she'd worried Lucy enough already with the things she'd told her about the toll house.

'I should have asked you first. Only, it was a spur-of-the-moment decision. We had to do something. We were in a bit of a panic.'

'It's fine. Dylan loves Nick. They get on fabulously.'

'Great. I'll let you know how things go at the hospital.'

'Good luck. Fingers crossed.'

She texted Nick as soon as Lucy rang off:

Thanks for taking Dylan.

He replied:

No probs. Day off. We're just heading to the park.

She re-read the text several times, trying to find meaning in it, knowing there wasn't any, other than the facts: Nick was taking Dylan to the park, probably sailing one of Nick's model boats on the lake or climbing trees or eating ice cream whilst stamping their feet against the cold. She smiled at the thought of the two of them together. Dylan would love it, spending the afternoon with Uncle Nick. And when she picked him up later, it would be a chance to clear the air.

She texted back, Sounds lovely. Meet you later at the house, then responded to the few remaining emails and tidied her desk. Eventually, with nothing else to do, she logged off early. Half past four. She'd pick up Dylan then go back to Lucy's, light the stove in the living room, snuggle down with a movie and mugs of hot chocolate. She shrugged on her coat, about to leave when the phone rang again: Cassandra calling from Paris.

'Kelda, thanks for holding the fort. How's it going?'

'Fine.' She swallowed her frustration and explained what had happened with the client, before patiently answering Cassandra's questions and listening to her stories about the hotel and the room service and the twins bouncing on the bed. As Cassandra droned on, she texted Nick on her mobile:

Sorry, held up. Be with you as soon as I can. Meet you at the house

Immediately she'd sent the message, a text arrived from Emma. She'd not heard from Emma since the hospital, only the odd phone call from Mum reporting on the surgery and how the two of them were getting on. *Fabulously*, according to Mum, though Kelda could hear the strain in her voice.

Hey, sis. Any chance you could drop my bag round
Mum's sometime?

It flitted through her mind that Emma was trying to escape.
Perhaps she'd tried to dupe Mum into giving her money and
Mum had had enough. She texted back about arranging a time,
locked up and went out.

Cassandra had kept her on the phone for twenty minutes and
it was getting late. It wouldn't be long before it was properly
dark. The town centre was heaving. A fair had arrived for half
term and the market square was awash with kids in skeleton and
witch outfits, swinging plastic pumpkins for Halloween. She'd
take Dylan there one night after work, watch him spin on the
rides and treat him to chips. It would be good to get out, do
something different, spend a bit of quality time together, make
up for the fact she had to work through half term. The fair had
brought in a crowd and the centre of town was closed to traffic.
She'd had to park several streets from the office this morning, and
it was easier to walk to Nick's place than fetch the car, but she
was glad of the extra time, still nervous as she climbed the stairs
to his flat, rehearsing what she'd say to him, how she'd act as if
nothing had happened, as if Emma hadn't said all those things.

'Hi.' He opened the door, hair still windswept from the park.

'It's so good to see you.' She hadn't meant to come out with
that straight away, but it *was* good to see him. It really was.

'You too. I wasn't expecting you . . . '

'No, sorry. Did you get my text? I was running late.'

'I haven't checked my phone for a while.'

'Dylan okay?'

He grinned. 'We had great fun in the park. We found a new
tree to climb and we played on the monkey bars. Come in.'

She followed him into the kitchen, wishing she had something to give him, a bottle of wine as a thank you for looking after Dylan. She heard the TV next door and imagined Dylan surrounded by Nick's models, absorbed in CBeebies.

They stood in silence. She didn't know what to do, whether to sit down or take her coat off or go and find Dylan. On the table was a hulled-out pumpkin with big teeth and gaping eyes.

'I'll make coffee, if you like?' he said.

'Lovely.' God, she sounded so formal. She tried to think what she'd normally do, how she'd normally act. She watched him select mugs from the shelf, boil water, heap the cafetière.

'How've you been?' she said.

'Busy. Really busy. Walter's got this idea for another conference. Our paper got published in a high-profile journal. It went down really well. In fact, we've become a bit famous.'

'Famous?'

'Famous in an academic sense. Not really famous.' He laughed. He was gabbling and she realised he was as nervous as she was. 'There's been loads of interest in our research. My research, really, but as Walter's the professor, his name gets slapped on everything too.'

'That's not fair when you've done all the hard work.'

He selected two mugs from the dish rack. 'It's the way academia works. Not that it matters. I've been asked to go to America.'

'Wow. America?'

'I know – crazy, isn't it? Head-hunted by a professor in Harvard.'

'That's great.' She sat down, feeling slightly sick. The thought of Nick not being here was all wrong. She stared at the pumpkin, at those big, jagged teeth. 'How's Alexa?'

'Fine. Apparently.'

'Apparently?'

He put the mugs on the table with the cafetière.

'We split up.'

'Oh, I'm sorry.' She didn't know what to think. Of all things, she hadn't expected this.

He sat down opposite and poured the coffee. 'It's the reason I haven't been in touch. I've been a bit of a mess, actually. Alexa and I argued after the party.'

She said nothing, just watched the top of his head, his hair falling messily from the crown, realising, achingly, how much she cared.

'I worked out a few weeks ago that the dates didn't match up.'

She frowned. She didn't know what he was talking about. It was her fault they'd split up. *Her* party. She should have worked harder to make things better.

'The pregnancy,' he explained. 'I remembered what the doctor said at the hospital, she was about three weeks gone. Which meant the baby was conceived around the time I was away in Brighton. I was in Brighton for two weeks. There's no way it was mine.'

He dragged his fingers through his hair and she saw the tiny creases of his knuckles. She realised how much Harvard mattered, how desperately she didn't want him to go.

'I wanted to tell you before. I was going to ask you for your advice when we went to the pub, but you seemed so happy about Simon, and it didn't seem quite right to tell you then.'

'It was fine. I would have been fine.'

'It was all a joke. The engagement. The pretence we were going to spend the rest of our lives together. I suspected the truth but I went ahead anyway. I knew I wasn't the only one, but I tried to make myself believe I could stop all that. How stupid was I?'

'You weren't stupid. Too forgiving maybe, but not stupid.'

'I *was* stupid. It was the same with Rachel. We married without really knowing each other. I can't believe I was about to make the same mistake again. Not that Alexa was the real problem. I mean, she's not the reason I hid myself away.'

'What do you mean?'

He picked up his mug and swirled the contents. 'After the party, I thought about what Emma had said, about me and you. Well, perhaps not exactly what she said,' he blushed, 'but the sentiment. And I realised she was right.'

She splashed too much milk into her coffee, watched as it dribbled over the side.

'Looks like I've been kidding myself for a long time.' He stretched his hand across the table, not quite touching hers. 'Sometimes you just don't see what's right in front of you, do you?' He curled his fingers like he didn't dare touch her. 'I'm sorry. I shouldn't be saying all this. Forget it.'

She didn't know what to say, wasn't sure whether to reach for his hand and tell him it was okay, that she *liked* it. Because, of course, Nick didn't know she was no longer with Simon; she needed to explain.

Suddenly, he scraped back his chair and snatched his coat from its hook. 'Let's go out for dinner,' he said. 'I don't know about you, but I could do with something a bit stronger than coffee.'

'Good plan.' She still couldn't meet his eye; couldn't even start to untangle the thoughts in her head. 'I've drunk too much caffeine today anyway.'

'My shout. We can take the cheeky monkey, too, unless he's busy?'

'Busy?' She wondered whether Dylan even realised she was here, with the noise of the TV next door. She'd been expecting him to tear in at any moment and tell her all about his afternoon. Thank God for Dylan. Right now, she could do with him babbling on about the park and Batman and whatever he'd been watching.

'Yes, you know – Dylan?' Nick grinned. 'He helped me do the pumpkin. Don't tell me you've forgotten about him already?'

'Forgotten?'

'I presume he's with one of his tearaway friends?'

'What do you mean? He's with you. Lucy left him with you.'

She tuned into the news channel next door. The news, not CBeebies.

Nick's face drained of colour. 'I ... I dropped him off at yours.'

'I don't understand. You mean you dropped him back at Lucy's?'

'No.' Nick frowned. 'I dropped him at the toll house. Just like you told me to.'

38

1864

The cart rattles to the market square in nauseating jerks. My hands are bound by a leather strap which makes sitting uncomfortable and I've the urge to unbutton my trousers and piss. The square is heaving, far busier even than on market day, and a throng of police constables makes way for the cart to pass. People shout over one another, jeering. Men and women on their way to work, with their baskets and wares; a family picnicking near the clock; fine women in silk dresses fanning themselves. According to the gaoler, some have camped here overnight for the best spot. I've drawn a crowd, become notorious. My story will be sold in newspapers across England.

The day is hot though it's only early morning. Flies hover over the dung heaps and the streets reek of shit. On the opposite side of the cart, a police constable keeps the mobs at bay, threatening them with his truncheon. Ahead of me, dizzyingly, in the centre of the square is the scaffold, a platform with steps and a rectangular wooden frame.

The cart halts, throwing me forwards.

'Time to go,' says the constable, like we're off for a day at the races. He lifts me to my feet by the leather strap and I stumble forwards, almost losing my footing. At the same time, I see something at the bottom of the cart. A slate-grey pebble.

'There!' I hiss. 'Over there!'

The constable looks at me, perplexed.

'The pebble.'

I see him spying the tiny stone with distrust.

'Please,' I say. 'I want to hold it. Put it in my hand.'

For a moment, I think he is going to ignore me, then, when he thinks no one's looking, he bends down and places it between my fingers.

'There,' he says, twisting his mouth into a sick smile. He thinks I'm mad.

I rub the pebble over and over, the leather strap chafing my wrists. Not as smooth as the ones Bella collected – I can feel a chink in the middle of it – but good enough. Solid enough.

Oh, Bella, my darling, to come back to me at this late hour!

The constable leads me down from the cart and through a gap in the crowd to the scaffold. The sun burns my face. The light hurts my eyes after so long in the gaol. My legs move mechanically. I rub the pebble over and over, imagining my fingerprints worn already into the surface, imprinting themselves for ever.

My darling! Give me the strength to bear it!

I climb the steps to the scaffold, seeing the noose waiting for me, hanging within its frame. Someone yells from the crowd, calling me a devil, but nothing matters anymore. The executioner grins a toothless grin and manhandles me into position above the trapdoor. He fits the noose around my neck, fiddling with the knot, placing it just so, to do the job properly, then he leans over to the crowd.

'This one won't keep us hanging around.'

The crowd roars with laughter. I see a gang of children pushing their way to the front, angling for the best view. A mother hugs her babe tight as if I might do it harm just by looking.

I roll the pebble between my fingers. I have nothing to fear from the rope. As long as I hold on to the pebble, I will bear what is to come.

The din dies around me as the crowd leans in to hear my final words, but I have nothing to say, nothing with which to satisfy the newspaper reporters or the gossipmongers. All I can think about is Bella. My words are for her alone. If this is the price I must pay to see her, then so be it. The executioner tugs a white cap over my head and pulls it low to cover my face. It smells of dust and something else. Something acrid. He tuts and struggles to set it straight, a perfectionist in his trade, yanking it harder. The sudden movement makes me drop the pebble. Panic threads itself like a web across my chest, squeezing my lungs, though the noose is yet to tighten. I imagine the pebble tinkling on the platform and rolling to a crack between the boards. My throat constricts, my stomach heaves. I'm transported somewhere else, though my legs are still steady, still firm on the trapdoor.

I'm in the bedroom at the toll house, seeing the dark green covers, Bella curled between the sheets, hands over her eyes.

Why Joseph, why? I'd found her talking with the shepherd and dragged her back inside, the rage and jealousy overpowering me, feeling like another man as she'd cowered beneath my fists. I try to comfort her but she turns away from me and weeps into the bedclothes. *I was talking, that's all, I was doing no harm.* The scene changes. I'm in the garden watching Bella pegging out the washing. Every now and then, she stops to rub her belly. Unlike the others – the babes who slipped away silently – this child is growing strong, defying me with every movement, with every roll and kick. *The pebbles are working*, she says to herself, rubbing them in her palm. Another scene, another summer's day: Bella and Helen in the garden together, sitting on the ledge, their heads bent together, whispering. Helen stands to leave and Bella reaches out to her. *Don't leave me*, she pleads with her eyes, *don't leave me with him.* But Helen doesn't understand and pulls away without a care.

Someone coughs in the market square. I see the slate-grey pebble rolling away from me in my mind, picked up by a child and tucked in his pocket as a souvenir. I see the pebbles in the toll house, rolling along the windowsills, circling Bella's death mask in the room upstairs. I think of all the times I'd thought I'd seen Bella or heard her or smelled her, only to be disappointed.

They weren't for you, Joseph, she whispers through the waiting crowd. *The pebbles were for me and the child. For our protection.*

There's the sound of feet on the platform, the billow of the chaplain's surplice caught by a freak breeze. I smell the acrid scent of the cap and realise what it is. Fear. Someone yells at the executioner to get on with it. Suddenly, the door beneath my feet swings open. I scream, but there is no sound, no breath.

The rope tightens. There's pain like someone thrusting a knife into my gullet. A horrible bulging tightness.

There is no Heaven, I think as I fight against the darkness. Bella is not waiting for me at all. There is only Hell.

39

※

NOW

Kelda shot up from the table. What the hell was Nick talking about?

Nick looked deathly pale. 'What? What is it?'

'We're staying at Lucy's. We haven't been to the toll house.'

'But you said you'd meet me there. You texted me. You said you'd meet me at the house.'

Kelda grabbed her keys from the table. 'Oh God. I didn't mean that. I was distracted. I meant I'd meet you here, at the flat.'

He scraped back his chair. 'I don't understand. We went to the toll house earlier. The back door was open. I saw your boyfriend, Simon . . .'

'Simon? Oh God.'

She ran to the door, breathing fast. Simon's words flashed

through her mind: *When you kill someone, it stays with you. It drives you mad. You wonder if you might do it again.* She remembered the last time she'd been to the house to grab their things, she was sure she'd locked the back door. Of course, she'd locked the back door! Or rather, it locked automatically on closing. And, of course, Nick didn't know they'd been staying at Lucy's. Dylan would just have gone along with it, presuming they were going back to the toll house after Lucy's hurried exit.

Nick followed as she ran down the stairs. 'We were in the park,' he said, running to catch up. 'It got too cold. We were halfway to yours, so we thought we'd walk, wait for you there.' He snatched his breath. 'We were going to play football in the garden to warm ourselves up until you got home.'

'But I haven't been home. I've been in the office.'

'I saw someone waving from the bedroom window. Dylan's bedroom window. And then I spoke to Simon. Dylan ran in and I spoke to Simon.'

'Spoke to him?' She felt ill. 'But we haven't seen each other for days. Simon doesn't even have a key.'

Nick shook his head. 'He said you were there, too, that you were in the bathroom. That you'd just got out of the bath. So I sent Dylan up the stairs to meet you and then I walked home.'

'Oh God.' Everything seemed to be tilting, the staircase, the banister, the breezeblock walls. The whole world felt like it was slipping away from her, like she was losing her grasp on reality. 'I wasn't there. I was still in work, stuck on the phone to Cassandra.'

He threw open the front door of the flats. Wind spiralled up the staircase. A little boy in a Halloween outfit ran past them on the street, hands raised above his head, making ghost noises.

'It was definitely Simon? The person you spoke to?'

Nick swallowed hard. 'Definitely. I saw him on the landing. I saw him plainly, like I'm seeing you now.'

She ran, swerving the fairgoers, the children lingering over hotdogs and pink fluffs of candyfloss, the mums and dads jostling pushchairs. Shouting at them to get out of her way, careless of the parents who stopped and stared, who grabbed their kids out of her path. Nick went in the opposite direction, to the shed at the back of the flats, to get his bike. With all the fair traffic, the bike might be quicker than the car, he said. He'd meet her there.

She pulled her car keys from her pocket, unable to stem the fear any longer. Dylan was in the toll house with Simon. Simon who'd tricked Nick into leaving him there. Simon who gave Emma the creeps, who'd killed a child, who – by his own admission – couldn't be trusted. She thought of the game of hide and seek Dylan had played in school. Played with the man. The same man he said he'd seen in the house, who wanted to break his neck. *Simon.*

She jumped in the car and rammed it into reverse, touching bumpers with the car behind, hearing the scrape of plastic against plastic. At the same time, her phone rang: an unknown number. She pressed answer and switched it to loudspeaker, thinking it might be Nick.

'Kelda.' Cassandra's voice sounded sour and disapproving. 'I rang the office again at four fifty-five but you weren't there. Can I remind you that I pay you until five o'clock?'

'For God's sake, shut up.'

She pressed the 'end call' button, then swung the car out into the road, driving erratically, beeping at pedestrians to move aside, jumping a red light, following the diversion signs from the fair to the north side of town, to the Old Turnpike Road.

You'll never manage. You're too young. You should hand Dylan over to an adoption agency.

Mum's words screamed in her mind, the words she'd said all those years ago when Kelda had mooted the idea of adopting her nephew.

It's nothing to be ashamed of. He'd have a better chance at a good life. A mum and a dad. Maybe a couple of siblings. You'd only be holding him back if you kept him. You'd be holding yourself back.

She pressed harder on the accelerator, speeding past the forty-miles-an-hour sign, out into the countryside. The toll house was a smudge in the distance, so isolated, a single building amongst the fields, crouched in front of the wood. She wondered how she could have stood living out here since the spring.

She parked beneath the bay window and ran from the car to the path, the little path that led through the gate and into the garden. She'd been this way so many times over the last eight months, to and from work, to and from sports groups, to and from the shops, but she'd never really looked at it closely, the old paving slabs, the pile of jagged rocks on one side.

The house was silent, no lights within, the back door ajar just as Nick had said. She pushed it wide, hearing it creak on its hinges. Immediately, there was a flutter of activity on the kitchen tiles. Mice scurrying from her footfall as she walked over a week's worth of post. The place stank. Mice and dust and dirt, and on the edge of it, lavender. She remembered what Mr Pritchard had said, about lavender being a warning, as she reached for the light switch. A faint buzz of electricity, a flicker of brilliant yellow that fizzled away to nothing.

She flicked her phone onto torch mode and edged forwards. Still only early evening, but the days were getting shorter, the darkness closing in, and it made her feel safer, seeing the white light reflecting off the front of the microwave and the gleam of the fridge and the magnolia walls. She saw the gash in the cavity wall, wider than ever, almost wide enough to reach right in and tear the mask from the wall. She crept past it, knowing the worst thing to do right now would be to call out for Dylan, to let Simon know that she was here too.

She flashed the torch into the lounge – empty – then tiptoed to the bottom of the stairs, tripping over Dylan's boots still cast aside from the football game. It was much darker here, no natural light except for the windows on the first floor, the tiny window on the left of the landing and a thin tail of light from her own bedroom window. The door to Dylan's room was closed but she knew, instinctively, he was in there, probably hiding beneath the duvet, wondering where she was. Or else Simon had him and had cornered him and had ... Oh God. She swallowed hard, eyes travelling up and down the swirling brown carpet, resting on the place where Emma had lain, where Glenys Pritchard had fallen before dying in the hospital. Suddenly, she sprinted, grabbing hold of the old banister, propelling herself upwards, no longer bothering to be quiet. Her mouth felt dry, her hand damp with sweat against the rail. Her shadow flashed up the wall in front of her, landing at Dylan's bedroom door. She raced up the steps to meet it.

'Dylan?'

She heard a sound beyond the door, whimpering like a puppy. She threw it wide. Dylan was on the floor in the corner beside the lava lamp, legs drawn into a ball, clutching his fluffy blue rabbit. She ran towards him, across the creaking floorboard, and cradled him in her arms.

'It's okay, it's okay, I'm here.'

He sobbed into her chest.

'What happened?' she said, thinking it was going to be all right after all. There was no one else here. No Simon as far as she could see. It had all been a terrible mistake; there'd be a rational explanation. Dylan was safe, that was the main thing. The *only* thing. 'What are you doing up here on your own?'

His eyes darted around her to the landing. 'It's him,' he said.

She gasped. 'Simon?'

He shook his head, confused. 'No, the other man.'

She felt an icy blanket of cold on her shoulders. 'What other man?'

'The man in the dark jacket. The one the woman told me to stay away from. The one who pretended to be Simon to Uncle Nick.'

She shook him by his arms, her mind clearing of one fear only to be replaced by another. 'Who? I don't understand. There is no man.'

'Yes, there is.' His eyes were wide, panicked. 'The man who wrote on the walls. He's still here.'

She thought of the lipstick scrawled all over the new paint-work; the pictures Dylan had drawn at school, the man with black holes for eyes.

'I'm sorry I didn't tell you. I was scared. He said he was going to kill me if I didn't get your lipstick. He made me give it to him. He wanted to write you a message. He wanted to tell you who you really were.'

She thought of the name in red on the wall: *Bella.*

'And now he's here again.'

'Where, Dylan, where?'

Dylan shook his head. 'I don't know anymore. He was on the landing, before. He wanted to come into my bedroom. He said I was in the way.'

She held her breath and inched around to face the door, expecting to see someone there. But there was nobody.

'Hold my hand,' she said, keeping the fear from her voice, wishing there was some other way out, that they didn't have to cross the landing and go down those stairs. 'I'm going to get you out of here. The car's outside. I'm going to take you away from the toll house and we're never coming back. You trust me, don't you?'

He looked at her, red-eyed, screwing Snuggy into his chest. 'But you're not my mum.'

'What?' The cold crept deeper, crept right into her core. 'Who told you that?'

'I heard you and Auntie Em arguing in the kitchen, the morning after the party.'

'Oh God.' She planted her hands over her face and breathed into her palms, fighting the urge to be sick. No, no, no, she screamed in her head. Lowering her hands, she saw the fright in Dylan's eyes, the confusion; she realised how lost he was. No wonder he'd got into trouble at school. No wonder he'd hidden himself in the games cupboard.

'Dylan, look at me,' she said, grabbing hold of him. 'Auntie Em was right, I'm not your biological mum, but I've looked after you ever since you were born. I rocked you to sleep when you were a baby, I watched you grow up, I was there when you took your first steps, and I've loved you all that time. Although I didn't give birth to you, I'm your mum in every other way possible. Just like Georgie and Ethan's mums. I've never loved anyone more in my life.'

She took hold of his hand and felt him squeeze her fingers like he was testing them out, wondering if he could trust her.

'Come on,' she said. 'Let's go downstairs. Go back to Lucy's. We can talk about it there. I can explain it properly. Ready?'

He nodded. She pulled him up and turned towards the door.

Something was creeping across the bedroom walls. A trick of the light, a dappled shadow. But the more she looked, the more she realised it wasn't just a shadow. It was real. Real substance. Something that looked like a spider's web but wasn't, spreading outwards, inching upwards towards the ceiling. Not white like a cobweb, but red. The red of blood.

'*Bella?*'

Her heart leaped in her throat. No voice she recognised, but one that sent shivers of dread through her body.

Dylan's hand trembled in hers. 'It's him,' he whispered.

'*I want the boy out of the way. Don't you understand?*'

She spun around, even now trying to think logically, trying to find the source of the noise. The bed. It was coming from beneath the bed. A low voice, crackly like it was being played through an old-fashioned radio.

She stumbled towards the landing, pulling Dylan along with her. Something rolled across the carpet, almost tripping her over: the microphone Nick had given Dylan for his birthday. She stopped where she was, halfway across the bedroom floor, and stared at it in horror, remembering how she'd taken the batteries from the back of it and thrown them against the wall.

'*I wanted you, not the boy. The boy is in the way.*'

The microphone wasn't flickering. There was no red light. It was completely dead. And yet, the voice was coming from it, louder now, growing in confidence. Not the woman's voice she'd heard before, but a man's.

'*I knew you'd come back to me. I've been waiting for you for a long, long time.*'

She kicked the microphone back under the bed and pulled

Dylan towards the door. 'It's okay. It's just a toy. Uncle Nick shouldn't have—'

'No, Mum!' Dylan tugged her backwards and pointed at the landing wall.

A shadow was moving towards them in the murky light from the little window.

'It's him,' Dylan sobbed. 'It's the man.'

'Why did you bring the boy here?'

This time, the voice came from in front, echoing across the landing and down the stairs. Her heart thumped erratically. She stared at the shadow in frozen horror: a head, a pair of shoulders, an arm raised high, fingers clutched around what looked like a knife. She gripped Dylan hard as the shadow edged closer, growing larger and larger against the landing wall, yet she couldn't see anyone or anything to explain it. She pulled Dylan behind her so that he couldn't see the shadow man, couldn't see the shadow knife, trying to think through the fog of terror.

Mum's voice clawed through the darkness in her mind: *You're too young, too inexperienced, you'll never make things work.*

Shut the fuck up, Mum, she shouted in her head.

She pulled Dylan back into the bedroom and slammed the door shut, wishing it had a lock on the inside like the ones in Lucy's house. But she doubted even a lock would keep the man out. She looked up and gasped. The walls of Dylan's bedroom were now entirely covered in bright red streaks and there was a smell, a horrid metallic tang, that reminded her of the time she'd cut herself peeling the orange, the bright red blood running into the kitchen sink.

She ran to the curtains and yanked them closed, pitching the room into darkness.

'Mum. I can't see you!'

'Shh. He can't see us now either. He won't be able to find us.' She crouched beside him, praying she was right, then tucked his toy rabbit under his arm, and whispered in his ear, 'I'm going to count to three and then we're going to run, okay?'

'Okay.'

'Do you trust me?'

A pause that made her heart ache.

She felt him nod. 'Yes.'

The bedroom door blasted open. Cold sliced into the room.

'Bella, where are you? Are you still angry? She was but a wanton woman, run off with a poor man.'

'One, two, three. Run!'

She dragged Dylan out of the bedroom and along the length of the landing towards the window at the far end. Behind her, she could hear the man groping about in the darkness, trying to find them, knocking into the bed, the wardrobe, stumbling against the landing wall. She felt her way with her fingers against the banister until she reached the dim light at the top of the stairs.

'Why do you run from me, Bella?'

A hand landed on her shoulder. She screamed. Fingers gripped her hard, bruising her skin.

'Are we not destined to be together for ever?'

'No!' she shouted into the dark. 'I don't want you. Get away from me. Get away from Dylan!'

She pulled Dylan forwards, feeling the top of the stairs with her feet. A feeling of utter dread that rooted her to the spot. Sorrow and anger and violence rolled into one. She felt like she would be there for ever, drowning in terror, in the awful events that had happened here a hundred and fifty years ago; that she'd never be free of them.

'Mummy?' Dylan was at her side, tugging her hand, jolting her back into reality. She threw her arms around him. She wouldn't stay here. She wouldn't become a victim. She needed to survive for Dylan.

She forced herself to smile down at him. 'Right, Batman, are you ready?'

'Ready.'

Fingers dug into her shoulder. Sharp bony fingers. She looked behind her and saw a man's face. Not a shadow this time, but real flesh and blood. Narrow lips. Sunken cheeks. Eyes like two dark hollows.

'Get away from us!' she shouted. 'I don't want you! I'll never want you!'

She felt his fingers in her back as she slipped, cradling Dylan, taking him with her down the stairs.

40

⌒

1863

It's the night the baby died.

Bella's lying on the bed in the toll house, not dead, just very, very tired. The birth has taken it out of her, the sorrow of the dead child so great, she doesn't even try to move. She couldn't move even if she wanted to, she's drugged by the herbs she imbibed, the herbs she took to ease the pain of labour. She bought them from a poor woman in town who specialises in plant magic, brewed them into a tea, and sipped them when the pains began. Then, when she awoke and found the babe dead in her arms and her husband curled at her side, she drank some more. But she finds they are too strong. So strong she cannot even lift her head; she should have trusted her own wisdom, her own knowledge of plants and flowers and their various properties, not the poor woman's. She should have drawn strength and protection from the pebbles as she has always done. But recently, she's been doubting herself. Doubting her husband more than ever. Sometimes she sees a shadow crossing his face when he catches her touching her belly, caressing the child within, and she wonders if she really knows him at all.

She loved him once, many years ago, when he'd shown her the marks his father made, the places where his flesh had been torn apart. She'd felt sorry for him, thinking she could make things better, thinking she could love all that pain away. But how wrong she'd been. She remembers their wedding night, the look in his eyes as he'd pinned her to the bed and pulled her hair, his desire for her unsatiable. No longer the shy young boy she'd first met, or the awkward youth, but someone she didn't know at all. She remembers his rage all those times she's visited her mother or her friends in the town. It's as if he wants her all to himself. She's even wondered if the beatings he gives her are somehow connected to all the children she's lost. But she has no one to ask save Helen, a spinster, who would not understand.

Now, she feels people around her, Joseph leaving her side, the doctor bending over her, saying there is no pulse. The words sing in her head but make no sense, all she can think about it that poor dead child. How much she would have loved it, cared for it, given it the best life possible. She'd hoped the child would soften her husband's anger, but recently she's feared more for the child than for herself.

Helen washes and dresses her with her tender hands. She knows all this, though she is so drugged she cannot open her eyes. She is just so sad, so very, very sad, she wouldn't want to open her eyes even if she could. Life has no meaning for her now that the baby is dead, though she supposes she will get over it as all women do. She will have to get over it. Life goes on, that's what her mother says. She hears the snip-snip-snip of scissors close to her head, as Helen takes a lock of hair, and doesn't question it at all.

Then, a few minutes later, or maybe it's hours, she hears her husband talking to the doctor, saying something about a mask.

They leave her in peace, and she tries desperately to sleep off the herbs. She needs to get better. She needs to make Joseph his supper for fear he will strike her. She needs to bury her child. She's worried what he might do to the poor thing if she's not there to see to it. She dozes for a while, but it's not real sleep, not at all restorative. She remembers what the poor woman said, something about the berries of the sleeping plant. Why hadn't she paid better attention to her words? Why had she been so distracted by her husband's jealousy of their unborn child? So distracted, she'd trusted a stranger more than her own judgement!

When she awakes, she feels something strange on her face. The doctor is speaking somewhere above her, saying something about bandages. She feels him pressing his fingers into her nostrils and she tries to cry out but finds that she cannot. Her skin feels heavy and wet, as though weighed by a great cloth. She cannot understand it, it feels so strange, so unnatural. She cannot understand what the doctor is doing, and she wonders if she's had a terrible accident. For a moment, she forgets about the baby, the labour, the sad silent years. She struggles to breathe as the doctor leaves her with his fool of a servant. She tries to raise a hand to tell him she is fading fast, that she cannot get any air, that the bandages, or whatever they are, are too tight, but she doesn't have the strength. She tries and tries and tries to raise her hand. The doctor's servant is killing her with all these bandages, she knows that, but she cannot make him understand. Where is her husband? For all she hates him and cannot abide his touch, he will know what to do. He will know she is suffering. He will peel off the bandages. He will save her, for he wants her more than anything.

She searches on the bed for the pebbles, but her fingers will not move, they merely press against the sheets and she remembers – oh, how she remembers – her husband last night when she needed them most, sweeping the pebbles to the floor!

41

NOW

Kelda came to, lying on the carpet in the hallway, a pain in her head where she'd knocked it against the banister, protecting Dylan. He was curled in a ball beside her, clutching Snuggy. Dazed, she pulled him upright and lifted him into her arms.

'Mummy?'

'It's okay.' She felt drunk, like she was going to be sick. 'You're okay. We're getting out of here, remember?'

She looked behind her, one final glimpse at the landing in the dying light.

Standing in front of the bookcase at the top of the stairs was a woman in a long dress, flowers tied at her waist, smiling down at them. Kelda smiled back, despite the pain, despite everything that had just happened. A feeling that the woman would do them no harm.

A shadow crossed the woman's face. She stretched out her arms, not to reach or embrace them, but as if in warning.

Go away from here, the woman seemed to say.

A moment later, she'd vanished, and in her place, shining like stars along the banister and up the stairs, were thousands of tiny white pebbles.

Kelda held Dylan tight and ran.

42

―∞∞∞―

It took Kelda three weeks to pluck up the courage to return to the toll house. She'd been staying at Lucy's whilst Lucy and Mike were up north, looking after their daughter. Their grandchild, a little girl, had been born that same night and was doing well. Tiny but thriving, Lucy cooed down the phone. Kelda remembered visiting Dylan for the very first time in hospital, his skin all wrinkly, his fingers bunched, his eyes the colour of the sea. She remembered standing in the hospital car park, Emma already huddled in the passenger seat, laying Dylan gently in the baby car seat with the newborn insert and kissing his forehead, promising she'd drive more carefully than she'd ever done in her life. Although Dylan now knew he was adopted, he hadn't asked for the details, though she guessed that would change as he got older. For now, all he wanted was the reassurance that she was still his mum and always would be.

It was Saturday afternoon, and Dylan was playing at Georgie's house. She still wasn't keen on their friendship but she'd come to realise there was only so much she could do; Dylan had to work it out for himself.

'Don't let him bully you,' she said, kissing him on the cheek before they rang the Wattses' doorbell.

'Mum!' He wiped off her kiss and grinned. 'Georgie's my best friend.'

'Still, you've got to stand up for yourself. Even best friends can be mean at times.'

To her surprise, Mrs Watts invited her in for a coffee. Normally, Mrs Watts was too busy to chat, or had other friends to entertain. Only occasionally she seemed bored enough to invite Kelda in. Today seemed like one of those occasions, until Kelda realised Mrs Watts just wanted to gossip. She'd seen the newspapers. The police had dug up two bodies in the field behind the old toll house. A man and a woman who – according to the forensic examination – had been heavily pregnant. Both bodies had been dated to the early 1860s, when the last toll man had lived in the cottage, the toll man who was hanged for murdering his sister-in-law. The police had so far drawn a blank, which was unsurprising given the age of the skeletons, but the link to the toll man was obvious. There was also the theory, impossible to prove, that the woman was the daughter of a local aristocrat who had disappeared in 1864 with a servant-lover.

'You're not living there, are you?' Mrs Watts's eyes gleamed with fascination.

'I'm staying with a friend. I suppose we'll have to go back eventually, until we manage to sell.' Kelda didn't want to talk about any of it; she wished Mrs Watts would let her go. She'd only meant to pop in for ten minutes and she'd arranged to meet Nick at the toll house in half an hour's time.

'Look,' Mrs Watts drew her fluffy slippers up onto the pristine white sofa. 'I don't want to interfere, but I've got a house just sitting there in the middle of town with no one in it at present. There are a few jobs that need doing before we find a long-term tenant. The house needs painting throughout for a start. How about you and Dylan stay there, do some painting for me? Peppercorn rent until you manage to sell?'

'It's very kind of you but—'

'My way of saying thank you.'

'Thank you?'

Mrs Watts flicked imaginary dust from the sofa. 'Georgie's a handful. He can be a complete nightmare at times. We've even had to employ a child psychologist. The only time he really seems happy is when he's playing with Dylan. Dylan's been a lifeline.'

'Really?' She didn't quite believe it.

'Georgie talks about Dylan all the time.' Mrs Watts laughed. 'Sometimes I think he wants to *be* Dylan. But it's not just that. There's another thing too. I feel a bit guilty.'

'Guilty?'

'Your friend, Simon.' Mrs Watts stared at her nails. 'When I met him at the party, I recognised his name. I'd heard something about him from a friend of a friend, something bad to do with his job. I told him to stay away from you, that you deserved better. To be perfectly honest, I was relieved when I heard you'd split up, though I still felt bad for making you unhappy.'

'It's okay. We weren't really going anywhere anyway.' She

didn't want to talk about that either, though she was strangely touched that Mrs Watts had decided to bring it up, that she had taken it upon herself to warn him to stay away. But she knew Simon wasn't a real threat. She'd had a bunch of flowers and a card from him since, a sorry card promising not to bother her again. More precious than the flowers had been the look on Cassandra's face when they'd arrived at the office. Cassandra had presumed they were for her, another gift from her husband; she'd even started to arrange them in a vase, then unceremoniously dumped them on Kelda's desk when she'd read the accompanying card. She hadn't brought up the subject of the after-work phone call, sensing perhaps, in a rare moment of empathy, there'd been something else going on. But Kelda knew it was only a matter of time before she found an excuse to dismiss her.

'Anyway, the point is, the house is there if you want it. Just send me a text.'

She still couldn't believe Mrs Watts's offer as she stood outside the toll house, watching the road, watching the weave of Nick's bike in the wind. That night, when she'd dragged Dylan from the toll house, she'd met Nick outside on the garden path; he'd had a puncture and ended up running. He'd helped them both into her car and driven them to A&E to get them checked over from the fall. Afterwards, he'd driven them back to his place and they'd sat up late, drinking wine whilst Dylan slept in Nick's bed, going over everything that had happened. The woman, Isabella Walton, had been trying to save them, Kelda was sure of it, that's why she'd seen her at the top of the stairs; Joseph had thought that Kelda was Bella and he couldn't understand why she'd chosen Dylan over him.

'Who knows what would have happened if you hadn't found us?' she'd said, leaning against Nick. He'd put an arm around her shoulder, and despite everything that had happened, she'd felt sleepy and content. 'Whether he'd have followed us down the stairs and finished what he'd started. Whether Bella would have had the strength to stop him. When Dylan first saw him in his room all those weeks ago, I smelled lavender. Lavender was used by the Victorians as a warning. She's been trying to warn me all this time, but I didn't realise. Not until it was almost too late.' She shuddered. 'The power of that man, to be felt all these years later.'

Nick had taken hold of her hand and smiled at her softly. 'You'd have found a way to save Dylan,' he'd said. 'Even if I hadn't arrived. Even if Bella hadn't stopped him. You're *way* more capable than you think.'

But although she'd formally put it to bed, the man on the landing was still there, stealing into her dreams. She was glad she was so busy in work with Lucy still on leave; it meant she fell asleep almost immediately she hit the pillow, only to wake at three o'clock in the morning, tossing and turning until the early hours. Sometimes she'd phone Nick, and despite her protest, he'd cycle over in the middle of the night and talk to her about America and hint they could come with him. And for the hundredth time, she'd say she'd think about it. But it was paper over the crack. She couldn't go on like this for ever. She was exhausted lying awake every night.

It was the reason she'd agreed to meet Nick at the toll house. There was something she needed to do, and she didn't want to have to do it on her own, and she couldn't sell the place, not with a clear conscience, until she'd done it.

'Hi,' he said, making her feel nervous and school girly despite all the things they'd been through together. 'Ready?'

'Ready.'

He swung his rucksack from his back, unzipped it and took out a short-handled axe.

The house was as she'd left it all those weeks ago. Wine glasses still unwashed in the kitchen from the party, Emma's holdall still on the table gathering dust. The last she'd heard, Emma had left Mum's after the operation, leaving a note on the table saying she'd gone back to Luke. That was after Mum had transferred £3,000 into her bank account for a catering course. 'Typical Emma,' Mum had said, trying to make light of it. Kelda had sensed her disappointment and promised she'd visit her soon with Dylan. She really meant it this time. She'd make a date, plan the trip; it was time to start afresh, put the past – all Mum's meddling, her old-fashioned ideas of right and wrong – behind them.

Nick checked the rest of the house whilst she stayed in the kitchen. Everything was in order, no blood on the walls like she'd seen that night with Dylan, though she knew Nick still believed her. He moved Emma's holdall onto the floor and together they dragged the table into the middle of the room, clearing the space in front of the cavity wall.

'Hideous, isn't it?' said Nick, looking at the death mask.

The hole was wider than the mask itself and cracks had inched right across the plaster.

'Right,' said Nick. 'Let's do this.'

He threw the axe over his shoulder and brought it crashing against the wall. She watched him work, bringing the plasterboard to the floor, then chipping around the mask until he was able to break it free. It fell to the floor with a light thud, glaring up at them – angrily, she thought – through its sleeping eyes. It could be anyone, a man or a woman, yet it filled her with such horror and for a flickering moment, she was back on the landing, her heart pounding, the hand gripping her shoulder. *Those eyes.*

'What now?' said Nick.

She took the axe from him. 'Stand back. I've never done this before.' She brought the axe down hard, splintering the face in two, a perfect crack running through the nose, splitting the mouth.

She stood upright, exhilarated. 'The wood,' she said. 'Let's bury it in the wood.'

They took a spade from the garden shed and made their way to the back of the toll house, passing the field and the place where the police had been digging.

It had been a long time since she'd been to the wood. She'd come here in the early days with Dylan, watching for rabbits and picking leaves for art projects. Her new life had been full of promise back then. They chose a spot in the middle and started digging, taking it in turns until they were a good metre deep. Kelda laid the two halves of the mask together before shovelling the soil back on top. She held Nick's hand, looking down at the newly laid ground, thinking she should say something, but not sure what. She wondered if she should kiss him, whether it would feel magical or wrong, remembering how Nick and Emma had kissed all those years ago. A drunken night, one of many in her student days, that threatened to wedge itself between them. She decided there and then to let it go.

The wind brought a flutter of leaves to their feet, over

the place they'd buried the mask, already hiding what had passed. Nick squeezed her hand, seeming to know what she was thinking.

This wasn't a grave, she thought, or a place to kiss. This wasn't a place to remember. This was a place to forget.

43

∽

1864

Early morning on a bright day in July, Dr Marsh pushes
open the front door of the toll house and walks inside,
clutching his package. He'd heard the house was open, the
locks broken by townsfolk come here to satisfy their curiosity:
the scene of the grisly murder. Not that he supposes there is
anything to see, just a house like any other.

There won't be another toll man, that's for sure, he thinks,
as he turns into the kitchen. The turnpike trusts haven't been
popular, and the railways and canals have replaced a lot of the
old trade routes. The tollgate has been open ever since the
day Joseph Walton threw Helen down the stairs. Dr Marsh
remembers the last time he was in here, attending to the body
of Joseph's wife. He remembers the death mask, his servant dip-
ping the bandages in the plaster and moulding them to Bella's

face. It had seemed wrong to him at the time, though he'd not said anything to Joseph and the money had been useful; it had seemed unnecessarily morbid. Why couldn't Joseph be satisfied with a lock of hair or a photograph like everyone else?

He remembered the night before that, being roused from his sleep by the midwife. A laudanum-induced sleep. He'd taken too many drops, more than the usual. It had become a bad habit, born out of a need to numb his mind after a hard day's work. The abrupt awakening had thrown him; he'd felt listless and annoyed and when he'd arrived at the toll house ... He shook his head, attempting to dismiss the memory, but it was there, bubbling below the surface of his mind. He'd ordered his servant to complete the mask, then he'd turned to leave and seen, out of the corner of his eye, the body — no, it wasn't possible, was it? — twitching. He should have gone back then, he should have checked, but he'd known it was all in his mind. The laudanum. He'd needed to get home to his surgery, to the bottle he kept in his desk; he'd felt the sweat on his forehead, running beneath his collar; he'd felt his hand shaking. He'd needed those drops more than anything ...

Now, he tours the ground floor first — nothing much to see — then makes his way to the landing. So, this is where it happened, he thinks to himself, fingering the blood stains. He is a medical man, used to death, yet still it disturbs him to think this is where Helen was stabbed. So much blood: on the walls, on the carpet at his feet. He wasn't in love with Helen, but she'd proved herself a loyal companion and, at his age, he couldn't ask for more. Such a shame, he thinks, straddling the rag-rug.

He takes the package into the larger bedroom, ignoring the child's room on the right, knowing this is where he will find what he is looking for. He only hopes he is not too late, that someone hasn't already carted it off as a souvenir. That's what he thinks has happened as he surveys the room. He *is* too late. He throws back the covers of the bed and upturns the pillows, then ruffles through drawers and in the wardrobe. Bella's dresses, unworn for nearly a year, smell of mothballs. He feels a deep sorrow as he rifles through them. He'd always liked Bella ever since she was a little girl, asking him how to mend a broken bird's wing. He'd taken her to his house and shown her pictures of anatomy in his books. Not a bird's wing but a human arm; maybe it would mend just the same? One day he'd found her by the river, collecting pebbles in her skirt. He'd told her how the pebbles had been worn away over millions of years. He remembered the look on her face as she'd rolled one in her hand as though it was treasure. He'd realised, then, that he loved her, though he knew it was never meant to be – she was too good for him, too young, too pretty – and some things, he realised, were better left unsaid.

He's just about to leave, when he sees something on the table beside the bed, covered in a lace cloth. He cannot believe he's been so stupid as to walk straight past it. Next to it is a photograph of Bella on her wedding day. Someone has taken a knife and scored out the man beside her, her husband. He pulls back the cloth and reveals Bella's plaster face, so uncannily lifelike, it makes him shiver. He takes it downstairs with his package and walks back into the kitchen, calling for his servant who has been waiting patiently by the front door.

'There,' he says, pointing to the brick pillar that divides the room into two.

The servant takes the package and pulls off the paper. Inside is another death mask, this one of Joseph Walton. Dr Marsh has several of these masks in his house, taken from the faces of hanged criminals. It always seems so pointless, the coroner's enquiry after a hanging – death is always by separation of the upper neck vertebrae or else more slowly, as in Joseph's case, by strangulation – but at least it allows him access to the body. It fascinates him, these plaster faces, the criminals in their death agony. He likes to measure the size of the skull, the length of the nose, the space between the eyes, looking for clues. If only criminals could be identified by their skulls, how much safer society would be!

But this mask, he doesn't care for. He's had nightmares ever since he hung it in his study alongside the others. It's as if the spirit of the dead man is trapped inside. He's felt this before, be it science or something else, the essence of the dead man contained within the plaster. He remembers the first mask he ever made, of a criminal hanged for poisoning his wife, how surprised he'd been when he'd held the finished mask in his hands and felt his fingers tingle. So many times since, he's felt the same tingling. It's not just his imagination. But the mask of Joseph Walton is worse than any he's experienced before. This spirit is powerful. It knows no bounds, emanating even beyond the mask itself. He's felt it following him around the house and even as he goes about his business in the parish. He's awoken at night, sweating, with the image of the mask in his mind. He's even heard footsteps in his study that cannot be explained. He knows he needs to get rid of the mask and thus end his troubles, and this seems to be just the place: a warning to others, a reminder of the darkness that has settled here.

He leaves his servant to plaster the mask into the pillar. It's not an easy job, but his servant has been with him a long time and has proved his worth. Dr Marsh knows that he will do the job well.

He walks back to the town, wanting the exercise. So decrepit that house. So unhealthy! He's been so much better recently with the laudanum, only taking what he needs to get him through the day, but this has jolted him back to a year ago. He thinks of the funeral, of Joseph smashing the coffin with the spade. He thinks of Helen whispering to him about Bella's other losses. He thinks of his fears about Joseph, his suspicions that the man was unhinged. It was the reason he'd sent Helen to the house in the first place, to prove her worth as a doctor's wife. If only he'd realised the peril she was in!

He stops by the bridge into town and watches the river rushing over the grey-white stones, collecting driftwood as it goes. He descends the bank and plunges his hand into the freezing water. He feels cleansed from the house, a different person, as he places Bella's death mask beneath the surface and allows the water to caress it, flowing over the nose and the eyelids and the soft round mouth, just as it caressed Bella's pebbles, releasing her spirit to wander wherever it might please. Perhaps, he fancies, thinking about the bird's wing, she will find her way to a place or a person that really needs her. As for him, he knows he has no need for this mask; he'd not wanted to make it in the first place. He remembers laying the bandages over her face, so overcome with emotion he'd had to give the job away to his servant. Bella was not a criminal, just a sweet young lady and his judgement was right: she was dead by the time he arrived at the toll house last August. There was no twitching body.

He gives a little gasp and sets the mask free – sets his mind free – watching it bob for a moment before disappearing for ever to the riverbed.

ACKNOWLEDGEMENTS

So many people have worked hard to make this book possible. My heartfelt thanks to:

My agent, Cathryn Summerhayes, for just being the best: believing in me, patiently responding to my emails, championing *The Toll House*, and holding my hand every step of the way. You deserve a medal.

My editor, Rosanna Forte, for seeing the potential in this story and helping me bring it to life with extra twists, turns and spookiness. It's been an absolute pleasure working with you.

The amazing team at Curtis Brown including Jess Molloy, Lisa Babalis, Grace Robinson and Katie McGowan. The equally amazing team at Little, Brown including Stephanie Melrose, Aimee Kitson, Thalia Proctor, Ben McConnell, Nico Taylor (who designed the most stunning book cover I've ever seen), my copy-editor and proofreader, and all the many others who have worked so hard behind the scenes. I am incredibly lucky to have worked with such professional and friendly people.

Anna Davies and the fabulous team at Curtis Brown Creative. Particular thanks to Suzannah Dunn, tutor extraordinaire, who taught me more about writing than any number of how-to books.

The 2017 online CBC cohort, with special thanks to the best writing group in the world: Joanne Clague, Emma Clark Lam, Sara Cox, Sarah Daniels, and Asha Hick. I wouldn't have got here without you.

Belinda Stephens for your enthusiasm and attention to detail.

Alison Seymour for heroically reading every single book I've ever written.

Sally and Annie for casting your midwifery eyes over Chapter Two.

Sara Sarre at Blue Pencil Agency and the Lucy Cavendish Fiction Prize for being part of my writing journey.

All the other wonderful people who have read my novels or offered words of encouragement over the years, including but not limited to Annie, Charlotte, Marie, Sarah, Maggie and Claire.

Last but not least, my family. My parents, Sue and Darrol, for always believing I could write, bringing me up in a house full of books, and supporting me one hundred per cent. My sister, Heather Davey, for being my writing buddy and best friend. We'll keep telling it like it is. My grandfather, 'Uncle David', for reading us his stories and filling our heads with dreams. My mother-in-law, Jill, for sharing her love of literature. My ever-patient children, Wilfred, Ebah and Taliesin, for being adorable. Mummy is proud of every single word *you* write. My husband, Steve, for believing in my writing more than I do, making me endless cups of tea, charging my laptop, being on hand for hugs and listening patiently to my plot ideas. Steve, this book is dedicated to you.

Read on for an exclusive preview of
Carly Reagon's thrilling new ghost story

HEAR HIM CALLING

COMING OCTOBER 2024

The boy looks up at the summit, at the white rocks and the concrete marker. He's lived in Gaer Fach all his life, but he's never been up there. Most days, he doesn't even notice the mountain range, or the startling clarity of the river as it rushes over stones and weeds, or the lush green fields. But today – maybe it's the heat, maybe it's the fact his parents are out and won't be back until teatime – he feels restless.

Across the yard, Cerys sits on an upturned crate, whittling sticks. She's wearing a dress the colour of the sun but it's streaked with dirt.

'Dwi eisiau ddringo i'r awyr,' he says. *I want to climb to the sky.*

Cerys pulls a face, her cheeks marked with the same dusty lines as her dress. 'Wyt ti'n crazy?'

He stares up at the concrete marker, what the grown-ups call the trig point. Is it really that crazy? All their lives they've been told to keep away from the mountain. They've been told it's dangerous. But it's the smallest mountain in the range. How dangerous can it be?

'Scaredy cat,' he pokes fun at his sister though she looks anything but, slicing a stick with the penknife – *his* penknife – alarmingly close to her thumb.

She puts the knife down. She's younger than him but just as fierce. 'What did you say?'

He smirks and wipes his hands on his shorts.

She stands up, scattering flecks of stick to the ground. 'All right then,' she says. 'Beat you to the summit.'

They run through the village, past the church and the pub, then take the mountain road that winds through a farmyard onto the footpath. The boy strips off his T-shirt and tucks it into his shorts, his white chest gleaming.

'Hey,' he calls, panting as Cerys scrambles ahead. 'Let's take this other path.' It's a cop-out, but he's tired. The mountain is harder than it looks, and they've been running for what seems like for ever. To his relief, Cerys doesn't argue, just follows him along the level track to the right, a sheep track rather than a real path. Looking down at the valley, they see their street, their house, their neighbours' cars like multicoloured beetles. Beneath them, about halfway up the mountain, is the place they call Y Twr Gwyn, *The White Tower*, that doesn't fit with everything else.

Eventually, the track ends in a cobbled yard.

He whistles. He's never seen this before, obscured as it is from the village by the tower. 'Look at this!'

In front of them is a rough stone cottage, no doors, no windows, just empty holes. They find sticks nearby and poke about inside, prodding at shadows, flicking the carcass of a dead bird in the fireplace. Cerys peers into a large box-like compartment at the back, whilst he sits in an old chair and pulls a packet of cigarettes from his pocket.

She turns. 'How did you get those? Mam will skin you alive.'

'No she won't. Not unless you tell her.' One, two, three strikes of the match. It flares in his hands, making him feel like a man, and the smoke flits upwards. A moment later, a crow screeches at them from the rafters, flapping its wings, fleeing into the daylight. He laughs to mask how startled he'd been, and makes shooting noises, aiming his fingers.

Then, everything changes. The sky darkens. A breeze tickles the nape of his neck.

He drops the cigarette and it burns a hole through his shorts, searing his skin. He jumps to standing, spins around. There's a figure in the doorway, a black silhouette against the afternoon sun. There's something about that figure. Something that makes the hairs on his head stand up on end. Maybe it's the way the figure is staring. Staring with such hate, with eyes that seem to leap from its body. Cat's eyes in the dark. Or maybe it's the glinting chain in its hand, one end wrapped around its wrist, the other end snaking to the floor.

'Rheda!' Cerys shouts from behind him. *Run!*

He takes his chance. There's a crack of light between the figure and the door frame, the gap just small enough for a boy like himself.

He darts into the sunshine and runs across the cobbles, onto the sheep track, his feet catching on the smaller rocks, not turning back until he reaches the mountain path. His thoughts gallop over each other. What is it he saw? What on earth is up there? And where is Cerys? He'd thought she'd followed him. He'd thought she was right behind. A cloud passes over, raising goosebumps along his arms. A buzzard sweeps overhead. And then he hears a ringing in the air. A sharp call of warning.

Somewhere on the mountain, Cerys is screaming.

1.

FIFTY YEARS LATER

Whichever way Lydia turns, the view is stunning, the same images she's seen on Google only bigger and better: the proportions, the expanse, the sheer brutality of the rocks. They're 250 metres up, standing on a ridge in the shadow of the tower, the mountain a mere mound compared to the rest in the range. Next to her, Kyle gapes down at the valley, seemingly as awestruck as she is.

She thinks of the address on the paperwork, tries and fails to sound the words in her head. 'I'm sorry,' she turns to the housekeeper, a woman in her mid-thirties with big curly hair, 'but what did you say the mountain was called again?'

Eleri beams down at Jamie on Lydia's chest, strapped in his carrier, facing inwards. She holds out a hand and encourages him to grip her finger. 'Mynydd Gwyn. It means White Mountain in English, though some would say it's not actually a mountain, just a big hill.'

'But why is it white?' Kyle leans over and fusses with Jamie's socks, pulling them up.

Eleri shrugs. 'The rocks, I suppose. And the old tale about the dragons. You know the one I mean? The white dragon and the red.'

Lydia runs a hand through Jamie's fine hair, hiding her ignorance. Her knowledge of Welsh myths is even worse than her Welsh pronunciation. She looks back at the way they walked earlier: a rough country track to their left all the way to the top. From the trig point, they'd had a good view of the house, a tower of white pebbledash with a grey slate roof. It had been Kyle's idea to climb the mountain first, before meeting Eleri – get a feel for the area, he'd said – and she'd enjoyed the shared challenge of carrying Jamie to the top. On the other side, they'd seen another valley, another sweep of mountains. Not a house in sight.

'I suppose you already know about the history of the tower?' Eleri sorts through a bunch of keys.

'Not really.' Kyle shakes his head, looking slightly embarrassed, like he *should* know the history of the place he's inherited. But the truth is, from what Lydia can gather, he barely knew his grandfather.

'It was originally meant as a viewing tower. An Englishman named Barker had it built in the 1930s, but he didn't keep if for long. He sold it to an artist who turned it into a retreat, added the kitchen and bathrooms, but it didn't take off. There's been a succession of owners since then, as well as periods where it's sat empty. I believe Mr Jeffreys, your grandfather, was the sixth person to live here.'

'I like it,' says Kyle, looking upwards to the roof. There are a couple of slipped tiles, which make Lydia uneasy, but she supposes it's inevitable with the place so exposed. 'At least, it's unusual.'

'Not really the place for a family,' Eleri says. 'Have you any idea what you'll do with it?'

Kyle reaches for Lydia's hand and gives it a squeeze. It was a surprise receiving the solicitor's letter. They'd not even known his grandfather had moved to Wales, let alone to a tower. As far as they'd known, he'd lived in Suffolk all his life. 'Not yet.' He smiles.

Lydia traces the route of their descent – from the summit down a track, through a farm and then a right-angle along another, rougher track to the place they're standing. She understands now why the mountain's called Mynydd Gwyn. The slopes are a patchwork of stone and purple heather and, from here, with the sun brushing the summit, the rock at the top *does* look white. From this angle, it seems impossible that they were standing there an hour ago, sunning themselves and taking selfies. It's too craggy, too difficult. The phrase flits through her mind: *too dangerous.*

'Shall we go inside?' Eleri fits a key into the door at the side of the house and swings it open. There's a smell of damp that immediately takes Lydia back to her student days. *I think I've seen enough already* she wants to say, but Kyle is pulling her in, bending his head though the doorway is higher than he is. She supposes it's the darkness of the place. The feeling that they're entering a cave deep underground.

'Light switch is somewhere. I haven't been here for a while. Aha, here it is.'

A chill runs up Lydia's arms and Jamie whimpers, pulling back from her chest. 'It's okay, little fellow.' Outside, it's baking hot, but in here it's like standing in the depths of winter. She cradles Jamie through the baby carrier as she makes out an L-shaped kitchen with dirty yellow units. There's a microwave that looks like an early model, an electric cooker encrusted with dirt and rust, and a fridge with its door wide open. The stumpy tail of the L is dominated by a sink and, above it, there's a small square window.

'I cleaned everything after your grandfather fell ill,' Eleri says, though it's hard to believe. She pulls back a curtain in the interior wall and steps through an archway into the next room. Then she folds back the shutters. Sunlight floods in, pooling on a coffee table and a couple of tatty armchairs.

'From London did you say?'

'That's right,' says Kyle.

'I bet there aren't many views like this in London.'

Lydia lingers in the kitchen, running her fingers over one of the worktops, gathering dust. 'Strange they only put big windows at the front of the house. Why make the kitchen window so tiny? It doesn't make any sense.' She thinks of the building from the outside. The south side, the side facing the summit, is completely devoid of windows bar this one. 'Why would you build a viewing tower with only half a view?'

She leans over the sink and presses her hands against the pane. She can see the top of the mountain and the cloudless sky, but it's as if she's holding a postcard rather than viewing the real thing.

Eleri's still fussing with the shutters on the other side of the archway. 'All I know is that Barker ran out of money. Or lost interest in the project. Or maybe both. It was quicker to finish the tower this way. Mr Jeffreys did some research, told me bits and bobs, and that's how I know. I think he was lonely. I used to clean up here once a week. It was about all the company he had.'

There's a heavy silence and she imagines Kyle thinking about the side of his family he doesn't really know.

'Do you want to see the rest?' Eleri opens a door into a hall-way and ushers them through, up a flight of stairs. The rooms are stacked one on top of the other, following the same stumpy L-shape as the ground floor. 'It's a strange design,' Eleri admits, 'but then, I'm no architect. This was Mr Jeffreys's bedroom here, with the en suite bathroom.'

There's an oppressive smell of old clothes and damp linen but Kyle doesn't seem to notice, testing the floorboards, whistling at the view. Lydia wonders if he's imagining his grandfather waking up in the old-fashioned bed, shuffling on the slippers that are still tucked beneath it. She glimpses the bathroom behind, filling the small protruding space above the kitchen window, the bath and overhead shower, the extractor fan, the faded baby-blue mat.

'And then, if you follow me up the next flight of stairs, there's a spare bedroom here with another en suite bathroom.' They peer into a space that mimics the one below but without the furniture. 'And then, on the third floor, which also has a wash-room, is the room Mr Jeffreys used to paint in.'

They follow her up the last flight of steps.

'Wow!' Kyle catches Lydia around the waist as they enter the painting studio and stare dizzily at the wide sweep of valley. Instantly, she forgets her earlier reservations. With the extra height, the view through the window is mesmerising.

'You can see Cadair Idris if you look far enough to the left. Snowdon's a little further around. That's the village of Gaer Fach below us, the one you drove through to get here. I run the village shop with my husband, Jon. It's a nice little community. Pub and a shop and not much else. It's very quiet. Did you say you're a sculptor?' Eleri looks at Lydia.

'That's right.'

'No doubt busy in London?'

Lydia smiles. Truth is, not busy enough.

Eleri fills the gap. 'I'm sorry about what happened. I found Mr Jeffreys on the doorstep downstairs. Heart attack, as I'm sure you know.'

'It's okay. We weren't close.' Kyle speaks to the window.

'Still, family's family.'

'Is it?' He turns towards Eleri, taking in the stacked canvases and paint-splattered easel. The paintings are traditional, country scenes: moonlight through the forest; a sleepy canal. 'Did you say there was a cellar?'

Lydia shivers. The last thing she wants is to explore underground. 'I think I'll take Jamie outside instead if that's okay?' She needs the warmth of the sun on her face, not another musty room. 'We'll wait for you in the garden.'

She leaves Kyle to nose around the house some more and takes the three flights of stairs to the ground floor. Jamie's fallen asleep, his head snug against the inside of the carrier. She spends a few moments ensuring he's comfortable, then steps outside. There's not much of a garden: a small patch of lawn that's knee high, an oil tank and a drystone wall bordering the steep rise to the summit. Adjacent to a garage, there's a barn that's padlocked shut. She stands on tiptoes and peers through a cobwebbed window at the space inside. It's bigger than she'd expected and she feels a quiver of excitement. This place would make a perfect studio. She imagines her workbench against the far wall, her tools laid out, her stones covering the floor, her favourite pieces on shelves and plinths. The idea of a space to herself thrills her. A space that she wouldn't have to pay rent on, or share with other people. A space with enough room to make a safe area for Jamie, where she can keep an eye on him as she works.

She steps back onto the lawn and lifts her gaze to the summit. There's something up there, halfway between the house and the ridge at the top. An outcrop of rocks or another building? In front of it, a man is waving down at the tower. No, not the tower. He's waving at *her*. She can feel it, just as she can feel the breeze in her hair and a chill on her neck.

She's about to wave back when Jamie cries out in his sleep. She leans over and rearranges the muslin cloth behind his head. At the same time, the house door creaks open.

Kyle appears, blinking in the sunlight.

'God, you gave me a fright!' She looks back to where the man was standing. Nothing there. Just a trick of the light, the hazy summer sun.

Kyle rubs her bare shoulders, sliding his fingers beneath the straps of the baby carrier. 'Here. Let me take that. You've been carrying him for ages.'

She shakes her head. 'He's asleep. Leave him be.'

'You all right? You've got goosebumps.'

'Just a breeze.' She hesitates. 'You're not seriously thinking about moving here, are you?'

Kyle sweeps flecks of dust from his hair. 'It's not that stupid, is it? Haven't we always dreamed of the country? Getting away from it all? Bringing up our family somewhere safe?'

She looks down at the crown of Jamie's head, then across to the valley. The same thrill as when she looked inside the barn. The possibility of escape, of getting away from London, from the crowds and the traffic, the feeling of being hemmed in, the panic attacks. And then, there's the potential of this place. She thinks of the view from the front of the house, the same view she's looking at now, the way it transforms the space inside.

'Think about it,' he says. 'Out here we'd have no rent. No mortgage. All this space for J-J to grow up in. All this healthy fresh air.'

'I thought I saw someone on the mountain,' she says, turning in the opposite direction, glancing up at the trig point and the jagged rocks. 'A man waving down at me.'

'A hillwalker, probably. Or a shepherd. Remember that farm we walked through earlier?'

'It freaked me out,' she says, though she knows it's stupid. 'Someone watching me like that. Watching Jamie.'

'There's bound to be tourists.' He grins and she knows he's right. *Of course* there are tourists. 'Come on. There's something else I want to show you.' He finds her hand and pulls her further into the garden.

'What is it?'

He doesn't answer, just leads her through the long grass, past the kitchen window and the rusted oil tank. A sheep bleats from the fields. A buzzard circles overhead, so close she swears she can hear the beating of its wings. 'It's on the other side of the tower. Something which makes this whole thing perfect.'